WHERE
LIES
THE
TRUTH

TROY ALLEN BROUSSARD

Layout and Design:

Variance Author Services

www.varianceauthorservices.com

Acknowledgments

I am exceedingly grateful to all who offered their time, feedback and support for this incredibly fulfilling project, especially my wife, Beth Broussard, my friends, Billy Parker, Kristi Loewer Simon, Reumae Knowles, and my editor, Tim Schulte of Variance Author Services.

To the late **Harper Lee**, whose masterpiece *To Kill a Mockingbird* and its story of racial injustice moved me spiritually, ultimately serving as the root inspiration for this work.

To the late **Carole Ann McCauley Fuselier,** my esteemed high school English teacher, who instructed me, encouraged me, challenged me and inspired me in the field of writing like no other.

To **my mother and father**, whose hard work, sacrifice, love and support made everything I am and everything I do possible.

To **my sons,** who gave me purpose in life that transcended all others.

To **my wife,** my force of nature, my one and only, my happily ever after.

AUTHOR'S NOTE

The reader will likely find some of the language and content graphic and in many respects offensive. In writing this novel, my intent was to portray realism through the medium of fiction. In doing so, I have attempted to be authentic and era-specific with language, to expose, to enlighten, to provoke, to inspire and to entertain, not necessarily in that order.

CHAPTER 1

St. Landry Parish, Louisiana
Summer 1976

As if playing a disorderly game of high-wire musical chairs, a small number of juvenile crows—barely constituting a murder—jostled and jockeyed for position on the sagging telephone line, croaking and clicking, their eyes cast downward, covetously. Below, resting upside down in the thick muck on the bank of the ravine, were the remains of their unfinished roadside repast, the fractured carapace of an ill-fated red-eared slider, its putrefying gristle and flesh simmering in the late morning heat, the stench hanging thick in the humid air.

Thwarting the ravenous intentions of the restless scavengers was the imposing figure of a large snowy white heron standing tall in elegant repose atop long, stilted legs, seeming to glow like a sylph in the lingering fog. Protectively, she hovered with perfect stillness above the commandeered spoils, her only movements from piercing yellow eyes that shifted to and fro as she predaciously perused the muddy shallows of the ravine.

Suddenly, her pupils dilated. Slowly—almost imperceptibly—she leaned forward, coiling her curiously long neck into an elongated "S" shape like a feathery snake preparing to strike. She watched intently as a small shadowy form appeared from behind a submerged clump of grass, its head preceded by disproportionately large pincers left partially open as if ready for battle. At the front of its tiny mouth, long antennules swayed randomly in the murky water as a multitude of twig-like legs delivered the creature's armored, bullet-shaped frame through the soft silt in the direction of the rancid fare.

1

As the keen-eyed crows stilled and waited for the drama to unfold, the Great Egret closely followed the wary movements of the crustacean as it slowly advanced, stopped and then retreated to its hiding place behind the vegetation, repeating this pattern twice more as the savvy huntress bided her time.

Finally no longer able to resist the putrescent seduction, the hungry crawfish left the safety of its cover and marched forward, oblivious to the impending peril. At the exact moment that it crossed the threshold of the hungry heron's striking range, she released herself like a tightly wound spring, lunging downward with blurring speed, her head completely disappearing into the muddy water. The crows fluttered and croaked with excitement as her head emerged with the partially crushed prey clamped firmly in her long, daggered beak, pincers and spindly legs flailing helplessly from either side as water dripped from her head feathers and beak.

As the Great Egret adjusted her hold on the crawfish through subtle coordinated movements of her beak and tongue, a loud clamorous chorus of caws erupted as the young crows took flight. Surveying her surroundings in reaction to the sounded alarm, the wary heron spied two figures in the distance. Uncomfortable with their approach, she quickly swallowed the crawfish and then took two gangling steps up the embankment to firmer ground before springing into the air, extending and contracting her vast wings to propel herself through the air. As she gained altitude, she let out a series of remonstrative croaks at the intruders while releasing the ample contents of her bowels to lighten her load.

The lean, heavily freckled boy who was narrowly spared the fecal assault guffawed and cackled as he skidded his refurbished Schwinn to a stop on the hot pavement. His pudgy companion braked and cautiously turned his English racer around in the road. "What's so funny?" he asked

"That big egret just crapped all over your back," the freckled boy answered through snorts and laughter.

"Nuh-uh!" the pudgy boy replied. "Please tell me you're lying, Ezra."

Ezra shook his head and suspended his laughter just long enough to reply, "Swear to God."

The pudgy boy grimaced and brought his oversized bicycle to a wobbly stop at the edge of the road. Balancing himself on the tips of his toes so as not to mash his testicles on the bicycle's top tube, he craned his neck to the left and back as far as he could and pulled at his shirt until he was able to see and smell the excrement for himself. He retched.

"Jesus, Giles, are you seriously going to throw up?" Ezra asked through unstifled giggles.

Giles looked up at Ezra with watery eyes. "I might," he answered.

Still giggling, Ezra laid his bike in the road and picked up a smashed, sun-faded aluminum beer can from the gravel shoulder. "Hold still," he said as he used the flattened can to scrape the thickest part of the bird droppings from Giles' shirt. "Okay," he said, "I got most of it."

"Thanks," Giles said, though his gratitude was somewhat lessened due to his companion's delight in his soiled misfortune.

Ezra wiped the can in the grass and then offered it to Giles. "Here," he said, "you have a little bit on the back of your cut-offs, but no way I'm touching your butt."

Giles accepted the scraper and attempted to remove the droppings from his cut-offs but only managed to smear it over a larger area. He looked up at Ezra helplessly.

"Let's just go," Ezra said as he pulled on one tube sock and then the other. "You can rinse it off when we get to Jagneaux's. There's a water faucet on the side of the building."

Giles threw the smashed can like a Frisbee toward the ravine. As he watched it turn this way and that before landing in a clump of cattails, something in the trough of the ravine caught his eye. "Hold on, Ezra. I think I see one," he said, pointing. "Look down there in the mud, right next to those cattails."

"I don't see anything," Ezra replied as he surveyed the area.

"I think it might be a 7up bottle," Giles said, pointing out a partially submerged green glass bottle that was well-camouflaged by the surrounding algae.

"Oh yeah, I see it now," Ezra said. After laying his bike down on the road again, he picked up a discarded survey marker and began shuffling down the embankment, leaning on the stick for support while using his free hand to swat at ravenous mosquitos emerging from the tall grass. "Christ!" he muttered as he slapped at one mosquito after another.

"Watch out for water moccasins," Giles called out from the shoulder of the road, nervously repositioning his wire-framed glasses on his nose.

Ezra took another couple of steps and then froze in his tracks, looking downward fretfully. "Oh shit," he whispered.

"What is it?" Giles whispered back.

Ezra remained frozen. "I thought I just felt a big one slither across the top of my foot."

"Holy crap. Really?"

"Well, I thought so," Ezra said, "but I must have been . . . *mis-snakin'*."

Giles rolled his eyes and shook his head with a smirk. "Dude, that's so lame."

Ezra let out a prideful chirp-like chuckle and continued down the embankment. After reaching the bottom and straddling the narrow trough of the ravine, he pulled hard on the bottle to free it from the mud's vacuum-hold producing a deep *blaarrppp* sound. "You heard that?" he said, "It farted."

Giles chuckled. "Yeah," he said, "that reminds me—do you know Keith Precht—the tall, skinny, red-haired dude in my class?"

"I know who he is, but I don't *know him* know him. Why?" Ezra asked as he flung the muddy 7up bottle up the embankment, landing it softly in the tall grass.

"Well, we had a sleep-over and Keith bet us that he could fart twenty times in a row."

"Nobody can fart that many times in a row," Ezra declared. "You would run out of gas, literally."

"Well, Keith can," Giles said. "He can suck air into his butthole and then he farts it back out. They're not super loud, but he can do it over and over."

Ezra chuckled and shook his head dismissively. "No way."

"I swear," Giles insisted. "I was there. I saw it—I mean I heard it—I mean I saw and I heard it."

Ezra looked at Giles with a furrowed brow, still very skeptical. Though Giles was not one to fabricate stories, Ezra suspected that the farts were likely a prank that he was too naïve to discern. "How can somebody suck air through their butthole, Giles?" he argued. "It's impossible."

"I don't know, but he can and he did. I was there."

Ezra scoffed.

"But wait, that's not even the best part," Giles continued. "So, Keith's bent over and has his pants and underwear pulled down—I guess so it's easier to suck in the air—and he's like trying to squeeze out fart number seven or eight when a tiny little turd-nugget shoots out of his butthole and lands on Jerry Carson's pillow."

Ezra guffawed. "No way!"

"I swear," Giles said. "Cross my heart and hope to die."

"You swear to God?" Ezra asked, still finding the story difficult to believe though also envious because he was not there to see it happen in person.

"You're not supposed to swear to God," Giles said.

"Then do you swear on your grandmother's grave?" asked Ezra.

"Which one?"

"The dead one, moron."

"Yes."

"Really?" Ezra said.

"Yes."

"Holy shit, that's hilarious."

Ezra had started to climb back up the embankment when he noticed the fractured turtle carapace on the bank of the ravine. He went to it and used the stick to lift it out of the muck. "Giles, check it out."

"What is that?"

"A busted turtle shell."

"From a loggerhead?" Giles asked.

"I don't think so. It looks like it's from a big yellow belly."

"Cool. You should bring it. We can nail it to the treehouse."

Ezra considered the idea for a moment before shaking his head. "Nah, it's still got some meat on the inside. It reeks."

"Well, we could put it in an ant pile and they'll pick it clean for us," Giles said.

"You want to carry it?"

"No."

"I didn't think so," Ezra said. As the young crows watched with interest from the top of a tall cypress on the other side of the road, Ezra tossed the carapace into the adjacent sugarcane field and began working his way back up the embankment.

CHAPTER 2

As Ezra straddled his bicycle frame and slid the muddy 7up bottle into the plastic Evangeline Maid bread sack hanging from his handlebars, the deep growl of a Plymouth Grand Fury announced its approach. "Watch out man," Giles cautioned as he gator-stepped his English racer to the safety of the gravel shoulder, "that car's coming really fast."

Ezra glanced at the approaching muscle car but disregarded Giles' warning, leaving his bike partially on the road as he re-tied the bread sack to his handlebars. "There's nobody coming from the other way," he said. "He can go around."

"He's not going around," Giles cried out. "Move, Ezra!"

As the Grand Fury reached the boys, the driver laid on the horn and swerved slightly into the opposing lane, the corner of his front bumper clearing Ezra's rear bicycle tire by less than a foot, the rush of air caused by the speeding vehicle nearly causing the boys to lose their balance.

"Holy crap!" Giles exclaimed, wide-eyed and unnerved. "You almost got hit!"

Ezra turned toward the car and raised a middle-fingered fist high into the air and then spit in its direction for added measure. The Grand Fury's brake lights lit and its tires screeched as the car came to an abrupt halt about two hundred yards down the road. When the reverse lights came on, Ezra quickly lowered his hand. The boys traded nervous glances. After the car remained stationary for several seconds, the reverse lights went dark followed by the brake lights, and the car began to idle forward.

Giles exhaled in relief. "Oh my God, I thought he was going to come after us for a second."

Just as the car began to gradually accelerate, Ezra stood on the tips of his toes and this time threw both fists and middle fingers as high into the air as he could, screaming as loud as he could, "Asshole!"

"Dude!" Giles pleaded, trying to grab Ezra's arms. "Don't!"

The Plymouth's brake lights lit again. The car screeched to a halt. The reverse lights lit and this time the tires began spinning, causing white smoke to rise from the pavement as the Grand Fury advanced rapidly in reverse toward the boys. Ezra chortled anxiously as he pushed his old Schwinn into motion, pedaling furiously down the road in the opposite direction with all of his might. "Let's get out of here!" he yelled.

"But I didn't do anything!" Giles protested as he awkwardly struggled to get his English racer rolling.

"Be sure and explain that to him after he runs you over!" Ezra called back over his shoulder.

As the reversing Grand Fury gained ground, the boys turned off the blacktop onto a rutted tractor crossing and then steered their bikes straight into the twelve-foot-high sugarcane crop. When the tall, dense foliage stopped his momentum, Ezra jumped off his bike and began frantically pushing through the thick cane. He heard a shriek and turned to see Giles lying at the base of the dewy cane with his legs tangled in the frame of his bicycle.

As the sound of the car drew nearer, Ezra retraced his steps and hurriedly pulled the English racer off of Giles and helped him to his feet. They grabbed their bikes and frantically pushed deeper into the cane. After advancing what felt like the length of a football field, they stopped to catch their breath, their hearts pounding from exertion and fright, their hair and clothes soaked with dew and perspiration.

Listening intently, crouched in the cane, the boys heard the Grand Fury's suspension creaking over the hardened tractor ruts. "He's coming," Giles whispered. He was on the verge of tears.

Ezra shook his head and put his finger to his lips. They waited, trying to breathe as softly as they could.

"Is he coming?" Giles asked, in a frightened whisper.

Ezra turned toward Giles and shushed him again, this time with a reproving scowl. "If he comes after us, we're gonna have to leave the bikes here and come back for 'em later," Ezra whispered.

Giles shook his head. "My daddy will kill me if something happens to my bike," he whispered back.

"Okay," Ezra replied. "You stay with the bikes. I'll come back for you later when the coast is clear."

"Hell no," Giles said, in an exceedingly rare exhibition of profanity. "You're not leaving me here by myself."

Ezra grinned. "Just relax, dude," he whispered. "He's not going to come in here after us. He's just trying to scare us."

"Did you recognize whose car it was?" Giles said.

Ezra nodded. "I'm pretty sure it's Blake Wyble," he answered. "He's a dope head that lives a few blocks from my house."

"I thought Blake Wyble was the dude who got killed in that three-wheeler accident?" Giles said.

"That was his younger brother Blair," Ezra replied. "Blake always drove a car. Blair always drove a truck two Rottweilers in the back, Attila and Hitler."

Giles furrowed his brow incredulously. "He named one of his dogs after Adolf Hitler?"

Ezra gestured for Giles to hold his voice down. "No," he whispered, "not after Adolf. He named him after Adolf's first cousin, Hubert. "He was a lot nicer. He raised bunnies and collected stamps."

Giles rolled his eyes. "Hubert Hitler," he whispered, chuckling to himself.

Ezra turned toward Giles and sniffed the air. "Did you shit your pants?"

"No!" Giles replied in a loud whisper.

"Relax, I was kidding," Ezra whispered back. Then he sniffed at the air again. "But you do smell like a raw biscuit when you sweat. You know that right?"

"Shut up."

For what seemed to them like an eternity the boys waited, watching beads of sweat appear and coalesce on their skin. They resisted the urge to slap at the blood-sucking mosquitos on their arms and legs so as not to give their location away. They listened anxiously for anything that sounded like someone creeping through the dense cane. Finally, they heard the sound of the Plymouth's transmission shifting into a different gear and then the car creaking back across the hardened tractor ruts, pulling out onto the paved road and then moving slowly back in the direction from whence it had come.

"We should wait a little longer," Ezra said. "He might be trying to bait us into coming out."

Giles pointed at Ezra's cheek. "You have a bunch of little paper cuts on your face from the cane leaves. Do I?" Giles asked.

Ezra looked back at Giles. "Yeah," he replied. "A few. I have some on my arms, too. These leaves are like little razor blades, man."

"Great," Giles said anxiously. "Now my mom's gonna know that we were in the sugarcane fields."

Ezra smirked. "So?"

"Then she's gonna want to know why," Giles replied.

"Just tell her we were chasing a rabbit or something."

"But we weren't chasing a rabbit," Giles protested, as if the act of lying to his mother would violate his genetic code.

Ezra rolled his eyes in exasperation. "Whatever," he said.

Giles sighed and began picking at a large wart on his knee, an unpleasant habit that usually manifested itself when he was anxious.

"Dude," Ezra said, "That's so gross. You can see the black seeds in it. You need to get that thing burned off."

"Do you know how much that would hurt?" Giles said.

"Well, then you should go see Trent Cormier's grandmother. She's a *traiteur*."

"A what?"

"You know, she treats warts and stuff like that," Ezra said.

"How?" Giles whispered.

"Trent said she takes a raw Irish potato and cuts it in half. She says a prayer over the wart and then rubs one of the halves of the potato on the wart and then buries it, and she gives you the other half to eat. And by the time the potato rots in the ground, the wart is gone."

"And it works?"

"Yeah it works."

"How much does she charge for that?" Giles asked.

"Nothing," Ezra replied. "That's the thing. It's a gift from God. They can't charge anything or they'll lose the gift."

After several more minutes with nothing heard but the buzzing of mosquitos, the chirping of grasshoppers and the distant birdsong of a meadowlark, Giles asked, "Do you think it's safe to get out now? I'm starting to get really itchy, and I think I've donated nearly two pints of blood to these mosquitos. Look at this one," he said, lifting his arm to let Ezra see a blood-swollen mosquito crawling across his arm, "he's too heavy with blood to fly."

"Damn."

"Can we go now?"

Ezra shivered and arched his back, letting out a high-pitched groan.

"What the heck are you doing?" Giles asked curiously.

Ezra sighed. "A huge bead of sweat just rolled all the way down my spine and into my butt crack."

"You are so gross," Giles said, wrinkling his nose in amused repugnance. "Let's get out of this jungle, please."

The boys picked up their bikes and retraced their steps back through the dense foliage. Upon reaching the edge of the crop, they stopped and Ezra peeked out cautiously.

"You see anything?" Giles asked.

"Nah, he's long gone."

"You sure?"

"Yeah."

"Thank God."

The boys pushed their bikes out of the sugarcane, across the tractor ruts and toward the road. They checked for the Grand Fury in either direction and saw nothing.

"Hey," Ezra said as they reached the shoulder of the highway, "would you drink a cup of my butt-crack sweat for twenty dollars?"

Giles grimaced and shook his head. "God no."

"What about half a cup for fifty dollars?"

"Nope."

"A quarter of a cup for a hundred dollars?"

"Nope."

"For how much then?" Ezra asked as he climbed back on his bike.

As Giles struggled to get his short leg over the tall top tube of his English Race, he said, "I wouldn't for any amount."

"That's bull and you know it," Ezra rejoined.

"Well, let's put it this way," Giles said. "You'll never have enough money to even tempt me."

CHAPTER 3

When they were convinced that Blake Wyble or whomever was driving the Grand Fury was not coming back, the boys resumed their bottle scavenging and then rode to Jagneaux's Superette. Giles used the water spigot on the side of the building to wash the bird poop off of his clothes before they rinsed out the bottles and then took them to a cashier for their refunds, collecting just under two dollars for their efforts. Giles purchased a pack of Pecan Twirls and Ezra a frosted honeybun before going outside to buy soft drinks from the vending machine. They sat in the shade on a parking bumper eating their snacks and taking turns swigging the contents of the ten-ounce bottles, competing to see who could manage the loudest belch.

Ezra regarded Giles for a moment curiously as though he were trying to figure something out.

"What?" Giles said.

"Do you know who you look like?"

"Who?"

"The snowman on *Rudolph the Red Nosed Reindeer*—you know, the one that glides around in the snow telling the story."

"Gee thanks," Giles said, with good-humored sarcasm. "Because of my glasses?"

"Yeah, but not just that," Ezra said. "It's also because of the way your eyes squint when you smile."

"Do you know who you look like?" Giles asked.

"Burt Reynolds?" Ezra guessed facetiously.

"Ha. Hardly."

"Tom Selleck?"

Giles chortled. "Not even close. And why are you picking men with mustaches?"

Ezra shrugged, not realizing that he had. "Mick Jagger?"

"No."

"I give up."

"Anson Williams," Giles answered.

"Who's that?"

"You know, Potsie Weber on *Happy Days.*"

Ezra snickered. "Nuh-uh!"

"You do," Giles insisted, "but with freckles of course."

"You suck."

Giles chuckled.

Ezra was about to comment further when they heard a curious plinking sound coming from across the parking lot. They turned to see a young colored boy rolling up on a metallic purple bike with long silver streamers coming out of either end of the chopper-style handlebars. The bike had a chrome sissy bar and a banana seat covered with a glittery gold vinyl.

The plinking sound was coming from the wheels. Short hard-plastic straws were fitted loosely on the spokes. As the wheels turned, the straws rose and fell, striking the metal base of the wheel on each downward cycle, the successive impacts produced a distinctive *plink-plink-plink-plink-plink-plink* sound.

The colored boy approached Ezra and Giles. He stopped his bike and balanced himself by resting his foot on top of a parking bollard. After repositioning the lime green pick in his tall, thick afro, he said to Ezra, whom he knew from school, "Hey, 'sup homie."

"Hey, 'sup Terrell," Ezra replied.

"Yo' man, you got a round *kahta* I could borrow?"

Ezra shook his head. "Nah, brah. I'm tapped out." He slapped the front pockets of his cut-offs to demonstrate that they were empty.

Giles looked at Ezra curiously. He had never heard Ezra talking to a colored person before and found it curious how his dialect seemed to mimic that of his dark-skinned schoolmate.

Terrell smirked at Ezra incredulously and then turned to Giles. "What about you, soul? Hook me up wit' a round *kahta*."

"A round what?" Giles asked, genuinely confused.

"Quarter," Ezra said, enunciating the word slowly.

Terrell leered at Ezra, narrowing his eyes and sucking his teeth as if to make clear that he did not require a translator.

"All we have left is a nickel," Giles said, then wondered if he should have called it a round nickel.

Terrell glanced at the snack wrappers and empty soft drink bottles lying next to Ezra and Giles and then looked up at them incredulously. Uncomfortable with the tension, Giles pulled the nickel out of his pocket and put it between his lips. Then he jammed both hands into his pockets and pulled the white linings out to show Terrell that they were empty. Removing the nickel from his lips, he offered it to Terrell. "Here, you can have it," he said.

Terrell looked at the coin for a moment as if he were deciding whether he wanted to touch something that had been in the white boy's mouth. Then, he reluctantly grabbed the coin and rubbed it on his pants before stuffing it into his pocket. Without speaking, he turned his bike around and pedaled off.

Ezra and Giles watched him until he and the plinking sound faded in the distance. "He didn't even say thank you," Giles said, when Terrell was out of earshot.

"What did you expect?" Ezra asked, clearly irritated. "Why did you even give it to him in the first place?"

"Because if I didn't, he would probably have told his older brothers and uncles and they might have come down here and stabbed us."

Ezra laughed mockingly and shook his head. "Dude, you're so lucky you don't go to my school. The coloreds would eat you for lunch."

Giles offered no disagreement. "So, why did he call it a round quarter?" he asked.

"That's just how they talk," Ezra explained. "It's a colored thing."

Giles nodded amused. "That's funny. Do they say round nickel and round dime and round penny?"

"No," Ezra answered.

"That's so weird."

"Y'all don't have any coloreds at all at St. Anne's?" Ezra asked curiously.

"Not right now. We had a colored girl in the second-grade last year," Giles replied. "She was the first one ever. Her grandmother is one of the lunchroom ladies, so Fr. Ewell let her come for free. But she didn't come back this year."

"Damn, you're so lucky."

Giles nodded.

"I mean, a lot of them are pretty cool and stuff," Ezra said, "but there's a lot who aren't and a lot of 'em pick on you just because you're white."

"Really?" asked Giles, genuinely disturbed.

"Yeah," Ezra said. "And they always want to fight you. Even the girls get in fights."

"Jeeze," Giles said, with genuine amazement. "Girls don't fight at my school. They just talk mean to each other sometimes."

"Y'all see that nigger-rigged bike?" A voice called from across the parking lot. Giles and Ezra turned to see Vance Duhon ride up on his skateboard, hop off, stomp on the kick tail and then catch it as it flipped into the air. "I'll bet there wasn't a single part on that bike that wasn't stolen," he added. "Who was that, anyway?" he said, directing his question to Ezra.

"Terrell Truitt," Ezra said.

"I thought so. I can't tell him and his brother apart."

"Terrell is always the one with the big fro," Ezra said. "Where you been anyway? I thought you were coming to find bottles with us."

"I had something to do," Vance said. Then he spat and watched the wad of saliva sail through the air, wrapping itself around a spoke on the wheel of a brand-new Oldsmobile Delta 88.

"Dude, that's Mrs. Duplechain's car," Giles said aghast.

"Who's that?" Vance asked with borderline disinterest.

"She works at St. Anne's. She's like everybody's favorite teacher."

"So?" Vance replied.

Giles began to reply but stopped short.

"Where's Bruce?" Ezra asked, realizing that Vance was without his canine sidekick.

"I had to bury him," Vance said. He was trying to sound matter-of-fact with no emotion in his voice but Ezra and Giles could see redness in his eyes.

"Are you serious, dude?" Ezra replied though knew the answer to his question. Then he realized that he had never actually seen Vance cry. Not even when he had broken his arm when he fell out of a tree.

Vance sucked his lips into his mouth and nodded without allowing his countenance to change.

Ezra and Vance had found Bruce, a shepherd-lab mix, several years earlier when he was still a puppy. He was emaciated and scavenging for food behind a Canal gas station on the south side of town. They surmised that he had made his way to Iris by following the railroad tracks from Opelousas. They fed him what was left of a Slim Jim that Ezra had in his pocket and he followed them home.

When Vance set him on the floor of the trailer, the puppy went straight to his mother who was lying on the couch with a cold rag on her forehead. She had just returned from her third round of chemotherapy after being diagnosed with colon cancer. Somehow sensing her suffering, the puppy laid his chin on her lap and gazed sympathetically into her eyes. It was the first time Vance's mother had smiled since her diagnosis.

After getting permission to keep him, Vance named the puppy Bruce after his favorite martial arts master, Bruce Lee. Ezra sometimes affectionately referred to him as *Bruces from Opelousas*.

Bruce was universally loved by all the kids in the neighborhood and went with Vance virtually everywhere. He also had a reputation for being a bit of a canine hero. There were numerous instances of him herding young trailer park children away from the busy street when their mothers were not keeping a close enough eye. And on one occasion, when they were walking a rice field levee, Bruce had knocked Vance to the side just as he was about to inadvertently step on a large cottonmouth. He then proceeded to aggressively harass the snake until Vance was able to smash its head with a piece of riprap. After Vance used his pocketknife to cut off the snake's head and then tossed it into the water, Bruce picked up the snake's decapitated body and pranced all the way home with it hanging from his mouth, stopping to show off his trophy to anyone willing to get close enough to inspect it.

"So, what happened?" Ezra asked sympathetically.

"Mr. Abel Mueller, the man who owns the trailer park, hit him in the head with a metal pipe," Vance said.

Giles and Ezra looked horrified.

"What? Why?" Giles exclaimed.

"Did you see it happen?" asked Ezra

Vance spat on the ground and then shook his head. "No, but Brett Francois did. He said Mr. Mueller came to the trailer park to check the septic system and Bruce was barking at him. After he got out of his truck, he grabbed a pipe out of the bed and hit Bruce really hard on the side of the head."

"Jesus." Ezra asked.

"Brett said he fell on his side and started squealing and bleeding from his ear. Mr. Mueller just left him like that. Brett went get his stepdad who put him out of his misery with his .22."

"Well, Mr. Mueller is a royal shitass," Ezra said. "We should go tell my dad. He'll arrest him."

Vance shook his head. "Bruce wasn't tied up. He would just say Bruce was trying to bite him."

"But that's horse crap," Ezra said. "Bruce has never bitten anyone."

"Yeah well, what comes around goes around," Vance said as he kicked an orange Fanta can across the pavement.

21

Ezra and Giles regarded Vance in silence. He had that look in his eye—that look that he was going to get even, somehow, some day. They glanced at each other, not knowing what else to say.

"Hey, y'all have any extra money for a coke?" Vance asked

After Ezra and Giles both patted their front pockets and shook their heads to indicate that they had no money, Vance pulled a quarter out of his front pocket, inserted it into the vending machine and selected a root beer.

"What the hell were you asking us for money for when you already had some?" Ezra asked.

Vance shrugged as he pushed his sweaty bangs out of his eyes. "I was saving it," he said.

Ezra was about to reply when someone called out from behind him, "Hey, fellas!" It was Rupert Robicheaux, a very gregarious, high functioning Down syndrome teen who lived across the street from Jagneaux's. He waddled over to the boys wearing an undersized Superman pajama top, baggy cut-off khakis and a New Orleans Saints beanie. When he reached the trio, Rupert stopped and vigorously shook each of their hands. "Pleased to see you," he said with a pronounced lisp.

When Ezra told him that he liked his hat, Rupert removed it and offered it to him as a gift. Ezra smiled and shook his head, explaining that he should keep it because it would look much better on him. Rupert smiled and agreed. He put the hat back on and then asked Ezra if it was on straight.

"Almost," Ezra said as he made a slight adjustment. "Now, it's perfect."

Rupert smiled and petted the top of his hat. "You let me know if you change your mind okay, Ezper?" He had never learned to pronounce Ezra's name correctly.

"I will, Ru," Ezra said, smiling warmly.

"You don't think it's too hot to be wearing a knit hat, Rupert?" Giles asked, worried that Rupert might become overheated.

"Nope. It's my magic hat," Rupert said. "My Uncle Randy gave it to me. He said it makes me strong in case I have to fight bad guys."

"Yeah, but Rupert," Vance said, "seriously man, it's nearly a hundred degrees today. Wearing a knit hat in this kind of heat is retarded."

Ezra and Giles both winced and turned red with embarrassment, scowling furiously at Vance.

Rupert regarded Vance curiously for a moment and then smiled affably and nodded. "I know," he said. "But I can count to twenty and I know my colors and shapes, and I can add numbers. Watch," he said proudly. "One plus one is two. Two plus two is four. Four plus four is five. Five plus five is six."

"That's really good, Ru," Ezra said.

"Yeah, Rupert, that's awesome," Giles added.

Rupert beamed with pride. "Okay, I have to go. My mom said I have to be back home in this many minutes," he explained, holding up seven fingers.

Ezra and Giles bid Rupert farewell and watched him walk into the store. "You know," Ezra said, turning to Vance, "you can really be a prick sometimes."

"Oh eat me," Vance growled. "He knows he's retarded."

"Still," Giles said, "he has feelings. And he knew you were making fun of him."

Vance grinned and regarded Giles for a moment before sniffing at the air on the side of his face. "Anybody ever tell you that when you sweat, you smell like biscuit dough?"

23

Ezra giggled. "I told you."

Giles did not reply. Instead, he threw his trash into the garbage can and began to ready his bike.

"Hey, you want to go frogging in the gully by the water tower?" Vance asked.

Ezra regarded Vance skeptically. "You can't ride your skateboard that far."

"I could ride on your handlebars," Vance retorted.

"Nah, it's too hot," Ezra said. "I'm going home to watch *Gilligan's Island*."

"So, you can beat-off to Ginger?" Vance teased.

"No," Ezra said in a tone that sounded a little too defensive. "I don't beat my meat. And I think Mary-Anne is prettier anyway."

"Whatever," Vance said.

"I'll see y'all later Ezra," Giles said as he climbed onto his bike and began pedaling away.

"Hold on, Giles, I'm coming," Ezra said.

Giles and Ezra road in silence for a couple of blocks before Giles finally spoke. "Sometimes it makes me wonder why we're friends with him. I mean, Jesus, making fun of a retarded person to his face. Who does that?"

Ezra shrugged. "It's just his way of getting attention."

"It's just his way of being a jerk," Giles retorted.

Ezra shrugged but offered no disagreement. "You want to go hunting tomorrow morning? I can ask my mom to drive us to the swampy woods past the water tower."

"I don't know. Maybe."

CHAPTER 4

Night was yielding to dawn as the aging Ford Country Squire rattled and creaked across the cattle guard and then rolled to a stop in the gravel. As its headlamp beams refracted in the thick fog, the passenger-side rear door swung open, and Ezra and Giles exited carrying air rifles and backpacks. While they readied their gear, Ezra's mother cranked down the window to remind them of the afternoon pickup time and to warm them to be careful. The boys responded with a series of nods and patient *yes ma'ams* and then watched the car pull away, melting into the fading fog to the sound of gravel popping beneath its weight.

The boys took turns jumping a small ditch and then tramped single file through the dew-soaked grass of a small clearing until reaching a large, low-lying wooded area. They stopped to load and pump their air rifles when the deafening roar of a crop duster's engine declared itself overhead. As the biplane tilted just above the canopy of trees, the boys could see through a break in the fog the goggled pilot nestled in his cramped cockpit, his hands pushing and pulling on the stick controls as he coaxed the aircraft through a sharp turn. Ezra lifted his rifle and aimed it in the direction of plane. His mouth contorted as he jerked the gun against his shoulder, simulating the firing of a high-powered rifle.

Giles sighed with relief and nervously adjusted his glasses as the plane. Ezra looked at him and smiled. "What?" he said. "As if I would have really shot at him, Giles."

"I didn't say anything," Giles replied.

"Look," Ezra said, pointing in the distance at a flock of large birds flying in formation just above the horizon.

"Are those ducks?" asked Giles.

"No, nigger geese," Ezra replied.

"How can you tell from here?"

"Ducks and real geese never stop flapping until they are getting ready to land. Nigger geese are lazy. They flap and glide, flap and glide the whole time they are in the air."

"Cormorants," Giles said.

"What?"

"Their real name is cormorants," Giles said.

"Nobody calls them that," argued Ezra.

"Well, that's what they are."

"Whatever."

As they entered the woods, the boys slowed their pace and surveyed their surroundings for any sign of game. Almost immediately, something rustled in a clump of tall grass near the base of a cottonwood. When Ezra kicked at the grass, a leopard frog leapt from its cover and then leapt twice more before stopping instinctively, relying on its natural camouflage to make it invisible. Ezra slowly crept toward the frog, stopped, and positioned the end of his barrel a few inches from its head. Just as the frog was about to leap way, Ezra pulled the trigger. The soft lead pellet struck its target splattering amphibian flesh, bone, blood and guts onto the surrounding leaves and pine straw.

"Dang!" Ezra exclaimed. "Did you see that?"

Giles frowned. "We're not supposed to kill things we don't plan to eat," he said, reprovingly.

Ezra looked at Giles and smirked. "Dude, relax. It's a leopard frog. There're millions of them. Nobody's gonna miss one."

"But still," Giles said.

"Well," Ezra said, picking up what was left of the frog's tiny hind legs, "if you're so worried about it, here, put this in the bag. We can fry it up when we get home."

Giles smirked. "Very funny," he said.

Ezra smiled and tossed the tiny frog legs into the grass as the boys continued down the footpath. They walked for several minutes without seeing anything to shoot before arriving at a ravine. Ezra found an old RC Cola can and hung it from the limb of a gum sapling. After getting bored with shooting the can they sat on a large log to eat the snacks their mothers had packed them.

Ezra began coughing and then spat out a piece of chewed-up pastry that had gotten lodged in his throat.

"Gross," Giles said.

"I was choking jackass, what did you want me to do?"

Giles chuckled. "This past Friday, I don't know if she had the flu or what, but Elaine Istre vomited on the sidewalk right after mass, and Sister Agnes picked the pieces of the Eucharist out of the vomit."

"No way," Ezra said.

"I swear," Giles said. "I was right there watching. Me and Seth Shenkan. Cade Hernandez was there too. We all saw. I almost gagged."

"Why would she do that?" Ezra asked, his face grimacing with disgust.

"She had to," Giles said. "That was the body of Christ. It's sacred."

"Does she follow y'all all to the restroom and take the digested pieces out of everybody's poop?"

27

Giles smirked. "Now you're just being stupid."

"I'm the one being stupid?" Ezra replied.

Giles was about to respond when Ezra's eyes widened and he lifted a hand to shush Giles. He pointed toward a crop of small trees in the distance as he lifted his gun.

"What is it?" Giles whispered as Ezra peered intensely in the direction he had pointed.

After a few moments, Ezra relaxed. "Never mind," he said. "I thought I saw something."

"Hey," Giles said, "did you hear that Ross Veillon is switching to St. Anne's next year?"

"Yeah, it's because his dad doesn't want him to have to compete against coloreds in sports when he gets to high school. He's like the fifth best athlete in our class, but at St. Anne's, he'll probably be a superstar because it's all white kids over there."

Giles nodded. "And we have the prettiest girls, too."

"Of course you do," Ezra said.

"Why do you say it like that?"

Ezra smirked as if the answer was self-evident. "Because only rich men can afford to send their kids to private schools, and men with money get the prettiest women, and the prettiest women have the prettiest daughters."

Giles shrugged. "Not always. I mean, my dad's a doctor and makes a lot of money, but my mom isn't that pretty and my sister looks like an overbred basset hound."

Ezra chuckled. "Exceptions to every rule. But at least Sarah Louise is nice. Most of the girls at St. Anne's are stuck up."

Giles nodded and pushed his glasses to the bridge of his nose. Then he kicked at an acorn in front on him. "Are you going to be a policeman like your dad when you grow up?" he asked.

Ezra shrugged. "I don't know. They don't make a lot of money. But they get to drive a police car and carry a gun, so I guess that kind'a makes up for it."

Giles nodded in agreement. "Has your dad ever shot anybody?"

"Sure," Ezra said, though he had no idea if he had.

"Really?" Giles replied, impressed. "Has he killed any bad guys?"

"Yeah, like two or three," Ezra lied.

"Dang," Giles said, "that's cool."

"Yeah, but the part that sucks is he's never home. He's always working."

CHAPTER 5

Always up with the roosters, as his grandmother was fond of saying, Terrell rose and put on the same clothes that he had worn the day before. He peeked into his mother's room to find the bed empty and her bedding in the same state of disarray it had been when he had checked it before turning in the night before. After finishing a bowl of cereal, he walked his bike through the front door and began pedaling down the street, making his way across the railroad tracks.

He rode through several neighborhoods on the white side of town to see if something of value might have been left out overnight. He spied a nice leather football glistening in the morning dew in the grass next to the driveway of a red brick home. After making a couple of passes up and down the street to see if his presence sparked any attention and observing none, he veered his bike into the driveway and was about to scoop up the football when he heard a screen door slam against its door frame. He quickly made a U-turn in the driveway and as he reached the street saw an elderly white woman shuffling across her front porch. She looked up and saw him and they held each other's gaze as he turned onto the street and rode away nonchalantly.

Terrell rode the white neighborhoods for half an hour before deciding to turn back, heading toward downtown. His tall afro swayed in the warm breeze as he zig-zagged through the Iris business district which, given that it was the weekend, was mostly vacant. He spotted a pristine, champagne-colored Cadillac Coupe Deville parked in front of a law office and steered his bike in its direction. Satisfied that he was not being watched, he stopped at each tire to remove the chrome valve stem caps, stuffing them into his pant pocket before riding on.

He hopped curbs, weaved around light poles and parking meters and stopped at every pay phone, soft drink and cigarette vending machine along the way to pull the return levers and check the change trays for coins, ultimately earning three dimes and a freshly minted Bicentennial quarter for his efforts. Upon reaching the storefront of the Ben Franklin Five & Dime, he stopped next to a new vending machine that stocked soft drinks in aluminum cans instead of bottles and gently leaned his bicycle against the wall. After making sure that no one was watching, he got down on his hands and knees, slid his long, skinny arm up the dispenser funnel, dislodged a soft drink can from the inner rack and then carefully withdrew his arm with an A&W root beer cradled precariously in his fingertips. After removing and discarding the aluminum tab, he thirstily guzzled the contents before dropping the can on the sidewalk, smashing it with his foot and kicking it into the storm drain. Then he climbed back onto his bicycle and continued down Main Street for another block before turning east and re-crossing the railroad tracks.

He pedaled down a potholed street distinguished by small, dilapidated shanties resting on brick piers, most sheathed with faux-brick siding and roofed with rusted tin. Almost without exception, the yards were small and unkempt, many littered with cigarette butts, empty beer cans, bicycle frames or discarded household appliances. A few had stripped-down automobiles sitting up on cinder blocks and skirted with overgrown grass. Some homes had dogs, mostly shepherd mixes or pit bulls, lying in patches of dirt, barking at passersby from the end of taut chains tethered to clothesline posts or car axles.

After crossing the entrance to the west side projects, Terrell rode past a lot upon which a rusted Sears's metal building sat. Liquor and cigarettes were being sold by an old man wearing thick-lensed glasses through a barred window. Several colored men sat on junked washing machines and dryers lying in the tall grass, smoking and sipping spirits from small brown paper bags, jawing and laughing. Most appeared drunk. The others appeared to be well on their way. He wondered if they had started drinking this early in the day or if they were still drinking from the night before.

A skinny, unshaven man wearing a ratty jogging suit recognized Terrell and called for him to stop, claiming that Terrell's father owed him three dollars. Terrell ignored him and kept riding. Laughing, the man yelled, "You tell yo' daddy that even royalty need to pay they debts," his comment inspiring a chorus of laughter and cackling from the other men.

The royalty reference was due to a nickname given to Terrell's biological father, Nedrick Watson, years before Terrell was born. After a long night of drinking and carousing, Nedrick came home to find his wife waiting for him in the kitchen with an opened bag of King Arthur flour sitting on the table. She pulled down his pants and underwear and then made him lower his genitalia deep into the bag of flour. Beyond inebriated, Nedrick did not have the wherewithal to protest. His penis entered the bag the same color as the rest of his skin but came out of the bag as white as driven snow, the flour sticking to the tacky vaginal fluid that coated its skin.

Before he realized what was happening, Nedrick's wife struck him in the head with a heavy cast iron skillet, knocking him unconscious. The neighbors found him lying in the front yard early the next morning, his pants and underwear still down to his knees and his conspicuous flour-coated phallus resting limply against his thigh. The bag of King Arthur flour lay partially crumpled at his side. Henceforward, he was known in the neighborhood as King Arthur.

After riding a few more blocks and making a couple of turns, Terrell reached a street with newer albeit modest homes. Some were of brick construction. Most had well-kept lawns and modest landscaping.

He felt his stomach grumble and decided to stop to see if his Aunt Dorothy might offer him something to eat. He rode his bike to a freshly painted yellow wood frame house with an early model Oldsmobile Cutlass sedan parked in the driveway. After hiding his bike behind the house where it was not visible from the street, he ambled toward the side entrance, practicing his strut along the way.

Through the screen door, he saw a heavy-set, middle-aged woman, his Aunt Dorothy, sweeping the floor with short, brisk broom strokes. At the kitchen table sat a huge teenage boy, his cousin Clayton, hunched over an open book, a pile of sandwiches and a tall glass of milk. Across the table from Clayton was Terrell's father, a skinny, grizzled man with matted hair and dirty clothes. He was sitting backwards in a kitchen chair with a large can of beer wrapped in a wrinkled brown paper bag on the table in front of him.

Nedrick spoke loudly and had a habit of licking his lips between thoughts. "Motherfucker unplugged my T.V. in the middle of *The Price is Right*," he said. "Can you believe that shit? Motherfucking white people want every fuckin' thing I got. Lord knows I ain't hardly got shit, but they still got to have it—got to have it all," he said, before taking a long gulp from the can of beer and wiping his mouth on his soiled shirtsleeve. "I ought to shoot that rent-to-own mother fucker in his sleep. Have 'em wake up dead and see what good that T.V. gonna do 'em then."

"How's he gonna wake up if he's dead, Uncle Ned?" Clayton asked, using a sandwich to hide his grin.

"You know what I mean, nigga," the man slurred. "And don't get smart with me Clayton, before I put my size nine boot up your big black ass."

Clayton's smile made clear without saying that he had no concern whatsoever that his skinny drunkard of an uncle would dare lift a finger toward him. For one, there was their size difference. Though only twelve years old, Clayton was nearly a foot taller and outweighed his diminutive uncle by forty pounds. For two, they both knew very well that Dorothy would use her broomstick or whatever other weapon she could find to bludgeon to a bloody pulp any person who attempted to harm so much as a hair on the head of any child in her family.

As if on cue, Dorothy, who up until this point had seemed to be ignoring her brother-in-law's intoxicated rant, stopped sweeping and propped her fist on her wide hip, her eyebrows raised high on her round, smooth face. "Clayton, you just eat your sandwiches and stop trying to stir the pot. As for you, Nedrick," she said, turning toward her brother-in-law and assuming a more menacing pose, "If you want to use language like that and talk about killin' people, you gonna have to go somewhere else with that. We don't condone profanity in this house. And we follow the Bible up in this house, Praise Jesus. Thalt shalt not kill."

"The Bible?" Nedrick said, wincing. "Ira Harris says if you read down deep, the Bible has rules about keeping slaves—how you like that?"

Dorothy sneered at Nedrick. "Last time I checked, Ira Harris is not a preacher trained in verse. And it ain't the Bible that's causing you trouble, Nedrick Watson. That's all on you. And all this talk about killin' innocent white folk—that ain't something I'm gonna listen to. Not under this roof. You hear me?"

"Innocent white folk?" Nedrick said, grimacing dramatically. "Innocent white folk? You find me one," he challenged. "You'd sooner find me some smeet-swelling cat piss."

"Smeet-swelling?" Clayton asked, unable to resist.

Dorothy chuckled. "Now, Clayton," she said with a wink, "you show a little respect. The aging mind is like a train that don't always stay on the right track."

Nedrick bowed up in his chair. "You ain't got no room to talk, Dorothy, you ain't exactly no fried chicken yourself."

"You mean spring chicken, Uncle Ned?" Clayton asked, stifling laughter.

"Yeah," Nedrick replied with a confused expression. "What I said? Shit, never mind. Anyways," he continued, "you know I was just playin', Dot. You know I ain't 'bout to kill nobody over a damn T.V." Then he paused to contemplate what might just motivate him to commit homicide. "Now if someone come for my Schlitz, they better be wearing a bullet-proof vest. That's all I got to say," he said, chuckling.

CHAPTER 6

When Ezra had mentioned his father's absence from home, he noticed Giles' cheeks flush and an uncomfortable expression appear on his face.

"What?" Ezra asked as he stuff his snack wrapper into his backpack.

"Nothing," Giles replied unconvincingly.

"Tell me," Ezra insisted.

"Nothing," Giles said even less convincingly.

"Giles," Ezra said, "if you don't tell me, I'm going to frog you in the butt when you're not looking."

"You better not."

"Well, then tell me and I won't."

Giles sighed. "If I tell you, you promise not to tell your parents that I told you?"

Ezra regarded Giles curiously. "I don't tell my parents anything my friends tell me."

"No, but this is about them," Giles said. "So, you have to swear."

Ezra regarded Giles warily for a moment. "I swear," he said.

"Well," Giles said before pausing as though he was having second thoughts.

"What?" Ezra demanded.

"I heard that your parents might be getting a divorce."

Ezra stared at Giles with a furrowed brow. "Who told you that?"

"I heard my mom telling my dad. She hears all kinds of stuff when she plays Bridge at the country club. My dad says the women over there are all a bunch of gossipmongers."

"Well, that's a load of crap," Ezra insisted. "They're not getting divorced. They don't even argue."

"That's what I thought. Those women are always—"

Ezra put his finger to his lips and pointed at a bird sitting atop a fence post behind Giles. "A robin," he whispered.

Giles looked over his shoulder and spotted the bird. "But they're illegal to shoot," he whispered back. "It's like a two hundred fifty dollar fine for just shooting one."

Ezra shushed Giles again and began creeping stealthily toward the robin using tree trunks and giant palmettos as cover. When a dry twig snapped beneath his foot, the wary robin chirped and flew about thirty feet farther down the fence line, landing on another fence post. Taking greater caution with his steps, Ezra crept closer to the bird until he reached comfortable shooting distance. As his father had taught him, he propped his rifle against the trunk of a tree, carefully took aim, exhaled and then gently pulled the trigger.

The pellet struck the robin in the breast causing it to flip backwards off the post, its wings flapping frantically as it fell to the ground. Several reddish-orange feathers floated in the air above it as the bird spun wildly in a circle in the tall grass. Ezra rushed to the bird, picked it up and held it gently but firmly in his palm. It shrieked and struggled to free itself for a few seconds before relenting and looking up at Ezra with helpless, frightful eyes, opening and closing its beak again and again as if gasping for air.

"It's suffering," Giles said. "Hurry up and put it out of its misery."

"I am," Ezra replied, handing his gun to Giles. He grabbed the bird by the head and rung its neck. On the second turn, there was a snap.

The bird's body went sailing lifelessly through the air and Ezra was left with only the bird's head in his hand.

"You don't have to do it so hard," Giles chided.

"Shut up, Giles, I didn't mean to," Ezra replied as he retrieved the bird's body from the tall grass. "Get the Ziploc ready," he barked.

As Giles pulled a plastic bag out of his knapsack, Ezra snapped the robin's wings off. Then he used his fingertip to puncture its abdominal cavity before widening the opening and removing the entrails. "The guts are still warm," he said. "You want to feel 'em?"

"No thanks."

CHAPTER 7

"What time yo' momma get back from work last night, Clay?" Dorothy asked.

"I don't know. She worked a double. I was sleeping when she came in."

"I never met a harder working woman," Dorothy said.

"You know when my daddy's coming home?"

"Yo' daddy got called to do a cross-country run, so he won't be back 'til next Wednesday. You and Cedric want to eat here tonight? I'm cooking some meatball stew."

"My momma had me take the leftover meatloaf out the freezer for me and Cedric for supper. We'll just eat that but thank you."

"Meatloaf?" Nedrick said with a hungry look in his eyes.

"Don't even think about it, Nedrick," Dorothy said. "You go bum food off of somebody else. Go see Melton, I think his boss be butchering a pig today. Maybe he'll set you up with some chitlins."

"Chitlins?" Nedrick said with disgust. "What you take me for Dot, some country-ass nigga?"

Dorothy ignored Nedrick and turned her attention back to Clayton. "Where is Cedric, anyway? I ain't seen him since yesterday."

"I ain't seen him either," Clayton said. Dorothy was about to say something else when she noticed Terrell standing outside the screen door. "Hey, Tee," she said. "Come on in, baby. You want something to eat?"

"No ma'am," Terrell answered bashfully.

Sensing that her nephew was just trying to be polite, Dorothy said, "Get in here, Tee. Auntie Dee gonna fix you a fried boloney sandwich and some milk."

Terrell entered the house but remained standing close to the door as if he did not want to get near his unkempt father.

"What's up, Tee?" Clayton mumbled through a mouth full of bread and bologna. Terrell lifted his chin to acknowledge Clayton's greeting but did not otherwise reply.

"Where's yo' momma, Terrell?" Dorothy asked.

"She at the Bingo hall," he answered sheepishly. "At least that's where she said she be goin'."

Dorothy, knowing better, tried to stifle a smirk as she laid a slice of bologna into the hot frying pan.

As Nedrick was leaning back in his chair to tilt his head back and drain the last few drops of beer down his throat, he lost his balance momentarily and nearly fell backwards. Terrell snickered and then quickly covered his mouth when Nedrick turned and glared at him. "What you laughin' at, you nasty lil' nigga?" Nedrick growled.

"Nothin' you need to worry about," Terrell muttered.

"What you said, boy?" Nedrick snarled.

When Terrell did not reply, Nedrick scoffed and shook his head disdainfully. "Look at you with those big ass teeth that's too big for yo' mouth and that big ass mouth that's too big for yo' face. I'll come over there and knock the stupid out of you is what I'll do."

Terrell tried to mask his hurt feelings by sucking his teeth insolently and leering back at Nedrick. "My momma said if you hit me again, she gonna call the *police* and send yo' sorry black ass back to jail." There was clear defiance in his tone.

"Which one's yo' momma?" Nedrick asked, though he knew the answer, the question designed to remind the insolent child that he was one of many insignificant children Nedrick had sired by many insignificant women.

"Fuck you, you sorry old bitch," Terrell replied in a wounded

40

tone.

"Hey, hey, hey, now!" Dorothy exclaimed as she handed Terrell a sandwich and a plastic cup filled with milk. "Both of y'all, now that's enough. Y'all need to watch yo' language up in here. I mean it."

"Well, I will tell you what," Nedrick said, wagging a scarred, bony finger at the young boy, "if he's mine, I will buss his ass when that ass needs bussin,' you hear me?" Then, addressing Terrell directly, said, "So you go tell yo' ho-dog of a momma, whichever one she is, that if she call the *police* on me her next call better be to the morgue because she be dead as soon as I get out. And you know I don't play nigga. Ain't gonna take no shit from nobody, not yo' momma and sure as hell not from a little snot-nosed punk-ass-bitch like you."

"You suck my dick, you drunk-ass cripple," Terrell said. Then, seeing Nedrick quickly slide his feet under himself as if to stand up from the table and give chase, Terrell hurried out of the house with milk splashing out of his cup and his sandwich flapping in this hand as the screen door slammed behind him. "Punk-ass King Arthur bitch!" he yelled over his shoulder as he disappeared around the corner of the house.

"Why you got to antagonize that poor child, Nedrick?" Dorothy asked in a chastising tone, wiping the spilled milk off the floor with a wet kitchen towel. "It's bad enough you don't claim him and his brother. Why can't you just let 'em be?"

"Fuck that little nigga," Nedrick said. "Him and his pumpkin-head twin. And you don't know they mine Dorothy. Everybody know they momma a ho. Ain't no tellin' who they daddy is."

Dorothy stopped sweeping and placed her hand back on her hip. "Nedrick you know you those boys' daddy, so don't run that nonsense up in here. And if you ain't gonna be a daddy to 'em, at least be kind."

Nedrick had stopped listening and seemed lost in thought.

41

"Motherfucker," he mumbled to himself as he scratched his head, ignoring his sister-in-law's remonstrance. "What I'm supposed to do with no T.V.?"

"That repo is on you, Nedrick." Dorothy declared.

"Dorothy Jane," Nedrick said, in an exasperated tone, "you know damn well it's the white man put me in this situation. I buss my ass at that rice mill, day in and day out, fifty, sixty hours a week for seventeen years. Then when my damn back finally give out on me, they just kick me to the curb wit' the rest of the broken equipment. No severance, no work comp, not a Got-damned mother fuckin' thing for my trouble."

Dorothy stopped sweeping and glared at Nedrick. "Yeah? Well, you would'a got yo' work comp had you not been on drugs, so don't be actin' all innocent up in here where we know the truth, Nedrick Wayne Watson."

Nedrick regarded Dorothy with a wounded countenance. "Dorothy J.," he said, "come on now girl. You know that drug stuff was some trumped-up bullshit. I hurt my back liftin' on a eighty-pound sack of rice seed 'cause they was too damn cheap to replace an old broke-down forklift. Me smokin' a little Mary Jane wit' my boys over the weekend ain't had a fuckin' thing to do with me hurtin' my back on a Thursday. You know that. I know that. They know that. They abuse me like a God-damned cheap shovel and then threw me in the tall grass when the handle got broke."

"Well," Dorothy said, "if you had finished high school and maybe went to trade school or something, you could have gotten yo'self a better-paying job where you didn't have to use yo' back so much."

Nedrick laughed derisively. "Woman, you don't know what the shit you talkin' 'bout. All da good jobs go to da white people. Jolly Riggins, he spent all the time getting' his GED and then went to apply to trade school. He told them he wanted to be a plumber. You know what da counselor lady told him?"

When Dorothy did not respond, Nedrick continued. "She told him he be wasting his time."

"That's Jolly. He dumb," Dorothy said. "He wasn't smart enough to pass the course, Nedrick."

"No. That wasn't it at all," Nedrick said. "How smart you got to be to clean-out some drains and run some pipe, girl? It's because most colored folk don't hire plumbers—they can't afford it, so they take care of that kind of shit themselves or get a friend or relative to. And ain't no white people gonna hire a black plumber because ain't no white people gonna let a nigga man up in they house. They let a nigga-woman come clean or cook or help take care of they kids, but they not lettin' no nigga-man up in they house. Electrician, same thing. T.V. repair, same thing. Appliance repair, same thing. So, all the good jobs go to the white people."

Dorothy scoffed and just shook her head.

"But" Nedrick continued, "if Reverend Jackson and them niggas in Washington hurry up with them ripruitions, I'll be in high cotton," Nedrick said. "I'll buy my own fuckin' T.V. A big ass motherfucker, big as a wall."

"It's reparations Uncle Ned," Clayton interjected.

"Reparations, yeah—what I said?" Nedrick replied, chuckling at himself.

"Reparations?" Dorothy asked, belly-laughing.

"What you laughin' at?" Nedrick asked. "You don't want to get paid? Shit, girl, if you don't want it, I'll take your check, too. Shit, they owe us."

"Who owes who?" Dorothy replied.

"You know what I'm talking about, Dot. Why you playin'

dumb?" Nedrick leaned back, sucked his teeth and said with authority, "White people owe black people for what they done to us with slavery and all that."

"When was you a slave, Nedrick?" Dorothy asked.

"How you wanna act, Dot? It don't matter that I was never a slave. I work for one white man for just enough money to give another white man, just to be able to eat and have a roof over my head. Shit, you know as well I do that the white man done been keepin' us niggas down—never giving us a chance—never since we got brought here. So yes, they owe us ripiri—ripari—shit, how you say it, Clayton?"

"Reparations," Clayton repeated, chuckling to himself.

"Yeah, reparations," Nedrick said triumphantly.

Dorothy stopped and regarded her brother-in-law with thinly veiled amusement. "Nedrick, look at your skin."

Nedrick knitted his brow and looked back at Dorothy in confusion. "What?"

"Look at the skin on your arm, fool," Dorothy repeated as she placed her fist back on her hip and waited for Nedrick to comply.

Nedrick looked at his arm and then back at her Dorothy, still confused.

"Your skin is lighter than half the Cajuns in this town. My boss, Mr. Fontenot, he white, and you as light if not lighter than him."

"So?" Nedrick replied, still not understanding Dorothy's point.

"So, that means you got a lot of white in you. Probably more white than black. So, if whites owe reparations to blacks, you better get out your checkbook nigga, 'cause you gonna be payin' more than you gettin'."

Nedrick twisted his mouth and rolled his eyes in irritation. "Girl, you done gone Pineville crazy on me. Why you wanna act like that? I ain't paying nobody shit. You know a nigga is a nigga, no matter how light they skin be. What the white folk say? You got one drop of nigga blood in you, you's a nigga. So, I'm in the *gettin' paid* line, bitch."

"Well," Clayton said after swallowing a gulp of milk, "you know technically, the word *reparation* comes from the root word *repair*."

"That's right," Nedrick said with renewed confidence. "The white people need to repair the damage they done caused us."

Dorothy smirked and tilted her head to the side for affect. "How they repair hundreds of years of oppression? Throwing some money at some niggas gonna repair all that? Ghetto niggas would have that spent in two months on booze and drugs and shit they don't need and when the money's gone, they still gonna be druggin' and thuggin'. Well-off niggas would just buy nicer cars and bigger houses. And then what? They gonna throw money at the next generation and the next generation after that? They ain't got the money to do that and even if they did, it ain't gonna repair a dog-gone thing. That's why it ain't never gonna happen if you ask me."

Nedrick regarded his sister-in-law as though she had just committed treason against her race. "Bitch, you talkin' crazy," he said.

"Coach Zaunbrecher," Clayton interjected, "he said if you really want reparations—if you really want to repair the situation in a truly honest way, you've got to put black people back in the position that they would have been in if the slavery had never happened in the first place."

Nedrick furrowed his brow, finding himself slow to follow, his confused countenance begging for elaboration. "What you mean?" he asked warily.

"He said if the white man had never gone to Africa and enslaved black people, then most blacks living in this country would not be here right now. He said African tribes did not have boats that could cross the ocean and so would have not migrated here on their own. So, if you want to genuinely repair of the situation, he says you have to give blacks one-way tickets back to Africa and let them have the life they would have had if the slave trade had never happened. All you would get is a grass hut and maybe a goat," he said.

"Coach Zaunbrecher really said that?" Dorothy inquired.

Clayton nodded. "Yep. I heard it straight out of his mouth."

"And he said that to the class?"

"No, he said it to Coach Schexnayder when they were in the coach's office drinking coffee. But the door was open, and I could hear 'em."

"He said that if American coloreds had to live like real Africans, you know, living in grass huts, having to watch out for lions and leopards when they go use the bathroom, catching malaria, they would realize how good they have it here."

"There you go, Nedrick," said Dorothy chuckling, "you better be careful what you ask for. Otherwise, the sixty percent of you that's white will be buying the forty percent of you that's black a one-way ticket to the Congo."

Nedrick regarded Dorothy and Clayton for a moment through glassy eyes and then chuckled. "Y'all fuckin' with me," he said. "Yeah, y'all fuckin' with me. Y'all crazy. I never said nothing about goin' back to no Africa. I just want my check."

Clayton nodded. "Maybe you can find out what African tribe sold your ancestors to the slave traders and go ask the Chief for reparations," he said to his uncle.

Nedrick scowled. "Ain't no African tribe sold my ancestors, nigga. That was all the white man."

"How you think the white man was gettin' most of the slaves they brought over here?" Clayton said. "African tribes were selling African people to the slave traders. Just like pigs and goats."

"What?" Nedrick said, sucking his teeth. "Boy, you so full of shit."

"No, I ain't," Clayton said. "That's a fact. You can read about it in the library. There were all kind of chiefs selling slaves, mostly for guns. Then they would take those guns, go conquer other tribes, enslave those people and then sell them to the slave traders for more guns."

"Nigga, you crazy. Ain't no African chiefs was selling African people."

"I'm telling you Uncle Nedrick. It's true."

"I'm telling you, it ain't," Nedrick retorted.

Clayton chuckled as he got up and walked out of the room and down the hall before locking himself in the bathroom, leaving Dorothy and Nedrick alone in the kitchen. Nedrick glared at his sister-in-law with tired, blood-shot eyes. He lifted the can to his lips and tilted it upside down but nothing came out. Dorothy started to say something and then stopped. She spotted crumbs on her otherwise spotless linoleum and bent at the waist to wipe them up, stretching the cotton floral print of her house dress to its limits as Nedrick watched with interest.

"You said Boosie ain't gonna be back for a few days?" Nedrick said to Dorothy.

"No. I said Horace was on a cross-country and won't be coming back on Wednesday. Boosie, he be back tonight. "Why?"

Nedrick stared at Dorothy with a changed expression on his face. His ire had dissipated. She turned around to resume her cleaning. As she moved to wipe off the sink and counter, she felt Nedrick's eyes on her. She stopped and looked over her shoulder to find Nedrick grinning back at her amorously.

"What you think you looking at, nigga?" Dorothy said confrontationally, holding the broom in one hand close to her large, curvy body.

"You know what I gots my eye on, bitch," Nedrick said, smiling slyly.

Dorothy cocked her head and lifted one eyebrow in bewilderment as she glared back at Nedrick. "The hell I do," she said.

Nedrick shot a glance down the hall to make sure that Clayton was still in the bathroom. "Some of that thick, sweet nookie," Nedrick said lowly, grinning through missing teeth.

Dorothy put her hand over her heart, her mouth agape, looking fixedly upon Nedrick in disbelief, wanting to believe that her ears had deceived her. "Nigga, I know you just didn't say what I think I just heard you say because if you did, you is one dead-ass nigga when yo' brother gets home."

"What?" Nedrick said, chuckling and feigning innocence. "What you thought I said, Dot?"

"Go 'head and play the fool, Nedrick. See where that gets you."

Nedrick smiled slyly. "What, Dot? What I did?"

"Never you mind, Nedrick. I ain't got no time for yo' games. You just best get yo' drunk ass out this house right now," she said as she turned her back on him and nervously started sweeping the area that she had already swept.

CHAPTER 8

Dorothy watched Nedrick shuffling out of the house and then heard the screen door slam shut. She peeked out of the window and watched him stagger down the driveway, mumbling something incomprehensible. A few minutes later, Clayton returned to the kitchen and sat back down at the table.

"Did you light a match up in there?"

"Yes, ma'am," Clayton said.

"And did you wash yo' hands?"

Clayton frowned and slid his chair back. He walked to the kitchen sink.

"No, no, no, boy," Dorothy said, "you bring yo'self back to the bathroom for that."

Clayton smirked and rolled his eyes but complied. When he sat back down at the table to finish his sandwiches, Dorothy grabbed a damp rag and began wiping the surface of the kitchen table, lifting Clayton's glass of milk and his plate to wipe under them.

"You want to end up like that fool?" she said. "Then ignore your schooling and hang out on the corner wit' the winos and the drug heads. They will gladly show you the path to that kind of life. You hear me?"

"Auntie Dee, you know you ain't got to worry about me," Clayton said.

"I better not," Dorothy replied, "the Lord Jesus knows I will tear the flesh off yo' ass if I see any sign of you going astray. That's the God's honest truth right there, without filter or fancy. And I don't care how big you get, Clayton Chaisson. You hear me?"

"Yes, ma'am." After a brief moment of silence, Clayton said. "Auntie Dee?"

"Yeah, baby?"

"What's Pineville crazy?"

"Do what?"

"Uncle Ned said you were being Pineville crazy."

"Oh," Dorothy said with a chuckle. "Pineville" is where the state insane asylum is at, you know, where they keep the looney-toonies. Nedrick thinks he being funny."

Clayton nodded just as a loud knock on the screen door reverberated through the kitchen. He and Dorothy both turned to see who was at the door just as it was opening. A dark-skinned, heavy-set colored girl with a large, unkempt afro and tattoos on her wrists entered carrying one toddler on her hip and dragging another by the arm, her face wrought with concern.

"What you doing here, Jayla?" Dorothy asked anxiously. "What's the matter?"

"Have y'all seen Cedric?" Jayla asked.

"He ain't at his house?"

"No."

"Well, I ain't seen him since yesterday before he left for work," Dorothy replied. "Why?"

"The nursing home be calling. D'Arius didn't show up for work today. Cedric neither. Nobody seen them since they got off work last night."

Dorothy looked at Clayton. "Cedric didn't come home last night?"

Clayton shrugged his shoulders. "I don't know. I spent the night at Pookie's."

Dorothy shifted her gaze back to Jayla. "D'Arius' momma ain't seen 'em?"

50

Jayla scoffed. "Jelsie? She shacked up with Chubby again. She can't be bothered."

"Chubby? I thought she was finally done with all that after he knocked her tooth out?" Dorothy said.

Jayla sucked her teeth and smirked. "Shit, she done worse than that to him. They both crazy. And as long as he be keepin' her high and she be givin' him what he want, they ain't gonna be done with each other no time soon."

Dorothy shook her head in disgust. "Lord Jesus."

"So, nobody seen Cedric or D'Arius then?" Jayla asked again, as if by repeating the question she hoped to get a different response.

Dorothy pursed her lips and exhaled anxiously. "Go look for your brother, Clayton. Check at home."

"I just come from there," Jayla said. "I knocked and knocked. Ain't nobody answered."

"Check anyway Clayton," Dorothy said. "Maybe he was sleeping. Maybe he was on the toilet. If not, check the park."

"Yes ma'am," Clayton said before grabbing the last sandwich on his plate and hurrying out of the house.

Dorothy and Jayla gave each other concerned looks. "I need to call Cedric's momma and let her know what's going on. I'll call you if I hear anything. You call me if you hear something."

"Okay," Jayla said. "But Dee—"

"What?" Dorothy replied.

"I got a bad feeling about this. I mean, it ain't nothing for D'Arius to not go home at night. I know he's gonna do his thing now and again. But Cedric? Something ain't right."

Dorothy's face assumed a concerned expression. "Girl, go on back to your house with them negative thoughts. I don't need that up in here."

Jayla didn't move. Her countenance was a conflation of apology and apprehension. She regarded Dorothy as if she wanted Dorothy to reassure her that there was nothing to worry about.

"Go on girl," Dorothy said, "before I knock you with my broom. I'll call you when I hear something."

"Okay."

CHAPTER 9

As the sun rose higher into the sky and the avian activity in and around the woods increased, so did the Ezra and Giles' hunting fortunes. By late morning, the Ziploc's contents included the breasts of two robins, three blackbirds, a grackle and a starling. As Giles was bagging the last breast, Ezra checked his watch. "My mom's going to be picking us up in about an hour," he said. "Let's go to the other side of the woods, closer to the highway. We can hunt the swampy area along the tree line while making our way back toward the cattle guard."

"Okay," Giles said as he followed Ezra through the brush.

They walked slowly and in silence, scanning their surroundings for any signs of game, Ezra taking the lead for a while and then Giles. Suddenly Ezra froze and gestured for Giles to stop and remain still. He pointed toward a thicket and made the sign for bunny ears to indicate that he had seen a rabbit. When the cottontail reappeared in a small clearing, Ezra lifted his rifle and took aim. Before he was able to pull the trigger, the cottontail disappeared into dense foliage and then after several seconds hopped back into sight on the other side of a large water oak.

As Ezra carefully adjusted his aim, the report of Giles' air rifle sounded, startling Ezra. A small tuft of the rabbit's fur flew into the air and it leapt skyward, flipping and landing clumsily before finding its feet and frantically racing off, zigzagging through the underbrush.

"Hey!" Ezra yelled angrily.

"I hit it!" Giles shouted. "I hit it! Did you see?"

"I'm the one who saw it first!" Ezra growled as they both sprinted in the direction of the rabbit, Giles following Ezra as they barreled through brambles and thistles in frenzied pursuit.

Just when they thought they had lost their quarry, the cottontail reappeared almost from under their feet and then just as quickly disappeared behind a large palmetto patch.

"Look," Ezra whispered, pointing at the ground at a droplet of blood, "he's wounded."

Giles beamed with pride. "I told you I hit him," he said.

Ezra shushed Giles. They paused for a moment to catch their breath, listening for any signs of movement. While Giles reloaded and pumped his gun, Ezra began creeping to the left side of the palmetto patch and gestured for Giles to circle around to the right. Giles nodded and complied, taking a wide berth so as not to flush the rabbit prematurely.

Moments later, Ezra heard a high-pitched shriek. He assumed that the rabbit had reappeared and startled Giles. He listened for the sound of Giles' air rifle but heard no shot. Quickly, he lifted his gun and readied himself to shoot just in case the rabbit ran in his direction. When nothing appeared, he called out to Giles in a loud whisper, "Do you see it?"

When Giles made no reply, Ezra surmised that the rabbit was still near and that Giles was attempting to creep toward it in silence. "Do you see it?" Ezra called out again, this time in a louder whisper, still holding his rifle up, ready to take aim and shoot. Again, there was no response. "Giles?" Ezra repeated.

When Giles did not reply, Ezra slowly circled back and quietly followed the route that Giles had taken through the brush and trees. He found Giles standing perfectly still near the edge of the palmetto patch, his back to Ezra, his gun in the mud at his feet.

"Giles," Ezra whispered.

Giles neither replied nor moved.

"What is it?" Ezra whispered, afraid to draw nearer, fearing that Giles might have stumbled upon a water moccasin or maybe even an alligator. When Giles didn't respond, Ezra carefully circled around and approached, cautiously peering over Giles' shoulder.

Directly in front of Giles, just a few feet away, was the cottontail. It laid on its side panting heavily with blood leaking from its nose. Ezra was about to exclaim with excitement when he noticed a muddy Converse high-top laying in the mud a couple of feet on the other side of the rabbit. The shoe was on a foot which was connected to a leg.

Slowly, Ezra stepped forward. When he gained a better view of what had captured Giles' attention, he stopped in his tracks, all of the air leaving his lungs. His heart began to beat wildly against his chest as adrenaline began pumping into his bloodstream. Lying before them in a contorted pile on the ground was a badly mangled colored boy. Much of the skin on his cheeks, nose and forehead was gone, exposing raw flesh and in some places bone. Where his front teeth had been only jagged, bloody stumps remained. Large patches of bloody scalp were visible in several places on the top and side of his head where clumps of his thick afro had apparently been ripped out by the roots. One eye was swollen shut and the other was open.

Adding to the frightfulness of the colored boy's appearance was that he appeared to be looking back at Giles and Ezra with the huge, macabre smile of a maniacal clown. Only he was not smiling. The impression of a smile was due to his lips having been severed from his face, fully exposing his bloody gums and what was left of his fractured teeth. The remaining skin and muscle tissue around his mouth had been cauterized, outlining the orifice with charred, bubbly flesh.

Ezra felt his body begin to quiver and then the sensation of wet warmth running down the inside of left leg. He grabbed Giles by the arm and gently tugged. The contact seemed to jar Giles from a state of shock and together they began to slowly shuffle backwards when suddenly the colored boy's body convulsed. Ezra's rifle fell to the ground as he and Giles shrieked and grabbed at each other in fright. They both turned and began sprinting through the woods in the direction of the highway, running faster than they had ever run before, leaping over fallen trees, splashing though swamp water and catching spider webs with their faces, impervious to thorns and brambles that tore at their clothes and flesh.

Finally, they reached the edge of the woods and then frantically climbed the highway embankment. When they reached the shoulder, they stopped and fell to their knees, gasping for air and pulling layers of sticky spider webs from their faces and hair. A tow truck driver who had just pulled a wrecked pickup from the roadside ravine saw them and stopped. After he calmed them down, they told him what they found. He rifled through his tool chest, found a can of spray paint and made a large silver arrow pointing in the direction of where the boys told him they had found the colored boy. Then he drove them to the St. Landry Parish Sheriff's Office in Opelousas.

CHAPTER 10

With the help of the deputy, the paramedics quickly moved the mutilated colored boy onto a stretcher, through the brush, up the embankment and into the ambulance. Upon radioing in the status to the dispatcher, they were instructed to transport the boy directly to University Medical Center in Lafayette. A surgical trauma team would be waiting.

As the ambulance was leaving the scene, additional St. Landry Parish Sheriff's Department personnel began to arrive. A stocky, bald-headed detective quickly took charge, instructing two deputies at the scene to help him conduct a careful sweep of the area, starting at the location where the colored boy was found and moving outward, using concentric arcs.

Within a few minutes a thin, beak-nosed deputy called out to the others that he had found something. The detective and a second deputy, an older, heavy-set fellow with a thick mustache followed his voice until they found the first deputy standing atop a short tree stump, gesturing toward a small swampy area approximately fifteen feet from where the disfigured colored boy had been found. As the detective and the older deputy drew nearer, they saw the distended body of another colored boy lying face down in the mud, all but hidden by a cluster of ferns.

"Don't think we're going to need an ambulance for this one Cecil," the beak-nosed deputy said.

The detective grimaced at the sight of the body. "Jesus," he said.

"Kirk," Cecil said to the beak-nosed deputy, "I need you to go back to the car and get on the radio. Have dispatch send for the coroner. Hampton," he said to the older deputy, "you stay here and help me to finish sweeping the area. There could be more. Be on the look-out for evidence, too."

"This is going to be a lot of paperwork boys," Hampton lamented.

Kirk began to walk back toward the highway and then stopped short. "Shit Cecil," he said, "you realize that we are just a few feet from the Evangeline Parish line, right?"

"I knew we were close," Cecil replied.

"Shit, he's right," Hampton said. "If the bodies were just a few feet in that direction, this would be their headache, not ours."

"Cecil," Kirk said, "if you give us the green light, me and Ham, we can move everything over there and let the Evangeline boys handle all the paperwork."

Hampton chuckled. "It ain't like them lazy sons of bitches wouldn't try to do the same thing to us."

Mostly just for kicks, Cecil examined the path to the estimated parish line. Quickly realizing that there would be no way to move the body across the political boundary without leaving very conspicuous tracks in the mud, he quickly dismissed the idea with a scoff. "Go call the coroner like I said."

"10-4," Kirk said before trudging through the brush back toward the highway.

"How long you think he's been dead, Cecil?" Hampton asked as he circled the body from a safe distance so as not to disturb the scene.

"Hard to say," the detective answered, scratching his chin contemplatively. "Might not be that long. When it's warm and damp like this, it can really accelerate the putrificationary process."

"I don't think that's a word," Hampton said teasingly.

"Well," the detective replied, smiling slyly, "I don't suspect they covered that word in school until the twelfth grade. Maybe if you would have finished."

"Oh, now that smarts Cecil," Hampton said, feigning hurt feelings.

"Well, you know the risks of messing with the bull, Hampton."

Hampton chuckled. "What were those kids who found the other one doing out here anyway?"

"Shooting their pellet guns," Cecil said. "One of 'em was Chief Brasseaux's son."

"Really?"

"Yep. I think the other one was Doc Poret's boy."

"Hmm, I'll bet they must'a shit their pants when they saw that other one. I mean Jesus, in on my years of doing this shit, I ain't never."

"Me neither," Cecil said.

CHAPTER 11

Ezra was sitting alone in a small conference room eating potato chips that a deputy had bought for him from a vending machine when his mother arrived.

"I'll give y'all some privacy, Miss Eve," the deputy who had escorted her to the conference room said as he closed the door.

Ezra was wearing the pants of the smallest police uniform that they could find, but they were still floated on him. A plastic bag containing his soiled pants lay on the floor next to his chair. His mother leaned over and kissed him on top of the head.

He looked up at her with a scowl on his face. "Giles' mom picked him up over an hour ago," he said.

"Oh, honey," she said. "I'm so sorry you had to wait for so long. Your dad's in Lake Charles for a training seminar, and I had already left to go pick y'all up at the cattle guard, so it was a while before I got the call at home."

Ezra did not respond.

"I was so worried when y'all didn't show up. Are you okay, baby? You must have been so scared." she said as she pushed his bangs out of his eyes.

Ezra pulled away from his mother's touch. "I wasn't scared," he said.

"Of course you weren't, baby," his mother said. "I didn't mean it like that." She rubbed his arm gently and said that he and Giles had been so brave and how they had saved that young man's life.

Ezra ignored her flattery. "Can we go home now?" he asked.

"Sure, honey."

As she drove toward home, Eve noticed an anxious look growing on Ezra's face that in turn made her anxious. "What is it, honey?" she finally asked in a gentle tone. Instinctively, she wanted to caress his face but decided that he would not be receptive and so refrained.

Ezra turned to look at her, instinctively wanting to see if the words of the answer she was about to give were going to match her body language. "Are you and Dad getting a divorce?" he asked.

Eve's brow furrowed as she withdrew her hand from Ezra's headrest. "No," she said, far too defensively to be reassuring. "Why would you ask that, honey?"

"Giles' mom heard it from the gossip monkeys at the country club," Ezra said.

Eve was too discombobulated to appreciate the malapropic humor in Ezra's response. When she did not respond immediately, Ezra repeated the question in an impatient tone, "Are y'all?"

"No, baby. Nobody is getting a divorce." she said.

Ezra's expression made clear that he was skeptical, but Eve felt helpless to ease his anxiety. She felt the strong urge to turn the car around and drive straight to Melody Poret's home and give her a piece of her mind. Instead, she stayed the course and decided she would deal with Melody later.

They road in silence most of the way back home. As they approached their driveway, Ezra finally spoke. "Can Giles sleep over tonight?" he asked.

"Oh baby," Eve said, as she parked the car, "with everything that's happened, I think it's best that you both get some good rest tonight. I'm sure his mom will feel the same way. Y'all can do a sleepover next weekend, okay?"

61

Ezra did not protest. Upon further reflection, he knew that Giles' mother would not let him come over tonight. "Okay, and I want to invite Vance, too," he said. "We can camp out in the backyard."

Eve hesitated. The risk of mischief always seemed significantly greater when Vance Duhon was part of their group. She started to say no when Ezra cut her off.

"Please Mom."

"We'll see."

"Mom," Ezra droned, "please."

"Okay, honey."

When Ezra's father returned home from his training conference, Eve filled him in on the details. She said that Ezra did not want to talk about it much—that he seemed a little traumatized.

"I'd be worried if he weren't after seeing something like that," his father said. "I'll talk to him in the morning. I'm sure he'll be fine." He grabbed a box of Cheerios from the pantry and set it down on the kitchen table.

"There are leftovers in the fridge," Eve said. "Smothered pork chops, rice and gravy, and sweet peas, if you would prefer that."

Bernard peered at Eve incredulously, almost grinning. She had never mastered the art of Cajun cooking, and he thought she had given up trying long ago.

"Oh, I didn't cook it," she said lightheartedly. "Your Aunt Shirley brought it over. I guess she still thinks you and Ezra are too skinny."

"She thinks everybody's too skinny," Bernard said as he opened the refrigerator to examine its contents. "I'll eat the rice and gravy tomorrow," he said. "I ate too much for lunch at the seminar." After putting the milk on the table, he grabbed a cereal bowl from the cabinet and a spoon from the drawer.

As he ate and perused the back of the cereal box, Bernard pretended not to notice that Eve was busying herself wiping down countertops that were already spotless. After a few more minutes of eating in silence while Eve organized things out in the kitchen that were already organized, Bernard could stand it no more and broke the silence.

"What is it, Eve?" he said without looking up.

She stopped what she was doing and turned to face him. "Well, I thought you might want to know—" When Bernard did not look up at her, she stopped, obviously wanting his full attention. She began again, this time louder and in a more commanding tone, "I was going to say that I thought you might want to know that Ezra heard a rumor about us."

"Okay," Bernard replied before shoveling more cereal into his mouth.

"Don't you want to know what the rumor is?"

Bernard shrugged. "Not really. I mean, if it's true, I'm sure I already know and if it's not true, I'm sure I don't really care."

"Well, maybe you can shed some light on whether it's true or not."

Bernard's only response was to continue eating his cereal.

Growing impatient, Eve continued. "He heard some gossip that you and I are getting a divorce."

Bernard stopped chewing for a moment and then resumed and swallowed. "Where did he hear that?"

"Giles Poret," Eve said. "Apparently Melody was gossiping about it and he overheard."

Bernard nodded subtly and went back to eating his cereal.

"Do you have any idea how the gossip may have gotten started?"

63

"Not a clue," Bernard answered in a mechanical tone, still not looking up.

"Well, it had to come from somewhere, Bernard."

"I suppose it did," Bernard replied. "What did you say?" he asked.

"I haven't said anything to anyone," Eve said indignantly.

"I meant what did you say to Ezra when he told you about the gossip?"

"What was I supposed to say, Bernard?"

"I don't know, Eve." Bernard sighed, trying to avoid a full-on state of exasperation.

"Well, what would you have said?"

Bernard turned to look Eve in the face. "It doesn't matter what I would have said because he didn't tell me. He told you."

"But what would you have said if he came to you about it? What will you say if he asks you?"

"Well, since he spoke to you first, I guess it would depend on what you've already told him, which is why I'm asking."

"Well, of course I told him it was not true," Eve droned.

Bernard signed and rubbed his temples.

"What?" Eve asked.

"Nothing."

Bernard stood and began washing his cereal bowl and spoon in the sink. Eve angrily threw the dishtowel on the counter and stamped out of the kitchen and down the hall. Bernard heard the bedroom door slam shut and he breathed a sigh of relief.

As was the norm, Bernard retired for the night in the guest bedroom. This had been the situation for as long as Ezra could remember. When he got old enough to realize that most married people slept in the same room, he had inquired about it. His parents told him that it was due to the fact his father often had to attend to police calls late into the night and their not wanting that to disturb Eve's sleep. Ezra had never given it another thought.

But the truth was that Bernard and Eve's sleeping arrangements had nothing to do with late work calls or sleep. The fact of the matter is that it had been many years since either had a desire to share a bed or any form of intimacy with the other. Their marriage was existing in a state of taxidermy—convincingly authentic looking on the outside but utterly devoid of life within. Although it had not always been that way.

CHAPTER 12

Introduced by mutual friends, Eve and Bernard met at Nick's Original Big Train Bar in New Orleans in the spring of 1957. A few years removed from completing a tour of duty in Korea, Bernard was a G.I. Bill senior studying criminal justice at Loyola University and Eve was a junior studying social work next door at Tulane. He, a staunch small-town southern conservative, and her, an unwavering progressive from the northeast, they were the living cliché that opposites attract and quickly fell in love. They dated for four months and, not having the support of Bernard's parents because Eve was not Roman Catholic nor the consent of Eve's parents because Bernard was not a Jew, eloped to Natchez, Mississippi.

Following their two-day honeymoon at the Monmouth Historic Inn, Bernard started his new job in Opelousas with Troop K of the Louisiana State Police and Eve began commuting to Lafayette to finish her degree at Southwestern Louisiana Institute before taking a job as an elementary school counselor.

Bernard quickly climbed the ranks to lieutenant with the state police before being offered the interim Chief of Police job in his hometown of Iris. He accepted the position and they moved to Iris in the spring of 1965. Later that year, their first child was born. Ezra Paul Brasseaux had his father's dark hair and gray-blue eyes, his mother's aquiline nose and his paternal grandfather's oversized ears. His ample freckles, a trait he had apparently inherited from Eve's mother's side of the family, would not appear until several years later.

Two years after Ezra was born and approximately three and a half months into her second pregnancy, Eve informed Bernard that she was going to New Orleans overnight to meet up with an old girlfriend from college who was in town for a conference. Bernard's mother had agreed to keep Ezra while she was gone.

When Eve returned home from her trip, she put Ezra to bed and then joined Bernard in the den. He was sitting in his favorite overstuffed chair with his feet propped up on an ottoman, drinking a beer and watching an episode of *Gunsmoke*. She turned the TV off and sat on the edge of the ottoman facing him. She said that she needed to tell him something. The expression on her face was grave. Bernard set his beer down, put his feet on the floor and sat up to give Eve his full attention.

Through tears, Eve told Bernard that when she reached New Orleans, she noticed that she was spotting and so she went to the emergency room. Struggling to get the words out, she told him that she was examined and was informed that she had lost the baby. She explained that she did not call him because there was nothing he could have done anyway and because she wanted to tell him in person.

All of the blood left Bernard's face. He took Eve's hands in his and asked her if she was okay as tears welled in his eyes. She assured him that she was and then they cried together before he picked her up in his arms and carried her to bed.

When more than two years passed without another pregnancy, Eve and Bernard were referred to a fertility specialist in Alexandria. After they both were subjected to a variety of tests, they met with the doctor who told them that they found a significant amount of scar tissue on Eve's fallopian tubes and that the chances of her conceiving again were virtually nil.

Eve and Bernard were both devastated. She leaned into him and he held her tightly as tears began to roll down their faces. Finally, Bernard gathered himself enough to speak. "The scar tissue—what would have caused that?" he asked as he gently squeezed Eve's hand supportively.

The doctor glanced at Eve as if to see if she was going to offer an explanation. When she did not, he began to formulate a response in his head, trying to choose his words carefully. "Well," he said and then paused and glanced at Eve again as if to give her one more chance to control the narrative. When she remained silent, he proceeded. In a tone that betrayed his discomfort he said, "The scar tissue is from a past procedure."

Bernard wiped the tears from his face and knitted his brow. He looked at Eve and then back at the doctor obviously desirous of further explanation. He felt certain that Eve had not had any procedures that would have affected her reproductive organs since he had known her. "What procedure?" he asked finally.

Again the doctor glanced at Eve to see if she was going to offer a response. When it did not appear that she intended to, he began to reply, but before any words were spoken, Eve pulled away from Bernard and straightened her posture. The doctor paused.

"An abortion," Eve said, trying hard to sound matter of fact and unashamed.

Bernard's face turned gray. He and Eve had engaged in friendly debates about reproductive rights on many occasions during their courtship, with Bernard always respectfully advocating the *pro-life* position and Eve the woman's *right to choose.* Because their discussions had always been philosophical and academic, or so he had assumed, it had never occurred to him that she had already had an abortion when they met. He felt certain that it would have come up or that Eve would have at least inadvertently tipped her hand during their debates. He now realized that he must have assumed incorrectly.

"Can I ask," Bernard said to the doctor, grabbing Eve's hand again, "how were we able to conceive our first child, you know, with the scar tissue and all? Did we just get lucky? Or did the hormones from that pregnancy maybe make the scar tissue worse?"

The doctor shot another uncomfortable glance at Eve as Bernard anxiously awaited the response.

As the sibling of an older sister with Rhett's Syndrome, Eve had grown up with a front row seat to her mother's life as the primary caregiver of a severely disabled child. She witnessed the utterly exhausting physical, mental and emotional toll that it took on her mother—the stress, anxiety and guilt, the stigma and isolation, the complete absence of normalcy. It was a fate that Eve was absolutely determined to avoid. Therefore, for each of her pregnancies, without telling Bernard, she requested amniocentesis. The results from the second pregnancy, unfortunately, confirmed that the fetus had a genetic disorder known as trisomy 13.

Eve's obstetrician explained to her that a baby with this particular genetic defect could be born with any combination of genomic malformalities, including heart defects, brain and spinal cord abnormalities, small and poorly developed eyes, extra fingers or toes, and a cleft lip and/or palate. He pulled out a medical textbook and showed Eve a number of photographs of children with trisomy 13. The images ranged from absolutely normal looking children to some with cleft deformities that were so severe as to render them barely recognizable as human. He also explained that that most infants with this condition fail to live past the first few days of life outside the womb and that less than five percent live beyond their first year. By the end of their meeting, Eve's mind was made up.

Before the fertility specialist could answer Bernard's question about how they were able to conceive their first child despite the scar tissue, Eve took a deep breath and staring at the floor in front of her said, "The abortion that I had was after Ezra was born."

The idea of his wife secretly having an abortion during their marriage seemed so implausible to Bernard that the implications of Eve's statement did not immediately register. He turned to Eve, his countenance wrought with confusion as if begging for her to explain that he had misunderstood her.

Eve sighed, still looking at the floor. She sensed Bernard's confusion. "I had an amniocentesis for each pregnancy," she told him. "The first one of course was normal. For my second pregnancy, the fetus had severe genetic defects. The doctor said it would be grossly deformed and probably wouldn't survive the pregnancy. I knew how strongly you felt about abortion, so I didn't say anything. When I told you I was going to New Orleans to spend time with my friend, that wasn't entirely true. I did meet my friend in New Orleans, but only to have her drive me to Pensacola. To a clinic."

Bernard glared at Eve. He was speechless, his thoughts and emotions running amok. He felt nauseous. He looked at the blank-faced doctor and then back at Eve. He felt like he was in the middle of a horrible nightmare.

"I told you what kind of life my mother had caring for my sister," she said. "I just could not bear going through all that, Bernard. I just couldn't. I didn't want that for me, or for you."

Bernard did not reply. He stood and walked out of the room. Eve found him in the parking lot, staring into the distance, a puddle of vomit at his feet. Neither spoke during the entire ride home.

The next morning, Bernard sat down across the kitchen table from Eve. He told her how betrayed he felt. He half expected to find her contrite and desirous of his forgiveness. Instead, she was dug-in, defiant and utterly unapologetic. They argued for hours, each saying things that would have been best left unsaid.

"I've had enough," Eve finally said, stepping toward the master bedroom. "I've got a terrible headache, and I'm going to lie down."

"Let me ask you one more thing," Bernard said.

Eve stopped and looked at him impatiently.

Bernard regarded her for a moment and then, in a very calm voice asked, "How did they do it?"

Eve looked perplexed. "How did who do what?"

Bernard spoke more slowly. "You know who and what." He repeated the question. "How did they do it?" Eerily, his tone was the same as it might be if he were asking her how the dry cleaners were able to get a stain out of a dress shirt.

"Are you being serious right now?" Eve replied, her voice barely above a whisper, the expression on her face mired in disgust and hurt, as if it was meant to shame her husband into withdrawing such an unseemly question. "Or is this just your way of trying to hurt me?"

A tear began to roll down Bernard's face. He took a deep breath and exhaled. In college, he was active in a Roman Catholic college ministry group. He became an organizer for its Pro Life committee and participated in several Right to Life marches. He had studied a number of articles on the different techniques that abortion clinics used. Some of the articles had been extremely graphic. They described the suction curettage technique where the physician "induces fetal demise" by injecting the fetal heart with sodium chloride before the physician enters the uterus with a

71

sharp instrument, literally slicing the fetus into pieces before using a vacuum device to extract them. Another technique was known as a dilation and evacuation procedure, usually performed with pregnancies that have reached the second trimester or beyond. It involves dilating the cervix before using a device to suck the dead fetus out whole, though sometimes the fetus is known to break up into pieces which are then extracted individually. And of course, there was the technique that had led to public outcry even amongst many supporters of reproductive rights, namely the so-called "partial birth abortion." With this procedure, the head and shoulders of the fetus are actually delivered and then its life is "terminated" by inserting a vacuum device at the base of its skull that is used to suck out its brains before the rest of its body is extracted from the uterus.

Standing before Eve, Bernard had these images flashing in his head—excruciatingly painful images of his own child's last living experience being so wretched and horrible, images of his or her body being violently ripped apart and sucked out of the womb, images of him or her being reduced to pieces before being discarded in a large, plastic-lined container filled atop a bloody pile of that day's fetal remains.

Matching the intensity of Eve's glare, and this time with a tone that demanded a direct answer, Bernard said, "I want to know how they did it, Eve. I have the right to know what happened to my child."

Eve's emotions were a confluence of disbelief, anger and outrage. She never thought Bernard capable of being so ignorant, so selfish and so cruel. Her nostrils flared as she leered at him in disgust. Then, somehow regaining her composure, if only for a moment, her face softened. She looked at him and delivered a hardened smile. "Go to hell, Bernard," she said coldly before turning and heading toward the bedroom.

Bernard followed, the corners of his mouth lifting ever so slightly, falling just short of a smirk over the irony of being condemned to hell by a woman who had paid someone to destroy her own child. "What's the matter, Eve?" he called out from behind her. "If you truly believe that there is nothing wrong with what you did, why are you so ashamed to tell me how it was done?"

Eve continued into the bedroom without responding or even looking back at Bernard. She quietly shut the bedroom door and began packing a suitcase. Several minutes later, she emerged from the bedroom and told Bernard that she and Ezra were going to spend some time with a friend in Baton Rouge. He did not object or try to stop her. He did not know whether she planned to return and in that moment, he did not know if he wanted her to.

Eve and Ezra returned home a few days later. During the time apart, the requited animosity between Bernard and Eve had only festered. After avoiding and ignoring each other for several months, they finally agreed to seek professional help. Unfortunately, the marriage counseling only succeeded in raking the coals and exacerbating the situation. They did however, with the counselor's guidance, manage to agree on a few things: to remain in the marriage for Ezra's sake, at least until he was out of high school; to not air their dirty laundry in public; and to not argue or exhibit hostility toward each other in front of Ezra. Thus was the genesis of the marital charade established for the benefit of Ezra and the outside world.

CHAPTER 13

Fatigued from a long week of work on her feet at the diner, Bernice Chaisson sat heavily in her living room chair, staring at the picture of the crucified Christ hanging on the wall, an empty coffee mug at her side. As she stood to return to the kitchen for a refill, she was startled by a firm knock at the front door. She was moving toward the door when the knocking repeated, this time louder. "I'm coming, I'm coming," she called out.

She opened the door to find a young St. Landry Parish Sheriff's deputy staring back at her anxiously. Two colored boys had been found a few miles south of town, near the St. Landry-Evangeline Parish line, one dead, the other in critical condition. The decedent had an Iris High I.D. in his wallet. The name on it was Cedric Chaisson. The school provided the police with this address, he explained.

Bernice looked the young deputy over. He could not have been more than twenty years old, she thought, maybe three years older than her Cedric. "Decedent?" she said finally, her tone making clear that she was not entirely familiar with the term.

The young deputy did not know how to answer delicately. "The dead one, ma'am," he said apologetically. She could get more details at the sheriff's office in Opelousas, he added as he gave her a card with the name of the detective who was assigned to the case. "I'm truly sorry, ma'am."

Bernice was dazed. She squinted her eyes as if trying to make sense of what the young deputy was saying. He recognized her confusion but was at a loss for what more to say. As he turned to walk away, Bernice spoke and he stopped and turned toward her.

"This must be a mistake," she said, shaking her head with vehemence. "That can't be my Cedric."

The deputy shifted his weight nervously. He regarded the woman sympathetically. It was his first time delivering a death notification by himself. He pulled a piece of paper from a folder and read aloud the description of the decedent's height, 5' 8", weight, 175 lbs. and the clothes he was wearing when his body was found, navy blue medical scrubs. "Your son worked part-time at the nursing home, right?"

Bernice stared at the deputy, still in denial. She opened her mouth to speak but no sound came. She looked down into the reflection of the deputy's shiny black shoes as if looking for her words and then looked up at him again, her expression begging the deputy to reveal his error or to admit that this was some sort of cruel joke, a joke which she could find in herself to forgive if only he would just confess it.

"Ma'am," the deputy said, extending his hand toward Bernice, "maybe we should find you a place to sit down."

But before the deputy could take Bernice's arm, her legs buckled and she fell hard to the ground, landing flat on her buttocks. The deputy tried to grab her to break her fall but it had happened too quickly. He stooped before her his hand on her shoulder asking her if she was okay, but she only hung her head and wept.

Unable to coax Bernice back to her feet, the deputy stayed with her in the doorway for nearly half an hour until her younger son, Clayton, returned home from football practice. The deputy gave him a quick explanation of what happened.

When Clayton too was unsuccessful in his efforts to talk his mother back to her feet, he lifted her in his arms and carried her to her bed. He then called his father at work to give him the news.

Cars and pickup trucks filled the gravel parking lot and lined both sides of the streets for three blocks. For two days visitors shuffled through the cramped spaces of the small funeral parlor. Neighbors delivered meals for the family and finger foods for the guests. Visitors expressed condolences, offering warm hugs and prayers and with moistened eyes if not flowing tears, took turns touching the shiny brass trumpet that lay delicately on a velvet pillow atop the closed lid of Cedric Chaisson's casket.

When loved ones approached Bernice to offer their condolences, she glared blankly through or past them and said nothing. When they put their hands on hers or their arms around her shoulders, she remained stiff and unresponsive. Periodically, her sisters lifted her from her chair and escorted her to the restroom. They begged her to eat, but she would not. Hour after hour she sat, staring at her son's casket, grieving in silence. Her sisters stayed close, taking turns wiping the tears from her face.

During the eulogy, the minister spoke of Cedric's exceptional musical talent and the fact that he had recently been awarded a full performing arts scholarship to Bethune-Cookman University in Florida, where he was to enroll in the fall. He credited Cedric's mother and father with teaching him about morals, virtue and work ethic, and with nurturing his relationship with God, contrasting them to other parents who seem more concerned with appeasing their children's material desires than with meeting their spiritual needs.

Dabbing sweat from his brow, he expressed empathy for the family's heartache and suffering while encouraging them to rejoice in the knowledge that Cedric was not just in a better place, but in a perfect place. He spoke of so many young people of Cedric's generation who had lost their way idolizing blaspheming musicians and money, getting caught up in drugs and sex and foolishly focusing on satisfying their hedonistic hungers, the effects of which would last but a second of eternity at the expense of forfeiting eternal salvation. Toward the end, he paused and turned back to Bernice. He spoke softly of a mother's love being fierce, interminable and unconditional—the closest thing to a Christ-like love that a human being is capable of sharing.

Though she did not return his gaze as he uttered these words, Bernice's face softened and her eyes moistened until a single tear welled in each eye and rolled down the prominent cheekbones of her tired face. The minister swallowed hard and choking back his own tears, turned his silent gaze to the ceiling as if he were questioning the wisdom of a creator who would cut so short the life of such a blessed soul and allow such suffering by such a loving mother. Bringing the eulogy to a close, the minister promised Cedric's parents that their son was—at this very moment— comfortably in the loving arms of Jesus Christ and that when their time was done and they were called, they would see this firsthand and bask with their son in the loving light of the Father, the Son and the Holy Spirit. He punctuated the eulogy with a triumphant "Amen" which was echoed by the standing room only crowd.

As the funeral director played a soulful recording of "Amazing Grace," Clayton and his sister Callie, prompted by their father, stepped to the closed coffin. Shoulder to shoulder, holding on to each other tightly, they stood. With his free hand, Clayton touched the frame of Cedric's portrait that sat atop the casket and then wiped tears from his eyes. Callie touched her lips with her fingertips and then touched the image of her brother's forehead in the photograph, sniffling and gently sobbing.

After a moment, their father stood and put his large hand on Bernice's shoulder and in a soft, deep voice encouraged her to rise and walk with him to the casket. But she remained seated, eyes forward, seemingly unaware of his touch and deaf to his words. With the encouragement of Bernice's sisters, Mr. Chaisson left his wife sitting and joined his children at the casket. He put his arms around them and they cried together, Callie burying her face in her father's massive chest. Then, their father released his hold on his daughter and placed his large hands on the casket above where Cedric's heart lay in restful repose. Tears streamed down his face.

As the hymn was nearing its end, the funeral director looked to Bernice's sisters to see whether she intended to visit the casket before it was removed. When she gave no response to their entreaties, the funeral director motioned for the pallbearers to approach. As they began to lift the casket from the stand there was a loud, wailing shriek from behind them as Bernice pushed through her sisters and began clawing at the lid, attempting to open the casket, screaming that she wanted to be with her "precious baby." She was sobbing and wailing and speaking incoherently to her dead son as her husband and children gently but firmly grabbed hold of her and pried her fingers from the handles. She struggled against them until finally her strength failed her. Letting out a final melancholy howl, she fainted, falling limply into the arms of her husband as Cedric's casket was carried to the hearse waiting in the parking lot.

CHAPTER 14

As the last of the late afternoon thunderstorms skirted past Iris, Giles and Ezra busied themselves with camp out preparations. Giles was unrolling the sleeping bags and organizing their provisions. Ezra was pounding the last of the tent stakes into the ground with the back of a hatchet.

"Just in time to help us set up," Ezra said sarcastically as Vance walked up with an old knapsack hanging from his shoulder.

"Yeah sorry," Vance replied. "My bitch of a stepmother waited until I was leaving to make me ride my bike to the Jagneaux's to buy her a carton of cigarettes."

A clap of thunder sounded in the distance and the boys, looking up and seeing dark clouds on the horizon, glanced at each other anxiously. "Is it supposed to rain?" Giles asked.

"I don't think so," Ezra said. "But even if it does, the tent is waterproof, at least so long as you don't touch the sides while it's raining."

"What's in the knapsack?" Giles asked.

Vance grinned. "Y'all come inside the tent and I'll show you."

After they all squeezed inside, Vance poked his head out briefly to make sure no one was approaching before reaching into the knapsack and pulling out two Miller High Life ponies with condensation beading on the glass bottles.

"Holy moly!" exclaimed Giles before he was shushed by Ezra and Vance.

"I've never tasted a Miller," Ezra said. "My dad lets me have a sip

79

of his Budweiser sometimes."

"Budweiser tastes like horse piss," Vance said as he used his Swiss Army knife to pop the metal cap off the stumpy bottle.

"How do you know what horse piss tastes like?" Ezra asked.

"Giles told me," Vance retorted as he took a big swig and then passed it to Ezra. Ezra took a small sip and grimaced at its bitterness before passing the bottle to Giles who took a swig, paused to absorb the flavor and then took a bigger swig.

"Easy Cookie Monster," Vance said as he grabbed the bottle from Giles. They repeated the process until the small bottle was empty.

"Man, I fill a little woozy," Ezra said, giggling.

"Me too," Giles said. "Are we going to drink the other one now?"

"Let's wait 'til we get back from nigger-knocking," Ezra said.

"But it'll get warm," Giles protested.

"Relax. I'll get a little ice chest," Ezra replied.

"We gotta do Old Man Melancon's house this time," Vance said. "I want to get him back for throwing that lawn mower blade at us when we were picking plums from his tree."

Giles groaned with trepidation. "I don't want to do him. After he did that my dad said not to go anywhere near his property. He said he's not mentally stable."

"Why did you tell you dad about that, idiot?" Vance scolded.

"I didn't," Giles said. "I told my mom and she told him."

"That's even worse."

Ezra chuckled. "That lawn mower blade didn't get within twenty feet of us, man. He was just trying to scare us."

"Still," Giles said.

"Relax dude, it'll be fine," Vance said.

While Ezra fetched an ice chest and some ice from inside the house, Vance made a fire and the boys roasted Vienna sausages while retelling their favorite dirty jokes. Finally, when the lights inside the house went out, predictably just after the ten o'clock news, they waited another ten minutes before jumping the chain link fence at the rear of the property and heading in the direction of Old Man Melancon's house.

After walking a couple of blocks, they noticed a dark-colored Plymouth in the driveway parked behind Mrs. Wyble's old Buick. Giles and Ezra stopped in their tracks. "It's him," Giles murmured.

"Yeah," Ezra said.

"Him who?" Vance asked, obviously out of the loop.

"Blake Wyble. He almost hit me with his car on Old Mill Road and then chased us into the sugarcane after I flipped him the bird," Ezra replied.

Vance chuckled. "Where was I?"

Ezra kicked at nothing on the ground. "That's the day we were collecting refund bottles—you know—the day that Bruce—"

"Oh yeah," Vance said.

"We should do their house," Ezra said. He checked the windows of the home to see if anyone was watching them and then walked up to the driver's side door. He drew a wad of phlegm from his nasal cavity into his mouth and hocked it on the car's door handle and then stepped back to admire his handiwork.

"Oh man," whispered Giles, "he's gonna be so pissed."

"Good," replied Ezra. "That's the point."

The boys tiptoed up the wooden steps and across the porch. Ezra took the lead with Vance holding onto his belt loop and Giles holding on the back of Vance's t-shirt, their protocol being that everyone had to be touching until the doorbell was rung. As they approached the door, they could hear muffled voices and see light flickering from a television.

81

Ezra turned and looked at Vance and Giles to make sure they were ready and then pressed the doorbell. Giggling and snickering, they turned to make their escape, Vance leaping over the hedges into the front yard and Ezra following Giles down the steps and across the driveway. Giles veered to the left and hid behind a row of bottle-brush shrubs that separated Mrs. Wyble's property from her next-door neighbor's. Ezra ran directly across the street and jumped into the bed of a pickup truck while Vance hurriedly climbed and hid in an oak tree in the next-door neighbor's yard.

As they anxiously waited, the porch light came on, the front door swung open and Blake Wyble stepped out of the house. Stopping at the edge of the porch, he scanned the area briefly and then walked to and around his car to make sure everything was in order. He grabbed the door handle and then quickly pulled his hand away, muttering profanities as he stooped down to wipe his hand in the grass. He stood and walked to the end of the driveway, taking his time to scan the area in every direction. Finally, he turned and began walking casually back toward the house only to suddenly change directions and begin moving quickly toward the shrubs where Giles was hiding.

Unable to see Blake approaching, Giles made no attempt to flee. Concerned that Giles might get caught, Ezra stood up in the bed of the truck and yelled, "Hey, faggot!"

Blake turned and began running in Ezra's direction as Ezra jumped out of the truck on the opposite side and ran between two houses with Blake in pursuit. Blake chased Ezra down the back alley for another fifty yards before finally relenting, bending at the waist to catch his breath.

"If I catch you, I'm going to beat the shit out of you," Blake yelled through the darkness.

"Eat me!" Ezra yelled back.

Blake turned and started walking back toward his home, stopping in the street to light a cigarette and peruse the area again before going back inside the house.

Aware that Blake might still be watching from a window, Vance waited several minutes before climbing down the backside of the oak tree and running to the street corner where he found Giles and Ezra waiting. "Ha!" he laughed as he strolled up, "I thought your ass was grass back there, Poret!"

"I know!" Ezra exclaimed, elbowing Giles. "I just saved your life, man!"

Giles shrugged, not realizing how close Blake had come to discovering him behind the shrubs. "I had a bad hiding place. I couldn't see anything."

"That was fun. Let's go do Old Man Melancon's house now," Vance said.

"I don't want to," Giles said, renewing his protest.

"I called it," Vance said.

"This will be the last one Giles, I promise," Ezra said.

Giles kicked at a pebble on the ground and put his hands in his pockets. "Y'all can. I'm kind'a tired. I think I'll just meet y'all back at the tent."

"Jesus, Poret," Vance scolded, "don't be a pussy."

"Yeah come on Giles," Ezra pleaded.

"Besides," Vance continued, "you're not going back to the tent by yourself with my beer in there."

"I wouldn't drink your beer without you," Giles said defensively.

"Well, we don't need to worry about that because you're coming with us," Vance said. His tone was uncompromising.

Ezra put his arm around Giles. "Come on. Just one more, dude."

"Okay," Giles said reluctantly. "But this is the last one. I mean it."

"Deal," Ezra said.

The boys walked a block and a half to Old Man Melancon's street and stopped at the corner to assess the layout. Across the street was a wide-open baseball park with virtually no cover. The houses in the area had sparse landscaping and the adjoining privacy fences on either side of the Melancon home prevented an easy escape toward the rear of the property. The house was without doubt a precariously positioned target.

Ezra gestured toward a sedan parked in the driveway of Melancon's next-door neighbor. That's our only good place to hide," he said.

Vance and Giles nodded in agreement. Vance volunteered to be the ringer since Ezra had already taken a turn and Giles was only reluctantly participating. As they started to cross the street Giles stopped and whispered, "Wait, I think I saw one of his curtains moving."

Vance and Ezra stopped and surveyed all of the windows but saw nothing. "Come on, you pansy," Vance whispered. "That old fucker probably goes to sleep at seven."

"Shhhhhh," Ezra warned as they crept across Old Man Melancon's front yard.

Vance grabbed Giles' wrist and held it firmly. "Let go of me," he said in a stern whisper.

Vance shook his head and tightened his grip. "I want to make sure you don't take off early," he said.

Cautiously, they climbed the front steps and began tiptoeing across the porch. Just as Vance reached the door, the porch light came on. Vance quickly jammed his finger against the doorbell button and they all turned to run. As they were racing across the front yard, Vance and Giles' feet became entangled. Vance stumbled but regained his balance and kept running as Giles fell clumsily into the thick St. Augustine. He hurriedly picked himself up and was moving his chubby legs and feet as fast as he could when he heard the front door swing open. Over his shoulder he saw Old Man Melancon step out onto the porch wearing stretched out cotton briefs and a tank top undershirt. He saw a single-barrel shotgun in his hands. He heard the old man garbling something unintelligible and then a booming report. Giles shrieked in pain as he felt dozens of projectiles strike his backside. "I'm hit!" he screamed to Ezra and Vance who, after hearing the gunshot, abandoned their hiding place behind the neighbor's car and began sprinting down the block as fast as their legs would carry them.

Ezra and Vance ran until they reached the next street, cut across several yards and turned down an alley. They stopped for a moment to catch their breath and wait for Giles, but when they did not see him after several minutes, they jogged back to Ezra's backyard. Several minutes later, Giles reached the fence, climbed it and hobbled toward the tent, his hand clamped to his left buttock. Ezra and Vance regarded him curiously. "What took you so long?" Ezra asked.

"I got shot and you jerks just left me there to die," Giles said angrily.

"Shhhhhhh," Ezra said, giggling. "You'll wake my mom."

"Are you kidding?" Giles growled in an exclaimed whisper, his cheeks flushed, his eyes blazing, "You'll have to wake her anyway. I need to go the hospital. I've been shot."

"Let me see." Vance said as he tried to stifle his laughter. "He stood up and tried to move Giles' hand.

"Don't touch it," Giles said. "I need to keep pressure on the wound. I could bleed out."

85

"Bleed out?" Vance said in a low giggling voice. "What the hell are you talking about? I don't see any blood. Turn around so we can put the flashlight on it."

"Hey," Ezra whispered emphatically, "I mean it, y'all need to keep it down before you wake up my mom."

"It was like a thousand angry wasps all stung me on the butt at the same time," Giles whined.

Vance finally convinced Giles to remove his hand but could find no evidence of an entrance wound in his pants, so they made Giles go into the tent and drop his pants and underwear. They used the flashlight to examine his backside. There was no gunshot wound; there was no blood. All they found on his buttocks was thirty to forty whelps, each the size of a pencil eraser. "I'm pretty sure you're not going to bleed out," Ezra said chuckling as Giles craned his neck to try to see for himself.

"It was probably rock salt," Vance said. "Our neighbor uses it to shoot stray dogs."

Giles pulled his underwear and pants back up, flush with embarrassment. "Well, it hurt like heck," he said.

Ezra and Vance poured out of the tent giggling, followed by Giles. Ezra stood and in an effort to parody Giles, cupped his buttock and began limping around the campfire and dragging his leg, dramatically whispering, "I'm hit! I'm hit!"

Vance giggled even more loudly and Giles' face grew redder. When Ezra repeated the pantomime the second time with even more exaggerated drama, Vance snorted which caused Giles to start giggling too. Covering their mouths in an effort to keep the noise down, they laughed at Ezra's performance and laughed at each other's laughter until their sides hurt, and then they laughed some more.

"Hey!" Giles whispered as the laughter subsided, "the beer!"

The boys followed each other back into the tent and finished the beer with less than three swigs each before coming back out and sitting around the campfire.

"I think I'm drunk," Ezra said.

"Me too," Giles said.

"Y'all are a couple of lightweights," Vance scoffed.

They bantered about their high jinx for a while and then decided to turn in when the mosquitos became too much to bear.

As they lay inside the tent, the boys were being serenaded by amorous tree frogs and cicadas, the volume of their piercing refrain repeatedly waxing, waning and then starting anew. Suddenly the chorus was interrupted by a loud explosion of flatulence inside the tent.

"Damn Giles," Ezra exclaimed, "that sounded wet."

Vance added. "Jesus, I'll bet you shit your drawers."

"It wasn't me," Giles protested. "It was Ezra."

"Oh my God!" Vance exclaimed in frightful laughter, covering his nose and mouth with his hand. "It's in my mouth! I can taste the Vienna sausages. I swear to God!"

"Me, too," Giles said, as the tent erupted in a cacophony of giggles, snorts and chortling.

Things finally got quiet again and the boys finally seemed to be settling into their sleeping positions when Ezra broke the silence, speaking barely above a whisper. "Giles, I wonder if that colored boy made it, you know, if he's still alive."

"Me, too."

"I feel really sorry for Clayton and his family," Vance added. "His brother was always so nice to everybody."

87

"Do y'all think coloreds have their own heaven, you know, separate from white people?" Ezra asked.

"Why would they?" Giles queried, somewhat amused by the idea.

"Well, it wouldn't make sense if they didn't," Vance interjected.

"What do you mean?" Giles asked.

"Well, I mean, heaven is supposed to be paradise, right?" Vance answered.

"Yeah, so?" Giles replied, not following Vance's logic.

"Well," Vance said, "how can heaven be paradise for white people if there are jigs in it?"

Ezra chuckled. "I never thought about it that way," he said. "And maybe vice versa is true too," he said. "I'm sure coloreds wouldn't want whites in their heaven. I mean, think about it. You think slaves would have wanted to see their masters in heaven when they died? Do you think coloreds today want a heaven with KKK people in it?"

Giles thought about pointing out that being a slave owner or a member of a murdering, racist hate group might serve as a disqualification for admission to heaven but because he was ready to go to sleep decided not to press the issue. "I don't know. I just hope there are dogs in heaven," he said instead.

"Me too," Ezra said.

"Me three," Vance added.

CHAPTER 15

The mutilated colored boy found by Giles and Ezra was identified as D'Arius Jaccard Cole. His vital records indicated that he was born in Iris, Louisiana, on October 6, 1961 to fourteen-year-old Jelsienne Beatrice Dupre. No father was listed on the birth certificate. His criminal records revealed two misdemeanor shoplifting convictions, an unprosecuted charge for disturbing the peace and three pending charges for possession of marijuana, one with the intent to distribute.

Further investigation revealed that D'Arius had repeated the sixth grade once and the seventh grade twice before dropping out of school when he turned sixteen. He had fathered two children before the age of seventeen, both with a Jayla Gibbs. Interviews confirmed that although Cedric and D'Arius were second cousins, they did not run in the same circles though they sometimes walked home together from work to keep each other company. Neither had been seen since working their evening shifts at the nursing home on September 3.

The medical records from University Medical Center noted that D'Arius had sustained significant blunt force trauma about the face, head, torso and extremities; he was severely concussed and bleeding from his left ear; one lung was bruised and the other collapsed; he had four fractured ribs; his left humerus sustained a compound fracture with bone fragments protruding through his bicep; his left tibular was shattered; his lower jaw bone were fractured; MRIs confirmed three lumbar vertebral fractures, spinal cord damage and swelling of the brain, the latter requiring a neurosurgical burr hole procedure; his penis had been severed and exploratory surgery on his perforated colon revealed a short piece of a wooden broom handle lodged in his rectum; and in addition to having five fractured teeth, his upper and lower lips had been sliced from his mouth with a sharp instrument and the surrounding flesh had been cauterized, presumably with a cutting torch.

In all, D'Arius spent a total of sixteen hours on the operating table and received eight units of blood as a team of vascular, orthopedic and general surgeons worked shoulder to shoulder, rotating in and out, trying to save his life and put him back together to the extent possible. He was wheeled to recovery with a total of one-hundred eighty-seven sutures over various parts of his body, his jaw wired shut, several skin grafts, and with pins, plates and screws in his tibular, humerus and spine. He remained in the hospital for sixty-eight days, the first twenty-two in the ICU.

D'Arius had sporadic visits from his mother. Jelsienne was a skinny, frail-looking woman with venous arms and legs. The homemade tattoos on her knuckles, neck and sternum were barely visible because of fading and the darkness of her pigment. She gave very little attention to her hygiene or grooming. Her frayed salt and pepper hair appeared as if it had not been touched by a comb or brush in weeks.

When she showed up at the hospital at all, it was not uncommon for Jelsienne to be drunk, high or both. She kept a cigarette in her mouth even when she was not smoking, which was not often. She was frequently belligerent with the staff and as a result had to be escorted from the premises on several occasions. The nurse's chart entries indicated that she struggled to grasp relevant care instructions that would be needed for D'Arius in a home setting. When the social worker assigned to D'Arius asked about his father and whether he might be able to assist with his care,

Jelsienne shook her head, scoffed. "If you know who he is, you know more than me."

As D'Arius' discharge drew near, a social worker met with Jelsienne and Jayla, the mother of his children, to explain that he had permanent and irreparable brain damage and an injury to his spinal cord such that it was highly unlikely that he would ever speak, walk or care for himself again. The social worker encouraged Jelsienne to have D'Arius admitted to a skilled care nursing facility where professionals could care for him around the clock. The social worker explained that her son would require twenty-four-hour care and total assistance with his ADLs.

"Aid-dee-who?" Jelsienne slurred inquisitively.

"A-D-Ls Jelsie," Jayla said, speaking slowly to make it easier for Jelsie to understand. "ADL stands for Activities of Daily Living. You know, going to the bathroom. Bathing. Brushing his teeth. Eating. Getting in and out of bed and in and out of a chair."

Jelsienne looked at Jayla suspiciously. "How you know all that, girl?"

"Because I'm a C.N.A. Jelsie. You know that. I used to work at the same nursing home that D'Arius worked at."

Jelsienne knitted her brow as if trying to recall but did not reply. Then she turned her attention back to the social worker, trying to focus through glassy eyes. "If he go to the funeral home, who gonna pay for that?" she asked before putting a broken cigarette in her mouth and rifling through her purse for a lighter.

"Do you mean nursing home?" the social worker asked.

"Yeah, that's what I said, huh?" Jelsienne replied as she lifted a cigarette lighter toward her mouth, looking at the social worker and then at Jayla for confirmation.

"You cannot smoke in here ma'am," the social worker said.

"What?" Jelsienne said with an insolent tone and a scowl on her face.

"You cannot smoke in the hospital. You have to go to a designated smoking area to do that."

Jelsienne stared back at the social worker with her crooked cigarette still hanging from her lips. "Who you?" she asked.

"My name's Myra," the social worker said, pointing to the name on the I.D. badge hanging from the pocket of her scrubs.

Jelsienne began looking for her lighter again, forgetting that it was already in her hand and then looked up the social worker as if just seeing her for the first time. "Mari, you got a light?"

"No, ma'am."

"Her name is *Myra*," Jayla corrected.

The social worker smiled at Jayla as if to say it was okay.

"Well Myra," Jelsienne said, "who gonna pay for the nursing home?"

The social worker patiently explained that given D'Arius' physical condition, he would easily qualify for Medicaid and Supplemental Security Income, what most people refer to as SSI benefits. Once he was admitted to a nursing home, the SSI money would be paid to the facility in compensation for the services rendered that were not fully covered by Medicaid.

Jelsienne threw her head back, laughing derisively. "Hell to the no on that," she snarled, bobbing her head with the utterance of each syllable, her broken cigarette flapping up and down in her lips as she spoke. "Ain't gonna be no nursing home taking my check. Y'all gonna send his ass home wit' me. I'll take care of him. Me and his baby momma," she said, gesturing toward Jayla.

The social worker started to object. "I don't think you realize—"

Jelsienne cut her off. "I don't give a shit what you don't think."

Jayla made eye contact with the social worker and shook her head apologetically, making it clear that it would be futile to push the issue any further.

On the date of D'Arius' discharge, Jayla dropped Jelsienne off at the entrance and waited in the car with her two young children. Jelsienne stumbled into the hospital, turned down the wrong hall and promptly got lost. Too confused and inebriated to explain why she was there, an orderly assuming that she needed medical care escorted her to the ER waiting room and sat her in a chair where she promptly fell asleep, not waking for nearly two hours.

When she awoke only slightly more sober, Jelsienne was able to get directions to the nurse's station of the appropriate ward. D'Arius was sitting in a wheelchair in the hall, his bed already occupied by another patient.

A heavyset nurse instructed Jelsienne to have the pick-up vehicle pull under the covered area near the entrance of the hospital where orderlies would assist with getting D'Arius loaded. However, when they all arrived at the pick-up area, Jayla's car was nowhere to be seen. The orderlies left D'Arius parked in his wheelchair next to a concrete bench and instructed Jelsienne to come get them if she needed help when the vehicle finally arrived. Jelsienne dismissed them with an irritated wave of the hand and then began rifling through her handbag for her cigarette lighter.

After a twenty-minute wait, Jelsienne recognized the familiar sound of a vehicle with a busted muffler coming around the corner of the hospital parking lot. A green, early model Ford Crown Victoria with a mismatched front quarter panel and a badly blistered vinyl roof came into sight and squeaked to a stop under the covered entrance, noxious black smoke spewing from the rusted-out muffler. Jayla was sitting behind the wheel with her two children bouncing around in the back seat, each sucking on a plastic straw from a Burger Chef cup and holding half-eaten hamburgers in the other hand.

"Turn the car off Jayla," Jelsienne barked. "You gonna choke us to death with all that smoke."

Jayla shook her head. "I can't. If I kill it when the engine's hot, it won't start again."

"Where you been anyway?" Jelsienne asked in a perturbed tone as she waived futilely at the smoke and walked toward the car. She peered at Jayla through the open window of the car. "We been waiting I don't know how long. It's hot as hell out here."

"I waited over an hour and you never came out so I went to Wal-Marts to get some diapers," Jayla answered. "How I was supposed to know how long you was gonna be?"

"Never you mind," Jelsienne replied. "Why you brought them kids, girl? You know we gots to have room for D'Arius."

Jayla scoffed. "What you talkin' about?" she said. "You knew we had the kids with us, Jelsie. They was in the car with us all the way from Iris to Lafayette."

Jelsienne smirked and sucked her teeth. "They must'a been hidin' in the back 'cause I sure didn't see them little niggas in the car on the way up here."

"Ain't nobody was hiding," Jayla mumbled.

"What?"

"Nothing."

"You shouldn't have brought them kids, Jayla. Where we gonna put D'Arius?"

Jayla rolled her eyes and sighed. "I didn't have nobody to watch 'em, Jelsie. What you want me to do?"

"Lord, have mercy," Jelsienne said.

"Y'all make room!" Jayla yelled at the kids. "We got to put yo' daddy up in here and you can't be jumping all around, bumpin' him and shit."

The children in the midst of a sugar rush, were jumping back and forth from one side of the backseat to the other, giggling and pushing each other, spilling their drinks on the seats. Jayla slapped her son hard on the back of his leg and exclaimed in a scolding tone, "You get yo' ass up against that door." The little boy froze and began to shriek, his eyes tearing and his mouth wide open, exposing partially chewed pieces of hamburger in his mouth. "I said get yo' ass by the door, D'Arial," Jayla snarled, slapping the back of his head, "before I give you something to cry about!"

The boy shrieked again and complied so as to avoid being struck again just as Jelsienne returned with the two young colored men in crimson-colored scrubs. The orderlies, who assumed that a more suitable vehicle would be used to transport D'Arius, exchanged concerned glances. "Y'all don't have access to a van or something?" the older one asked.

"We look like van people to you, nigga?" Jelsienne rejoined. "Just put him in the back seat so we can get ourselves the fuck out of here."

With considerable effort, the orderlies maneuvered D'Arius into the rear seat of the vehicle, positioning his casted leg across the bench seat and leaning him precariously against the rear passenger side door. When they got D'Arius as comfortable as could be managed under the circumstances, Jayla opened the opposite door and instructed the two kids to sit on the floorboard and not to touch their father.

CHAPTER 16

Ezra and Giles halted their game of rock-paper-scissors upon hearing the loud smacking of shoes against the asphalt street. They looked up to find Dewey Bordelon running full speed in their direction, his backpack slamming rhythmically against the small of his back with each stride, his eyes and round, pimply face animated with excitement.

"Damn Dew, where's the fire?" Ezra asked as the husky boy stopped and bent at the waist, panting profusely, trying to catch his breath. Finally, he gestured for Ezra and Giles to follow him a short way down the sidewalk away from the other kids at the bus stop. Giles and Ezra paused and smirked at each other, then followed.

"Have y'all heard?" Dewey asked, still breathing hard.

Ezra's instinct was to respond with a smart-ass answer such as "what, that you're finally getting a sex change operation? Or, "what, that your testicles finally descended?" But suspecting that Dewey might have some juicy gossip, he refrained. "Heard what?" he asked.

"Y'all know Kim and Kelly Mueller, right?"

"Duh," replied Ezra.

"I don't," Giles said unashamedly.

"Yes you do," Ezra asserted. "They're twins. Cheerleaders at Iris High. Probably the finest girls in the whole town. Tall, long dark hair."

"Yeah, total foxes," Dewey added.

"Oh, okay," Giles replied. "I know who they are. I just didn't know their names."

"So, what about them?" Ezra asked, curiously.

"Well, Kelly got raped by a couple of niggers."

Ezra and Giles both reacted with incredulity. "You're lying," Ezra replied.

"Swear to God," Dewey replied, crossing his heart.

Ezra glared at Dewey, trying to get a read on him. "You *swear to God* swear to God?" he queried.

"Stick a needle in my eye if I lie," Dewey said with as much solemnity as a twelve-year-old could muster.

Ezra and Giles looked at each other and then back at Dewey who was clearly gloating.

"Holy shit," Ezra said, though still somewhat dubious. "How did you find out?"

Dewey spat on the ground, relishing the attention. "My mom and Taylor Prudomme's mom meet for coffee and cigarettes in our kitchen every morning. I heard them talking."

"Dang," Giles said. "I've never heard of anybody around here getting raped before."

"Fuckin' niggers," Dewey said, "my dad says we should ship all them som' bitches back to Africa." As he said this, he gestured toward the west.

"Africa is that way genius," Ezra retorted, pointing toward the east.

"Well," interjected Giles, "if you want to be technical about it, since the earth is round and you could get to Africa taking a surface route in either direction, y'all are both right. But if you are trying to point directly at Africa, you're both wrong because with the earth's curvature you are both actually pointing into outer space. Africa is actually in that direction," he said, pointing diagonally at the ground in a slightly eastward direction.

"You are such a nerd, Poret," Dewey said, rolling his eyes.

"You're one to talk," Giles retorted, pointing to the calculator holster on Dewey's belt.

"Man," Ezra said, still trying to wrap his head around the rape story, "I was right behind Kim and Kelly in line to go to communion last Sunday."

"I know. I saw 'em in church too," Dewey joined in. "I was sitting next to the middle aisle and got to watch both of them walk the whole way to communion. I had a hard-on for the rest of mass."

"That's not saying much," said Vance, who had just walked up, always the last to arrive at the bus stop. "You catch a hard from watching Daphne on *Scooby Doo*."

"That's a damn lie!" Dewey said a bit too defensively.

"Hey, did you hear about Kelly Mueller?" Ezra asked Vance.

"Yeah," Vance said. "The rape? Yeah. I heard my stepmom talking to somebody on the phone about it this morning. It's apparently all over town."

"I heard that Kelly was leaving the Jagneaux's parking lot when the colored men jumped into her car," he said. "One had a knife and made her drive to the baseball park, and they raped her right there in the Little League dugout."

Ezra gasped. "Jesus," he said. "Both of them?"

"Yep," confirmed Dewey. "At least that's what I heard. After school, me and Matt Lafleur are going to go see if there's any blood or anything on the dugout benches. Y'all wanna come?"

"Did they stab her or something?" Ezra asked.

"No," Dewey answered. "I don't think so."

"Then there's not going to be any blood, dumbass."

"Yeah-huh," Dewey said, "from her getting her cherry popped."

Ezra and Giles exchanged confused glances. Neither were versed in matters of sex to the level of Vance and Dewey, both of whom had much older brothers.

"I mean it's one thing to get raped," Vance said, "but to get raped by a nigger? Jesus."

"Is Kelly still going out with Perry Fuselier?" Ezra asked. "I wonder if he knows yet."

"He ought to be worried about her being stretched out so bad that he won't be able to even hit the sides," Vance said, chuckling.

The other boys regarded Vance with disgust.

"Hey, I wonder if it was Queep." Dewey said.

"Who's Queep?" Giles asked.

The others all looked at Giles as though he must have come from a different planet. "You don't know who Queep is?" Dewy asked.

"No," Giles replied, unembarrassed by his ignorance.

"Queep's the retarded colored dude who walks around town talking to himself and pulling on his huge wang all the time," Ezra said.

"Yeah," Vance added, "Shane Courville said he saw him looking at some women's panties in Howard Brothers and his pecker got hard and was sticking out of his underwear above his belly button. They say it's like twelve inches long and as big around as a tuna can."

Giles grimaced in disgust as Ezra and Vance laughed.

The boys all moved closer to the shoulder of the road as a jacked-up Ford F100 with mud tires and a roll bar passed, followed by a large brown delivery truck.

"I'm going to get one just like that when I get my license," Vance said.

"A UPS truck?" Dewey teased.

99

"Yeah," Vance retorted, "I'll need something that big to be able to take your mother parking."

The boys all let out a collective gasp and then laughed, including Dewey who had long since come to the conclusion that negative attention was better than no attention.

"I sure hope they catch those colored dudes," Giles said, redirecting the discussion back to the rape.

"When they do, there're definitely going to get the gas chamber," Vance said.

"Louisiana doesn't have the gas chamber," Giles said. "We have the electric chair."

"Even better," Vance replied. "Kentucky Fried Nigger."

Giles and Ezra grimaced. Dewey chuckled. "Yeah well, that's if Mr. Mueller doesn't get to them first," he said. "My dad said that he's crazy."

Ezra was about to reply when they were interrupted by the approach of the St. Anne's school bus. As it came to a stop, the loading doors squeaked open and a half dozen boys and girls wearing parochial school uniforms got in line to climb the steps and find empty seats. Giles gave a quick wave to his friends and got in line.

Just as Giles reached the steps of the bus, a car suddenly pulled up and stopped directly in front of the bus. The driver's side door swung open and the angry-looking, long-haired driver slid out and marched toward Ezra, Dewey and Vance with a cigarette in his mouth. It was Blake Wyble.

Blake poked Ezra in the chest. "You're the little faggot who shot me the bird that day on Old Mill Road and nigger-knocked my house," he growled. Then he pointed at Giles who had stopped on the first step of the bus and added, "and I recognize your little fat friend, too."

100

Giles turned white and hurried onto the bus. Ezra regarded Blake anxiously, terrified about the prospect of getting pounded into the pavement in front of all of his schoolmates.

"Not so brave now, are you?" Blake said to Ezra before taking a puff of his cigarette and blowing the smoke in Ezra's face.

Ezra leaned back, trying to avoid the smoke. "I didn't know it was you Blake, I swear," he replied anxiously, his voice cracking. "I thought it was somebody trying to hit us with their car."

Before Blake could respond, a loud yell came from the direction of his car. "Hey, dickhead!"

Everyone turned to see Vance standing on Blake's car with one foot on the front bumper and the other on the corner of the hood. "Leave him alone."

The other kids watched with awe. Blake turned red in the face but did not move. "Get the fuck off my car, Duhon!"

Vance remained steadfast. His expression revealed no fear. "Leave him alone unless you want a size nine footprint in the middle of your shiny hood, motherfucker."

Blake looked around and found everyone staring at him, waiting for him to react. Nervously, he glared at Vance, uncertain of his next move. When Vance lifted one of his feet into the air as if he were about to stomp on the hood, Blake quickly threw his hands up into the air and yelled, "Okay, okay, okay, stop! I was just fuckin' with him. I wasn't gonna hurt 'em. Just get off my car."

The old bus driver had put the bus in park and on old, arthritic knees, gingerly made his way to the last step on the bus. "What's going on here?" he grumbled. When nobody responded, he looked at Blake and said, "Young fella, you're gonna need to move your car so I can get moving."

101

Blake glanced at the bus driver and took a drag from his cigarette. "Hold your horses, old timer." He started walking back to his car. Vance eyed him for a moment and then hopped to the ground on the opposite side of the car.

"You better watch yourself Duhon," Blake muttered as he checked his hood for dents and used his shirt tail to gently wipe off the dusty footprint left by Vance's shoe. He took one last drag on his cigarette and flicked it in Ezra's direction before sliding into the driver's seat, slamming the door shut and speeding off, his spinning tires leaving a cloud of smoke in their wake.

As the bus driver slowly hobbled back up the steps of the bus, Ezra found Giles watching through one of the open side windows and walked toward him. Giles was still pale with fright.

"That's one reason," Ezra said, smiling triumphantly.

"That's one reason for what?" Giles replied, confused.

"That's one reason why we're friends with Vance, moron."

CHAPTER 17

A loud rap on his office door startled Bernard in his chair. "Come in," he said, not trying to mask his irritation.

The door swung open, and a beefy man donning a flattop and an affable smile poked his head in. "Hey, Chief," he said with a shit-eating grin.

"God damn it, Curtis," Bernard said, "you nearly made me choke on my butterscotch. Why can't you knock normally like a civilized person?"

Curtis reacted with the mischievous smile of a boy who liked being told that he didn't know his own strength. "Sorry Chief," he replied with a southern drawl that seemed very out of place in Iris, where most people spoke with a flat, Cajun French accent.

"Well?" Bernard said impatiently, his eyebrows raised and his forehead skin bunching up in tanned wrinkles below his widow's peak.

"Oh, Chief, I was just checking in," he said. "Wanted to see if Ezra and the little Poret fella were doing okay."

"They're fine," Bernard said, suddenly feeling guilty for admonishing his sergeant now that he was aware of the purpose of the visit. "Thank you for asking."

"You know," Curtis said. "I gotta think, I don't know, at their age finding that boy all beaten and mangled like that in the woods—that must have scared the bejesus out of 'em, you know?"

"Oh, it spooked 'em pretty good, that's for sure," Bernard replied.

Curtis began to giggle. "Spooked 'em . . . that's funny Chief."

"That's not how I meant it, Curtis," Bernard said.

"Anybody ever tell you that you look like Cary Grant when you turn serious, Chief?"

"No Curtis, I can't say that I've ever heard that before."

"Well, you sort'a do. At least I think so, probably because of the way you do your hair. Gil, he says no, but I think you do."

Bernard stared at Curtis as if to invite him to leave if his business was done.

"Well, one thing's for sure," Curtis said, not getting the hint, "they saved that colored boy's life, you know that, huh Chief? The paramedics said that if he had been out there even just another hour or so, he would have probably died for sure."

"Yeah maybe so," the chief said, reluctant to bestow hero status on his son.

"And praise Jesus that they didn't find the other one, huh Chief? That would have been even worse," the sergeant said, emphasizing his words with a short whistle. "I talked to of the sheriff deputies; he said the dead one was bloated out to here and his skin was already starting to bust open. I would hate for them boys to walk up on something like that, you know?"

"Yes," Bernard said, "they are lucky in that regard I suppose. Speaking of which, did the coroner come up with a cause of death yet?"

Curtis nodded. "From what I'm hearing, the word is that he was drowned and then got dumped out there."

"Drowned?"

"Yep," Curtis affirmed. "So said, he had enough pond water in his lungs to fill a five-gallon aquarium. Really sad, if you ask me. From what everybody says, he was one of the good coloreds, you know?"

"And what about the Cole kid, were they finally able to get in touch with his family?"

Curtis scoffed and nodded. "I heard they sent a couple of deputies out to his mother's residence in the projects. Nobody answered the door. Finally, Cole's girlfriend showed up with a baby on each hip— can you believe he already has two kids? He's seventeen years old for Pete's sake. Anyway, she let the deputies in and they found the mother laying on the floor of her bathroom, half-naked, high as a kite. A stray cat had jumped in through an opened window and was licking half-chewed CheeWees from the inside of her mouth."

Bernard grimaced. "That must have been quite a sight."

"Kirk Dronet—he was one of the deputies that was sent over there—he said he recognized the girlfriend. Jayla Gibbs is her name, you know, Harvey Gibbs' older sister. You remember him? She was arrested few years ago after she followed a projects nigger into the Western Auto and beat him down with a sock filled with golf balls. Apparently, he had been bullying Harvey."

"Where did a teenage colored girl get a bunch of golf balls?" Bernard asked, curiously.

Curtis chuckled. "The hell if I know. Maybe Harvey was one of them little jigs that fishes the balls out of the ponds at the golf course to sell back to the golfers."

Bernard nodded and began to skim through pages of a report with the hope that Curtis would get the message and excuse himself.

Curtis lifted his head and began to sniff the air. "What is that, Chief? Old Spice? Brut?"

"No. I'm not wearing cologne, Curtis."

"You sure?"

"It's called Irish Spring," Bernard replied in a patronizing tone. "It's a soap, Curtis. It helps to not smell like wet ass when you work in an office where there are other people, especially in a setting where most of the people still have their olfactory senses intact. You should try it."

"Old factory senses?" Curtis asked, scratching his bulbous nose.

"Never mind," Bernard said, as began rummaging through the clutter on his desk. "So, is there anything else I can do for you, Curtis? As you can see, I've got a lot to do."

"Actually Chief, before I go, I wanted to tell you that they finally got my cable installed."

"Good to know, Curtis. Good to know."

"Well, they have this channel, WTBS, and they're showing three Clint Eastwood movies back-to-back tonight. Me and some of the guys we're getting pizza and beer. Thought you might wanna come."

"Gonna have to pass but thanks, Curtis."

"Aw Chief, I thought you were a big Clint Eastwood fan?"

"I like him just fine. I just can't tonight. I've got testimony prep for the Malveaux trial."

"Malveaux?" the sergeant asked, furrowing his brow. "I thought that he had pled?"

"No, there's no plea yet."

"Hmm. Maybe it fell through," Curtis said, scratching his head in bewilderment. "What's the deal Ellis offered him anyway?"

"Three years and time served."

"Shiiiiit, that's a sweet deal. What's he expect? Dealing drugs to high school kids? I'd send his ass straight to the chair if it was me. That's what I'd do."

"I know you would, Curtis."

"Hell yeah I would," Curtis said with amplified self-assurance. "Wouldn't hesitate a second, that's for damn sure on that one. You know it wasn't too long ago that they would lynch niggers for less than that. I ain't seen it myself, but my Uncle Jimmy from Ferriday, his grandfather on his momma's side was an Exulted Cyclops in the Klan. He got to see a nigger hanged from a tree when he was in middle school. Them ole boys, they didn't play around. You think those redbones and piney woods fellas are crazy and foul? They ain't nothing compared to the Delta hillbillies—especially when it comes to hatin' niggers."

"You didn't see any hangings when you lived up there?" Bernard asked.

"Nah," Curtis replied. "I wasn't but six years old when we moved. I missed all the good stuff. My uncle, he still has a piece of the rope that they used at the hanging. After they cut the nigger down, the hangmen would cut the noose rope into little pieces and hand them out as souvenirs."

An incredulous look appeared on Bernard's face. "Is that true?" he asked, hoping it was not.

"Hell yeah it's true. I seen the little piece of rope myself. And according to my Aunt Vivian, in the old days, when she was a young girl, they sometimes would have picnics when a nigger was being lynched, and even women and children would come to watch."

"Jesus," was all Bernard could think to say.

"Yep."

"Hey, I meant to ask you earlier, have you come up with anything on the rape of the Mueller girl?"

"No, sir. Not a damn thing. There was no rape kit done and Abel won't let us interview her, so there's that. So we got nothing except hearsay and scuttlebutt."

"Well tell me this. Those two colored boys found off the highway—is there any reason to believe that they were somehow connected to the rape?"

"Oh no sir, none whatsoever," Curtis said. The Mueller girl supposedly said the jigs who raped her were in their late 20s to early 30s and really big and muscular and both with real dark complexions. The boys they found in the woods were teenagers. One was real small and the other was short and chubby, and both high yella—barely darker than me and you."

The Chief nodded thoughtfully. "Okay." He stood up and walked around his desk. He put his hand on the back of his loquacious sergeant and nudged him through the door. "Thanks for stopping by Curtis. Y'all enjoy movie night."

"Okay, thanks, Chief."

CHAPTER 18

In January of 1976, the lead felony prosecutor at the St. Landry Parish District Attorney's Office was found dead at his desk. The autopsy indicated cardiac arrest as the cause of death. Lacking any suitable candidates for a replacement, the District Attorney published an ad for the open position in the American Bar Journal.

Weary of New England winters and the tedious prosecution of traffic violations and misdemeanors, attorney Isabella Vadas was one of dozens of applicants who submitted an application and curriculum vitae. After a two-hour telephone interview and a thorough review of several writing samples, Vadas was offered the job and accepted. Two and a half weeks later, with everything she owned packed into a small U-Haul trailer, she climbed into her Subaru Star and drove south, putting the Fairfield County District Attorney's Office and the snow-capped streets of Danbury, Connecticut in her rearview mirror.

A few weeks into the job, Vadas attended a political fundraiser for the incumbent mayor of Opelousas. It was held on the outskirts of Washington, Louisiana, at the antebellum home of William Barrow and his wife Flora. Upon meeting Vadas and learning that she was new to the area, Flora insisted on giving her a personal tour.

"My husband's sixth great grandfather was Robert Ruffin Barrow—maybe you've heard of him?" Flora queried.

Vadas pondered the name for a moment. "I don't think so."

"Well, he was the largest landowner in this region in the 1800s," Flora boasted. "He owned sixteen plantations total, mostly in Louisiana, though a few were in east Texas. Anyway," she continued, gesturing toward the impressive dwelling, "he actually built this home for his daughter Ingrid and her husband Benjamin as a wedding gift in 1858. The main home sat in the middle of that large grove of live oaks that you passed on the drive. It was twice the size of this home. Unfortunately, it was razed to the ground in 1865."

Vadas frowned. "That's unfortunate," she said. "I'm sure it was a sight to behold."

Flora nodded and smiled bitterly. "Reportedly the fire was set by a horde of newly emancipated slaves. Of course," Flora continued, "there was no homeowner's insurance in those days and with all the financial uncertainty caused by the war, Robert Ruffin chose not to rebuild. Instead, they moved to one of his homes in Texas where of course they did a much better job of managing the newly enfranchised."

"Ah," Vadas replied as they progressed toward the steps leading to the front porch. "I've noticed that you don't have a Cajun accent. Are you not from this area?"

"Oh, no," Flora said with a hint of pretentiousness. "I grew up in New Orleans, uptown, and William is from Birmingham. We met at Ole Miss actually."

"Ah, a real Rebel romance," Vadas said, feigning delight, "How charming."

Flora smiled proudly and gestured toward the home's façade. "Anyway, the architecture is French Creole, but you'll notice that the millwork has a Scandinavian motif, which was to pay homage to Ingrid's maternal ancestry. "So," she said as they entered the parlor and accepted a couple of iced teas from one of the colored waiters, "at the height of its operation, there were as many as seventy-five slaves on this property alone. In fact, it was the second largest plantation in Louisiana."

Vadas' face flushed. She could not help but peek at the colored waiter behind Flora to see his reaction to her comment. He responded with a very subtle smile acknowledging Vadas' empathetic glance. Oblivious to the muted exchange, Flora moved into the den and pointed to a pair of old metal tools with long wooden handles and large metal blades that hung crisscross above the fireplace. "Have a look. Those are called billhook knives," she said. "The adult male slaves used them to harvest the sugarcane crop by hand."

Vadas gazed at the implements as if in a daze, finding it so eerie and a bit nauseating that she was standing on property where human beings had actually owned other human beings—where men, women and children toiled day in and day out just for the privilege of sustenance and not being whipped.

"Can you imagine how powerful they had to be? To cut that thick cane with those things by hand all day long?" Flora queried.

"Yeah," Vadas replied, her eyes fixated on the wooden handles worn smooth by the hands of slaves who labored in fields just a stone's throw from where she stood, "humans who were so powerful and yet so powerless, right?"

"Well," Flora said, her tone somewhat contrarian, "that's the crux of the matter right? The question of humanity. I mean, not to be overly anthropological but by and large most slave-owners were good Christian people. And to be fair, in that era, Negroes were regarded as, well, subhuman, right? So, you could argue that there was really no sinful intent."

Vadas bit her tongue, struggling to mask her disdain. She chose her words carefully so as not to offend her politically connected hostess. "No doubt it was a different time," she said.

After bringing Vadas through the main rooms of the home and showing off various antiques and pieces of art, Flora ended the tour on the back porch which overlooked a large courtyard. The area was shaded by a canopy of three-hundred-year-old live oaks all draped with Spanish moss, some with limbs so massive and long that they required carefully placed metal supports to prevent them from splintering away from the trunk due to their leveraged weight.

As they descended the back steps, Flora introduced Vadas to her husband William, before taking leave to welcome some new arrivals. After a modicum of small talk, William was pulled into a conversation by the guest of honor, leaving the young prosecutor to her own devices. She meandered through the crowd and found an opening at one of the long tables topped with mounds of boiled crawfish, potatoes and corn. After accepting a beer from one of the waiters, she turned her attention to the crustaceous delicacy about which she had heard so much.

As she wrestled with her first crawfish, Vadas' attention was grabbed by a young female vocalist belting out Cajun French lyrics in time with a fiddle and accordion. As she watched and listened with interest, a distinguished looking man standing across the table from her took notice and leaned in. "Do you understand French?" he asked.

Vadas turned to face the man and smiled. "Marginally," she replied. "I took four years of French in high school. But you know how it goes, if you don't use it, you lose it. I probably understand just enough to get me into trouble. Is she singing something about passing through a rear door?"

"Very good," the man said. "That's actually the name of the song, "The Back Door." It's a song by D.L. Menard, who's basically the Elvis Presley of Cajun French music," the man said in jest.

"Oh okay," Vadas said. "I like it. It's very catchy."

112

"It's about a young man who routinely gets into drunken mischief at night and then sneaks back into his home through the back door and continues this routine until his shenanigans lead him through the back door of the local jailhouse."

Vadas smiled and nodded. "Huh, yes, okay."

"I'm Bernard, Bernard Brasseaux," the man said. "I'd offer you my hand but as you can see, it's a bit of a mess from peeling crawfish."

Vadas smiled and nodded. "I'm Isabella Vadas. My friends call me Isa."

Bernard nodded curiously. "So, what kind of name is Vadas, if you'll forgive my curiosity?"

"Not at all," Isa said. "It's eastern European. I'm told that I come from a long line of very poor but very proud Hungarian rapeseed farmers," she said, chuckling.

"Interesting," Bernard said with a genuine smile. "Judging from your accent, I'm guessing you're not from around here?"

"No, I'm not. I moved here from Connecticut. But I do have a lot of relatives in central Texas, which is where my Dad grew up."

"Ah," Bernard said. "And what brings you to Cajun country?"

"Work," Isa said. "I'm the new A.D.A. for St. Landry Parish. "Lead felony prosecutor," she said with facetious pride.

"Ah yes," Bernard said, "now that you mention it, I had heard that Harry was bringing in a hired gun from the east coast."

Isa let out a girlish snort. "I'm hardly a hired gun."

"Well, welcome to Acadiana, and I hope the job turns out to be everything that you'd hoped."

Isa smiled. "Thank you. I'm hoping to get some good experience, though I'm not sure how many felonies are actually taking place out here. From what I can tell, it's seems pretty quiet."

"Well," Bernard said with a peculiar expression, "you might be surprised what lies lurking beneath the cover of darkness, even in these friendly little Cajun towns."

Isa furrowed her brow. "You sound like you speak from experience. Are you a criminal?" she asked playfully.

Bernard smiled. "Doesn't hunger make a thief of any man?"

Isa's countenance displayed pleasant surprise. "Ah, a Pearl S. Buck partisan?"

Bernard shrugged. "Once upon a time I guess," he said, "when I actually had time to read for pleasure."

"And what occupies your time now?"

"Law enforcement."

"Oh, in what capacity?"

"Chief of Police in Iris."

"Oh, wow, yeah. I've been there a couple of times. Charming little town."

"Yeah," Bernard said, winking, "so if you ever get caught going thirty in a twenty-five, I'm the man to see."

Isa smiled. "I'll keep that in mind."

Bernard pointed at the crawfish in Isa's hand. "Hey, how about I give you a quick lesson on how to peel those things?"

"Please," Isa replied gratefully.

"Okay," Bernard said. "The first rule is don't eat the dead ones."

Isa snorted. "Seriously? Aren't they all dead?"

Bernard smiled. "No, I mean yes they're all dead, but don't eat the ones that were dead before they were boiled."

"How do you tell the difference?"

"The dead ones have straight tails." Bernard picked through a pile of crawfish and found one with a straight tail. "Like this, see?"

"Okay."

"The ones that were alive when they went into the water will have curled tails."

"Ahhh."

"Next," he said as he selected one of the larger specimens from the steaming pile, "hold it by the head in one hand and twist the tail off with the other. Then you want to suck the head—"

"Wait, wait, wait," Isa said, chuckling dubiously, "you're not serious."

"—like this," Bernard said smiling, as he put his lips on the open cavity of the crawfish head and sucked hard, pulling the flavorful fat and juices into his mouth as the young woman watched with intrigue. Bernard picked up another crawfish, removed the head and pointed inside of the cavity. "You see that yellow stuff? That's the fat. That's really where all the best flavor is."

Isa eyed Bernard warily as if she suspected he might be pranking her but then noticed a couple of other people at the long table sucking the heads as well. "Okay," she said, nervously. Cautiously, she placed her lips on the open end of the crawfish head and sucked. "Mine didn't have any," she said. "And now my lips are burning!"

Bernard chuckled. "You'll get used to the spice. And you have to suck really hard," he said, demonstrating on another crawfish head.

Isa took a swig of beer to cool off her mouth and then put the crawfish head back to her lips and this time sucked much harder. Her eyes suddenly widened and her expression brightened. "Ooooh," she said. "That's actually pretty tasty."

Bernard nodded knowingly. As he began to show Isa how to peel the crawfish tail, they were interrupted by a stocky, narrow-eyed man wearing blue jeans and starched khaki shirt. "How're the crawdads?" he asked, putting a large hand on Bernard's shoulder.

"Excellent as always," Bernard said. "Isa, this is Abel Mueller. Abel, this is Isabella Vadas. She came down here all the way from Connecticut to put our felons behind bars."

"I know who she is and where she comes from," Mueller said. His tone was neither friendly nor hostile.

"Nice to meet you, Mr. Miller," Isa said.

"*Mueller*," he corrected.

"Mr. *Mueller*," Isa said, in an apologetic tone. "Sorry about that. I'm still getting used to all the Cajun names."

"It's not Cajun," Mueller replied.

"Oh okay," Isa replied. "Strike two, I guess."

Mueller did not laugh at the joke or even smile. He turned to Bernard. "You hear what's going on with the niggers in Ville Platte?"

"I heard something about it," Bernard answered.

"We're not going to stand for that kind of shit over here," Mueller declared.

Bernard lifted his chin to acknowledge Mueller's declaration. "I don't think we have to worry about anything like that in Iris, Mule," he said.

"Oh, I'm not worried," Mueller said as he patted Bernard on the back with a sly grin. "If they bring that kind of nonsense here, they're the ones who will need to be worried."

Bernard forced a smile but did not otherwise respond.

Mueller's expression changed as if he had just remembered something. "What about that ticket I gave you to get fixed in Avoyelles Parish. Is that all good?"

"I put in a call to the sheriff up there," Bernard said. "I'm waiting for him to call me back. Shouldn't be a problem. He owes me one."

"Good. Keep me posted," Mueller said before walking off without another word.

Bernard turned back to Isa and found her looking at him wide-eyed. "Well he's a little intense," she said with a touch of sarcasm.

Bernard grinned and nodded. "That's one way to put it."

"You two close?" she asked.

A conflicted expression appeared on Bernard's face. "No, not exactly," he said.

"Oh?" Isa rejoined in a tone that made it obvious that she would be interested in more detail.

"It's a little complicated," Bernard explained. "We grew up together but were never exactly friends. Then we served together in the same battalion in Korea."

"Wow, okay."

"Yeah. He probably saved me from getting run through with a bayonet a time or two in Kangwon Province, so there's that."

"Kangwon Province?" Isa replied. "Really? The Battle of Pork Chop Hill?"

The corners of Bernard's mouth turn up slightly and his head tilted in admiration. "You know your history."

Isa smiled. "I'm my father's daughter."

Bernard nodded. "So anyway, yeah, he's very connected politically, so it pays to stay on his good side if you rely on politics to keep bread on your table."

"Good to know, I guess," Isa said. "So, what's going on in Ville Platte that's got the gallant war hero's panties in a wad?"

"Oh, a couple of Black Panther wanna-be teachers at the public high school got the colored students all riled up over a prom king election."

Isa knitted her brow. "How so?"

"Well, from what I heard, there was a run-off to elect the prom king between a white boy and a colored boy. The colored boy is supposedly very popular, a straight A student, student council vice-president, a three-sport letterman. He lost out to a white boy who was a C student, not on student council, doesn't play any sports and whose only organizational affiliation is a local hunting club."

"I'm guessing the white boy got voted king by a majority white student population?"

Bernard nodded.

"So, what happened?" Isa asked.

"Well, two colored teachers organized a walk-out."

"Well, good for them, right?" Isa said. "So, what happened?"

"The school board got involved and decided to recognize both boys as co-prom kings for this year."

"Ah, a diarchy," Isa said, obviously pleased with herself for remembering a term from her political science studies that she never anticipated using in the real world.

Bernard nodded. "And they didn't announce this yet because they are waiting for tensions to die down, but going forward, there simply will be no queens or kings for prom or homecoming. They'll just have a homecoming court with seven white girls and three blacks to match the student demographics."

"Okay," Isa said, "so why is Mr. Mueller so concerned about a student protest in another town?"

Bernard shook his head and rolled his eyes. "Well, probably because one of his daughters will be this year's homecoming queen. But also, that's just Abel. Let's just say that he has no tolerance for coloreds trying to assert themselves."

Isa grimaced but said nothing. "Welcome to the south I guess."

"Something like that," Bernard said, smiling apologetically.

After an awkward silence, Bernard forced a smile and said, "Enough of all that—how 'bout we get back to the crawfish peeling lesson?"

"Sure," Isa said.

"Alright. Pull off the tail, peel off the top two segments of the tail shell and then pinch the bottom to squeeze the meat out, like this," he said as he demonstrated.

Isa complied. "Wow, it worked! What's that little black line running down the middle of the tail meat?" she asked.

"That's the flavor vein," Bernard replied with a mischievous grin. "You eat that last, like a dessert."

"Really?" Isa asked suspiciously.

Bernard laughed. "No, that's the digestive track—the poop."

Isa's eyes widened with surprise and then she squinted at Bernard. "You're evil," she teased.

Bernard chuckled. "Just pull on it. It'll come out altogether in a little string."

Isa grabbed the end of the black string with her fingernails, pulled it out and flung it into a pile of refuse.

"Now, you can eat the tail plain or dip it in the sauce," Bernard explained, pointing at a salmon-colored concoction in a small container.

"What's in the sauce?" Isa asked.

"Ketchup, mayo, Tabasco, and a splash of Worcestershire."

"Hmm, I think I'll try one plain first." She smiled warily and then slid the bare crawfish tail into her mouth. She paused to allow her taste buds to weigh in. "Mmmm! That's good!" she exclaimed, surprised by how much she liked the taste. "Really good!"

Bernard smiled and nodded. "So, aside from acquiring a taste for our mudbugs, how are you otherwise liking Cajun country so far?" he asked.

Isa smiled and nodded, covering her mouth until she swallowed. "I'm still getting used to the heat and humidity, but the people have been so amazing."

Bernard smiled and nodded as if he were not at all surprised.

"I've lived in quite a few places because of my father's work," Isa continued, "but I've never experienced anything like this. People here go out of their way to be so nice and helpful. And the food—Oh my God— the boudin, the cracklin', the gumbo, the sweet dough pies—it's all so incredible. I've already gained eight pounds. I don't know how anyone can stay trim down here."

Bernard nodded and chuckled. "It takes some effort," he said. "But I'm glad you're being made to feel at home. Cajuns take a lot of pride in their hospitality."

"So, what's your favorite Cajun dish?" Isa asked.

Bernard thought about it for a moment. "That's a tough one. It's probably a tie between rabbit sauce piquant and seafood gumbo," he finally said.

"I had seafood gumbo in New Orleans a few years ago when I was there for a conference," Isa said. "I wasn't crazy about it."

Bernard smiled. "That's not authentic seafood gumbo," he said. "New Orleans advertises Cajun food as part of their tourism, but you'll only find real Cajun food in Acadiana."

"Got it," Isa said as she noticed Flora and William posing for a photograph with several local politicians. She gestured toward them with her chin and spoke in a hushed tone. "Are you close friends with our esteemed host and hostess?"

Bernard chuckled and took a sip of his beer. He lowered his volume to match Isa's. "Let's just say that we don't exactly run in the same circles."

"No slave-owners in your family tree?" Isa queried, mostly in jest.

Bernard smiled and shook his head. "Thankfully, no. Slaves were never a part of the Cajun culture. And Cajuns would have been too poor to own any regardless."

As Isa was about to follow up with another question, an elderly man in a seersucker suit interrupted and asked if he could borrow Bernard for a moment to discuss a private matter. Bernard told Isa that he was delighted to have made her acquaintance and excused himself.

CHAPTER 19

A couple of months after meeting Isabella Vadas at the crawfish boil, Bernard was called as a witness in a criminal trial in a case in which he had made the initial arrest. The defendant was accused of statutory rape in connection with numerous sexual encounters he allegedly had with his children's teenage babysitter. It was Vadas' first felony trial. Her presentation of the case was flawless and the jury deliberated for just fourteen minutes before returning a guilty verdict, convicting the defendant on twenty-seven counts. In celebration of the victory, the District Attorney bought dinner for his entire prosecutorial team at Toby's Little Lodge in Opelousas. Bernard was invited.

When dinner was over, a few in the group decided to extend the evening by having drinks in the lounge where live music was being played. After a couple of cocktails, the D.A. and several others decided to call it a night. When Bernard announced that he would say goodnight as well, Vadas asked with him to stick around for one more drink. "Don't leave me here to celebrate my victory alone," she pleaded. He reluctantly agreed to one more drink.

As they talked and laughed, one drink turned to two and then three.

"I never asked," Vadas said. "But it's a small town, and I was just wondering if you knew the perp in this case, you know, before you made the arrest?"

"Sort of," Bernard replied. "He was several years older than me. His younger sister was in my graduating class."

"I really thought I was being pranked by Harry when I was assigned the file," Vadas said.

"How so?" Bernard asked.

Isa grimaced. "Because of his name, silly."

Bernard feigned a puzzled countenance "What about it?"

"Seriously?" Vadas said.

Bernard maintained a serious expression. "Ms. Vadas, you mean to tell me that you had a hard time believing that John John Johnson was his real name?"

Vadas chuckled. "Please call me Isa. And yes. It may be the dumbest name I've ever seen or heard," she said. "So, what's the story behind it? Do you know?"

Bernard took a sip from his beer. "The story I heard is that his mom and dad each wanted to name him after their own father."

"And?"

"And both of their fathers were named John."

Isa guffawed. "That's hilarious. So, which one got the first name and which one got the middle?"

Bernard snorted, shaking his head. "Good question. No idea."

Isa rose from the booth. "I need to run to the little girl's room," she said. "Don't leave."

Bernard nodded and finished what was left of his beer while she was gone, planning to make his exit as soon as she returned.

"You know," Isa said as she slid back into the booth, obviously beginning to feel the effects of the alcohol. "I've been thinking."

"About?"

"Well, I see the wedding band on your finger, so I assume there is a Mrs. Brasseaux, right?"

A guarded expression formed on Bernard's face. "Yes, there is a Mrs. Brasseaux," he said.

"But I've never seen you with her and you've never mentioned her." Isa wore a probing expression on her face. "I don't even know her name."

"Well, her name is Eve," Bernard said. "And I can assure you that if I haven't mentioned her, it was not by design."

"Hmm," Isa replied, smiling with incredulous flirtation, her inhibitions in her wake, "you don't strike me as the type of person who is predisposed to inadvertence."

Bernard was about to reply and then segue into an excuse to leave when the band began to cover "When a Man Loves a Woman" by Percy Sledge. Isa shrieked with excitement and threw up her hands. "That's my new favorite song," she said. "Come on Chief Brasseaux, dance with me."

Bernard looked like a deer in headlights. He started to decline and announce his plans to depart when Isa hopped out of the booth, grabbed him firmly by the hand and began to pull him toward the dance floor.

"I really don't dance," Bernard said, blushing and glancing around the room to see if there was anyone present that he knew.

Isa put her finger to his lips and shushed him, leading him away from the table. She found an opening on the floor amongst the dancers. She turned back toward him, placed his right hand on the small of her back and pressed her body against his. Bernard knew that he should step away but did not. He found himself swaying to the music with Isa's head resting comfortably on his shoulder and the fingers of her free hand positioned gently on the back of his neck. He became self-conscious about whether Isa could feel the heavy thumping of his heart or detect the weakness in his knees as they danced.

When the song came to an end, Isa leaned back and stood on the tips of her toes and kissed Bernard, partly on the cheek, partly on the corner of his mouth. Then she whispered into his ear, "You lied."

Bernard pulled his head away and looked at Isa curiously, still holding her hand. "About what?"

"About not being a dancer."

Bernard felt his face flush and released Isa's hand. He thanked her for the dance and congratulated her for her trial victory again before bidding her goodnight.

In the days that followed, Bernard found his mind completely preoccupied with thoughts of Isa. His emotions vacillated between giddiness and guilt. He told himself that she was only being flirtatious because of the alcohol and that she was too young and had too much going for her to be genuinely interested in someone of his age and status. He reminded himself that regardless of the emotional demise of his relationship with Eve, they were still married. And even more importantly, there was Ezra to consider. He decided that if he kept his distance and stayed busy, the infatuation—and it was nothing more than that, he assured himself—would fade with time.

For the next several weeks, Bernard sent subordinates in his stead when the IPD was called to attend meetings at the D.A.'s office. He avoided political and civic events that Isa might be expected to attend. He turned and walked the other way when he saw her in the hallway of the courthouse or around town when he had business in Opelousas. On the couple of occasions when he was unable to avoid her, he made it a point to interact with her in a very business-like manner and to excuse himself promptly. But despite holding fast to these rules of engagement, there was no indication that his feelings for her were waning. In fact, it appeared to be just the opposite.

CHAPTER 20

The feelings that Isa had stirred in Bernard became the catalyst for much introspection over the next couple of months, particularly as it related to his marriage and his future. He ultimately decided that he had sacrificed his own happiness for long enough. Though still his highest priority, he reasoned that Ezra was resilient and old enough to understand that sometimes marriages do not work out. He realized, or perhaps rationalized, that Ezra's well-being and his own happiness did not have to be mutually exclusive.

Eve was sitting in front of the television folding a load of laundry when Bernard came home from work. It was the day after his fortieth birthday, though he and Eve were well past acknowledging much less celebrating such things.

"Where's Ezra?" he asked.

"Sleep-over at Giles' house," Eve replied without taking her eyes off of the program she was watching.

"Good," he said, turning off the volume of the television. "We need to talk."

"About what?" Eve asked. She assumed it was about their finances as that and Ezra were about the only things they ever seemed to discuss anymore.

Bernard decided to be direct. He took a deep breath and exhaled. "About an exit strategy," he said.

A surprised and confused expression appeared on Eve's face as she laid a folded washcloth on a stack of others. "An exit strategy? What are you talking about, Bernard?"

"Us, Eve. This dead, loveless marriage," he replied, trying to sound compassionate but resolute. "We are still relatively young. We can both start over. Don't you think that we each deserve to be happy?"

Eve glared at Bernard in silence for a few moments. "Where is this coming from?" she finally asked.

"What do you mean?" Bernard asked. "It's coming from me. From right here," he said touching his chest. "I know you are as lonely and unhappy as I am. Surely you want and need more than this, too?"

Eve looked hard at Bernard through probing eyes. "Is there someone else?" she asked. She did not expect a truthful answer but wanted him to suffer through the experience anyway.

Bernard shook his head. "Eve, there's me, there's you, and there's this huge void that used to be us."

Eve chortled. "That's very poetic. Is that a line from a movie?"

Bernard ignored the jab. "I know we said we would try to stay together for Ezra's sake, but I'm no longer convinced that's the right thing to do. We're not setting a good example for him, and I feel like we are both just withering away emotionally and that by the time he's out of the house and we have the opportunity to move on, there won't be anything of us left to share with anyone else."

Eve offered a subtle nod. "I see," she said. There was an eerie calmness in her tone. "So not even the unflappable Bernard Brasseaux can turn forty without succumbing to a midlife crisis, huh?"

"It's not a midlife crisis, Eve," Bernard argued.

"Yeah," Eve replied, "that's obvious."

Bernard ignored the sarcasm.

"It feels like there's more to this than you're telling me," she said, holding his gaze.

Bernard shook his head. "No, not really."

"Not really?" Eve said, grinning bitterly.

"Come on, Eve," Bernard pleaded.

Eve smirked. She realized that if there was more to the story, Bernard was not ready to share it. "Can we continue this discussion later? I suddenly have a terrible headache."

Bernard sighed. Claiming a massive headache had been Eve's escape hatch in undesirable situations since he had known her. "Fine."

The next day, Bernard waited for the dam to break, but Eve went about her day as if nothing had happened. If anything, she appeared slightly more cheerful than usual. It was more of the same the next day and the next. Bernard decided to let sleeping dogs lie for a while.

Several weeks later, Bernard saw Isa in the lobby of the St. Landry Parish courthouse. This time he did not turn and walk in the other direction.

"Well, hello there," Isa said in a tone and with an expression that made it clear that she was very happy to see him. "I was starting to wonder if you'd gotten lost in a corn maze or fell into a well."

Bernard blushed and smiled. "Not a lot of corn fields or exposed wells in these parts," he said. "How are you?" he asked.

"I'm doing fine," Isa said, "though very busy. Thank you for asking. How are you?"

"Good," Bernard said. An awkward silence followed his reply.

"Yeah," Isa finally said, "I guess you were right. My felony caseload is keeping me much busier than I anticipated—oh, and I joined a tennis league."

"A tennis league?" Bernard replied. "I didn't know Opelousas had one."

"It's actually in Eunice," Isa said. "I was doing some research at the LSUE library and met one of the faculty members. The conversation somehow turned to tennis and how we both play, and well, she invited me to join."

Bernard looked impressed. "I didn't know you were a tennis player," he said.

"Yeah," Isa said, chuckling, "well there's only so much you can learn about someone over a few crawfish tails and a couple of beers, right?"

Bernard smiled bashfully and looked down at his feet, then back up at Isa. When their eyes met again, he felt his heart pounding in his chest and he sensed that she might be feeling something similar. "I guess so."

"If you want to remedy that," Isa said, smiling demurely. This time it was her turn to blush as she awaited his response.

Bernard felt his stomach flip. The corners of his mouth turned upward as he tried to suppress a smile.

"I know a great little spot in Lafayette. It's downtown on Jefferson Street. They turned an old filling station into a diner. The food is amazing and the beer is ice cold."

Bernard nodded. "Actually, that doesn't sound too bad."

"Great. I could meet you there at six?" Isa said.

"Tonight?" Bernard replied, a little surprised.

"Sure. Unless tonight is bad for you."

"No, no, I can make tonight work," Bernard said after thinking about it for a moment.

"The place is called Tee Nah Nah's. It's right across from the old federal courthouse."

"I know where that is," Bernard said. "I'll see you at six."

"Outstanding."

Bernard found Isa at the back of the diner and slid into the booth across from her. They were both trying to hide their nervousness and excitement.

"You decided not to invite Mrs. Brasseaux?" Isa asked, deciding to break the ice with an industrial grade maul.

Bernard blushed with embarrassment. "I don't think she would have enjoyed herself. She has an aversion to seeing me smile," he said with a subtle grin.

A waiter appeared and they ordered beers and fried alligator appetizers. When the waiter excused himself, Isa wasted no time inquiring about Bernard's marriage. She listened intently as he reluctantly shared the story, sparing virtually no detail. In turn, she shared that she had ended a long-term relationship before leaving Connecticut. "He didn't want kids," she said. "In the beginning, I didn't think I wanted them either. But that eventually changed."

"That's probably not that uncommon," Bernard said.

"So," Isa said, "let me ask you this. If the opportunity presented itself, would you want more? Children, I mean."

Bernard's face flushed. Isa's directness caught him off-guard again. "Wow," he said.

"I'm not putting the cart before the horse or anything like that," she said, "it's just something I'd like to know up front."

"No, no, I don't mind. It's a legitimate question," Bernard said. "I actually had wanted a house-full when we first got married. But since all the stuff with the—" He still found it hard to utter the word *abortion*.

"I get it," Isa said, trying to spare him.

131

"It's just that I—I just assumed there would be no more. So, I haven't thought about that in forever. But to answer your question, yes, yes, I would definitely be very open to that."

Isa smiled warmly.

As the evening progressed, it became clearer to Bernard and Isa that their connection was real and that one way or another—the details of which would have to work themselves out—they would pursue a relationship. Over the next few months, they saw each other as much as discretion allowed. And their feelings for each other grew very strong.

On the same day that news broke of the Mueller girl's rape, Isa telephoned Bernard at the office. "Did you hear about the rape?" Bernard asked right off the bat. "Looks like you're gonna be busy for a while."

"I did," Isa replied. She went on to say that she had just received word of her favorite aunt's passing and that she would be making arrangements to go to the funeral in Austin. Bernard expressed his condolences and said that he wished he could go with her.

When Isa returned from Austin, she and Bernard made plans to picnic at Chicot State Park, north of Ville Platte. Under the canopy of an old willow tree on the north, less frequented side of the lake, they sat on a small wooden pier and hung their bare feet in the water, holding hands and sipping wine, allowing small bream to nibble on their toes. Bernard pointed out a large alligator on the near side of the lake taking in the last of the afternoon sun on a large cypress log.

"Wow, how big do you think it is?" Isa asked.

"Nine, maybe nine and a half feet," Bernard answered.

"Whoa. How big do they get?"

Bernard shrugged. "The females usually tap out at about nine feet. The males get a lot larger, up to twelve, sometimes thirteen feet."

"Good grief."

"Yeah."

"Should we be letting our feet hang in the water like this?"

Bernard chuckled. "We're fine. They want to keep their distance from us as much as we want to keep our distance from them."

As the sun began to set, they watched a pair of snowy egrets glide across the lake just inches above their white shimmering reflections, their ghost-like forms in stark contrast to the backdrop of cypress trees adorned with ample tangles of Spanish moss, some hanging just inches above the surface of the water. "So beautiful," Isa remarked.

Bernard nodded in agreement.

After a period of silence, Isa took a big sip of wine before clearing her throat and squeezing Bernard's hand. "I've got some news," she said, unable to mask the anxiety in her voice.

"Okay," Bernard said with slight trepidation.

"It's not bad news," she said, reassuringly.

"Okay," Bernard replied, though his tone suggested that he would reserve judgment.

"My aunt that passed away—she never had kids, and well, she pretty much left everything to me."

Bernard's eyebrows climbed his forehead. "Really?"

Isa grimaced, as if slightly embarrassed by what she was about to say. "Yeah. And she was wealthy. Very wealthy actually. And my inheritance incudes this really beautiful lakefront home on a sixty-acre horse ranch in the Texas foothills, north of Austin."

"Double and triple wow," Bernard said as he waited for the other shoe to drop.

"So," Isa said, but she did not finish her sentence, hoping that Bernard would anticipate her question so that she would not have to ask it.

"So?" Bernard replied, declining to take the bait.

"So, how would you feel about us living there?" Before Bernard could answer, Isa continued. "It's so incredibly beautiful, Bernard. And there's so much to do. Horseback riding, hiking, fly-fishing, mountain biking, hunting, you name it. And she left me so much money, we wouldn't even have to work. Though if you wanted to, I know that with your resume, every law enforcement agency in the tri-county area would be champing at the bit to hire you."

Bernard looked like a rabbit caught in the beam of a spotlight. He opened his mouth to reply but Isa cut him off. "And of course I've thought about Ezra," she said. "He would absolutely love it out there. It's a young boy's paradise. He could even have his own horse. He could hunt and fish every day if he wanted to."

Bernard had a pained look on his face. "But Eve would never agree to let him come live with us out there, Isa."

"I know," Isa said, "at least maybe not in the beginning. But I've thought about it. You could come back for visits as often as you want, and we could fly him back and forth anytime he wanted to come stay with us. And he could come for longer visits during school breaks and during the summer. That's really not that uncommon these days, you know?"

Bernard sighed and stared out across the lake contemplatively. Isa gently put her fingers under his chin and turned his head toward her. "Look at me," she said. "Pretending that there's still a marriage and prolonging the inevitable is not doing Ezra any favors. Trust me. My mom stayed married to my dad for years after she should have left him, and my sister and I are the ones who paid the price. Our therapists can vouch for that."

"So, you've already decided that you're not going to work anymore?"

Isa smiled. "I won't have to. I mean, I'll still want to dabble in the law a little. I think I'll do some *pro bono* work here and there but not much more than that."

Bernard nodded. "It's nice to have options."

"Yes," Isa said. "It's nice for both of us."

Bernard smiled bashfully and nodded. "I want nothing more than to be with you, Isa."

"But?"

"It's a lot to think about. Mainly because of Ezra. Almost exclusively because of Ezra, really."

"I know."

Bernard sighed. "Let me ask you something," he said.

"Sure."

"If for whatever reason I decide that I need to stay here, at least for the time being, would you stay too or would you still move?"

Isa paused for a brief moment, trying not to let her countenance reveal her uncertainty, and then smiled. "I'm not going anywhere without you, Bernard Brasseaux," she answered.

Bernard held her gaze for a moment, not entirely convinced.

While Isa was away, Bernard tried to look at the situation from every angle, especially from Ezra's perspective. He ruminated. He prayed. And just when he believed he had reached a decision, uncertainty would creep into his thoughts, and he would wipe his mental slate clean and start his deliberations anew, only to come to the opposite conclusion the next time. The news of the Mueller girl rape and then, just a couple of days later, the discovery of the colored boys in the woods, was almost a welcome distraction.

After several days of vacillating, Bernard went to bed certain that he would have to decline Isa's proposal, at least until Ezra graduated high school and went off to college. Ezra would need some time to adjust to the idea of his parents divorcing, and that would be difficult without also having to deal with his father moving hundreds of miles away. His mind was made-up.

But the next morning, it was as if his subconscious had reanalyzed the situation while he slept. He woke feeling certain that not giving life with Isa a chance would be something that he would deeply regret. Isa was his happily ever after. Living in Iris was not a reasonable alternative because Isa would almost certainly face much undeserved "homewrecker" blowback, particularly from the women in the community. And Ezra was young and resilient. He would adjust, and he even might eventually convince Eve to let him come live with them in Texas. The situation would not be without some challenges, but they could make it work. They *would* make it work.

Feeling confident in his decision, Bernard telephoned Isa and told her yes, that he was willing to move to Texas. She was beyond elated. She asked how soon. Bernard said that he would probably need a couple of months or so. He would need to get things in order at the police station and prepare Curtis and the staff for the transition. He would have to pack and put some things in storage. And most importantly he would have to try to sort things out with Eve and Ezra.

He said that he had two weeks of paid vacation that he would lose if he resigned without using it, so after getting everything in order at the station he was going to take his remaining vacation days to spend some extra time with Ezra before his resignation would become effective. If all went according to plan, he would be ready to make the move by the end of the year.

"I really think it would be best to let you get completely moved to Texas before I announce my intentions. You're obviously going to have to be part of the explanation and I don't want to make you an easy target."

"I appreciate that but I can take care of myself, Bernard."

Bernard smiled. "I don't doubt that for a second."

After he ended the call with Isa, Bernard summoned Curtis and his administrative assistant, Paula, into his office and sat them down. "Happy Tuesday," he declared.

"What's so happy about it?" Paula asked.

"Well, it's not Monday," Curtis offered with a chuckle.

Bernard nodded and smiled. "That's right. Some things are good for what they are not."

Paula and Curtis exchanged curious glances. Bernard was acting peculiarly. They waited for him to begin. Bernard told them that he was going to be taking a two-week vacation in the near future and that he wanted Curtis to start taking a more active role in the administration of the police department. He said he wanted to make sure that everything was being handled properly while he was away.

Curtis and Paula exchanged glances again, wondering if there was more to the story. Bernard had never even taken a one-week vacation, and when he had taken vacations, it was never with all of this preparation.

Suddenly Paula's jaw dropped and her hand rose to cover her open mouth. With a look of dread on her face, she whispered, "Oh Chief, is it cancer?"

Bernard chuckled. "No, Paula I do not have cancer. It's nothing like that. I'm just trying to get our house in order, that's all."

Paula did not seem reassured. "Are you sure, Chief? Because Lynette Thames just got diagnosed with pancreatic cancer. They say she's got two months at best."

"I do not have cancer, Paula."

"Well, ain't this a big bucket of bear shit?" Curtis said, finally inserting himself into the conversation. "So, I'm going to have all these extra duties on top of everything I'm already doing?"

Bernard scoffed. "If, by everything you mean riding around town eating donuts and boudin all day, then yeah Curtis, maybe so."

Curtis huffed. "Now that smarts, Chief."

"Well, it's time you learn this side of the operation."

CHAPTER 21

When Mr. and Mrs. Chaisson went to the St. Landry Parish Sheriff's Office in Opelousas a couple of months after being notified of their son's murder to inquire about the status of the investigation, they were told by the lead detective that the sheriff had signed off on the decision to suspend the criminal investigation. As the detective explained, they were simply unable to develop any leads. There were no witnesses. No prints. No one with an identifiable motive. They could not even explain how the boys had arrived at the location where they had been found with no footprints or vehicle tracks leading to or from the area.

Unwilling to give up hope of finding their son's murderer, the Chaissons drove to the Iris Police Department and requested an audience with Chief Brasseaux. When they sat across from his desk, Bernard could see that Horace and Bernice were both still extremely grief-stricken and altogether downtrodden.

The Chaissons cut to the case, inquiring as to whether the IPD had any involvement in the investigation of their son's murder. Bernard explained that because their son and the other boy were found outside of Iris' corporate limits and because there was no report of a crime being committed within its corporate limits, the IPD had no jurisdiction.

The Chaissons implored Bernard to reconsider. They explained that their son was an honor roll student and that he had never been in trouble a day in his life. That the boys were last seen walking home from their jobs at the nursing home in Iris and that Cedric would have never left Iris on his own volition or without permission from them. And that any route they could have possibly taken to walk home would have been well within the corporate limits of Iris. Therefore, they insisted, something criminal must have happened to the boys in Iris regardless of where their bodies were ultimately found.

Bernard took a moment to consider their argument and then leaned forward in his chair, resting his elbows on his desk. "I hear what you are saying, and while your theory is very plausible, we still don't have any evidence of anything criminal occurring in our corporate limits. So, I'm sorry, but my hands are tied."

"But Chief," Horace pleaded, "how do you know there's no evidence if you don't investigate?"

Bernard appeared stumped for a moment then cleared his throat and leaned back in his chair. "Well, normally an investigation is prompted by a complaint or by someone reporting that they found evidence of a possible crime. But in this instance, no one reported a crime here or even finding any evidence of anything criminal happening in Iris."

Horace was about to reply when Bernard raised his hand to stop him. "But" he said, "I hear what you're saying. I do. And I'll tell you what I'm going to do. I'm going to put Jarvis Lewis on this for a few days. I'll have him poke around, you know, talk to the people at the nursing home where the boys worked and to the people in the colored community. I know the St. Landry Parish detectives already did all of that, but maybe the people in the colored community will be more willing to speak freely with a colored officer. If Jarvis comes up with anything that points to a possible crime committed in Iris, I'll open a formal investigation and devote more resources to it. That's absolutely the best I can do for you."

The Chaissons let out a collective sigh and thanked Bernard profusely. In turn, he cautioned them against getting their hopes up. They said they would be in touch but asked that he keep them informed if they developed any leads. He promised that he would as he escorted them out.

As Bernard re-entered the station, Paula stopped him. "Chief, Sue Mueller was here to see you while you were meeting with the Chaissons."

"Sue Mueller?" Bernard replied with confused expression.

The woman nodded. "When I told her you were in a meeting with the Chaissons and that I didn't know how long you would be, she said she would come back later. She asked that we not say anything to her husband about her coming here. She really seemed out of sorts, Chief."

"Okay."

"And I don't mean out of sorts from her daughter getting raped. At least I don't think it was that. She seemed—I don't know—afraid."

"Okay. Well, let me know if she comes back. And if I'm on the phone or in a meeting, come pass me a note."

"Yes, sir."

CHAPTER 22

Auzenne's neighborhood grocery was the designated bus stop for elementary and middle school children living in the Batiste Addition, a residential area on the east side of Iris occupied almost exclusively by colored residents. While waiting for the bus, the young boys were running back and forth across the parking lot, laughing, shouting and throwing acorns at each other and sometimes at passing cars. When a customer was accidentally hit in the head by an acorn and went inside to complain, the store owner came outside and scolded the boys, calling several of them out by name and threatening to tell their mothers. In response, the boys apologized and settled down, but only until the owner went back inside.

The play of the young girls by comparison was tame. In the shade of a large water oak, a dozen girls, mostly dark-skinned and dark-eyed and mostly wearing brightly colored dresses and brightly colored barrettes, were sitting in clusters of four playing the "Rockin' Robin" clapping game. Off to the side, sitting alone was a lighter-skinned girl, more golden in tone, with straighter, rust-colored hair and green eyes. She pretended to be preoccupied with the hem of her skirt, occasionally looking up with envy to watch the darker-skinned girls singing, clapping and laughing. She was careful to avoid eye contact with them, her feelings still smarting from recent teasing.

The day prior, the girls in her class had been taking turns naming which fifth grade boy each thought was cutest. When it was the lighter-skinned girl's turn, she named Billy Hollier. The other girls shrieked and laughed, expressing amused disgust at the idea that a colored girl would find a "stringy-haired white boy" attractive. They mocked her unmercifully, exclaiming, "Awwww! Celee a sugar roach! Celee a sugar roach!" She had not spoken to any of them since, though none of them seemed to care.

While refastening one of her barrettes, Celee heard a grunting noise a short distance behind her. Curious, she turned and saw that the sound was coming from an older boy with large, bulging eyes. He was rubbing his pelvis against the corner of the building as he stared at her, drool running down the side of his chin. Celee was horrified, but too shocked to turn away.

Suddenly, a hard slap was delivered to the side of the boy's head, causing slobber to spray from his mouth. He squealed and covered his head with his arms, cowering against the building. "What I told you about doing that where people can see, Queep?" The admonishment came from an older girl who held a baby on her hip. She raised her hand as though she were going to strike Queep again but did not.

Biddable by nature, the chastised boy peered up at the girl and muttered something unintelligible but apologetic in tone, to which the girl said, "You better be." She grabbed him by the shirt collar and pulled on it to make him stand tall. "Now go over there with the rest of the short bus kids," she instructed, pushing him toward a bench where two other mentally handicapped children were sitting quietly.

The girl shifted the baby to her opposite hip and then ambled over to where Celee was sitting. "Don't pay him no mind," she said. "He retarded. He don't know no better."

Celee nodded and put her head back down, too embarrassed to say anything in response. Then, as the older girl started to walk away she found the courage to ask, "Is he your brother?"

"Nah," the girl said. "He just live by me on Mt. Dump." Mt Dump referred to the housing project adjacent to the Batiste Addition. Its name was a euphemism derived from the fact that it had been constructed atop a buried landfill, giving it the highest elevation in the tri-parish area. "We all try to help look after him."

Celee nodded.

"You Deidra's lil' sister, huh?" the older girl said.

Celee nodded.

"How come she ain't been around?"

"She has mono."

"The kissin' disease?"

"Yeah, I guess."

"Who she been kissin'?" the older girl queried. "I might want to catch it and stay home from work," she joked.

Celee blushed and smiled. "I don't know."

"Well," the older girl said as she shifted her fussing baby from one hip to the other, "tell her Jayla said hey and that I still want to borrow her pink jellies. She probably think I forgot about 'em. I didn't forget."

"Okay, I'll tell her," Celee said, watching the curly haired infant squirm in his Jayla's arms. "Is that your little brother?" she asked.

"No, he mine," the girl said. "Her name D'Arienne," she added, showing Celee the name tattooed in script on her left forearm. "She three months. My momma watching my son, D'Arial," she said, pointing to the corresponding tattoo on the opposite forearm. "He almost two." Jayla could see that Celee was trying to do the math in her head. "I had D'Arial when I was still twelve," she said, smiling proudly.

Celee nodded, not wanting to say what she was thinking and not knowing what else to say. Jayla pointed with her chin to the group of girls singing and playing the clapping game. "Why you ain't playin' with dem?"

Celee shrugged. "They don't want to play with me, I guess."

Jayla scoffed. "Don't let that bother you. They just jealous because you bright, that's all."

144

Celee looked confused. "Delida makes better grades than me," she said, gesturing toward the little dark-skinned girl sitting closest to them.

"I'm not talking about bright-smart, I'm talking about bright-light," Jayla said. "You know, your skin is lighter than theirs, so they jealous."

Celee looked at the skin on her arm and then compared herself to the other girls but did not reply.

When she got home, Celee mentioned the incident involving the retarded boy to her mother. Her mother shook her head sympathetically and hugged Celee. "Just don't pay no mind to that foolishness, baby. That poor boy ain't got the sense God gave a June bug chasing headlights at night on the highway. He ain't trying to be bad—he just don't know no better."

"But if he's not bad, why does he do that?" Celee asked. "I've seen plenty retarded people, and none of them do that."

Celee's mother shook her head and sighed, pulling her lips inside her mouth as she contemplated how to respond. "You remember that talk we had about male animals gettin' with female animals to make baby animals?"

"Yes, ma'am."

"Well, God makes it to where all people eventually want to get together and make babies. It's not supposed to happen until you're all grown up and married, you see, but sometimes that drive to make babies comes out in people too soon and too powerful and they have a hard time controlling it. Queep, he's all messed up in the head and everything, you know, from being retarded. I guess he's messed up with that part, too."

"Well, it's really gross," Celee said, grimacing.

145

"I know, baby. But he can't help it. Just like you can't help that you so sweet and cute," her mother said as she smiled and pinched Celee's cheek.

Celee blushed and smiled but then the smile left her face as quickly as it had come. "Momma?"

"Yeah, baby?"

"What's a sugar roach?"

Her mother raised her eyebrow. "Where did you hear that, baby?"

Celee told her mother about the teasing. Her mother told her that those girls were ignorant and to ignore them, but Celee pressed her for an answer. Reluctantly, her mother told her that a sugar roach was what some people call a colored girl who wants to be with white people. When Celee seemed not to understand the metaphor, her mother explained that the roach symbolized the colored girl and the sugar symbolized white people.

Celee grimaced with offense. "That's ugly," she said. "I'm not filthy and nasty like a roach."

Her mother shook her head vigorously. "No indeed you are not baby girl. You are clean and you are kind and you are beautiful and you are smart. And those mean girls are just jealous of you because you are Creole and their skin is darker than yours."

"That's what Jayla said. How come they so worried about that?" Celee asked.

"Aw, baby," her mother said. "That's a complicated thing you asking right there. I guess mostly, it's because they think that colored people are lower than white people and because Creoles are lighter-skinned than other coloreds we are whiter than them. So, they probably assume that we think we are above them, and it makes them mad."

"I don't think that, Momma."

Her mother smiled and kissed Celee on the forehead. "Aw, I know you don't, baby girl. You too sweet to have such thoughts. But, that don't stop them from thinking you do. There's just a lot of foolishness out there child," she said, caressing her daughter's cheek. "But after this school year, you won't have to see those mean girls no more. It's gonna be different in California."

Celee nodded. "I can't wait 'til we move."

CHAPTER 23

"Damn," Vance said, mostly under his breath but loud enough to be heard.

"What?" Ezra and Dewey asked in unison, looking around curiously.

Vance pointed with his chin to the opposite side of the cafeteria. "Dessa Ardoin is wearing her white Calvin Klein jeans."

Ezra and Dewey looked over their shoulders and saw Dessa taking a seat with a group of girls.

"You still talking to her?" Vance asked Ezra, his tone suggesting that he might decide to pursue Dessa if Ezra was no longer interested.

Ezra shook his head. "Nah. I mean, she's fine and she's really nice but she's too Holy Roller for me."

"Hmm," replied Vance. "Well, my uncle said the Holy Roller chicks are usually the first ones to put out because their parents keep them all cooped up until they just want to explode."

"Well, I'm not going to stick around long enough to find out. They're too weird."

"Weird how?" Dewey asked.

Ezra shrugged. "They invited me to their church and her mom was speaking in tongues. It was really creepy. And her dad was talking all crazy about colored people having dark skin and afros because of a curse God put on them."

"Well, that part's true," Vance said. "That's the curse of Ham. God cursed him and all his descendants because he looked at Noah when he was naked."

"Where did you hear that?" Ezra asked.

"My step-mom is in a Bible study. I heard them talking about it."

"Well, I never heard of that," Dewey said, "and I go to Catechism every week and mass every Sunday."

"Me, too, I never heard of that either," Ezra said.

Vance shrugged as if he could care less. He tapped Ezra on the arm. "Hey after school, get Giles and y'all meet me at the treehouse."

"What for?" Ezra asked.

"It's a surprise," Vance replied as the bell to go to class sounded.

"Can I come?" Dewey asked as everyone was getting up from the table and collecting their food trays. Ezra and Vance pretended not to hear him.

In his next class, where seating assignments were in alphabetical order, Ezra sat directly in front of Clayton Chaisson. When Clayton walked to his seat, he gave Ezra a friendly tap on the shoulder. "What's up, Lil' Brass?"

"Not too much," Ezra answered. Then he recalled seeing Clayton and his family pulling out of the driveway of a house that was for sale in his neighborhood a couple of days before. "Hey, I saw y'all at the Andrus house the other day. Are y'all thinking about buying it?"

Clayton nodded. "Yeah, ever since my brother—" he stopped short of finishing his thought, "—my parents want to move to a safer neighborhood. We supposed to be moving in next month."

Ezra's face lit up with delight. "Aw man, that's awesome. Let me know if y'all need help. We just live three blocks over."

"Will do."

After school, Ezra rode his bike to Giles' house, finding him trying to pump air into a flat bicycle tire. "That's not going to do any good," Ezra said. He leaned over and pushed the value stem to the side to reveal the problem. "The valve stem is cracked."

"Poo," Giles said.

"Ride your sister's bike," Ezra said.

"No way," Giles said. "I'm not riding a girl's bike."

"What difference does it make?"

"You ride it and let me ride yours," Giles said.

Ezra chuckled. "I don't think so."

"What difference does it make?" Giles asked.

"It's not going to make any difference because I have a bike to ride," Ezra replied.

"Double me?" Giles asked.

Ezra sighed. "Come on, hop on."

Ezra pedaled and steered with Giles sitting on the handlebars, resting his feet on the front forks. The start was wobbly, and they nearly crashed a couple of times before Ezra was able to build up enough speed to stabilize the bike.

"Don't go too fast," Giles said.

"I'm not."

They rode to the edge of town where neighborhoods ended and rice fields and soybean fields began. They followed a levee to a tree line and then turned down a dirt path that led to a small wooded area. Upon reaching the hidden treehouse, Ezra leaned his bike against a tree and they climbed the ladder to meet Vance who was already inside.

"What took y'all so long?" Vance asked.

"I had to double Giles because he had a flat."

Giles opened a wooden box and pulled out an *Iron Man* comic book.

"Hey, I was just talking to Joey Guidry," Vance said, "guess who got his pecker sucked by a *negresse* behind the movie theater last night."

"Joey Guidry?" Ezra queried curiously.

"No. Sean Bellow."

Ezra grimaced. "I'm not sure who I'm more grossed out for, Sean or the colored girl."

"What do you mean?" Giles asked.

"Sean's got warts all over his hands and his knees."

"Well, she wasn't sucking his hands or his knees," Vance said.

"Men can get warts on their peckers and women can get them on their vaginas," Giles said without looking up from his comic book.

"No way," Vance said in disgust.

"It's true," Giles insisted. "I read about it in a pamphlet at my dad's office."

"Who was the colored girl anyway?" Ezra asked.

"I don't know," Vance answered.

"Would you let a colored girl give you a blowjob?" Ezra asked.

"Who, me?" Vance asked.

"Yeah."

"Depends," Vance declared. "If it was Chelsea Frank, yeah."

"Yeah, but she's barely colored," Ezra said. "What about a really pure looking one like Brenda Jackson?"

"Blue-gum Brenda?' Vance replied. "I don't think so."

"I bet Giles would," Ezra said teasingly, winking at Vance.

Giles looked up from his comic book upon hearing his name. "Would what?"

"Let a colored girl suck your pecker," Ezra said.

"Shit," Vance said. "You know he would sixty-nine that all day long."

Ezra and Vance noticed the blank look on Giles' face and chuckled at his expense. "Giles, you don't even know what sixty-nine means, do you?" Ezra said.

"No," Giles admitted without embarrassment.

Vance and Ezra snickered in unison. "For somebody who makes straight A's, you sure are dumb," Vance said.

"So what is it?" Giles asked.

"It's when you eat a girl's twat while she sucks your cock," Vance explained.

Giles' face squeezed together as if he had bitten into a lemon. "Gross!"

Vance and Ezra giggled.

"Hey," Ezra said to Vance, "where's the surprise you were talking about?"

"Oh yeah," Vance said. He reached into his back pant pocket and pulled out some folded papers. "Check this out, suckers." He unfolded them and laid the first one the plywood floor of the treehouse. "Look, but don't touch," he said.

Giles and Ezra were mesmerized. They left their milk crate chairs and sat up on their knees to get closer while heeding Vance's instruction not to touch. Staring back at them was a beautiful fully nude woman with long sandy-brown pigtails sitting against the wall of a dilapidated barn with her legs spread and her back arched. One slender-fingered hand held the brim of a well-worn straw cowboy hat that sat tilted atop her head while the other hand rested just below her flat belly, her fingertips barely reaching the edge of her pubic hair. The caption identified her as "Tawny" and said that she grew up in Indiana and loved horses.

After what seemed like a long time, Giles finally broke the silence. "Her nipples are gross—they're too big," he said.

"I like 'em," said Ezra who seemed as smitten as Giles was disgusted.

"That's nothing. Look at this one," Vance said as he pulled out another page from his pornographic trove. The model was a dark-skinned colored woman with a prodigious afro. She was holding a wooden spear while standing on a sandy beach with the ocean at her back. She was wearing nothing but a crocodile tooth necklace. Mouths agape, Ezra and Giles stared at the enormous areoles that nearly covered the entirety of the woman's undersized breasts. The caption identified her as "Zoya" and stated that she was a descendant of a Zulu priestess from the Ivory Coast of West Africa.

Vance pointed at the large pile of pubic hair between the colored woman's legs. "Would you eat that black pussy, Giles?"

Giles shook his head vigorously. "Gross. No way."

Vance grinned. "I think you would," he said.

"I wouldn't eat a vagina no matter what the color," Giles proclaimed vehemently.

"Well, that's too bad," said Vance.

"Why is that?" Giles asked, puzzled.

"Because" Vance explained, "you only have two choices in life: either eat pussy or suck cock. So, I guess that makes you a cocksucker."

Giles defiantly shook his head. "I can choose neither," he said. "And besides, the stuff they wrote about her is all wrong. The Zulu tribe is from South Africa, not the Ivory Coast. Those regions are thousands of miles apart, like from here to Alaska."

"You're fucking reading the words when there is a picture of a naked woman in front of you?" Vance asked, exasperated. "What kind of faggot are you?"

"The kind that knows his geography apparently," Ezra said, chuckling. Then he felt guilty for not coming to Giles' defense.

The next morning, Vance rode his skateboard over to Ezra's house to see if he wanted to go to the rope-swing at the bayou. Ezra said that his mother was grocery shopping and that he would have to wait until she returned to ask for permission. While waiting under an oak tree in Ezra's backyard, Vance took out his pocket-knife and showed Ezra how to make a whistle out of an acorn. When they got bored blowing their new whistles, Vance pulled a can of smokeless tobacco from his pocket and offered some to Ezra.

"Where did you get that?" Ezra said, looking around to make sure there were no witnesses.

"I found it between the seat cushions in my dad's truck," Vance said as he put a pinch of tobacco between his gums and cheek and then watched Ezra do the same.

"It tastes like wintergreen," Ezra said, "but it burns."

"Well, yeah," Vance said as if Ezra were stating something that should have been common knowledge. "You've never dipped Skoal before?"

"Yeah but it's been a while I guess," Ezra lied.

Vance spat a wad of brown tobacco juice into the grass. "I'm going to see if I can bring some new pictures the next time we go to the treehouse," he said.

"Cool," Ezra replied, trying to pretend that he was enjoying the tobacco experience after accidentally swallowing some of the juice.

"Fucking Giles," Vance said, "Can you believe he was bothering with reading the words instead of looking at the pictures?"

Ezra chuckled. "Yeah, but maybe you shouldn't tease him so hard about being queer." As he said this, Ezra leaned over, plucked a blade of grass from the ground and placed it in the path of a foraging roly-poly. When the bug climbed onto the blade, Ezra lifted it from the ground, allowing it to crawl onto his hand.

"What's the big deal?" Vance asked.

"I think it might hurt his feelings."

"Shit," Vance replied, before spitting another wad of tobacco juice into the grass, "I call everybody a faggot."

"Yeah, but Giles might think you mean it when you say it to him."

Vance regarded Ezra curiously. "Why? Do you think he really might be a faggot?"

"No," Ezra said, though there was a hint of uncertainty in his voice.

"Didn't he say he might want to be a priest?" Vance asked. "Aren't most priests secret faggots?"

Ezra shook his head as he lowered his hand to the ground to release the roly-poly back into the grass. "Yeah. I mean no, I mean, yes he's talked about being a priest, but no, most priests aren't faggots. And regardless, I don't necessarily think Giles is queer."

"Not necessarily?" Vance replied, "Well wouldn't you want to be sure? I mean, wouldn't you want to know if one of your best friends might be secretly wanting to suck your dick the whole time y'all are hanging out?"

Ezra grimaced. "Dude, I feel nauseous." His complexion was turning a pale shade of green. "I think I need to throw up."

Vance laughed and spit on the ground again as Ezra hurried around the side of the house to vomit. When he was done, he walked back

155

and found Vance on his knees. He had captured a large insect and was precariously holding it between his index finger and thumb.

"What are you doing with that mosquito hawk?"

"My cousin from Texas calls these dragonflies," Vance said.

"Yeah, my mom calls 'em dragonflies, too. But my dad says mosquito hawk, and me too. Don't they remind you of those double-winged crop-dusters?"

"Watch this," Vance said, ignoring Ezra's question. He carefully manipulated the large insect's body into a full circle and positioned the tip of its tail against its mandibles. Immediately the mosquito hawk began to voraciously consume its own tail.

"Dude," Ezra said "that's so cruel."

"What?" Vance replied. "He's hungry."

Ezra smirked. "Stop. It's just mean."

"Whatever," Vance said before tossing the mosquito hawk into the grass.

CHAPTER 24

A freshly washed beige Buick slowly pulled into the gravel parking lot at Andrus' Feed & Seed right at closing time. The car stopped in front of the warehouse just as the owner, a short, well-built man in Dickies and a faded denim work shirt was pulling the sliding doors closed. The balding, pot-bellied driver stepped out of the car wearing a practiced smile.

"I was just closing up," the owner said.

"Actually," the pot-bellied man said, "I'm not here for feed, Mr. Andrus. I'm Willard LeBas, the president of the Laurent Addition Home Owners Association. I just need a few minutes of your time."

"Concerning?" Andrus asked warily.

"To discuss the purchase agreement that you recently signed on your parents' home in the McCarron Addition," LeBas said.

"What about it?" Andrus asked in defensive tone.

Lebas produced a copy of the M Addition neighborhood covenant and laid it on the hood of his car. Using his stubby index finger, he directed Andrus' attention to paragraph 14 and proceeded to read it out loud:

> ... hereafter no part of said property or
> any portion thereof shall be ... occupied
> by a person not of the Caucasian race, it
> being intended hereby to restrict the use
> of said property ... against occupancy
> as owners or tenants of any portion of
> said property for residential or other
> purposes by people of the Negro or
> Mongolian race.

Andrus shook his head, stating that he had spoken to an attorney from the bank and was advised that racial restrictions on property covenants were no longer enforceable. In response, LeBas stated that the HOA's attorney has given them the exact opposite opinion. He went on to state that if the contract was not cancelled within twenty-four hours, both Andrus and the prospective buyers would be served with a lawsuit to block the sale and to enjoin the colored family from moving into the neighborhood. He intimated that there might be protracted litigation. He explained that if the HOA was forced to file suit, it would include a claim against Andrus for fines and associated attorney fees for violations of the neighborhood covenant not just for attempting to sell the property for occupancy by non-Caucasians but also for seventeen other documented violations that had previously been "overlooked" by the HOA. "To date," he said, "the fines total over $3,700, and that does not include the HOA's attorney fees that would be recoverable as collection costs."

"So, this is how you operate?" Andrus asked angrily. "Threatening people with lawsuits? I didn't see this kind'a bullying going on when Pierre Quebedeaux sold his house to those two queers right across the street from my parents' house."

"With all due respect sir," LeBas replied, "I think you are smart enough to understand where we are coming from. I think you know that when it comes to residential values, homosexuals are a bit different from coloreds."

"Well," Andrus responded, "queers is worse if you ask me. It's not a sin to be colored. Color is not a choice."

LeBas smiled sympathetically. "Mr. Andrus," he replied, "you might have a point there if this were purely a matter of morality. However, this is a legal matter and the difference here is that the neighborhood covenant does not exclude homosexuals."

When Andrus did not offer an immediate rejoinder, LeBas seized the opportunity to continue. "And surely you understand the devastating impact that having one colored family move into a white neighborhood can have. Think about it Mr. Andrus. Barbecues with twenty to thirty people spilling over into the street and the neighbors' yards. Loud music, drinking and smoking and hooting and hollering until all hours of the night. Drugs, cars on blocks in the front yard. Crime. Surely you heard about those coloreds raping that little white girl on the north side of town. So you can see why this is important."

Andrus continued to glower in silence, staring at nothing in the distance. Finally he said, "If I break the contract, I will owe them $150 earnest money."

LeBas smiled, took out a checkbook and promptly wrote a check to Andrus for $150 on the HOA account. He set it down on the hood of his car. Andrus stared at it for a moment and then picked up, folded and slipped it into his front shirt pocket. LeBas thanked Andrus for his time before squeezing himself into his car, his large belly mashing against the steering wheel. He nodded a thank you to Andrus, started the car and slowly drove off.

On the following Monday, Ezra saw Clayton at his locker and renewed his offer to help his family move into their new home. Clayton dejectedly explained that they were not buying the house after all. The owner had backed out of the deal.

"How come?" Ezra asked, obviously very disappointed.

Clayton seemed reticent to answer. He shrugged his shoulders. "Something about them not wanting coloreds in the neighborhood."

Ezra felt simultaneously embarrassed and angry. "Who's *them*?" he asked.

"I'm not really sure," Clayton said.

After getting home from school, Ezra rode his bike straight to the police station. He told his father about the seller reneging on his contract with the Chaissons because someone did not want a colored family living in their neighborhood. He wanted to know if there was anything his father could do to help them. By his reaction, Ezra sensed that his father was already aware of the situation.

"I'm afraid there's nothing that can be done, son," his father said. "I'm sorry."

"But why?"

"It's very complicated, son."

Ezra glared at his father, making it clear that he was unsatisfied with the response.

Bernard regarded Ezra for a moment in silence, struggling to find the right words. Then he pulled his keys from his pocket and told Ezra to follow him as he walked outside to his Ford Bronco. Ezra regarded his father for a moment without moving. "Where we going?" he said. There was a hint of defiance in his tone.

"Just get in, son," Bernard said, his tone and expression making it clear that it was not a request.

They drove south, mostly on back roads, passing through several small towns before getting onto Highway 167 and finally reaching the City of Lafayette. They continued south on the Evangeline Thruway until reaching Willow Street where they turned left, entering one of the older sections of town.

Bernard drove slowly to give Ezra an opportunity to take in their surroundings. While stopped at a traffic light they saw two colored men standing on the shoulder of the road, both shabbily dressed, sharing a bottle of liquor packaged in a brown paper bag. To their left stood a colored woman on the street corner, scantily clad, smoking a cigarette and screaming angrily at two similarly dressed women on the opposite corner, one colored, the other white, who responded with laughter and vulgar gesticulations.

As they drove on, Bernard and Ezra saw an older colored man leaning against a utility pole, talking to a very skinny white woman with poorly applied makeup and bleached hair accented by a generous layer of dark roots. The old man turned and watched as a neatly dressed light-skinned colored girl, holding the hand of a like-hued young boy, walked past at a quick pace, her head down so as not to invite attention. He said something to the girl, smiling mischievously. The girl ignored him and quickened her pace, pulling the stumbling boy along.

As the Bronco rolled to a stop at the next intersection, Ezra saw several middle-aged colored men standing in the side parking lot of a convenience store. Some were drinking. Some were smoking. Some were doing both. One seemed to be telling a story and was acting out a fight as his buddies laughed and egged him on. When one of the men pointed at the lingering Bronco, some of the others looked in their direction. Bernard turned right on Agapanthus Avenue and drove for several blocks before coming to a stop on the side of the road next to an empty lot.

After putting the Bronco's transmission in park and turning off the engine, Bernard gestured toward an old Acadian-style house on the opposite side of the street. The wood frame dwelling was mostly white with pale green trim though much of the paint was peeling, exposing prior paint colors, primer and in many areas bare wood. Two of the downstairs windows were boarded up with repurposed wooden signs, one urging voters to *Elect Herman "Pappy" Latiolais for City Alderman, No. 13,* the other, more faded, bearing an advertisement that read, *Blair House, the Original Zyde-Cajun Restaurant.*

Unpainted wooden steps led to a large porch where an old grizzle-faced colored man was sound asleep in a metal lawn chair, his head cocked to one side. In front of the house was an early model Oldsmobile Toronado, its bare wheels resting on cinder blocks. A Rottweiler mix was chained to the rear axle. When the dog noticed the strange vehicle pull to a stop, it lazily crawled out from under the car to let out a warning bark, rousing its owner from his slumber.

Wanting to avoid eye contact with the old man, Ezra turned his head in the opposite direction and looked out of his window where two young colored men were leaning against a rusted-out propane tank, both looking back at him. Above them hung drooping power lines attached to a leaning creosote pole. Hanging from the lowest line was a pair of green Converse high tops tied together by their laces.

"Those look brand new," Ezra said, pointing at the shoes. "Why would someone throw brand new shoes on the telephone wires?"

Bernard looked at the shoes dangling from the line. "You'll see shoes hanging like that every few blocks or so," he said. "That's how drug dealers mark their territory."

"Really?" Ezra asked skeptically.

"Yes, sir. That's why there are so many shootings and knifings in this area. It's mostly fighting over drugs and drug territory."

Ezra turned his attention back to the two young colored men. One was sucking hard on a crinkled, hand rolled cigarette. Ezra continued to watch as the first man passed the cigarette to the other man before exhaling a thick plume of white smoke through his mouth and then letting his head fall to the side in a relaxed pose. The other man pulled his oversized pants up with one hand as he brought the homemade cigarette to his lips with the other, sucking on it for what seemed like several seconds. The first colored man said something that caused the second man to laugh and cough out plumes of white smoke with each hack.

"Are those men doing drugs?" Ezra asked.

Bernard looked out of Ezra's window at the two men for a moment and then shifted his gaze in a different direction. "I suspect that they are, but don't stare."

"Aren't you going to arrest them?" Ezra asked, still watching them through the glass.

"No," Bernard said. "I don't have jurisdiction here."

"Are you going to go report them to the Lafayette police?"

"No."

"Why not?"

"Because that's not why we came here."

Ezra turned and leered at his father. "Why did we come here?"

Bernard subtly gestured back toward the house where the old man was sitting on the porch. "This house is where my maternal grandparents lived when I was your age."

"Mama and Papa Bergeron?" Ezra asked. He mostly remembered them from photos, his great grandfather passing long before he was born and his great grandmother dying when he was only three years old.

Bernard nodded.

Ezra studied the house and the surrounding area but did not respond immediately. Finally, he said, "I didn't know they were poor."

"They weren't," Bernard replied. "Papa Bergeron had his own hardware store. They weren't rich, but they were very comfortable. This used to be a beautiful home in an immaculately kept neighborhood where

163

nice, hardworking people lived and kids played in the streets without any worries." Bernard allowed his son a little more time to take in the scene before asking him, "Would you feel safe living here now?"

"No," Ezra said.

"Why not?" Bernard asked.

"What happened?" Ezra asked, avoiding his father's question.

Bernard pointed to the two young colored men standing across the street, then to three young colored girls yelling and chasing each other down the sidewalk further up the block, then back at the old man slouched in his chair on the porch. "*They* happened," he said.

Ezra kept looking back at the two colored men. They had finished smoking their peculiar looking cigarette and were now leering at Ezra and his father through heavy eyes. He thought that they had stepped closer to the Bronco, but he was not sure.

"It's not that we don't like colored people, son," Bernard explained. "But we know from experience that when colored families start moving into a white neighborhood, things start to deteriorate and get more dangerous. We just want to protect our families and protect our property values. That's all."

"Can we leave now?" Ezra asked apprehensively, keeping his eye on the two colored men, one of whom was now pointing at the wheels of his father's Bronco. Bernard nodded and started the engine.

Ezra sat in silence most of the way home staring aimlessly out of his window at acres and acres of pasture and farmland—mostly crops of rice, cotton and sugarcane. He spied redwing blackbirds balanced on cattails, red-tailed hawks perched on the tops of telephone poles and egrets standing on the backs of cattle lazily grazing on thick grass in the hot sun. When he grew bored with the scenery at eye level, he gazed up at the sky looking for images in the clouds. Finally, he asked, "If colored people are so bad, why do you make me go to school with them? Why can't I go to St. Anne's?"

Bernard sighed. "I don't think all coloreds are bad, son. Just like I don't think all white people are good. And second, we can't afford the tuition at St. Anne's."

"Why didn't you turn?" Ezra asked as they passed up the road leading to their neighborhood.

"I thought you might want to get some ice cream," Bernard replied, hoping to inspire some good will.

"I don't want any," Ezra said.

"You sure?"

Ezra nodded. "Are you and mom getting a divorce?" he asked. He turned toward his father to gauge the reaction on his face.

Bernard remained silently stoic for a moment. "Didn't you already discuss that with your mother?"

"Are y'all?" Ezra repeated.

Bernard wanted to choose his words carefully. He wanted to be honest with Ezra, but in fairness to Eve, he decided that she needed to be part of the conversation. "Your mother and I have a complicated relationship, son."

Ezra smirked. There was that word again, he thought. "Who will I live with?" he asked.

"Come again?"

"When you and mom get divorced, who will I live with?"

Bernard let out a frustrated sigh. "Buddy, if we get to that point, you'll be the first one to know. But we're not there."

"I don't get it," Ezra said, refusing to let it go.

"You don't get what?"

"Well, Jimmy Theriot's parents got divorced because they fought all the time. You and mom get along just fine."

"Well," Bernard said, "oaks can pass for elks in just the right light."

Ezra knitted his brow, not comprehending his father's reference. "What is that supposed to mean?"

"That's an old expression my dad made up when Uncle Jack and I went with him on an elk hunt in Missouri when we were younger. It was almost dark and Uncle Jack shot at some oak tree branches thinking that they were the antlers of an elk. The expression means that things are not always what they appear to be," Bernard said.

Ezra turned away and stared out of the window.

When they pulled into the driveway of their home, Bernard killed the ignition and turned to Ezra. "Do me a favor, Sport. Don't harass your mom about this divorce stuff. Give us a chance to figure some stuff out and then we'll talk to you and let you know where everything stands, okay?"

"Yes, sir."

CHAPTER 25

"Come in," Bernard said, in an irritated tone without looking up from his paperwork.

His secretary poked her head in, hiding her portly figure behind the door. "I'm sorry, but Mr. and Mrs. Chaisson are here to see you, Chief."

Bernard sighed deeply and rubbed his temples. "Tell them they need to make an appointment, Paula."

"They do have an appointment, Chief," Paula replied.

"Well, apologize for me and reschedule. I really don't have time right now."

"But Chief—"

"What is it, Paula?" Bernard snapped and then immediately regretted his tone. "I'm sorry. What is it?"

"It's just that you made me reschedule their last two appointments."

Bernard removed his reading glasses and covered his face with his hands. "Alright. Give me a minute and then bring them in."

As the Chaissons were getting settled into their chairs across from Bernard's desk, he apologized for not being able to meet with them sooner. They were very understanding but also eager to find out if there had been any developments in their son's case.

Bernard explained that, as promised, he put Jarvis Lewis on the case. He told them that Jarvis had interviewed every employee at the nursing home and made inquiries with numerous people in the colored community, including several confidential informants. Jarvis had also visited business owners and residences along the route the boys would have taken from the nursing home. Unfortunately, other than getting confirmation that the two boys were last seen leaving the nursing home following their evening shift, no one had seen them since or had any helpful information. The Chaissons listened intently and were very disappointed.

"But that doesn't mean you should abandon all hope," Bernard said. "Sometimes we get lucky. Somebody ends up saying something to the wrong person. Somebody gets arrested and informs on somebody else to cut a deal. It happens more often than you might think. But those things usually take time to develop. We just have to be patient."

Horace shifted in the wooden chair causing its legs to creak under his considerable weight. He leaned forward and rested his elbows on his knees, looking Bernard in the eyes. "Chief, we know the police want to believe that this was some kind of drug deal gone bad, but we don't believe that's what happened. Nobody in the colored community thinks that. We've been talking to people who know the game and all the so-called players in town. They all sayin' the same thing. This wasn't drug related. Cedric was squeaky clean. D'Arius smoked and peddled a little dope here and there, but he had two kids and was workin' a full-time job. He wasn't involved in nothing serious."

Bernard nodded and pursed his lips. "Now Horace, I'm not saying this was for sure a drug thing or that Cedric was involved in anything illicit. But you would not by a long shot be the first parents to be completely surprised by what their child was up to, especially when it comes to drugs. Even the best kids sometimes get into things they shouldn't and without the parents knowing a thing. I've seen it a hundred times over the years."

Bernice shook her head. "I know what you sayin', Chief Brasseaux. I do sir. And I'm not some simple-minded mother blind to her children's misdeeds. I know who my Cedric was. And I'm telling you there ain't no way no how my boy was messing around with drugs or drug dealers. He wasn't using. He wasn't selling. And he wouldn't be hanging around nobody who was. And, with all due respect sir, that's not an opinion. That's fact."

Bernard nodded, trying hard to avoid any appearance of condescension. He sensed that Bernice had more to say and so remained silent.

Bernice shifted in her chair and leaned forward, putting a hand on the edge of Bernard's desk as if to prevent herself from falling over. It was obvious that the stress from losing her son had taken an enormous toll on her. Normally a vibrant, attractive woman, she appeared gaunt, haggard and frail. She peered at Bernard through tired eyes. "Chief Brasseaux," she said in a failing voice, "respectfully, we need you to look at what was actually done to these boys and use some common sense. Little D'Arius was tortured and mutilated. He has brain damage. His lips were cut off of his face, sir. A broom handle was jammed up his rectum. He was castrated. And my baby," she paused to wipe tears from her face before continuing, "my baby, God bless his beautiful soul, was drowned like a rice bin rat. The autopsy report said they found mud up in his nostrils and muddy water in his lungs."

Bernard grabbed a box of facial tissues and gently set it in front of Bernice. She nodded her gratitude and used one to dab her nose and eyes but did not stop talking.

"I been living in the colored world too long sir. I've seen so much. And one thing I know is that drug dealers ain't gonna bother with doing all that cruel nonsense. They are very practical. They'll just stick a knife in

169

you or put a bullet in you and be done with it. No sir, this was not about drugs. This was some high-level hatefulness. And I mean no personal offense, but we know and we think you know too that this was some angry white people who did this. And if you're not willing to consider that as a distinct possibility, then shame on you sir."

Bernard's affect flattened. He could not dispute Mrs. Chaisson's logic. There was evidence of real malevolence here, real psychotic animus, atypical of any local drug-related violence he had ever seen or heard of. "I hear what you're saying Mrs. Chaisson," he said, "and I don't necessarily disagree with you, but I don't know what you expect me to do. I simply don't have any evidence to go on. No evidence, no leads, no suspects."

Horace's wide nostrils flared with anger. When he opened his mouth to speak, his wife reached over and put her hand on his arm. When he turned and looked at her, the grief on her face derailed his anger. Realizing that he was on the verge of alienating the only person in a position of authority who seemed to care even a little bit about what happened to their son, he leaned back in his chair and swallowed hard before speaking.

"The day before Cedric and D'Arius went missing," Horace said, making it a point to speak in a very soft and calm voice, "it was going all around town that that little white girl—you know who I'm talking about—claimed that she got herself raped by some colored men. White boys and men was riding around the colored section of town in pickup trucks, hollering racist things and throwing rocks, eggs, half-empty cans of beer and whatever else they could find at colored people walking on the side of the roads. At least three people I know got hit. Willie Senegal was hit in the back of the head with a beer bottle and had to get six stitches. Miss Yolanda Batiste got a beer can filled with pea gravel thrown through her

170

living room window. All we saying is that maybe you could look into that side of it."

Bernard leaned back in his chair. "Horace," he said, "I don't doubt that any of those things happened or that it was motivated by the news of that girl being raped by colored men. But there's a world of difference between some young jackasses blowing off some steam by throwing things and what happened to Cedric and the Cole boy. And furthermore, who would you have me investigate? Every white male in the tri-parish area?"

"Nobody said that." Horace said. "But what about that little girl's daddy? He's supposedly mean as a snake and maybe a little battle-touched from Korea. You could at least question him, couldn't you?"

Bernard forced a smile in an effort to hide his frustration. "Look," he said, "it's perfectly natural for civilians to second guess the police. As a civilian, you can think and say anything you want. But as a police officer, I have to follow the law. People have Constitutional rights, and I took an oath to protect and uphold those rights. I can't go accusing someone of a crime when I have no evidence or even reasonable suspicion to believe that they were personally involved. I have to play by the rules. And I don't have any evidence that the girl's father or anyone else had anything to do with this, Horace. I want to help you, but my hands are tied."

Bernard could see the utter disappointment on the Chaissons' faces. He recognized that their theory was entirely plausible. He could think of more than a few white men in Iris and the surrounding area who were prejudiced enough and brazen enough to be involved in some sort of racial pay-back vigilantism—men who literally valued Negro life even less than that of stray dog or a feral cat. And he had to admit to himself that he would easily put Abel Mueller at the top of that list. But there was simply no evidence, or at least that is what he kept telling himself. And of course, though he could not admit it to the Chaissons, there was the issue of what

171

Abel Mueller might be capable of doing if he got so much as an inkling of suspicion that Bernard was investigating his potential involvement.

Obviously disheartened, Horace nodded politely before rising to his feet. He took Bernice by the arm and gently helped her out of her chair. She looked so fragile that Bernard thought for a moment that Horace would have to carry her out. When Bernard began to stand, Horace gestured with his hand to indicate that they did not need to get up. Out of respect, Bernard stood anyway but stopped short of escorting them out of the office. He watched as Horace gently placed his large hand on the small of his wife's back and guided her out of the police station.

CHAPTER 26

"Where's Ezra?" Bernard asked upon returning home from work and finding Eve cutting out coupons at the kitchen table.

"I brought him and Vance to the skating rink," Eve said without stopping what she was doing or even looking up.

"On a school night?"

"He didn't have any homework, so."

Bernard pulled out a chair and joined Eve at the table. Every time he had played out the conversation in his head it had ended poorly, so he decided to just get to the point.

"I'm ready to move on," he said, with no preamble.

Eve did not stop cutting. "What are you talking about?" she asked.

Bernard saw through the feigned ignorance. "I want to move forward with filing for divorce," he said with as much compassion as he could muster.

Eve's face twitched and her head titled slightly to the side. "Do you want to tell me where this is coming from, Bernard?"

Bernard regarded Eve for a moment. "We've already talked about this, Eve. We've been in a loveless marriage for so long that I'm afraid I'm going to forget how to love, or how to be loved. I just want to be happy again. I deserve a chance at that. And frankly so do you."

Eve pulled a cigarette case out of the pocket of her housecoat. Her hands were shaking as she wrestled to remove a cigarette from the pack, finally managing it. She lit it quickly and sucked hard on the butt, the nicotine instantly helping to settle her nerves.

"When did you start smoking again?" Bernard asked.

Eve scoffed and blew a thick plume of smoke directly above Bernard's head. "Is there someone else?" she asked. When Bernard swallowed hard and did not respond immediately, the corners of her mouth turned up slightly in a malevolent grin. "There is, isn't there?"

It was not in Bernard's nature to lie. "I am seeing someone," he said, "but this is not about her, Eve. It's about us."

"Of course," Eve said sarcastically as she flicked ash into a large ceramic ashtray. "Who is she?"

Bernard pursed his lips as he thought about how to answer. He did not want to drag Isa into his personal drama with Eve, but he knew the information would come out eventually. And he did not want to appear ashamed. "Her name is Isabella Vadas. You don't know her. She's not from around here. I met her through work."

"Through work?" Eve asked in a snarky tone. "That's very vague, Bernard. Was she someone that you arrested? Is she a prostitute?"

Bernard rolled his eyes. "Come on, Eve."

"Why don't you come on, Bernard?"

"Look, I don't want this to be ugly. It doesn't have to be. She's not a prostitute. She's an attorney."

Eve nodded and smiled. "How serious is it?"

"It's serious," Bernard said uncomfortably. "She has some property in Texas. She asked me to move there with her. I said yes."

Eve's face pinched with ire. "Texas? What about Ezra? Or do you not give a shit about your son anymore?"

Bernard regarded Eve, trying to maintain a softened countenance. "If we can't be civil, I'm not going to take part in this conversation," he said.

Eve snorted and let out a truncated guffaw. "Are you being serious right now? You announce to me that you want to break up our family to follow a fling to Texas and I'm supposed to handle it like Donna fucking Reed?"

Bernard took a deep breath. He did not respond.

"We agreed to stay in the marriage at least until Ezra was out of high school, Bernard," Eve said.

"I know we did."

"But?"

"I thought that was best at the time. But things have changed. I know it's going to be an adjustment for Ezra, but we can work through it."

Eve took a long drag on her cigarette and exhaled, trying to remain as calm as possible. "So, how are you supposed to have a relationship with Ezra when you are living in Texas?"

"I'll visit on a regular basis, and I'll fly him over any time he wants to visit there. He can come for holiday breaks and during the summer."

Eve shook her head in disbelief.

"It'll be a hell of a lot better than what he's been getting from us, Eve. He has no memory of us being happy—of us having a real marriage. We simply co-exist. What kind of example are we setting for him?"

"Oh, so you're doing this for him, are you?" Eve said with a titter.

Bernard resisted the urge to retaliate.

Eve took another extra-long drag on her cigarette and held it, glaring at Bernard scornfully before blowing the smoke through her nose. "So," she said, "when's all this going to happen?"

Bernard scooted his chair back from the table in order to avoid the heaviest concentration of smoke. "I think we should tell him when he gets home."

"No, I mean when are you moving?"

"Probably within a month or two. I've got two weeks of vacation coming to me so I'll take that and spend some extra time with Ezra. I would like him to come visit over the Christmas break."

"Ezra is going to be home with me for Christmas."

"Fine, he can come for New Year's then."

Eve started to object to that as well but stopped short. "Have you turned in your resignation already?" she inquired.

"Not officially, but I've let the mayor know that it's coming."

Eve glared at the wall for what seemed like a long time. "I want a little time to think about the best way to tell Ezra. We can talk to him tomorrow afternoon."

"Let's not put it off, Eve. Please."

"One day Bernard," Eve said, indignantly. "Is that really too much to ask?"

Bernard sighed. "No."

"And you'll be hearing from my lawyer," Eve said. "I want the alimony and child support resolved before you leave."

"We don't need lawyers, Eve."

Eve scoffed. "You don't get to tell me what I need."

Bernard gritted his teeth and nodded. "Alright. I'll see you tomorrow afternoon."

"You can sleep at the fishing camp," Eve said. "I don't want you sleeping another night in this house."

Bernard started to object but then realized that some physical separation would be best. "That's fine."

Eve picked up Ezra and Vance at the skating rink just as it was closing.

"Mom, can Vance sleep-over?"

"Not on a school night," Eve said. "He can sleep over this weekend."

"But we don't have any homework."

"Not on a school night," Eve repeated. There was no give in her tone so Ezra relented.

As they entered the house, Ezra dropped his skates on the floor by the front door. "Is there anything to eat?" he asked. "I'm starving."

Eve ignored the question. She told Ezra to sit down at the kitchen table. He noticed for the first time that her eyes were red and swollen. "Have you been crying?" he asked.

Eve forced herself to smile. "There's no easy way to tell you this so I'm going to just tell you straight out, the way I think I would want to be told if I were in your shoes, okay?"

Ezra regarded his mother warily. "Okay."

"I was wrong," Eve began, her voice quivering as tears beginning to well in her eyes. "I didn't know."

"You didn't know what?" Ezra asked anxiously.

"You asked me if your father and I were splitting up. Well, your dad informed me today that he wants a divorce."

Ezra was stunned. He opened his mouth to say something but no words came.

"He has a girlfriend," Eve continued. "He's moving to Texas to be with her. I just found out this afternoon. I didn't know, honey, I swear."

Ezra felt his stomach flip and thought for a moment that he was going to vomit. Fighting back tears, he turned and walked to his room without saying a word.

"Ezra?" Eve called out.

Ezra closed his bedroom door without responding.

CHAPTER 27

After his discussion with Eve, Bernard drove to the mayor's house to discuss the transition at the department. Bernard and Mayor Tracy "Tee" Laurent had been friends since middle school. It was Tee, then a City Councilman, who spearheaded the recruitment of Bernard for the interim Chief of Police job more than a decade earlier.

Bernard and Tee usually saw eye to eye on things, and Tee was on very short list of people in town who Bernard felt comfortable talking to about personal issues. It also did not hurt that Tee was on his third wife, which made Bernard less apprehensive about being judged relative to a failed marriage.

They sat on oversized rocking chairs on the back porch so that Tee could smoke a cigar while they talked. "So do we have a last day on the job pinpointed yet?" Tee asked.

"Not exactly," Bernard answered. "I'm shooting for some time between Thanksgiving and Christmas, but that's not written in stone. There are some housekeeping matters to see about and a few loose ends on a case or two that that I want to tie up before I leave."

Tee sensed that there might be something more. "And?"

Bernard shook his head and sighed. "I'm just a little worried about Ezra. I want to make sure we're okay before I head out."

"Does he know yet?"

Bernard shook his head. "We're going to sit down with him tomorrow afternoon and talk to him about everything."

Tee nodded. "He'll probably take it pretty hard, but he'll adjust in time. Kids are resilient," Tee said.

Bernard nodded. "I hope so."

"Don't you have some vacation coming to you? Why don't you use that to spend some quality time with him before you leave?"

Bernard nodded. "That's the plan."

Tee stepped back into the house and came back out with two partially filled whiskey glasses. He handed one to Bernard before retaking his seat.

"Thank you," Bernard said. He swirled the whiskey around in the glass and then held it to his nose to catch a waft of the aroma. "Johnnie Walker Black?" he guessed.

"Blue," Tee said with a smug smile.

Bernard turned and looked at Tee with a surprised countenance. "Seriously?"

Tee smiled. "It was a wedding gift," Tee said.

"Which marriage?" Bernard asked with a grin.

"The second one," Tee said. "I've been rationing it for over a decade."

Tee lifted his glass to Bernard who reciprocated. "You've been one hell of a police chief and an even better friend," Tee said. "I'll be sorry to see you go."

Bernard nodded and thanked Tee for his kind words then took a small, slow sip, allowing his palate to adjust to the smooth Scotch blend. He nodded his approval and then took a slightly larger sip.

Tee followed suit and then leaned back to savor it before taking another puff from his cigar and blowing out several rings of smoke, watching them dissipate one after the other. "How confident are you that Curtis can handle the job until we can rig a special election?" he inquired.

Bernard tilted his head and raised a brow at the mayor.

Tee chortled. "I'm joking, Bernard."

Bernard raised his other brow to express his incredulity.

"Mostly," Tee said, chuckling.

"I think he'll do fine," Bernard said. "He's lazy, but capable."

Tee smiled and nodded. "That's pretty much how I see it too."

The next morning, Bernard informed his subordinates of his plans, wanting them to hear it from him first. Everyone genuinely seemed sad to learn that he was leaving, though Curtis seemed to have mixed emotions, obviously somewhat excited about the prospect of serving as interim chief, which he knew would give him an advantage against any opposition in the special election that would follow.

When Bernard returned home that afternoon, Eve was sitting on the porch with a lit cigarette in one hand and a half-empty cocktail glass in the other. Her eyes were glassy and she had a sly look on her face that made Bernard feel very ill at ease. He stopped at the bottom of the steps. "I'm sorry I'm a little later than I said I would be. My afternoon got away from me."

Eve did not speak but gestured as if to say that his tardiness was of no consequence. She took a sip from her glass and then another drag from her cigarette.

"Did Ezra make it home yet?"

"He did, but he left again," Eve answered nonchalantly.

"Where to?"

"To play with his friends."

"Didn't you tell him we needed to talk to him?"

"He doesn't want to talk to you, Bernard," Eve said before taking another sip of her cocktail.

Bernard's initial confusion quickly turned to anger when he surmised what had occurred. "Why not? Did you say something to him?"

"He already knew, Bernard," Eve said smugly. "Apparently you and your lover weren't quite as discreet as you thought you were."

Bernard's face flushed with anger. "He already knows what, exactly?" He kept his voice low, trying to control his temper.

"That you're quitting your job; that you're leaving; that you're moving to Texas with your whore," Eve said in a haughty tone as she flicked her cigarette and watched the ashes fall onto the porch.

Bernard sighed. He knew it was Eve who told Ezra, but he wanted to avoid an unwinnable argument, especially when she had obviously had too much to drink. As he turned to leave, he heard Ezra riding up on his bicycle.

"Hey, Sport," he said in a friendly tone.

Ezra dropped his bike in the front yard, climbed the porch steps and walked straight past Bernard without replying. Bernard glared at Eve for a moment before following Ezra into the house.

"Leave him alone Bernard," Eve called out.

Bernard found Ezra in his room lying in his bed, pretending to be occupied with a model airplane. "We need to talk, Ez," Bernard said in a gentle tone.

Ezra ignored him and continued to randomly inspect his model. Bernard was about to speak again when he felt Eve's presence behind him. He turned to find her standing in the threshold of Ezra's room, still smoking her cigarette. "Can you give us some privacy?" he asked politely.

"This is my house," she answered defiantly. "And he's my son."

Bernard turned back to Ezra and then sat on the edge of his bed. When he tried to rest his hand affectionately on Ezra's foot, Ezra drew his legs up against his body. "Ezra," Bernard said, "I'm sorry you found out the way you did. I wanted to be the one to tell you myself."

"So it's true," Ezra said without looking up.

Bernard heard Ezra's voice crack as he spoke and realized that he was on the verge of tears. "What's true is that it's been many, many years since your mother and I have been happy together, many years since this has felt like a real marriage. And I just feel like we both deserve a chance at finding happiness again."

"And for your daddy," Eve interjected, "finding happiness apparently means moving to another state and starting another family."

It took every ounce of self-restraint that Bernard had to abstain from responding to Eve's vitriol, to not retaliate with an explanation that it was his mother's decision to have an abortion when she was pregnant with Ezra's brother that destroyed their marriage in the first place. He took a deep breath and exhaled. "I have met someone very special, and yes, we are moving to Texas. I'll be getting a job there. But that doesn't mean you and I aren't going to still spend a lot of time together, even more than we have in the past since I am not going to have to work nearly as much. And, I think you're really going to love it out there when you come to stay with us. We'll be living on a ranch in the foothills. They'll be horses, fly-fishing, mountain bikes and—"

"I'm not going to Texas," Ezra said. "Ever."

"I know you feel—"

"And if you try to make me," Ezra interrupted, "I'll run away. I swear to God I will."

Bernard could feel Eve's self-satisfied smirk from behind him but resisted the urge to look at her. "Okay, Buddy, well—"

"I'm not your buddy," Ezra said, his tone filled with insolence.

Bernard started to reply but then thought better of it. He rose and turned to walk out of the room when Ezra spoke. "And I hope your new girlfriend gets tired of you and leaves you so that you know how it feels."

Bernard shuttered and turned to face Ezra. "Son, I'm not—"

"Just leave, Bernard," Eve interjected. "You're just going to make things worse."

"I just—"

"Just go," Eve said.

Bernard took a deep breath. He opened his mouth to say something but then stopped and walked out of the room.

CHAPTER 28

Courtesy of Eve's well-placed confidences, the gossip mill in Iris was soon running amok. Bernard ignored the glares and whispers of neighbors, courthouse staff and passers-by, trying to focus his attention on getting things in order at the station. When he was not working, he tried to see or contact Ezra, desperately wanting to disabuse him of the notion that he was abandoning him, but Eve's interferences and Ezra's recalcitrance made it impossible.

At the top of Bernard's list of objectives before leaving the department was to follow through on his promise to the Chaissons. Though he felt certain that his efforts would be for naught, he wanted to be able to satisfy them, and himself, that he had done all that he could to find whoever was responsible for their son's murder.

He began by instructing his assistant to go to the St. Landry Parish Sheriff's Office in Opelousas and check-out the file on the Cole/Chaisson investigation. An hour later, there was a knock on his door, and the stout assistant entered Bernard's office with a smaller than expected file and a large mug of coffee. "I figured you might want a fresh cup," she said.

"Thank you, Paula."

"I thought you were supposed to be on vacation this week, Chief?" Paula said as she laid the mug along with the file on Bernard's desk.

"I am," Bernard said as he opened the file. "I'm fly-fishing in Montana as we speak if anyone asks for me."

"Yes, sir," she said before closing the door behind her.

After perusing the investigative report, Bernard removed a large stack of photographs from a manila envelope and spread them out across his desk. He noticed that there were no foot or tire tracks leading up to or away from either of the bodies. The closest footprints to either body were smaller ones, those made by Ezra and Giles. They appeared to be approximately seven to eight feet away from where D'Arius Cole was found lying against the trunk of a cypress tree.

Bernard also noticed there was a significant disturbance in the brush and mud for several feet on only one side of each body. He oriented the photographs directionally and determined that the disturbances were on the side of the bodies closest to the highway. He deduced that the boys' bodies were propelled through the air from the direction of the highway, landing in the mud and skidding and/or rolling several feet southward— away from the highway—before coming to rest where they were eventually found. D'Arius Cole's body had been stopped by the cypress tree which explained while the Chaisson boy's body had been found ten to twelve feet farther from the highway.

Bernard set the photographs aside and went back to the first page of the investigative report. He scribbled the mile marker number on a piece of paper and stuffed it into his front shirt pocket. He reassembled the file and tucked it under his arm, grabbed his keys. He drove toward the scene, heading north on Highway 4408 until he found the correct mile marker. He pulled over onto the shoulder of the highway, located what was left of the crime scene markers and followed them to where the bodies had been found.

Though intervening rains had all but erased the soil disturbances, Bernard used the photographs to approximate the direction from which the bodies had arrived at their final resting points. Then he slowly walked the area using a concentric arc pattern, starting from the location of where the bodies were found and moving in the direction of the highway. About twelve feet from where Cedric Chaisson's body was found, he discovered two cottonwood saplings snapped in half about four feet above the ground. He found another in the same condition a few feet farther along, this one with a small piece of blue cotton material wedged into its splinters, the same color as the nursing home scrubs that the boys were wearing the night they went missing. He also found a similar pattern of disturbed brush, limbs and saplings leading to where D'Arius Cole had been found.

As he drew nearer the highway, Bernard found deep ruts in the soil and mashed sugarcane remnants. He also saw broken glass and shards of metal scattered about indicating a recent motor vehicle crash. The size and number of the ruts and yaw marks on the pavement suggested that at least one of the vehicles involved in the crash had been a tractor-trailer. The sugarcane debris indicated that it was probably a sugarcane hauler.

When Bernard returned to the station, he called the records department for Troop K of the State Police. He requested all motor vehicle accident reports for any crashes occurring within two hundred yards in either direction of mile marker 14 on Highway 4408 between August 1 and October 30, 1976. The clerk asked him to hold for a moment while she cross-referenced the request with a map.

"That's going to include accidents on both sides of the Evangeline Parish-St. Landry Parish border," the clerk said.

"Correct."

"I'll get right on it, Chief."

The clerk called back less than an hour later, reporting that only two crash reports met Bernard's request criteria. "The first is dated August 22, 1976 and documents a single vehicle accident investigated by the St. Landry Parish Sheriff's Office," the clerk said. "According to the report, it occurred approximately three-hundred twenty feet north of mile marker 14 in St. Landry Parish and involved a twenty-two-year-old male operating a 1972 Honda XL250. It says he lost control of the motorcycle, left the roadway and collided with a tree. His injuries were fatal."

"Okay let's go to the next one, please," Bernard instructed.

"Let's see," the clerk said. "The second report documents a two-vehicle collision that occurred on September 3, 1976 and was investigated by the Evangeline Parish Sheriff's Office. The estimated time of the accident was 2:48 a.m. The location was fifty feet south of mile marker 14, just inside Evangeline Parish. Vehicle 1 was a Peterbilt tractor-trailer sugarcane hauler with a single occupant. Vehicle 2 was a 1969 GMC pickup with two occupants. The report includes a written statement from the driver of the semi indicating that he was traveling at approximately fifty miles per hour through the curve of the highway when the oncoming vehicle crossed the centerline causing a head-on collision. There were no traces of alcohol or drugs in his system. The driver of the pickup was severely injured and the passenger is noted as a fatality."

"Who were the occupants of the pickup?" Bernard asked, as he took notes.

The clerk paused as she flipped through the pages of the report. "Let's see. Hold on, okay, here it is," she said. "It identifies the driver as a Ferrell Pugh, and the passenger as an Errol Frey."

After a short pause, Bernard asked, "Is there registration information on the pickup listed in the report?"

"Yes sir," the clerk replied. "The pickup was registered to an Abel Mueller. That's Mike, Uniform, Echo, Lima, Lima, Echo, Romeo."

"Son of a bitch," Bernard muttered under his breath.

"Sir?"

"I'm sorry, I was talking to myself."

"Do you need me to send a copy of this to your office?" the clerk asked.

"No, I'll just pick it up next time I'm in Opelousas," Bernard said.

"Okay. I'll have it ready for you. Just ask for Meagan."

"Thank you, Meagan, I'm grateful for all your help."

"Any time, Chief Brasseaux."

After Bernard ended the telephone call with the clerk, he called Curtis into his office.

"What's up, Chief?" Curtis said, sensing that Bernard appeared to be on edge.

"Well a couple of things actually Curtis," he said. "Have a seat."

Curtis gingerly lowered his stout body into the office chair as if he had a stiff back. He took a deep breath as though the task of sitting down had winded him. Bernard leaned back in his chair and regarded his portly subordinate for a moment.

"You okay?"

"Oh, yeah, Chief."

"Curtis, this needs to be kept strictly confidential, okay?"

"Roger that, Chief."

"I mean just you and me, and not another God-damned soul unless I expressly give you the green light, understand?"

"Perfectly," Curtis said, assuming the most serious countenance he could muster, which was not terribly serious looking at all.

Bernard leaned back in his chair and sighed. He regarded Curtis for a moment longer as if to reassure himself that Curtis was capable of maintaining a confidence. Finally, he said, "I think Abel and his crew had something to do with what happened to those two colored boys."

188

Curtis looked a little surprised by the comment and then stifled a snicker. "Shit Chief, that was my theory from the get-go."

"Based on what?"

"Hell, we both know—shit, you better than me with y'all growing up together—that having his daughter raped ain't nothing Abel Mueller was likely to take sitting down."

Bernard nodded. "Yeah, but I don't just mean I suspect him. I mean I have some evidence that might implicate him, his brother-in-law, Ferrell, and his dead buddy, Errol Fry."

A curious but not surprised expression appeared on Curtis' face. "What kind of evidence?" he asked.

"Well, it's all circumstantial, but God damn it, it's pretty compelling," Bernard said. He went on to explain what he was able to piece together from the photographs, his findings at the scene and his research of the crash reports in that area. He told Curtis that everything pointing to the colored boys being ejected from a vehicle from the direction of the highway, that Abel's pickup, occupied by Pugh and Frey, was involved in a crash in that exact area about thirty-six hours before the colored boys were discovered.

"So, you think Pugh and Frey were going to dump them colored boys somewhere when they had the head-on with that big cane hauler?"

Bernard nodded. "That's exactly what I think."

"And the boys got ejected from the bed of the pickup upon impact and ended up in the woods?"

"Correct."

"And what about Abel? How do you think he was involved?"

"I'm not exactly sure. But you saw the pictures of the Cole boy. Whoever did that to him was one sadistic son of a bitch, and I don't know anyone more sadistic than Abel Mueller, or anyone with more motive."

"So, why do you think he wasn't he in the truck with the other fellas?"

"Well, I figure that all they did to the Cole boy would have made quite a mess. I'm thinking maybe Abel stayed behind to clean up, you know, get rid of any evidence."

Curtis nodded. "Makes sense."

"Makes a lot of sense," Bernard affirmed.

"You have any idea where?"

"Well, you gotta think they needed a place where they were sure no one would see or hear what was going on. And we know the Chaisson boy was drowned in muddy water, so what does that tell you?"

Curtis nodded. "Abel's got all those crawfish ponds on his property, and he's got barns and pump sheds scattered around out there. Most probably it was somewhere out there, huh?"

"That's what I'm thinking," Bernard said.

"So, what are you going to do?" Curtis said. "If you go accusing Abel of these crimes, he's not likely to be very understanding. Especially, if you're wrong."

"I know that," Bernard said.

"And I mean, Abel ain't exactly the type to say, *Oh, that's okay, Chief, I know you were just doing your job*, you know what I mean?"

Bernard nodded. Curtis had never seen him looking more stressed.

Then suddenly an anxious expression appeared on Curtis' face. "Whoa, whoa, whoa, wait a minute," he said excitedly, "with you about to resign, that would leave this mess squarely in my lap as the acting chief."

Bernard nodded, his expression apologetic.

"God dammit Chief, if we accuse Abel and we can't prove it, he'll make it his mission in life to destroy me. Maybe worse."

190

"That's why I'm bringing you in on this now Curtis," Bernard said. "If we act on this, there's going to be potential consequences for both of us, maybe more so for you. But I really think we owe it to the Chaissons to follow through on it. Don't you?"

Curtis glared at Bernard. "Well," he said after giving the situation a moment's thought, "if I get a say in this, I say we just as well let dead dogs lie, Chief. Like you said, all the evidence is circumstantial. We ain't got no proof that Abel or Pugh or Fry had anything to do with any of this. And not only will going after Abel do nothing to bring the Chaisson boy back or erase what happen to the other one, but I don't think either one of us wants to do anything that's gonna put us in Abel's crosshairs, especially not over a couple of dead niggers. Well, I know one ain't dead but he's probably worse than dead, so. Anyway, you know what I'm trying to say."

Bernard sighed but did not reply.

"When's your last day anyway?" Curtis asked.

"I haven't decided exactly," Bernard said. "If we're going to act on this, I'd like to see this through as much as I can before I leave."

Curtis scooted to the edge of his chair and looked at Bernard plaintively. "I really think we should let this be, Chief. I really, really do."

Bernard looked at Curtis intently. "You're serious?"

"As a heart attack."

"And you'd be okay with that, you know, morally, ethically?" Bernard asked.

Curtis scoffed and chuckled, regarding Bernard condescendingly for perhaps the first time since they had met. "Oh, Chief," he said, "I think I'll be able to sleep at night just fine. Definitely way better than spending the rest of my days looking over my shoulder for Abel Mueller."

Bernard nodded as he held Curtis' stare. "Let me gnaw on it for a bit. I won't do anything without talking to you first."

"Okay, Chief. Thank you. I appreciate you letting me weigh in."

After Curtis left his office, Bernard sat in his chair staring out of the window. He had never felt so conflicted. After a couple of minutes, he swiveled in his chair and found the framed copy of the oath he had taken when he was sworn in as Chief of Police hanging on the wall behind his desk. He read it silently to himself.

> *I solemnly swear to always uphold the Constitution of the United States of America; to never betray my badge, my integrity or the public trust; to serve my community; to protect lives and property; and to maintain the highest ethical standards in the fulfillment of my duties, so help me God.*

Bernard knew that his integrity and the aforementioned ethical standards dictated that he follow through on the investigation of Mueller, Pugh and Fry. However, he also knew that their being convicted of the crimes against the colored boys was far from a cinch. First, he well understood the reluctance of getting any jury to convict in a case based solely on circumstantial evidence, even more so when it would be a predominately white jury being asked to convict white men. Second, he knew that Mueller had been instrumental in getting the St. Landry Parish District Attorney elected, which would certainly influence the D.A.'s decision regarding whether to bring charges in the first place.

Bernard walked to the restroom and threw cold water on his face. He looked at himself in the mirror. He felt ashamed about even considering not pursuing the investigation or at least sharing his findings with the St. Landry Parish Sheriff's office. He returned to his desk without having made up his mind about what he was going to do.

At the end of the day, Bernard grabbed his keys and was headed out of his office when his telephone rang. He started to walk out without answering but then turned around and grabbed the receiver. "Chief Brasseaux," he said.

"Well, hello there, stranger," said the voice on the other end of the line.

Bernard smiled. "Back at you," he said sweetly.

"We got the first snow of the year up here last night," Isa said. "I wish you were here to see it."

"Really? It's still so warm over here. It seems crazy to even be thinking about snow."

"Any idea when you'll be heading this way?"

"I'm still trying to figure that out," Bernard said. "I'm going to move the rest of my stuff out of the house tomorrow."

"How's that old fishing camp bed treating your back?" Isa asked.

"Fine," Bernard said.

"And how's it going with Ezra?"

Bernard sighed. "Not fine. Not good at all. At least when I was still in the house, it made it difficult for her to poison him against me. Now, she has full reign."

"I'm sorry, Bernard. I know it's hard. But he'll start to see through all that eventually, and he'll come around. You'll see."

Bernard contemplated how unlikely that it all seemed at the moment and how he had so terribly miscalculated Ezra's anger and resentment. "I don't know."

"I do," Isa said. "He will."

Bernard did not reply.

"I can't wait to see you," Isa said.

"Me too," Bernard replied, though he sounded distracted.

"Is there something else, Hon?" Isa inquired.

Bernard sighed. "There's some police work stuff I'd like to sort out before I leave, that's all. It's a bit complicated. I'll tell you about it later."

The next day was Saturday. Bernard was running errands when he spotted Ezra at the pubic tennis courts, hitting a tennis ball against the practice wall. He parked and began walking over to Ezra.

"Hey Sport," Bernard said, "how about we go get a burger and shake at Stark's?"

Ezra ignored the invitation and continued to practice against the wall.

"Look Ezra," Bernard said, "I know you're upset. I get that. But it's very complicated."

Ezra huffed as he continued to hit the tennis ball against the practice wall. "Is it?" he replied.

The question surprised Bernard, and he was unsure of how to respond. "I really want to spend some time with you before I leave," he said. He was trying not to come across as desperate as he was feeling.

Ezra caught the tennis ball in his hand and turned to face his father. "Is it true that y'all are planning to get married and start a new family in Texas?"

Again, Bernard was not anticipating the question and did not know how best to respond. "We haven't made any definite plans about any of that, son," he answered. "And I promise—"

It was not what Ezra wanted or needed to hear. Profound dejection immediately registered in his countenance which stopped Bernard midsentence. Ezra dropped his tennis racket and the ball and began to walk off the tennis court toward his bicycle.

Bernard wished he had been better prepared. He was ready for more obstinacy and resentment but not probing questions. He picked up the tennis racket and followed. "Ezra, stop," he said. He immediately regretted how stern he sounded.

Ezra climbed onto his bicycle and began to ride off.

"Ezra?" Bernard said, walking toward Ezra. "Son, let's just sit down and—"

"Mom was right about you," he yelled. "And I never want to see you again."

"Ezra, you don't mean that," Bernard replied.

Ezra skidded his bicycle to a stop and turned back to face his father with a hate-filled glare. "I've never meant anything more in my entire life," he said before restarting his bike and riding off.

When Bernard got back to his office, his private line was ringing. "Hello?" he answered.

"Chief Brasseaux, this is Rhett Hebert in Opelousas. You probably don't remember me but you helped me out of a jam quite a few years back involving a traffic stop in Iris. I'm repaying the favor."

"How so?"

"Well I don't normally make these types of calls. I doing this as a courtesy, to let you know that I've been retained by your wife to represent her in the divorce and child custody proceedings."

"Okay, I appreciate the heads up, Mr. Hebert."

"Do you have a lawyer, Chief Brasseaux?" Hebert asked.

"I do not. I wasn't planning on getting one."

"With all due respect, you're going to want to change those plans, sir."

"Why's that?"

"Eve has asked me to file for sole custody of your son. She also wants to legally change his last name to her maiden name."

Bernard was stunned. "Are you serious?"

"I just wanted to give you forewarning of what's to come. Hire a lawyer, Chief Brasseaux."

"Okay."

"Goodbye, sir."

Bernard sat back in his chair dumbfounded, growing angrier by the second. He picked up the telephone to call Eve, dialed the number and then slammed the receiver down against the base so hard that a piece of the phone chipped off and flew across the room. "To hell with you, Eve," he growled. "To hell with Iris. To hell with all of this."

CHAPTER 29

When Bernard missed his first two appointments at the station the following Monday, Paula reluctantly called his house. When Eve answered, Paula apologized for bothering her and explained that she was trying to reach the chief. Eve said she had not seen him since he had come to get his things on Saturday.

Bernard did not make an appearance at the station on Tuesday or Wednesday either. "Still no sign of the chief?" Curtis asked Paula when he returned from his morning donut run.

"Nope."

"When was his two weeks of vacation supposed to be up?" Curtis asked.

"Last Friday," Paula answered. "He's got meetings on his calendar every day this week."

Curtis shook his head. "It's just not like him to not show and not call in."

Paula nodded. "Surely he wouldn't just leave for Texas without telling us, right?"

"Normally, I wouldn't think so. But I'm not at all sure where his head is these days. I've been in his shoes more times than I'd like to admit. A man in his situation can get all out of sorts. So honestly, it wouldn't surprise me at all if he just decided to take off without a lot of fanfare. You know how he hates goodbyes and people getting sentimental."

Paula nodded. "Well, I'd sure be very disappointed in him if that's what he did."

When no one saw or heard from Bernard be the end of the week, Paula started going through his things in his office. She found a signed letter of resignation sitting in his top drawer. It was dated the prior Monday. She showed Curtis. "Well, I guess that settles it," he said.

Curtis met with the mayor later that morning to explain the situation and show him Bernard's letter of resignation. "I'm surprised and not surprised," the mayor said. He immediately appointed Curtis as interim chief and sent a written order to the registrar of voters to schedule a special election.

Horace Chaisson telephoned the police station the following Monday morning, asking to speak to Chief Brasseaux. The call was put through to Curtis.

"Chief Doyle," he answered.

There was a pause on the other end of the line.

"Chief Doyle," Curtis repeated.

"Oh I'm sorry," Horace said. "I was calling for Chief Brasseaux."

"Bernard Brasseaux is no longer with the I.P.D.," Curtis said. "I'm acting as interim Chief. Is there something I can help you with, sir?"

Horace paused before responding. "No longer with the I.P.D.?"

"No, sir."

"I don't understand."

"He resigned."

"Okay."

"Is there something I can help you with?"

"We had met with him a couple of times about our son's case. We were calling to check on the status, to see if there were any developments."

"Yes sir. I'm familiar with the case, Mr. Chaisson. In fact, I spoke to Chief Brasseaux about it before he left."

"Oh, okay," Horace said. "Well, we are sorry to bother, but—"

"No bother. No bother at all," Curtis said, "As I think you were aware, we put Jarvis Lewis on the case, and he did a very thorough investigation. He interviewed everybody under the sun and even a few that were hiding under rocks. But no one saw or heard anything."

"Nothing?"

"Nothing at all, sir," Curtis answered. "In fact, Chief Brasseaux signed off on the decision to close the investigation before he left."

"Close the investigation?" Horace said, clearly disheartened.

"Yes, sir."

Curtis could hear someone talking in the background through a hand that covered the telephone's mouthpiece. After a short, garbled exchange Horace said, "What about that little girl's daddy? Did y'all question him?"

"What little girl?" Curtis asked, feigning ignorance.

"The little girl who got raped," Horace said, trying to manage his frustration.

"Oh no, Mr. Chaisson, we didn't have probable cause for that," Curtis said. "Best we can figure, sir, is that the Cole boy was probably involved in some kind of drug situation and your boy unfortunately was just in the wrong place at the wrong time. I'm very sorry but that happens more often than you might think."

Curtis could hear a woman's voice on Horace's end of the line but could not make out what she was saying. "So, you saying nobody even questioned the little girl's daddy?" Horace asked.

"Correct," Curtis said firmly. "Like I said, there was no probable cause to. Now if there's nothing else I can help you with, I've got other police business that needs attention."

Curtis hung up the phone and asked Paula to bring him the Cole/Chaisson file so that he could document his discussion with the family of one of the victims. She indicated that Bernard had been reviewing the file when she last saw it. They did a thorough sweep of his office and could not locate it.

"Well, ain't that a fine kettle of fish?" Curtis said.

Paula shrugged and began to walk back to her desk.

"Paula," Curtis called out.

"Yeah?"

"Call the St. Landry Parish D.A.'s office and get me a forwarding telephone number for Isabella Vadas."

A few minutes later, Paula found Curtis in the kitchen pouring himself a cup of coffee with one hand and holding a half-eaten link of boudin in the other. "I called the D.A.'s office. Ms. Vadas didn't leave a forwarding number."

"Well hell's bells," Curtis said.

"I'm sure the chief—I mean Bernard—will be in touch eventually," Paula said. "I'll remember to ask him about the file."

CHAPTER 30

The following Saturday morning, Vance woke and made his way down the length of the trailer to the small kitchen to find something to eat. He found an opened box of Cocoa Puffs on the table. His younger half-brothers, ages four and six, were sitting Indian style on the braided area rug in front of the console television watching Saturday morning cartoons, each with a bowl of cereal in front of them.

As Vance rifled through the freezer looking for frozen waffles, an argument broke out between his half-brothers over whether to change the channel from *Super Friends* to the *Bugs Bunny Road Runner Show*.

"Hey, shut up before you wake up Dad and he comes out and beats both your asses," Vance scolded in a hushed tone.

"But we already saw this one, Luke," the older brother whined.

"So!" retorted Luke.

"Just do *eenie meenie miney mo*," Vance suggested.

Neither brother objected. "I'll say it Bo," Luke quickly said. "You always mess it up."

"Na-Uhhhh!" Bo complained.

"Shhhhhh!" Vance warned. "Luke, just let Bo do it this time."

The boys faced off, each pushing forward a foot such that their bare toes were almost touching each other's. Hunching over his knee, Bo began. "Eenie . . . meenie . . . miney—"

"You're doing it wrong!" Luke interrupted. "You don't start on your own foot. You have to start on mine."

"Okay, okay," Bo said, and then began again, this time touching his brother's foot first. "Eenie . . . meenie . . . miney . . . mo . . . catch . . . a . . . nigger . . . by . . . the . . . toe . . . if . . . he . . . hollers . . . make . . . him . .

201

. pay . . . fifty . . . dollars . . . every . . . day . . . and . . . my . . . momma . . . said . . . you . . . are . . . not . . . it."

"I won! I get to pick!" Luke exclaimed as soon as Bo touched his foot on the last word.

"No!" Bo argued. "You are *not it*. That means you are not the one who gets to pick."

"No, no, Bo," Vance said from the kitchen. "Luke won. He gets to pick."

Tears welled in Bo's eyes and his face turned red with anger. He stood and kicked Luke's cereal bowl over, splashing milk and soggy chocolaty puffs across the area rug and against the wall.

"Oooooooh! You're in trouble now!" Luke exclaimed.

"Shut up, Luke!" Bo yelled before turning and running out the front door, slamming it behind him.

"You better clean that up," Vance said to Luke. "You know he's gonna blame it on you."

Luke looked at the mess and then back at Vance seemingly confident in the fact that he had the truth on his side. He crawled to the television and turned the knob several notches just in time to watch Wile E. Coyote hurriedly paint a roadway landscape onto a dead-end rock face just before the Road Runner zoomed through it as if the picture had magically transformed into a real road only to have Wile E. slam into the rock face with a loud, injurious crash as he tried to pursue.

Not wanting to be present when one of the adults came out to find the mess, Vance grabbed a banana and his skateboard and hurried out of the trailer.

Vance rode his skateboard to Ezra's house and knocked on the front door several times before the door finally opened. Still in her pajamas and smoking a cigarette, Mrs. Brasseaux's eyes were swollen and her hair was mussed. Seeing the normally attractive woman unmade caused Vance noticeable discomfort, as if he were peeking into the dressing room of a famous movie star and discovering that her beauty was mostly manufactured. "Hi Miss Eve," he said, avoiding eye contact. "Is Ezra here?"

Eve did not speak. She opened the door wider for Vance to enter and gestured with her cigarette hand toward Ezra's bedroom. As he approached, Vance could hear a repeating *thud* sound getting louder and louder. When he knocked and entered, he found Ezra lying face-up in his bed throwing a tennis ball against the ceiling and then catching it, over and over again.

"Hey, you wanna go walk the bayou and catch turtles?" Vance asked, trying to snap Ezra out of his funk.

"Nah," Ezra replied without taking his attention away from the tennis ball and the ceiling.

"Well, do you want to go find Giles? Maybe go to the treehouse?"

Ezra shook his head with disinterest.

"So, what do you want to do then?" asked Vance.

"I'm pretty much doing it," Ezra said as he tossed the ball at the ceiling again.

Vance finally relented. "Well, I'm going ride my skateboard. Come find me later if you feel like it."

Ezra did not reply. He continued what he was doing as Vance began to show himself out. When Vance reached the door, he stopped and turned back, regarding Ezra for a moment. "I know it's not the same," he said, "but when my mom died, I pretty much felt the exact way that you do right now."

"It's not even close to the same," Ezra said in a dour tone. "Your mom didn't choose to leave."

Vance nodded. He wanted to argue that although his mom did not choose to get colon cancer or to die, God had chosen to take her and that the he felt the same anger towards God that Ezra was feeling toward his father. But he remembered being in the throes of grief and how nothing anyone told him, no matter how true or how profound, made any difference to him. So he refrained.

Over the ensuing weeks, Ezra's anger toward his father began to wane. He began to miss him. And he felt guilty for being so hateful towards him when they last spoke. He always tried to be the first to the telephone when it rang. When his mother answered, he would listen to see if it was perhaps his father calling. When he heard a vehicle in their driveway, he would peek out of a window hoping to find his dad's Bronco pulling up to the house. Finally, he asked his mother if she had a telephone number for his dad, but she said he had not left or forwarded a phone number or an address.

A couple of months later, when Ezra's twelfth birthday came and went without so much as a card or a call, his longing for his father was replaced with bruised feelings and a renewed sense of bitterness and resentment. He also began to feel like people were judging him. Once he had held the favored status of the son of the well-respected Chief of Police. Now he was the boy from the broken home, the apple that surely had not fallen far from the philandering tree. These feelings, combined with his transition to adolescence, effected dark changes in his behavior and personality. Over the next few years, his grades suffered. He stopped going to church. He quit playing sports. He neglected his hygiene. And with the exception of occasionally hanging out with Vance and Giles, he all but withdrew from his circle of friends, settling into a melancholic, mostly solitudinous existence.

On the first day of school following the Mardi Gras break of his junior year of high school, Ezra found a stranger nestled comfortably between the giant roots of the live oak under which he and Vance normally met before the morning bell. The girl, cute and petite, was engrossed in a thick, well-worn book, seemingly oblivious to the world around her. The girl suddenly lifted her head and caught Ezra staring. He blushed, instinctively looking away, trying to give the appearance that he had been looking at anything but her.

"Oh fuck, did I steal your spot?" she asked apologetically, looking up at Ezra with large, wide set eyes that were of a light blue hue that Ezra had never seen before.

A girl using profanity would have normally been very off-putting to Ezra. But there was something about this girl that immediately seized him, something that rendered the vulgar language immaterial. Never in his young life had he felt so irretrievably spellbound and disarmed, and it was all so instantaneous. For the first time in years, Ezra felt an intensely sober self-consciousness about his appearance and even more so about his hygiene, gravely regretting that he had come to school without shaving or washing his hair in more than a week.

"Um, no, I mean, me and my friend usually hang out here before school starts, but it's no big deal. We'll hang somewhere else."

As he started to walk away, Ezra thought he heard the girl say, "I like your freckles." He stopped and turned toward her, not certain that he had heard her correctly. Plenty of people had teased him about his freckles over the years. No one had ever complimented them. "I'm sorry?" he asked.

The girl smiled demurely, glanced down at her book and then back up at Ezra. "I said that I like your freckles."

Ezra was not sure how to respond, uncertain of whether the new girl was being flirtatious, sarcastic, or just matter of fact. Before he could ruin the moment, she saved him. "They remind me of my favorite constellation. Are you familiar with the story of Perseus and Andromeda?"

Ezra's face suddenly lit up with confidence. "Yeah, sort of," he said as he tried to picture his face in his mind to determine for himself whether there was any credence to the girl's comparison, or whether she was just bullshitting him.

"Really?" the girl replied skeptically.

"Yeah. Poseidon gets pissed off when he learns that Queen Cassiopeia was bragging about her daughter Andromeda being more beautiful than Poseidon's sea nymphs and so he sends a sea monster to destroy their city. Cassiopeia and her husband, the king, figure that the only way to avoid this fate is to sacrifice Andromeda to Poseidon, so they have her chained to a large rock at the edge of the sea. But just Poseidon's sea monster appears and is about to devour her, Perseus swoops down on his flying horse, slays the monster and rescues Andromeda."

The girl smiled and nodded. "Not too shabby. I'm guessing you're a voracious reader like me."

Ezra shook his head. "I read a little. But remembered all that stuff from the movie."

"Movie?" the girl asked.

"Yeah, you know, *Clash of the Titans*."

"Oh shit, okay," the girl said. "I haven't seen it. We didn't have a movie theatre in the little piss-ant town where I was living. I didn't think there was one here either."

"There's not, but there're two in Opelousas, which is only about fifteen minutes away," Ezra said, pointing in a southerly direction.

"Cool."

"Yeah, but make sure not to go on a Tuesday."

"They're both closed on Tuesdays?"

Ezra shook his head. "No, but Tuesday is Nigger Night."

The girl's eyebrows arched with surprise.

"What?" Ezra replied, noticing her disapproving look. "That's what everybody calls it. Tuesday is half price night, so that's when they all go."

"Duly noted," the girl said. "And just so you know, I'm not a big fan of that word."

Ezra regarded the girl curiously. "Where are you from?"

"Oregon," she replied. "A little town called Klamath Falls."

"Wow. Okay."

. "Before we leave the subject entirely," the girl said, "did you happen to know that Andromeda was black?"

Ezra shook his head dismissively. "No, she was definitely white. She was white in the movie, and I've seen paintings of her in books, and she's white in all those."

There was a hint of condescension in the girl's smile. "Well, the movie and the paintings that you saw are all wrong," she said. "Andromeda was an Ethiopian princess, and as you probably know from all the news coverage about the famine going on over there right now, Ethiopians are very black. Andromeda being depicted as white in the movies and in paintings is fucking horseshit. It's a prime example of whitewashing. It's racial bias."

Ezra looked perplexed. His instinct was to argue, but he sensed that he was intellectually outgunned, and by more than a little. Just then, a cute red-haired girl greeted him as she walked by. "Hi, Ezra," she said, smiling warmly.

"Hey, Bobbi Lee," Ezra replied, lifting a hand to wave.

The girl sitting between the roots waited for the red-haired girl to get out of earshot and then turned to Ezra. "That's so fucking crazy," she said.

"What?" Ezra asked.

"That girl being named after a confederate general," she said.

"What are you talking about?"

"General Robert E. Lee," she said.

Ezra looked confused for a moment then chuckled and shrugged his shoulders, having never considered the origins of Bobby Lee's name. "What's the big deal?"

"What's the big deal?" she girl asked with disgust. "He was the head of the motherfucking confederate army."

Ezra regarded Ava with amused curiosity.

Ezra's wide-eyed reaction in turn amused Ava. "What?" she said in a challenging tone. "Girls around here aren't allowed to cuss?"

Ezra shrugged. "I wouldn't say girls aren't allowed to cuss so much as—well—they just don't." *Except for the trashy ones,* he thought to himself, though for a reason that he could not figure out, this girl seemed to have the ability to cuss without sounding low class. "While we're on the subject of names, what's yours?" Ezra asked.

"Ava," the girl said, and not quite ready to move on added, "And for the record, I don't support the idea that there is such a thing as cussing. I mean, who ever had the authority to decide that some words are proper and some are profane? Think about it. We are taught that saying vagina and fornication is proper speech but saying pussy and fucking is vulgar when they mean the exact same thing. It's so imbecilic."

Ezra winced and looked around as he raised his finger to his lips to caution Ava to hold her voice down. "Whether you think it's bullshit or not, you can get in trouble if a teacher hears you."

"Sorry," Ava said, lowering her volume. "But it all stems from elitism really," she continued. "The so-called upper classes wanted to separate themselves from the common folk so they label the poor people's language as vulgar, profane, common, and nasty. Then, of course the Church jumped on the band wagon and took it a step further by making profane words sinful. How utterly fucking asinine is that?"

Ezra continued to stare at the girl blank-faced, overwhelmed and dumbfounded, not understanding half of the words she was using. He smiled. "You're really weird, you know that?" he finally said in an endearing tone.

Ava chuckled. "I'll take that as a compliment. I like weird. Normal is boring and lacking in luster."

Ezra smiled and shook his head. "So, why did y'all move here from Oregon?"

Ava's countenance immediately soured. "Well, my mother's ass-wipe of a boyfriend got transferred here for his job. She followed him down here and dragged my younger sister and me kicking and screaming the whole way."

"What about your dad? Why didn't you stay with him?"

Ava scoffed. "That's a long, not terribly interesting story. Let's just say that my father still lives in Neverland."

Ezra nodded and decided not to press the issue any further. He certainly did not want to open the door to any questions about his father.

"So, Ezra, what's up with your Hebrew name?" Ava asked. "I thought everyone around here was Christian?"

"Actually, most people here are Catholic," Ezra said.

"Aren't Catholics Christian?" Ava asked, confused by his response.

"Yeah, but around here, when people say they are Christian, they mean Protestant. If you're Catholic, you don't say you're Christian, you just say you're Catholic."

"Bizarre, but okay."

"And to answer your question, Ezra was my great, great grandfather's name. My mom is Jewish."

"Ah, okay," Ava replied.

Ezra looked at his watch. "The bell's gonna ring in a second and I have to walk all the way to the other side of campus for my homeroom, so I guess I'm gonna get going. It was nice to meet you."

"Okay, yeah, ditto," Ava said as she slipped her large book into her backpack and began to get up. "Hey, do you want to meet for lunch or something?"

"Sure," Ezra said, "if you don't mind sitting with my idiot friends."

"Bigger idiots than you?" Ava teased.

"Arguably," Ezra replied.

"I guess I'll risk it. I'll look for you in the cafeteria?"

"Cool."

As Ezra turned to leave, an elderly custodian walked by carrying a five gallon bucket and a mop-stick with a nail protruding from the end, policing the ground for litter. "*Comment ca va, Monsieur Brasseaux?*"[1] the old man said to Ezra.

"*Ca va, Mr. Cliff,*" Ezra replied. "*Et vous?*"[2]

"*Aww, comme-ci comme-ca,*"[3] the old man answered with a warm smile, rotating his wrist back and forth.

Ezra smiled and nodded. The old man tipped his cap to Ava and continued on his way.

"You're fluent in French?" Ava said to Ezra as they walked for a while in the same direction.

"No," Ezra said. "I know a lot of words and a few phrases, but that's it. French was the first language of my grandparents on my dad's side, but they would get punished by the Anglos-Saxon teachers for speaking French in school, so their generation pretty much stopped teaching the language to their children and grandchildren."

"That's so sad," Ava said. "Fucking British imperialism at its finest, huh?"

Ezra was not sure what she meant but did not want to appear ignorant so he agreed and quickly changed the subject.

---

[1] *How are you, Mr. Brasseaux?*
[2] *It's okay* (meaning *I'm doing okay*) *and you?*
[3] *Aww, like this, like that* (meaning *not too good but not too bad*).

CHAPTER 31

Ava squeezed her way between crowded tables and set her lunch tray down in front of Ezra's while he was still settling into his chair. "Hey, where are your friends?" she asked as she pulled out a chair.

"Well, Dewey had to check out for an orthodontics appointment and Vance got detention."

"Ah, okay. So it's just me and you?"

"Looks like it."

"Hey, you want this?" she asked, gesturing toward the slab of meatloaf dripping with thick brown gravy at the center of her plate.

"You don't like meatloaf?" Ezra said, stabbing the slab with his fork and dumping it onto his own plate.

"I don't eat meat," Ava said.

"Hmm," Ezra said. "I've never met a vegetarian before."

"Well, then you still haven't," Ava said. "I'm pescatarian."

"What's that?"

"I don't eat meat, but I eat fish."

"Ah," Ezra said. "What about crawfish?"

"Um, no, nor anything else that lives in the mud."

Ezra smiled. "You don't know what you're missing."

Ava grimaced. "Well, that's a state of ignorance I'm happy to embrace."

Ezra quickly bowed his head, made the sign of the cross, said grace under his breath and then made the sign of the cross again as Ava watched with intrigue.

"Are you super religious?" she asked with genuine curiosity.

Ezra shrugged. "I'm not a Holy Roller or anything, if that's what you're asking. Why, are you?"

Ava winced. "God no."

"Why are you making that face?"

"Sorry, I didn't mean to."

"But you did."

"Well, I just don't get it."

"What? Religion?"

"Yeah. Christianity in particular."

"What's not to get?"

"I really don't want to offend you," Ava answered in a sincere tone.

Ezra chuckled. "You can't offend me. What don't you get?"

"Well," Ava said, "let's break it down. A Hebrew god impregnates a young girl to father a son whom he sacrifices to himself in exchange for forgiving all people for sins committed thousands of years earlier by a man and woman who were duped by a fallen angel masquerading as a talking snake. And this god holds all of mankind responsible for the sins of these two people, and to obtain his forgiveness, all humans are required accept his dead-but-still-living son as their savior, in which case they are granted blissful immortality in an invisible paradise. Oh, and if they don't agree to these terms, the consolation prize is that they still get immortality, but they spend it in an invisible fiery hell, weeping and gnashing their teeth for all eternity."

Ezra stared at Ava with an expression rife with dubiousness and intrigue. He was aghast at her blasphemy. He literally pulled back from the table to get further distance between himself and her as if, subconsciously, he was afraid of an impending lightning strike.

"And frankly," Ava continued. "I could make the argument that the cornerstone of Christianity is rape."

"Rape?" Ezra replied incredulously.

Ava nodded. "Yes. Sex without consent is rape, right? And when Jesus was conceived, Mary was like fourteen—clearly still a child. Given that she was a devout Hebrew and He was her God, there's no way she thought that saying no was an option. I mean, read the Old Testament—if you defy Yahweh, you'll mostly likely be stoned to death or burn in hell. And everyone knows that only adults can give legal consent, right? So, having intercourse with someone too young to give their legal consent is rape."

Ezra laughed. "But, God didn't have intercourse with Mary. She became pregnant with Jesus through the Holy Spirit," he argued.

"Well yeah, that all sounds fine and dandy, but biologically, Jesus was a real person, and to be conceived, somebody had to get some sperm to Mary's egg," Ava countered.

"So, you're really serious?" Ezra asked.

"Hell yeah I'm serious," Ava replied.

Ezra smiled and resumed eating.

"Do you have any siblings?" Ava asked.

Ezra shook his head, not wanting to speak with food in his mouth.

"An only child, huh? That's trouble," she said, teasingly.

Ezra shrugged.

"What's your dad do? Seems like everybody's dad around here either farms rice or sugarcane or works at one of those big gas plants."

Ezra's face grayed, though he tried to show no reaction. "I don't have a dad," he said, trying to sound casual.

Ava furrowed her brow. "What do you mean you don't have a dad? Were you a test tube baby?"

"No," Ezra replied. "He left us when I was in middle school."

"As in, I'm-going-to-get-a-pack-of-cigarettes-and-never-came-back left?"

"Something like that. He hooked up with this lady from work and they up and moved to Texas. We haven't seen him or heard from him since."

"Well, that fucking sucks a whale wang," Ava said empathetically.

Ezra chuckled at the expression. "We would say it sucks a donkey dick, but yeah. It is what it is."

"You and your mom get along pretty well?" Ava asked.

"I guess," Ezra said. "As long as I put out the trash and save my clothes, she pretty much leaves me alone."

"Save your clothes?" Ava asked curiously.

"Yeah. You're mom doesn't make you save your own clothes?"

Ava giggled. "What does that even mean? Like from drowning, or from a fire?"

Ezra rolled his eyes. "No, silly. Like when you put them where they belong—like in your dresser or chest of drawers, or whatever."

"That's hilarious."

"I'm glad you find me so amusing," Ezra said.

"Me too," Ava said in a tone and with a look that Ezra felt sure bordered on flirtation.

"So how are you liking Iris High so far?"

Ava shrugged. "People are really nice but no offense, you guys are a couple of grades behind in pretty much every subject down here."

"Yeah, well," Ezra said, "that's mostly because of the coloreds. The teachers have to dumb everything down so that they can keep up. One of my best friends goes to St. Anne's. It's all white except for maybe one colored student in the whole school. They're way ahead of us in everything too. Well, everything but sports. The coloreds make us better in sports. But, I think I would rather suck in sports and not have most of the coloreds."

Ava frowned disapprovingly. "Everyone down here is so prejudiced," she said. "It's really disheartening."

Ezra shrugged. "Well, why don't you wait until you've been down here for a while. You'll be prejudiced too."

Ava decided to change the subject. "My mom's boyfriend says if you're from south Louisiana, you're called a coon-butt."

Ezra laughed. "It's coonass."

"Yeah, that's it. What's a coonass?"

"It's supposed to be a derogatory slang term for a Cajun," Ezra replied, "but a lot of Cajuns refer to themselves as coonasses, so they've basically adopted the term."

"So, what's a Cajun, exactly?" Ava asked. "I mean, I know about Cajun seasoning and the *chank-a-chank* Cajun French music, but I'm still not clear on what a Cajun really is."

Ezra smirked. "One of the few things you haven't read about?"

Ava smirked back. "One of the many, actually. A necessary element of wisdom is being aware of your ignorance, as paradoxical as that might sound."

Ezra chuckled. "You are such a geek."

"I know. So, what's a Cajun?" Ava repeated.

Ezra shrugged as if to indicate that he might not be the best person to ask. "Basically, there were French people who had settled in what is now Nova Scotia, Canada, which, back then, was called Acadie. A bunch of these Acadians eventually migrated to south Louisiana. The descendants of the Acadians are called Cajuns."

"Why did they leave Acadie?"

"The British came in, stole their land and put them on ships with whatever they could carry."

Ava listened contemplatively. "Man, that's awful.

"Yep."

"It would probably be pretty difficult to find a group of people that the British haven't ass-raped at some point at one time or another."

Ezra shrugged and smiled. "I guess," he said. "Hey, do you want to go get pizza tonight? I mean not like a date or anything, just to hang out."

"You have a car?"

"Kind'a."

"What's that mean?"

"I have an El Camino. It's half car, half truck. It was my grandfather's."

"Cool. Yeah. I can do pizza."

Their cultural and philosophical differences notwithstanding, Ezra and Ava became fast friends, and their friendship quickly morphed into romance. Ava had managed to pull Ezra out of his reclusive existence. Her time spent with Ezra made Ava feel less homesick. He introduced her to beignets, bayous and Blackfoot Sue. She introduced him to marijuana, mushrooms and the Melvins.

After a couple of months of heavy kissing and petting, Ava was no longer willing to wait for Ezra to take things to the next level. While they had the house to themselves and were making out on the couch, Ava unbuttoned Ezra's jeans and began to pull the zipper down when he stopped her and sat up.

"What's wrong?" she asked.

An embarrassed expression covered Ezra's face.

"It's okay, you can tell me," Ava said assuringly.

Ezra covered his face with his hands.

"Ez?" Ava said, trying to pull his hands down to be able to look him in the eyes.

Ezra took a deep breath. "This is so humiliating."

"Whatever it is, it's okay," Ava whispered. "I promise. Just tell me."

Ezra closed his eyes while trying to muster courage. He glanced up at Ava and then hung his head again, not wanting to make eye contact with her while saying what he was about to say. He spoke slowly and clearly, not wanting to have to repeat himself. "Please do not laugh."

"I won't. I promise."

He sighed. "I only have one testicle," he said.

Ava knitted her brow and smiled warmly. "Jesus-Fuck, Ezra, is that it?" she said. "I was worried that it was something really, really bad. I mean back home one of my friends was dating a boy with a micropenis."

"What is that exactly?"

Ava giggled. "It's an iddy biddy little baby penis on a grown dude."

Ezra grimaced. "Well, that would suck worse for sure, but having only one testicle is still pretty damn bad for a guy."

Ava kissed him on the hand and then kissed him on the tip of his nose. "I'm sure you wish you had two, but it doesn't matter to me even a little bit," she said. "I mean, for fuck's sake, if you're going to go through life with a missing body part as a dude, that would be the thing I would pick. No question about it."

"Good to know," Ezra said.

Ava giggled, kissed him hard and recommenced pulling on his zipper.

Ezra and Ava eschewed their junior prom on principle, electing instead to drive around in the country listening to a homemade cassette tape of their new favorite artists, including General Public, Modern English and the BoDeans. With the El Camino's windows rolled down, they took turns swigging on a bottle of Boone's Farm Strawberry Hill and singing at the tops of their lungs. When they grew tired of singing and driving, they drove out into the country, turned down an old dirt farm road and parked in the middle of a soybean field. They made a pallet out of quilts and lay in the bed of the El Camino, smoking grass while watching for shooting stars.

"Ooooh, ooh, ooh! I see one," Ava exclaimed in a whisper, as if her normal speech volume might scare the meteorite away.

"Where?" Ezra asked.

"There, look—oh my God, it's zig-zagging!" Ava declared with amazement.

"That's a firefly," Ezra said before bursting into laughter.

Ava blushed with embarrassment and then joined in the laughter. They laughed and then giggled and then just when it seemed that the tittering was about to subside Ava snorted and it started anew.

As Ava continued to survey the sky for falling stars, she noticed Ezra examining his fingernails. "What are you doing?" she asked.

Ezra sighed. "I was just thinking about how cavemen and cavewomen kept their fingernails short. They didn't have fingernail clippers and, you know how if you don't cut them they'll just grow and grow and grow into these gross, curly things to where you can't even grab shit or use your hands for hardly anything."

Ava giggled. "Well, I'm sure they had some flint tools that they used to keep them from getting too long."

"But what about before they developed tools?" Ezra challenged.

"Then I guess they would just bite them, you know, like a lot of gross people still do today."

"Okay, but then what about their toenails?"

Ava looked stumped for a moment and then grinned. "I guess their mate would have to bite them for them."

"Gross!" Ezra exclaimed. "Can you imagine how nasty a caveman's toenails would be? And having to put that in your mouth?"

Ava chuckled. "True love, huh?"

Ezra grimaced. "I guess."

"I'm sure of it."

"Hey," Ezra said, "are you going on the class trip?"

"God, no. You?"

"I was gonna, but Vance can't go, so I thought I might do something with him instead."

"Is Vance going to college?"

Ezra shook his head. "Nah, he's joining the Army."

"Ew! I wouldn't think Vance would do well with being told what to do all the time."

"I wouldn't either. He'll either get kicked out in three days or drink the Kool-Aid and get turned into a bad ass killing machine to be cut him loose in Grenada or Lebanon or some other military hotspot where he'll wreak a special kind of havoc the likes of which those poor bastards have never seen."

"Well, I hope it's the former."

Ezra was about to reply when he spotted a shooting star. He pointed it out and told Ava to make a wish.

"I saw it," Ava said. "What did you wish for?"

Ezra sighed. "I made my wish under the big oak tree the first day that I met you, and it's already come true. So, I didn't make one. I didn't want to be greedy or take away any of its power that might be used to make your wish come true."

"That's so sweet," Ava said, kissing Ezra on the lips and then pulling back to look into his eyes.

"What was your wish?" Ezra asked.

Ava grinned slyly and then moved her mouth to his ear. "Take my clothes off and you'll find out," she whispered.

CHAPTER 32

There was a loud rap on Vance's bedroom door. "What?" he answered, expecting it to be one of his annoying half-brothers or worse, his unbearable step-mother. The door opened and Ezra entered with a huge grin on his face. "What are you doing here?" Vance said, surprised. "I thought y'all were leaving for Panama City this morning with the rest of the class?"

Ezra shrugged. "I decided last minute not to go. Everybody says class trips are lame anyway," he lied.

"Is that what they say?" Vance asked incredulously.

"Yeah," Ezra said. "Everybody just gets drunk on the beach the first day and passes out in the sun, and then they are too sunburnt to do anything the rest of the trip."

Vance scoffed and smiled. "So, what are you going to do?"

"Not *me* Kemosabe, *we*," Ezra replied. "Get some extra clothes and your toothbrush together. I'm throwing you a military bachelor party."

"Where are we going?" Vance asked.

"You let me worry about that."

"Is Giles coming?"

"No, his parents won't let him."

"Good, so it's just Batman and Robin."

"Yep."

"I'm Batman," Vance declared.

"Not a chance," Ezra replied. "You can't be Batman without a Batmobile."

Vance smiled and nodded. "You got me there, Bruce."

As they drove the stretch of country highways between Iris and Opelousas, Ezra and Vance stared out of the window taking in the seemingly endless acres of rice that had just begun to flower, its rich golden panicles swaying in the breeze. "Probably not the amber waves of grain that we sing about, huh?" Vance asked.

"Probably not," Ezra replied. "Though it sure is pretty."

After stopping to purchase a couple of links of boudin and a bag of cracklin at Ray's in Opelousas, they headed east on Highway 190, passing through Port Barre and Krotz Springs before crossing the Atchafalaya River and then the Morganza Spillway. They left Highway 190 at Lobdell and took the entrance ramp to Interstate 10 before finding themselves stuck in bumper-to-bumper traffic on the large cantilever bridge that spanned the Mississippi River between Port Allen and Baton Rouge.

Ezra read the small dedication sign at the foot of the bridge. "Who the fuck was Horace Wilkinson?" he asked rhetorically, knowing there was no chance that Vance knew the answer.

"No clue," Vance said.

"I've never even heard it called that," Ezra said. "Everybody just calls it the new bridge."

"It doesn't look very new," Vance observed.

"You feel that?" Vance said as they sat in stopped traffic at the apex of the bridge. "The whole damn bridge is swaying."

"Freaky," Ezra replied.

When traffic began to flow again, they drove east for another hour before crossing Lake Pontchartrain and finally reaching New Orleans. So awestruck by the size and symmetry of the Superdome were they that they circled it twice before moving on.

They drove down Poydras Street in heavy traffic, marveling at the skyscrapers, statuaries and neoclassical municipal buildings. They saw pigeons foraging for scraps of food in the streets and smartly groomed businessmen with fancy briefcases sharing the sidewalks with raggedy clad pedestrians pushing shopping carts filled with all of their earthly possessions.

Ezra ruffled Vance's hair. "Country has come to town," he said.

Vance grinned and nodded.

Ezra parked the El Camino in a dirt median under an overpass. After relieving themselves between two concrete pillars, they walked several blocks down Canal Street, taking in the scenery along the way. Suddenly, Ezra put his hand on Vance's chest, gesturing for him to stop.

"What?" Vance said, looking down to see if he was about to step in hobo excrement.

"This must be it," Ezra said, pointing at the sign that read Chartres Street.

"What?" Vance asked.

"Do you smell that?" Ezra asked.

"What?"

"The Mississippi. The fresh bread. The bourbon. The old brick. The beginning of the French Quarter," Ezra said with an excited twinkle in his eye.

The young men advanced, ambling along cobblestone streets, admiring the rich colors and ornamentation of historic hotels, storefronts and quaint Creole residences. They marveled at the military statues and grandiose fountains. They gawked at the wide assortment of people with whom they shared the sidewalks and streets.

When they came upon St. Louis Cemetery, they casually strolled through what seemed like an ocean of above-ground gravesites. They noticed a small crowd of tourists gathered around one of the larger tombs. Ezra tapped a woman on the perimeter of the crowd. "Excuse me," he said, "what's so special about this one?"

"It's the tomb of Marie Laveau," the woman said with a British accent. "You know, the famous Voodoo queen."

"Ah," Ezra said, "Okay, thank you."

"Can you see her skeleton or anything?" Vance asked, trying to understand why the site was so popular.

"No," the woman answered. "You can only see the tomb. But, it's quite fascinating all the same."

"It's funny how all the tombs are above ground," Ezra said.

"The guide told us that it's because New Orleans is below sea level. They originally tried in-ground burials, but when there were big floods, there would be bodies floating all over the city."

"Jesus," Ezra said.

When it started to rain, Ezra and Vance dove into a pastry shop where they ordered eclairs and coffee. When the rain stopped, they strolled through residential areas of the French Quarter. The homes featured an abundance of lush ferns and flowers that hung from cast iron mezzanines and large gas lanterns that flickered in the shadows of old brick-walled courtyards. They noticed two men enter one of the courtyards holding hands.

"Did you see that?" Ezra whispered.

"Yeah. I just threw up in my mouth," Vance replied.

"Supposedly there's almost as many queers that live here as in San Francisco," Ezra said.

"Lovely," Vance replied.

As they moved toward the center of the Quarter, the boys were awed by the mass of humanity. Tourists meandered in every direction, on sidewalks, down and across streets, in and out of shops, bars and restaurants. Many hung from balconies and out of hotel windows. More than a few had reached or at least were well on their way to reaching a comfortable if not stupefied state of inebriation.

Feeling parched and empty-handed, Ezra and Vance entered a bar. They proudly produced their driver's licenses showing that they had both recently reached the age of eighteen and bought a couple drinks before resuming their self-guided tour. They spent the afternoon walking, drinking, people watching, harassing pigeons and riding streetcars. They each ordered a shrimp-on-a-stick from Takee Outee and strolled around Jackson Square to watch street artists draw caricatures and paint portraits of tourists, stopping briefly to stroke the muzzles of perspiring, over-worked carriage mules lined up on Decatur Street.

By late afternoon, ready to rest their feet, they hobbled into the plush panoramic pinkness of Poodle's Patio, ordered Long Island Iced Teas and sat on a pink leather sofa against a pink wall. They lost themselves to the barrelhouse piano blues of Leon Gros, a/k/a Archibald, and fell in love with and bought drinks for a slender Creole backup singer who flirted with them from the stage.

After they emerged from Poodle's an hour or so later, the sun had set, and the energy of Bourbon Street had undergone a dramatic transformation. Tap-dancing, bucket-drumming and tromboning street performers busked from virtually every street corner. Live jazz or blues music blasted from every door and window of every bar. Smartly attired and hatted touts stood at every door, exuberantly cajoling passers-by to patronize their establishments. Beautiful and not-so-beautiful transvestites wearing grossly exaggerated fake eyelashes, extravagant wigs and glittery dresses strolled about, enjoying the gawping and jeering of tourists; and on occasion young and sometimes not-so-young inebriated females lifted their blouses to display breasts of all shapes and sizes to groups of wheedling males on balconies who encouraged them with promises of throwing down Mardi Gras beads.

As they were taking in all the sensorial delights, Ezra and Vance stopped and shared a glance of mutual amazement, collectively gleaning that this merry amalgam of gleeful debauchery and celebratory *joie de vie* was something unique—something that probably did not exist anywhere else in the world. And at that moment, they felt very fortunate and privileged to be a part of it.

Eventually, finding their stomachs growling again, Ezra and Vance purchased hotdogs from a Lucky Dog vendor and Sazeracs from a walk-up bar. They sat on the edge of the sidewalk in front of a t-shirt shop to eat and drink, enjoying a front row view of the tourists and locals of every hue and height, every age and level of affluence—male, female and ambiguous—filing in and out of bars and clubs, wandering aimlessly up and down the intersecting streets, laughing, crying, yelling, singing, flirting, haggling, arguing, stumbling, passing out and on occasion vomiting in the street.

"Look at that one," Vance said, pointing to an overserved fraternity boy leaning precariously against the wall of a jazz club. "He pissed himself."

Ezra nodded and chuckled. "That's unfortunate."

They witnessed a couple of greasy, older men hitting on a group of young women who were part of a bachelorette party who in turn were flirting with street musicians blowing trumpets and trombones. They saw men who dressed like women and women who dressed like men and people who barely bothered to dress at all. They grimaced in reaction to the noxious body odors of passing pedicab drivers and wondered how their passengers could stomach the smell.

As they were finishing their Lucky Dogs, a pair of young black boys, no more than eight or nine years old, stopped a well-dressed middle-aged man and his much younger female companion in the street. The shorter boy stepped in front of the man, lifted his money up and said, "Mister, I'll bet you this here five-dollar bill that I can tell you where you got your shoes."

The man chuckled, smiled confidently at his female companion. "Okay, I'll take that bet," he said, pulling a five dollar bill out of his wallet and showing it to the boy.

The colored boy smiled. "Mister, you got your shoes on Bourbon Street, New Orleans, Louisiana." As he said this, he held his hand open for payment.

The man turned red in the face, but unwilling to risk looking chintzy in front of his female companion, reluctantly handed the five-dollar bill to the boy. "Good one" were the words that came from his smiling mouth, though his angry eyes said *now, get the fuck out of here.*

"Dumbass," Vance muttered.

Ezra chuckled.

As they ambled along Carondelet Street, they heard the chatter of shoppers and merchants and smelled the fresh breads and spices emanating from the French Market. Vance watched a panhandler hastling some tourists while Ezra stopped to buy a bar of fudge from a vendor, then they continued down St. Peter.

They eventually reached Cabildo Alley and a row of candlelit tables occupied by women reading Tarot cards. At the first table was a bald Creole woman wearing a rastacap and huge hoop earrings. A small sign on her table indicated that the price for a reading was three dollars. Ezra offered her five dollars for two readings, one for him and one for Vance. Before she could answer, Vance pulled Ezra aside and said, "I'm not spending money on that bullshit."

"Relax," Ezra said, "I'm paying. It'll be fun."

"You are wasting your money," Vance argued.

Ezra stepped back to the table and held out five dollars to the woman, which she reluctantly accepted. Ezra pushed Vance into the chair across the table from the woman who was eyeing him curiously.

"You are skeptical, yes?" the woman said in a thick Caribbean accent.

Vance shrugged, not wanting to give the woman any clues about his background by hearing his accent. After having him cut the deck of cards, the woman closed her eyes, took a deep breath and then slowly flipped the top three cards onto the table in a neat row, explaining that the first card represented Vance's past, the second, the present and the last, his future.

After studying the cards for a few seconds, the woman told Vance that his past involved much darkness and a huge void. That he was is a state of transition and that he would very soon be experiencing big changes in his life, including some type of journey which would involve many new faces. Vance grinned skeptically. He stood, gesturing for Ezra to take his turn.

After the reader flipped Ezra's first card, a peculiar expression appeared on her face. She studied the card for what seemed like a long time before flipping the second and third cards. Finally, she looked up at Ezra and regarded him for a moment as if she were second-guessing her reading. "What is it?" Ezra asked.

The woman told Ezra that his reading was very both curious and complicated, that the cards revealed that he had lost someone very close to him but under very unusual circumstances that were not as they had appeared.

Ezra regarded the woman skeptically. "What does that even mean?" he asked.

"The cards are urging you to look beneath the surface," she said.

Ezra knitted his brow. "I don't understand. What surface? And what am I supposed to be looking for?"

The woman shook her head. "That is not clearly revealed," she said. "But according to the cards, this person who is lost to you desires to be found."

Ezra snorted. "Well, if it's who I think it is, he surely knows the way home."

The woman regarded Ezra curiously and then her expression became piteous. "This person who wishes to make contact is no longer in the physical world," she said.

A confused look appeared on Ezra's face as he took a mental inventory of people in his family who had died, which included both of his paternal grandparents, his maternal grandfather and an aunt, none of whom he could imagine would be trying to make contact with him.

The woman then reached into a leather satchel and pulled out a highly polished piece of ebony. After rubbing it between her fingers for a few seconds, she laid it on the table. "For five dollars," she said, "I can make contact with this person's spirit. You can ask one question."

Ezra sneered at the woman. "That's a lot of money. And I don't have any questions."

As Ezra was stepping away from the table, a strange expression appeared on the woman's face and she closed her eyes as if she were listening to something in her head. Then she opened her eyes and looked into Ezra's. "Oaks can pass for elks in just the right light," she said, enunciating each word carefully in her thick accent.

Ezra's body stiffened. He stared at the woman, his mouth agape. "Where did you hear that?" he asked.

"Have you changed your mind?" the woman asked, smiling confidently.

Ezra stepped back to the table, holding the woman's gaze. He reached into his wallet, pulled out a five-dollar bill and set it on the table.

"No, the woman said sucking her teeth. "You rejected my five-dollar offer. My new price is ten dollars."

"Come on," Vance said, grabbing Ezra's money, "this bitch is trying to milk you."

The woman smiled proudly. "This bitch's price just went up to fifteen dollars."

"Let's go," Vance insisted, pulling Ezra away from the table in an effort to break the woman's hold on him.

"Wait," Ezra said, freeing himself from Vance's grasp. Then he lowered his voice so that the woman could not hear. "I want to do this."

Vance smiled and shook his head. "Dude, my uncle was in the Navy. He said they have these people at virtually every port they would stop at. They are highly skilled scam artists. They say really general stuff that happens to just about everybody. It's only personal because that's how

231

you interpret it. Think about my reading—going on some type of journey and meeting new people. That's fucking everybody at one time or another. It's all bullshit, dude."

"But what about the saying about the oaks and elks?" Ezra argued. "That was really specific. My dad used to say that."

"Yeah," Vance said, "it's probably just an expression that they used in the old days. She just played the odds and got lucky."

"No," Ezra said, "it wasn't. That's a saying in our family from when my Uncle Jack—when he was a kid—mistook the branches of a scrub oak for elk antlers and shot at it."

Vance was still skeptical. "Look, I'll tell you what. Let's go sit down and have one drink so you can clear your head, and if you still want do it after that drink, I'll come back with you. And by then, she will have cooled off and we can probably negotiate her back down to five dollars."

Ezra finally capitulated. They walked half a block to a shotgun saloon, sat at the bar and drank a beer. Ezra drank fast, and when they were done, he insisted on heading back to the card reader. Vance finished his beer more quickly than he wanted to as Ezra stood tableside and waited impatiently.

When they turned the corner at Cabildo Alley, Ezra's face fell. The woman was gone, as were her chairs, her table and her cards. "Son of a bitch," he said, looking around to make sure that the woman had not moved to another spot in the long row of card readers.

"I'm sure she'll be back later, dude," Vance said as he pulled Ezra in the direction of the river. "She's probably just going eat or something. Come on, let's go for a walk. We'll circle back later."

Ezra asked several of the card readers who were not with customers if they knew when the woman with the large earrings would be back, but they each acted if they did not know who he was talking about and offered to give him a reading. Dejected, Ezra finally followed Vance toward the river.

After reaching the river walk, Ezra and Vance leaned on the railing to gaze upon the Mighty Mississippi and the clutter of barges, tugs and riverboats that occupied its murky expanse. A homeless man wreaking of urine and sour, alcohol-infused perspiration shuffled up to them and asked for some change. He said that he needed just a few more dollars to buy a bus ticket to visit his daughter in Houston. She just had a baby, his first grandchild, he said. When Vance ignored him, the homeless man put his hand on Vance's arm and gave him a gentle squeeze. "Come on, man," he said, "I ain't asking for much. Just a little change to go see my grandbaby."

Vance stiffened and drew his arm away. "Don't put your hands on me, motherfucker," he warned sternly.

Ezra quickly put his hand on the man's back and guided him away from Vance. He could feel the man's rib bones through his shirt and jacket. He reached into his pocket and gave the man some change.

"God bless you, young man," the homeless man said.

Ezra stepped back to where Vance was standing. "Just an old man down on his luck."

"Yeah well, ain't no telling what he's been touching with those grubby-ass hands."

Ezra forced a smile and then gently punched Vance's arm, gesturing for him to follow.

"Where are you going?" Vance asked.

"We can't have a bachelor party without going to some strip clubs, can we?"

Vance's eyes lit up as he grinned from ear to ear. "No sir," he said. "I wouldn't think so."

CHAPTER 33

They saw a poster advertising an "Electrifying One Woman Show" by "The Legendary Chris Owens." Ezra suggested that they start there but the plan was quickly aborted when they learned that the photos on the posters were nearly twenty years old and that Owens, who was now in her mid-fifties, did not actually strip.

Eschewing gentlemen's clubs with cover charges, they targeted low end strip joints with no covers, one-drink minimums and subprime strippers, stingily tipping with one dollar bills or not at all. As they watched a small-breasted Oriental woman twirl awkwardly around a pole, a strung-out Creole dancer with a *fleur de lis* neck tattoo and thick silver nose ring squeezed in between them at the bar and began running her fingers through Vance's hair. "You're cute," she said with a tired smile.

"And he's hung like a mule too," Ezra interjected, causing Vance to blush.

"Oh," the stripper said, her eyes widening, then I might have to charge you a little extra."

"Charge me extra for what?" Vance asked.

The stripper smiled. "For a blowjob, honey."

Vance grinned. "What's your name?"

"Dawn."

"How much, Dawn?" Vance asked out of curiosity.

"Fifteen dollars," she said.

"I'm normal sized," Ezra said. "How much would it be for me?"

The stripper examined Ezra for a moment and said, "Fifteen dollars."

"Why do I have to pay extra, too?" Ezra asked indignantly.

234

The stripper smiled mischievously. "I charge extra for freckles."

Ezra turned red with embarrassment as Vance giggled at his expense.

"Do you take I.O.U.'s?" Vance asked.

The stripper furrowed her brow, then smiled warmly and pinched Vance on the cheek. "You're cute, but not that cute," she said before standing and moving on to the next set of patrons.

"I gotta take a piss," Vance said. "You?"

"I'm good. I want to watch this one," he said, gesturing toward a young, pink-haired stripper who had just climbed onto the stage.

When they were finally ready to call it a night, the sun was beginning to rise and shopkeepers were emerging with garden hoses to wash litter, spilled cocktails and, in some areas, vomit or urine from their storefront sidewalks. At the same time, a big, noisy street sweeper rolled around the corner, scrubbing the curb with large, rotating metal brushes. Directly behind it was another vehicle, just as large, which used a large vacuum system mounted under its chassis to swallow the juicy street waste.

After stopping at a shotgun grocery to buy a juice drink and aspirin for their headaches, the boys zig-zagged through the Quarter to Café du Monde. They waited in line for several minutes before they were finally seated by a humorless Vietnamese hostess. They ordered hot beignets and chicory flavored café au lait. They ate and drank and watched the early morning tourists coming and going, some stopping to drop coins into the bucket of a colored man with a beat-up trumpet playing Louis Armstrong covers on the sidewalk.

Their digestive rumblings satisfied, they followed Decatur to Canal and back to the overpass under which they had parked. They pulled sleeping bags out of the cab, spread them out in the bed of the El Camino, and slumbered for several hours in the shade of the overpass, senseless to the ceaseless sounds of the city noise.

When they woke in the early afternoon, they walked to a Burger King and washed their faces and armpits in the lavatory. After going back to the car to change shirts, they window shopped on Canal for a while before heading back to the French Quarter to resume their revelry, albeit at a more measured pace.

As the afternoon sun was beginning to set, a couple of coeds wearing Ole Miss apparel, one dark-haired and petite, the other fair-haired full-figured, flirted with Ezra and Vance from a mule-drawn carriage. After Ezra and Vance lied about being freshmen at LSU, the girls invited them to hop aboard for the remainder of their ride. When the tour ended, the foursome walked, talked and took in the sights, stopping for raw oysters before landing at Pat O's where they drank Hurricanes and sang along "Piano Man" and "American Pie" with the dueling pianists and the rest of the mostly inebriated crowd.

After getting their fill of the piano bar, the girls led Ezra and Vance to The Cat's Meow Karaoke bar where they persuaded Ezra to sing Rick James' "Super Freak." He performed so badly that he was booed off the stage, the loudest boos coming from Vance and their new friends.

As Ezra took his walk of shame off the stage, the full-figured coed grabbed her friend by the arm, said something in her ear and then discreetly pointed across the bar. The coeds exchanged anxious glances and then gestured for Ezra and Vance to follow them out. The girls stumbled out onto the sidewalk giggling and cackling.

"We know another place—The Tropical Isle—it's not too far. Come on," the petite coed said, grabbing Ezra's hand.

"So, what was up back there?" Vance asked as they followed the narrow sidewalk toward their new destination.

"We saw someone from our sorority, and we didn't want her to see us," the full-figured coed answered.

"She's a party-pooper or something?" Ezra asked out of curiosity.

"It's not that," the petite coed said.

"Then what?" Ezra asked, curiously.

The girls exchanged conspiratorial glances. Then the taller girl said in a loud, giggling whisper. "She dates niggers."

"Oh," Ezra said, feigning disgust. "How did she get into your sorority in the first place if that's the case?"

"That's just it. Nobody knew," the petite girl said. "We only just found out a couple of days ago. The guy she's dating is on the football team and everything, but still. Our sorority council is going to have a meeting next week. She's surely going to get kicked out."

After they entered the next bar, Ezra motioned Vance to follow him to the restroom.

"What's up?" Vance asked once they were inside.

"I don't want to hang out with these bigoted bitches anymore," Ezra said. "Let's ditch 'em."

Vance grimaced. "Are you fucking serious?" he said. "They don't want nigger lovers in their sorority—so what? Man, before you started hanging out with Ava, you never—"

"—I just don't want to hang out with them," Ezra interrupted.

"Look, it ain't like we're lookin' to marry 'em, bro. Pussy is pussy. Who gives a rat's ass whether they're prejudiced?"

"I kind'a do," Ezra replied apologetically.

"Come on man," Vance urged. "These girls are ripe. And what kind of friend cock-blocks a buddy on his military bachelor party?"

237

Ezra opened his mouth to retort and then stopped. He sighed. "Okay, fine." he said.

They made their way back to the girls who had just ordered Hand Grenades. "Hey," the larger girl said, her face lit up as if she had just come up with a grand idea. "Y'all want to get tattoos?"

"Tammy Lynn Woodley!" the petite girl exclaimed in her exaggerated southern drawl. "Your momma and daddy would kill you!"

Tammy laughed. "Not if they never saw it. I would get it down here," she said, smiling demurely and pointing to the area just below her bikini line.

"What would you get?" Vance asked, curiously.

"I don't know. What do you think I should get?"

"Let's go check out that freaky looking bar around the corner, first," the petite coed said.

After showing their IDs to the bouncer, the foursome followed each other single file through the dark, narrow corridor of an establishment befittingly called The Dungeon, eventually working their way up to the crowded bar area where they ordered more drinks and danced to alternative music until they could dance no more.

After they stumbled out onto the sidewalk, Tammy pushed Vance against the wall and kissed him hard on the mouth as Ezra and the petite girl watched with amusement. Then the petite girl turned to Ezra, stood up on her toes and gave him a quick but sensuous kiss on the mouth. "We have a room at the St. James on Canal Street, unless yours is closer," she said, grinning amorously.

"No, the St. James is a lot closer than where we're staying," Vance interjected between kisses.

"Okay," the petite girl said, smiling and kissing Ezra again, this time a little more forcefully. Then she took him by the hand and began walking in the direction of the hotel with Tammy and Vance in tow.

"Where are y'all staying, anyway?" Tammy slurred.

As Vance struggled to formulate a lie, Ezra blurted out, "at the Casa El Camino. It's near the overpass, that way," he said, pointing in the opposite direction. It's really small."

"Yeah, super small," Vance said, chuckling, "and kind'a shabby, actually."

"I wouldn't say it was shabby," Ezra said defensively. "It's modest."

Ezra and Vance arrived back in Iris on Monday just after lunch, exhausted and malodorous. Ezra stopped the El Camino in front of Vance's trailer and put it in park. Vance grabbed his things out of the bed and stopped in front of Ezra's opened window.

"Did you have a good time?" Ezra asked.

Vance smiled and leaned in, lifting his hand toward Ezra's face. "Smell my finger," he said.

Ezra cackled and fought to keep Vance's hand away from his face until Vance finally relented.

Ezra looked at his watch. "I'll pick you up in the morning at 6:30 a.m. sharp."

"I'll be ready."

The next day, Ezra picked up Vance and they drove straight to Opelousas. They ate breakfast at the Palace Café and then drove on to the Trailways bus station where Vance purchased a one-way ticket to Fort Benning, Georgia.

After completing boot camp and Army Ranger training, his battalion would be deployed to Iraq to assist Saddam Hussein's forces during the final stages of the Iraq-Iran War. Four years later, after Iraq invaded Kuwait, his battalion would be redeployed to Saudi Arabia as part of Operations Desert Shield and Desert Storm to fight a war against the same Iraqi forces he had previously helped to train and support.

Following his final tour, he was transferred back to Fort Benning, where he would serve as a training instructor for six years, then to Enid, Oklahoma where he would work as an Army recruiter until he qualified for and accepted full military retirement at the age of forty-one.

CHAPTER 34

In the spring of their senior year in high school, Ava had received and accepted a full academic scholarship to the Rhode Island School of Design in Providence. Ezra, who had hoped that they would both attend LSU, was disappointed though supportive. For the first couple of months of their freshman year, they wrote to each other religiously and spoke on the telephone every Sunday, Ezra's mother limiting the long-distance calls to fifteen minutes a week to keep the costs in check.

Toward the end of the first semester, Ezra noticed that the letters from Providence began coming in less often and that Ava was beginning to be less faithful to their weekly call schedule. When she returned to Iris for the Christmas break, he instantly sensed that things were off. The amorous synergy they had shared before Ava left had been replaced with physical awkwardness and neither, at least initially, proved willing to address the elephant in the room.

After Ava got settled and had dinner with her mother and sister, Ezra picked her up and they went for a drive. They talked about their respective college experiences, eventually making their way to Eunice where, for lack of anything better to do, they stopped at The Purple Peacock. They drank a beer and danced to a couple of songs on the crowded dance floor though neither seemed to be terribly engaged. They sat at a table and had another beer before heading back to Iris.

On the drive home, Ava seemed mostly disinterested when Ezra described all the craziness and partying associated with campus life at LSU, SEC football and the Baton Rouge college bar scene. Though she did not come out and say it, Ezra got the impression that she viewed it all as superficial and sophomoric. In contrast, she spoke of RISD with great affection, lauding the quality of people she was meeting, gushing over the

241

beauty of Providence and making it clear that she did not miss the south. Ezra became frustrated.

"Okay, if you're not going to say it I will," Ezra said.

"What?"

"Something's off," he said. "Between us, I mean."

Ava nodded. "I know."

"What is it?"

Ava adjusted her position to face Ezra. "I'm not sure how to say this, so I'm just going to spit it out, okay?"

"Sure," Ezra said.

Ava paused which made Ezra even more anxious.

"Well," Ava said, "I don't want to break up exactly, but I don't think we should be exclusive anymore," she said.

Ezra looked at Ava for a moment and then stared straight ahead through the El Camino's windshield, gripping the steering wheel much tighter than was necessary.

Ava hung her head. "I'm sorry," she said. "I just don't think this long-distance thing is fair to either of us."

Ezra took a deep breath and exhaled before responding. "Are you seeing someone else?" he asked.

Ava shook her head. "It's not about anyone else, Ezra. It's about us being so far apart for so long when we are at a stage in our lives where we should be free to explore and, you know, be adventurous. That's all."

Ezra glared at her, finding himself perturbed by her evasiveness. "*Is* that all?"

"Yeah," Ava said, albeit unconvincingly.

"Are you seeing someone else?" Ezra repeated very slowly, trying to contain his anger.

Ava glared back. "Am I on trial or something?" she said defensively.

"I'm just asking a question."

"And I answered it," she said, glaring at Ezra.

"Yeah okay," Ezra said, scoffing under his breath, "I guess you did."

"I thought you would appreciate my honesty," Ava complained.

Ezra chortled. "You know, when you start seeing someone else before you breakup with your boyfriend, it's not exactly an exhibition of honesty, is it? It's called cheating."

"And when you talk to someone you supposedly love like that, it's called being an asshole," Ava retorted angrily. "You can just bring me home now."

"You cheat on me and I'm the asshole?" Ezra rejoined.

"Well, what about you? Like you didn't hook up with anyone when you and Vance went to New Orleans."

"So you admit that you cheated?" Ezra argued.

"Do you?"

"We hung out with some girls, but I didn't really do anything," Ezra said, giving himself a pass for the passionate kissing in light of his decision to ultimately forego a full-blown sexual encounter.

Ava scoffed. "Yeah, right. Just take me home."

Ezra obliged by making a sharp U-turn in the middle of the highway and speeding back toward Ava's house. After rolling through a couple of stop signs and making several sharp turns, the El Camino came to a screeching stop in front of her driveway.

Ava opened the door and was getting out when Ezra blurted out an apology and asked her to stay in the car so that they could talk, but she slammed the door shut behind her and walked into the house without speaking or looking back. Ezra punched his steering wheel and screamed in frustration before putting the El Camino in drive and peeling out on the asphalt.

On his way home, Ezra saw a large colored man in a black suit walking on the sidewalk alongside the main highway. As he grew nearer, he recognized him as Clayton Chaisson. When he pulled over and offered him a ride, Clayton gratefully accepted, explaining that his car had broken down a few blocks back and that he only needed to go as far as Junior's, the only twenty-four convenience store in town, to use the pay phone to call his father. When Ezra offered to bring him all the way home, Clayton smiled and said that Ezra did not want to do that, the implication being that it might not be entirely safe for a white boy to be riding through the black section of town after dark.

"What are you so dressed up for?" Ezra inquired.

"I was at a funeral and then a reception at my Aunt's house," Clayton replied.

"Oh, I'm sorry. Who died?"

"It was actually a double funeral. My Uncle Nedrick and his son, Jerrell."

"Ah. Jerrell was one of the twins that was a couple of grades behind us in school, right?" Ezra asked—he was the one who always wore the big giant afro?"

"It was Terrell who had the big hair," Clayton said, smiling sentimentally. "Jerrell was the other one. Their momma always made Jerrell keep his hair short so people could tell them apart."

"Ah, okay," Ezra said. "Well I'm sorry to hear that."

"Thanks."

"How's Terrell doing?"

"Believe it or not," Clayton said, "Terrell actually got his act together. In fact, he just got accepted into the police academy."

"You're shitting me," Ezra replied.

Clayton shook his head, smiling. "No, sir."

"Wow," Ezra said. "Good for him.'

Clayton nodded.

"So, what happened to Jerrell and his dad?" Ezra asked. "Car wreck?"

"Nah," Clayton replied, shaking his head with disappointment. "They were both drunk at a barbeque and Jerrell was jawing at Nedrick, you know, the same old tired shit, hammering him for not steppin' up as a father. And some of his podnas were eggin' him on, you know stirrin' the pot. Ole Nedrick—the little banty rooster that he was—he just wasn't havin' it. It just kept escalating until they both end up pullin' pistols from their cars and starting shootin' at each other. Jerrell took one in his heart and died on the spot. Nedrick took one in his lung and one in his spleen and died in the hospital the next day."

Ezra grimaced. "Jesus man, that's horrible. I'm truly sorry for your family."

Clayton nodded a thank you. "That's just life in the hood, man." Then he chuckled to himself.

"What?"

"I was just thinking about the irony you know, of two people killing each other being buried together in the same grave."

"They were buried in the same grave?"

"Sure was."

Ezra nodded. "Yeah, I'll bet that hasn't happened very many times. Were they buried near your brother?"

Clayton nodded. "Right across the row from each other."

"What about you?" Clayton asked, eager to change the subject. "How you been?"

Ezra shrugged and gave some thought to telling Clayton about being dumped but decided against it. His problems seemed so insignificant by comparison. "Not too bad," he said.

"You sure?" Clayton asked, sensing that there was something lurking beneath the surface.

"Yeah," Ezra said unconvincingly.

"Alright then," Clayton said, not wanting to pry.

"Can I ask you something, Clayton," Ezra said.

"Sure."

"Did y'all ever find out who was responsible for what happened to Cedric and your cousin?"

"Nah man, we never did."

"That sucks," Ezra said. "I know y'all would liked to have had some closure on that."

Clayton nodded. "Yeah, when the sheriff's office closed their investigation, my parents went talk to your dad. He tried to help, but—" Clayton stopped himself and then as if he decided not to say what he was thinking, said, "—but nothing came of it."

"You were about to say something else," Ezra said

Clayton shook his head. "Nah, it's nothing."

"No, go ahead."

Clayton shrugged. "I was just going to say that when my folks called to follow up on the investigation, they were told that your dad had resigned and moved out of state or something like that and the new Chief said he had closed the investigation before he left. It just left us all confused and—I don't know, I don't need to unload this on you, man. I just need to quit talking."

"No," Ezra said, "it's okay. I can't say I'm surprised." He scoffed. "In the end, my dad wasn't exactly known for finishing things he started. You know what I mean?"

"You haven't had any contact with him since he left?"

Ezra shook his head. "Nah. I mean, I guess some of that's on me. He tried to talk to me a bunch of times before he left, but I was too angry to want to have anything to do with him. I said some pretty awful things. Really awful, actually."

"Well, you were just a kid in a really tough situation. Don't be too hard on yourself, man."

Clayton noticed Ezra's countenance darken. "I'm sorry, Lil' Brass," he said. "I didn't mean to dredge up—"

"Nah dude, it's fine," Ezra said. "I mean, he broke his wedding vows to my mother. He abandoned me. He obviously swept what happened to Cedric and your cousin under the rug. I've just come to accept that he was not a very good person. It's as simple as that, really."

When Ezra dropped Clayton off at Junior's, he splurged on a six-pack of Heineken and drove around town until he finished it. When he got home, he stumbled to the closet in the spare bedroom where his mother kept a few of his father's things. He located an old wooden box and set it on the bed. Inside, he found his father's birth certificate, his baptismal certificate and his Social Security card. In the corner was his father's high school graduation ring with "IHS" engraved on one side and a screaming eagle on the other. Under a couple of black-and-white photos of Ezra's grandparents was a small glass case. Inside the case was his father's Bronze Star, awarded during his combat service in Korea.

He shut the box and returned it to the shelf in the closet where he had found it then staggered down the hall, through the kitchen and out the back door. He walked across the backyard until he reached the base of an old Chinese tallow tree at the rear of their property where he unceremoniously tossed the medal in the dirt between two large roots. Struggling to keep his balance, he unzipped his pants and proceeded to relieve himself, watching the medal and ribbon all but disappear beneath the froth of his urine.

CHAPTER 35

Ezra re-entered the house through the back door barely mindful of the noise that he might be making that could wake his mother. He found a stash of Oreo cookies hidden in a repurposed plastic Country Crock container and ate several with a tall glass of milk. He left the half-empty glass and the opened container of cookies on the kitchen table and made his way to his room where he collapsed onto his bed face-up and staring at the ceiling. He gave a moment's thought to getting up to brush his teeth then owing to his maudlin state summarily dismissed it.

His encounter with Clayton had brought back some unpleasant memories about his father, memories that he had until now managed to compartmentalize. He called to mind how his father refused to intervene on the Chaissons' behalf when the HOA interfered with their purchase of the Andrus home and how he attempted to justify their actions by bringing Ezra to a blighted section of Lafayette where his great grandparents had once lived. He wondered how deeply his father's bigotry ran and about the types of racist people with whom he had associated. He pondered whether his father was guilty of more than just sweeping the investigation of the crimes against Cedric and his cousin under the rug—whether he had perhaps actively participated in the cover-up before leaving town or worse yet, whether he might even have been directly involved.

He contemplated how his father's racial prejudices had influenced his own perspective on race, a perspective that Ava, to her credit, had tried very hard to reshape. He realized that Ava had shone a spotlight on his bigoted beliefs and attitudes and had helped him to be more open minded. But he knew that she had not entirely cured him. On some level, he understood that the years of cultural indoctrination, especially during his formative years, had been too powerful and were too entrenched to be quickly undone by one very smart and very pretty girl from Oregon preaching social enlightenment. Though still she deserved credit for trying.

Then it suddenly occurred to him that he had assumed that Ava's new boyfriend was white. And this led him to the shameful realization that the boyfriend's race actually mattered to him.

As it often did, Ezra's imagination began to run wild. In his mind's eye, he pictured Ava's new boyfriend to be tall and light-skinned with a square jaw, bright white teeth and greenish-gray eyes. And he would of course be an athlete, though not one playing a conventional sport, at least not conventional for black athletes. Rather, it would be something like lacrosse, cross-country running or water polo. And he would come from a wealthy family and naturally would have a name that reeked of pretentious alliteration like Mason Mills, Grayson Greer or Hayes Hoffman.

He pictured them together, laughing, holding hands, kissing, wrestling in the nude under silk sheets at Mason-Grayson-Hayes' family's lake house "in the Hamptons," wherever that is. These images drove him to a profound state of nausea. He got out of bed and walked to the bathroom, knelt over the toilet and waited for the vomit. When it did not come, he went to the sink and splashed cold water on his face. He put a folded bath towel to his mouth and let out a muffled scream, trying to drive the painful images out of his head, desperate for some emotional respite. He rifled through the medicine cabinet and found a bottle of Tylenol PM. He swallowed three of the pills and shuffled back to his room. He turned on the small black and white television that sat on edge of his dresser, crawled back into bed and fell asleep watching a *Cheers* rerun. He slept hard and dreamt.

Everything was normal with Ava and they had made plans for him to visit her in Rhode Island. He had arrived by boat and was anxiously waiting at the port for her to pick him up. Just when he was ready to accept that she had forgotten, she turned the corner riding a tandem bicycle, donning a brightly colored sundress and a beautiful smile. They rode up and down hills and through quaint market streets, he sitting in the back doing most of the pedaling while Ava carelessly wove through pedestrian and vehicular traffic, her dress flaring in the wind, exposing her bare buttocks as she navigated the winding streets to a brightly painted three-story house.

The first floor of the house was occupied by at least a dozen college students of every conceivable ethnicity. They were sitting beneath a cloud of thick smoke passing around a huge blunt. Ava introduced Ezra as her Christian friend who preferred to be called Catholic and they all laughed except for one androgynous looking character who leered inquisitively at Ezra through wire-rimmed glasses while eating freshly cut cantaloupe out of an upside down fedora. Ezra nodded at the group and then followed Ava up a spiral staircase and then down a long hall to a spare bedroom.

After freshening up, Ezra ambled out of his room in search of Ava, following various halls that seemed to lead to nowhere. Eventually, he heard screams. As he continued down the hall, the screams became louder and louder. Upon reaching the door at the end of the hall, he opened it and spied Ava, naked, sliding, clawing and caroming atop a mountain of sweaty ebony flesh. Huge dark hands appeared from either side of her hips, their long dexterous fingers wrapping themselves like tentacles around her small buttocks, squeezing them tightly, lifting her up and pulling her down as Ava let out a rhapsodic rhythm of moans, gasps and incoherent copulatory utterances that culminated in a seemingly unending sequence of squeals and shrieks. And then, for just a second, there was an eerie moment of silence followed by post-climactic heaving and panting as Ava collapsed onto her side, her hair falling over her eyes, leaving only her nose and heart-shaped mouth exposed as she gasped for oxygen like a recently boated bream, her cheeks flushed, framing a satiated smile.

Ezra stood paralyzed, demoralized. He felt his nausea grow and felt certain that he was going to vomit. He shifted his gaze to the offending mound of fleshy obsidian glimmering in the light, watching the man's chest rise and fall with labored breaths. It was not until the man turned to face Ezra that he recognized him. It was a darker, more chiseled version of Clayton Chaisson.

"What's up, Lil' Brass," Clayton said in a voice that was his but not his. Ezra did not respond. He looked at Ava, who upon hearing his name, pushed her hair from her eyes and smiled contentedly as her arm fell across her quivering belly. She rolled over allowing her legs to spread open. Simultaneously smoldering and ambrosial, her coital effluvia seized Ezra's olfactory senses. Both aroused and repulsed, he wanted to go to her and run from her in the same instance.

As he struggled with indecision, Clayton climbed out of the bed with his huge phallus hanging heavily to one side. He patted Ezra on the top of the head affectionately as he passed. Ava giggled as she rolled herself up in the bed sheet like a mummy. She called out Ezra's name in a voice that was deeper and raspier than he knew hers to be. A familiar voice. When he did not come to the bed, she lifted and tilted her head, smiling at him as her hair fell across her face in the opposite direction than it had been. Again, she called his name. "Ezra? Ezra? Ezzzra?"

Ezra startled at the loud rap at the door. He lifted his head and looked about the room in time to see the door open. "Ezra, I have breakfast on the table for you," his mother said in an exasperated tone.

Transitioning through the momentary discombobulation that exists between the dream state and consciousness, Ezra pulled the covers over his head and groaned. "I'm not hungry."

"Well, you need to eat something."

"My stomach hurts."

"Well, drinking to excess has a tendency to cause that young man, as well as number of other conditions adverse to your health."

"I wasn't even drinking last night Mom," he lied, though not putting much effort into the deception.

"And Elvis was spotted buying sweet potatoes at the Winn Dixie again," his mother retorted, trying to match his absurdity.

"I swear."

"The little Lord Jesus is watching you son," his mother called back as she walked back to the kitchen.

"You're a Jew, Mother. Your people rejected Christ, remember?"

"Fine. Then Elijah is watching. Come eat."

As he continued to lay in bed, Ezra's thoughts turned back to Ava and the images in his dream that he could not shake. He was studying Karl Jung in his psychology class, and he wondered if his dream was some sort of manifestation from the collective consciousness. He gave some thought to calling Ava and telling her about it but knew it would make him sound crazy and jealous and even worse, racist.

"What are your plans for the day?" Eve asked as Ezra pushed his scrambled eggs around on his plate without eating them.

253

"I've got to go interview this man about the Cajun Mardi Gras. It's for a term paper. Giles is going to come and take pictures for me."

"Who are you interviewing?"

"His name's Ferrell Pugh. Aunt Bertie said he used to be the president of the Iris Mardi Gras Association and knows a lot about the history."

"Yeah, I know him. Actually, I knew his wife better. She just passed away a few months back. He's always been very nice."

CHAPTER 36

As the tires of the El Camino crackled across the oyster shell drive, Ezra and Giles were greeted with a friendly smile from a gangly, thick-haired man in khaki coveralls sitting in a rocking chair on the porch of the old wood-frame house. After setting his coffee cup down on the small table, the man rose using a cane for support.

Ezra pulled in further, lowered his window and called out, "Mr. Pugh?"

The man smiled and nodded. "Y'all get down," he beckoned in a friendly tone.

Giles followed Ezra up the porch steps. They shook hands with Pugh and then followed him inside, watching him walk with a painful limp. "I've got arthritis in my hip bad, bad from a car wreck several years ago," he explained. "Some days it's worse than others. Today it's not too bad."

"Take your time," Ezra said.

After cursory introductions, Pugh gestured for Ezra and Giles to sit at the kitchen table while he poured them each a fresh cup of coffee and served them homemade biscuits with butter and fresh figs on the side. "I picked these this morning," he said proudly. "I got two trees in the back. It's always a fight with the birds to see who's gonna get to the ripe ones first."

"Delicious," Giles said. Ezra nodded in agreement.

Pugh apologized for the clutter. "My wife would not be too happy to see her house like this," he said. "She passed about eight months ago," Pugh said. "The cancer got her."

"I'm sorry to hear that," Ezra said. Giles nodded in agreement.

"Give me your name again son," Pugh said to Ezra in a friendly tone.

"Brasseaux," Ezra said. "Ezra Brasseaux."

A look of recognition appeared on Pugh's face. "Our Chief of Police a while back was a Brasseaux," Pugh said. "Bernard Brasseaux. Any relation?"

Ezra's countenance turned ashen. "He was my father," he said matter-of-factly, there being no indication of pride or affection in his tone or expression.

"Oh, okay. Yeah, I can see a resemblance."

Ezra was tempted to explain that he had not seen his father in years and had essentially disowned him, but not knowing if Pugh and his father had a history and if so, whether it was positive or negative, he refrained.

"Yeah, I was several years ahead of your father in school, so I didn't know him very well. But he was a good Chief of Police," Pugh said. Then he turned his attention to Giles. "And tell me your name, son."

"Giles Poret," Giles answered, "I'm just the photographer," he said, holding his camera bag up for Pugh to see.

"Poret?" Pugh repeated, "Who's your momma and daddy?"

"Roland and Melody," Giles answered.

"Doc Poret?"

"Yes sir," Giles replied.

"I'll be damned," Pugh exclaimed with a smile. He pulled the zipper down on the front of his coveralls to reveal a large scar on his sternum. "I had a triple bypass in 1984. Your daddy, he did the plumbing."

Giles smiled and nodded.

"Well," Ezra said, seizing the opening, "how about we let Giles get a few pictures of you—maybe one of you in your kitchen and another just sitting down wherever you feel comfortable, and then we can start the interview."

"Shit," Pugh said in a jestful tone, "If I had known you were going to be taking my picture, I would have gotten my hair cut."

The boys chuckled. "Your hair looks fine," Giles said reassuringly.

Ezra began the interview by asking Pugh about his Cajun heritage. Pugh explained that his surname was actually Irish, but that his mother was an Hebert from Vermilion Parish, a large Cajun French family who had essentially adopted his father as one of their own. "That's how it was," he explained. "The Cajun French culture was strong, strong like that, especially back then. If you married a Cajun girl, that was it, you became Cajun, too. That's how we had all these non-French people that considered themselves Cajun when, by blood, they were Irish, German, Spanish or English. Hell, nowadays, we have the McGees, the Bollichs, the Ortegos, the Johnsons, and a bunch of others that consider themselves just as Cajun as the Aucoins, the Boudreauxs, the Broussards and the Holliers."

Ezra nodded as he took notes. "Have you ever been to France, Mr. Pugh?" he asked.

Pugh shook his head. "And I have no desire to go. Cajuns are of French decent, but there's a world of difference in those cultures and from what I've heard, I want no part of theirs."

"I always thought it was curious how everybody says people from France are so rude, but Cajun French people are so friendly," Ezra said.

"You know why?" Pugh said.

"No, sir."

"Well, that actually started with the Micmaq Indian tribe in Canada. If it wasn't for the Micmaq, the original French settlers in Acadie

257

would not have survived their first winter up there. They didn't know how to fish those waters, how to hunt or trap the game there or what crops to grow. It was the Micmaq who taught them everything they needed to know in order to survive. They took the Acadians in. They treated them like family. And that—how you call it—hospitality, it got absorbed into the Cajun culture."

Ezra nodded and continued to take notes as Pugh spoke. As the interview turned to the history of the Cajun Mardi Gras, Pugh explained that the traditions associated with the rural Courir de Mardi Gras went back hundreds of years, beginning with the peasants of rural France. "Mardi Gras," he explained, "translates as Fat Tuesday. It's the last day to feast and you know, *revel* before the forty-day Lenten season."

When Pugh began to discuss the history of the motley costumes donned by Cajuns on their Mardi Gras runs, Ezra seized the opportunity to steer the interview toward the issue of race, inquiring as to whether there was any association between the tall, pointed capuchons worn by the Cajun Mardi Gras revelers and the pointed white hoods for which the Ku Klux Klan was so well known. Given that his college professor for whom he was writing the paper was black, he thought that coverage of this issue might gain him favor.

But Pugh vehemently disputed any connection between the Cajuns and the KKK. "A lot of people don't know this," he said, "but the Klan is not only anti-colored, but also very much anti-Catholic. And of course, the majority of Cajuns are staunch Roman Catholics you see."

"I was not aware," Ezra said, "I mean, about the anti-Catholic thing."

"I'll tell you another thing," Pugh said, "and not very many people realize this either, but when coloreds want to talk about how the whites enslaved them and all that, well, that wasn't the Cajuns. The Cajuns had nothing to do with all that. They were living in Canada when the slave trade got started over here. And even after they was exiled and came down here, they had nothing. They couldn't afford to buy a horse or a cow much less a slave. So, people can think what they want, but the Cajuns were never a part of all that."

"That's interesting," Ezra said. "I never thought about it that way."

"Well, it's true," Pugh said. "Now, if they had money, would they have bought some slaves? Maybe so. Maybe not. We'll never know."

"So, the capuchon, how did that get started?" Ezra inquired.

"From what I read, the capuchon comes from the early Mardi Gras celebrations in France. The poor people wore them to, you know, mock the nobles," he explained. "It was to make fun of the ladies in waiting who would wear those tall, pointed hats."

"Interesting," Ezra replied.

"You see this right here?" Pugh said, pointing to a jagged scar that was nearly hidden in layers of wrinkles that ran across the left side of Pugh's eyebrow, "I got that on my very first Mardi Gras run. I was twelve years old, and it was the first time I had been drunk," he laughed. "My uncle could stand on the saddle of a horse and ride like that from here to Point Blue, sober or drunk—it didn't matter. I decided to try and got a little too confident a little too fast. I fell and cut my face on the spur of the man riding next to me. I bled like a stuck pig," he said, laughing at himself.

Ezra and Giles smiled and nodded.

"You see this scar?" Pugh said, seeming to point to the same scar above his eye. Upon closer examination, Ezra and Giles could see that there were actually two scars, one diagonally intersecting the other. "I got this one two years later. Same eye," he laughed. "I was chasing a chicken and fell headfirst into a barbed wire fence. I untangled myself and took off

259

after the chicken again, but there was so much blood in my eyes that I couldn't see where I was going, and I ran headfirst into a pine tree. Knocked me out cold," he said, chuckling.

"Goodness," Giles said.

"I woke up in the bandwagon with fiddle and accordion music blaring in my ears. They had butterflied my laceration with some strips of duct tape they had gotten from a farmer. They gave me a beer and put me right back on my horse."

Ezra and Giles chuckled. "That's hardcore," Ezra said.

"Those were some crazy times for sure," Pugh added.

"I imagine," Ezra said, "that over time as the Cajun culture has become more known to the outside world, you get people from all over who want to participate—you know, get drunk and chase the chickens, just to say that they did it."

"Oh yeah, for sure, we've had plenty of that," Pugh said. "And as long as they respect our traditions and customs, we don't mind. But if they don't," Pugh quickly slid one palm across the other and made a whistling noise with his mouth, "we don't hesitate to give them their walking papers."

"Did the blacks ever try to come up with their own version of a Courir de Mardi Gras," Ezra asked, "you know, like how they took Cajun French music and put their own style to it to make Zydeco music?"

"No, not really," Pugh said. "And we were never worried about that. The coloreds were never too organized. And we didn't care what they did so long as they kept to themselves."

"Y'all never had blacks try to participate in your courir?"

"No," Pugh said. "Well, I lied. I remember one year, I was working the sign-up table when one came with—what's his name—Clifford Dronet's grandson—wait, no, not Clifford—Clyde was his name—yeah, it was Clyde Dronet's grandson. He was at some college in Maryland or someplace up there in the northeast and he brought a group of friends home, like you said, to come experience our Mardi Gras. Well, they had a little nigger in their group. We told them thank you but no thank you. This is a private organization, you know. We don't have to take nobody we don't want."

"I think I remember something about that," Giles said. "The Dronet kid wrote a letter to the editor of the Daily World about how ashamed he was to be from the south and how ignorant the people in Iris were for turning that black boy away. And it was printed in the paper."

"Yep," Pugh said, "a lot of people were upset about that boy trying to embarrass his hometown like that. His grandfather especially. But you know, it's not that we have anything against coloreds. We just want to keep our traditions intact. That's why we don't take women either. I got nothing against women, mind you. None of us do. But our Mardi Gras has been men only going back as far back as you can go. We drink, we cuss, we fight, we piss in front of each other on the side of the road. You can't have all that with women present. They would want to turn it into a tea party," he said, chuckling.

Ezra smiled. "That's true."

"Do you speak French, Brasseaux?" Pugh inquired.

"Not really," Ezra replied. "I mean, I know a lot of words and phrases, but I'm nowhere close to being fluent."

"How about you, Poret? *Vous parlez francais?*

"No sir."

"Well, that's because the English-speaking school teachers had such a rough time with little Cajun kids who only spoke French. To make sure they were practicing their English, they would punish them for speaking French in school. Eventually the parents, they wanted their kids

261

to do good in school, so they stopped teaching them French altogether. It's sad but it's true."

Ezra frowned and nodded in agreement.

"But language is the backbone of a culture," Pugh continued, "so you should make it a priority to learn. The Cajun culture is on the verge of dying. If you young people don't do something, we're in jeopardy of having nothing left of it but Cajun cookbooks and recordings of dead Cajun musicians."

"I agree," said Ezra.

Trying to steer the interview back towards race, Ezra inquired as to whether, in Pugh's experience, Cajuns and blacks had ever bonded over the fact that they were both persecuted by the KKK.

Pugh admitted that he had never thought about it. "You know," he said, after giving the question some thought, "I can tell you for sure that there's definitely no bond between the Cajuns and the real niggers—you know, the dark ones, how you call 'em—the untamable ones—the ones that mostly live in the ghetto part of town. But you know, the Creoles—the high yellas we call 'em—most who have French last names, they're different. A lot of them speak French, and they're good, clean people. Civilized. Cajuns get along with them just fine. My son was good friends with one—a Papillion. They would go rabbit hunting together and stuff like that. He would come eat at our house. It ain't to where I would, you know, let my daughter marry one of 'em, but they're good people. Not like the dark ones that live in town."

"I remember," Ezra said, "when we were in middle school, some blacks had raped a white girl. She was a few years older than us—real pretty. I remember we—you know, the whites—were so angry, we wanted to see all the blacks strung up."

When Ezra mentioned the rape, Pugh's face fell. He nervously

262

lifted his coffee cup to his mouth only to realize that it was empty and then set it back down, avoiding eye contact with Ezra and Giles. The change in his demeanor did not go unnoticed. There was an uncomfortable silence for several seconds before Ezra spoke again.

"Mr. Pugh, are you okay?" Ezra asked.

Upon hearing his name, Pugh seemed to snap out of his trance. "Come again?"

"Are you okay?"

"Oh, yeah. I'm good. I just get these little dizzy spells sometimes. It's my blood pressure pills that cause that. It's nothing."

"Mr. Pugh," Ezra said, "you're probably worn out from all these questions. I can't thank you enough for being so helpful. I think I have everything I need, so we'll be getting out of your hair."

"Okay," Pugh replied in a fatigued tone. "Y'all come back and visit sometime, you hear?"

"Yes, sir, we will," Ezra replied as they left the house.

As he watched Ezra and Giles backing out of the driveway from his kitchen window, Pugh picked up the telephone and called his brother in law.

"Hello?"

"Mule?"

"Yeah?"

"You remember I told you a college kid was coming to interview me about the Cajun Mardi Gras?"

"Yeah."

"Well, guess who it was."

"I don't feel like guessing, Ferrell."

"Bernard Brasseaux's son."

263

After a short period of uncomfortable silence, Ferrell said "Mule, you there?"

"Yeah."

"It was Bernard Brasseaux's son that came to interview me."

"I heard you, Ferrell," Abel said.

"Well, that don't make you nervous?"

"Did he say anything about his daddy?"

"No. In fact, when I put it together that that's who his father was, he seemed embarrassed of him. He didn't seem to want to talk about him at all."

When Abel did not reply, Ferrell said, "Mule?"

"What?"

"I don't know. I just wanted you to know."

"Alright," Abel said before hanging up.

CHAPTER 37

"That guy really knew his shit about the Cajun Mardi Gras, huh?" said Ezra. "I'm going to kick ass on this term paper."

Giles shrugged. "Yeah," he said but with a conflicted tone.

"What?"

"I don't know," Giles replied. "I guess it's just hard to reconcile so much niceness and prejudice in the same person."

"Is *niceness* a real word?"

"I think so."

"Well you have to remember that he's from a different generation," Ezra argued. "I mean think about it, everything was segregated for their whole lives and then the federal government comes in and forces integration down their throats, and they've got blacks all of the sudden in their faces demanding this and that. That had to be a tough pill for them to swallow."

"Well, there should never have been segregation in the first place," Giles countered.

"Easy for you to say. You went to a Catholic school your whole life with all white people. You never had to deal with them. If y'all didn't have a black maid, you probably would never have even talked to a black person before you got to college."

"That's not my fault," Giles retorted.

"I didn't say it was," Ezra replied. "I'm just pointing out that you lack a certain perspective."

Giles knitted his brow. "Are you saying you wish everything was still segregated?"

"No, that's not what I'm saying," Ezra said, after thinking about the question for a moment longer than Giles thought that he needed to. "But, I am saying that I understand prejudice. It's not like white people just randomly decided to be prejudiced against black people for no reason."

Giles' felt his stomach rumble. "I'm getting hungry," he declared.

"I could eat," Ezra said. "You want to make a detour and hit Stark's?"

"Sounds good."

"Cool."

"But, you know," Giles said, getting back on topic, "it's not just the old people."

"What are you talking about?" Ezra asked, not entirely understanding his reference.

"The prejudice. When I come home and run into people our age who are still here, it's the same thing with a lot of 'em. *Nigger this, nigger that.* It's embarrassing."

"I think a lot of that is just straight-up indoctrination," Ezra said. "When you're around it for so long, it gets imbedded in your subconscious."

"Yeah, I think that's probably part of it." Giles said. "My dad used to fill in for the medical director at the nursing home on occasion. I remember him talking about how it was not uncommon for old people that he had known for years who were really nice and respectful and who hadn't used racial slurs for decades, but, when they started showing signs of dementia, they would revert back to calling black people niggers and coons. It was a big problem because most of the nurse's aides and orderlies who took care of them in the nursing home were black, and the administrators were concerned that the blacks would get angry and take it out on the residents."

266

"Damn," Ezra said. "Can you imagine? A black nurse's aide has to clean shit off the ass of an old demented white person and gets called a nigger in the process, thank you very much."

"I know."

"Do you think you're still racist?" Ezra queried.

"I don't think so. Not consciously, anyway. What about you?"

"No," Ezra answered, though with reticence. "I mean, I have black friends and I would go out with a black girl if the opportunity with the right one presented itself. I wouldn't have said that a few years ago."

"I have a question. When did we stop saying *colored* and started saying *black* instead?" Giles queried.

"Huh. I don't even know."

Ezra grimaced as they approached the entrance to the Stark's drive-in. "Jesus, would you look at the line."

"Dang," Giles replied.

"Do you know what you want to order?" Ezra asked.

"Cheeseburger, tots and a strawberry shake. Here," Giles said, pulling four dollars from his wallet and handing it to Ezra.

"*Merci.*"

As they sat in silence, Ezra read a bumper sticker on the back of the minivan in front of them that said *Pray the Rosary.* "So, do you still pray?" he inquired.

Giles shook his head. "No, not really."

"When did you stop? I mean I remember when we were young you were so religious that you were thinking about becoming a priest."

Giles snorted. "Yeah, maybe for like a week or two."

"So, when did you stop praying?" Ezra asked.

"I don't know," Giles said. "I guess it was a gradual thing. I mean other than having a psychological benefit for the person doing the praying, sort of like mediation, do you really think that prayers alter the course of events in any way? Do you really think that God and/or the saints who people pray to are sitting up in heaven and deciding where a hurricane will pass and who will get cured of cancer and who will not based on prayers?"

Ezra shrugged. "I certainly don't think it hurts."

Giles nodded. "Me either. I'm saying I don't believe it works at all. The fact of the matter is that people could pray to a cucumber and have the same statistical success of getting what they want or need as compared to praying to God."

Ezra was about to reply when someone caught his eye. "Look," Ezra said, pointing to a group of older black teens walking through the parking lot. "Do you recognize the tall one wearing the Walkman?"

"No," Giles said. "Should I?"

"Do you remember the little black dude that you gave that nickel to at Jagneaux's when we were kids? You were scared that if you didn't, he was going to ride back to Coontown and get all his cousins and uncles to come to stab us. Remember?"

"Yeah, okay. The kid with the tricked-out bicycle? That's him?"

"Yep."

"I probably saved your life by giving him that nickel," Giles said, chuckling.

"That's what you said back then."

"His name is Terrell. He had a twin brother named Jerrell, but Jerrell died in a shoot-out with their dad at a barbeque not too long ago."

"Really?"

"Do bears shit in the woods?" Ezra asked rhetorically.

"Not polar bears," Giles replied.

Ezra rolled his eyes.

"Nor bears that live in zoos."

"Okay," Ezra conceded.

"Or that travel with circuses."

"Okay, okay," Ezra said in a surrendering tone, "point sufficiently driven home, parked in the garage, washed and waxed."

Giles grinned triumphantly.

CHAPTER 38

Ezra and Giles shared a dorm room at LSU on the twelfth floor of Kirby Smith Hall. The first people they met at the dorm were their suitemates, Miller Dobbs from Clinton, Mississippi, and Todd Robert Coley from Harrison, Arkansas, both of whom had more traditional thick southern accents and predictably, an affinity for bourbon.

During the first night in the dorm, Miller and Todd Robert sprung for cheap beer and threw a small party in their room. A couple of freshman coeds wandering the halls heard the commotion and joined the party. They played a game of quarters until the beer ran out at which point they began doing shots from a fifth of Wild Turkey that Miller pulled out from the top of his closet.

"Where are the girls?" Miller asked upon returning from the bathroom.

"Bitches took off as soon as the bourbon ran out," Todd Robert slurred.

"Fucking mooches," Miller said with a scowl. Then he turned to the group and announced that he had come up with a "grand idea" while sitting on the toilet.

"I can't wait to hear this," said Todd Robert.

"I propose," he stammered, "a twenty dollar winner-take-all sexual conquest contest."

"A what?" Ezra asked, so inebriated that he had to lean against the wall so as not to fall over.

Miller spoke more slowly. "A sexual conquest contest."

"Sexual conquest contest, sexual conquest contest," Todd Robert repeated, "say that five times as can as you fast."

"This is how it will work," Miller continued, struggling to keep his eyes open. "We come up with a point system for ranking girls that we bang. A regular girl—one point. A Goth—two points. Asians—three points. I girl from one of the hottie sororities—like Tri-Delta or Chi Omega—four points."

"Cool," said Todd Robert. "And if she happens to be a virgin, you add two points to whatever she was worth otherwise."

"Yeah, I like that," Miller said.

"But the virgins have to be bona fide," Giles chimed in. "None of these *I only take it up the ass so I'm technically still a virgin* virgins."

The others all looked at Giles curiously.

"Have you ever met someone who was having anal sex and claiming to be a virgin, Giles?" Todd Robert asked.

"Yeah," Ezra joined in, "inquiring minds want to know."

Giles blushed. "No, I mean, not that I know of. I was just saying."

"Are you taking it up the ass and claiming to be a virgin?" Miller asked.

Giles blushed and laughed. "Not recently," he said in jest. The others laughed.

"I know it would take a miracle," said Ezra, "but let's say that for an LSU cheerleader, a Golden Girl or a gymnast, you get five points."

"I like it," Todd Robert replied excitedly.

"Agreed," Miller replied with crooked smile.

"And let's say fat chicks count for a negative one point," Ezra added.

Everyone chuckled. "Yeah, fine," Miller said, before resuming his slurred recitation of the ground rules. "Score will be kept on the honor

271

system, and whoever has the most points at the end of the semester gets the entire pot."

"How much do we each put in?" Giles asked.

"Twenty dollars," Miller repeated.

"Damn, that's a lot of money," Ezra said. "Let's do ten."

Giles and Todd Robert nodded. "Yeah," Todd Robert said, "ten is plenty."

"Fine, you tightwads," Miller said, "ten per person."

"How many points for banging a nigger?" Todd Robert asked, mostly in jest.

"Minus five," Miller declared, and they all laughed and agreed.

"What about a dude?" Giles queried.

"Huh?" Todd Robert asked, unsure of what Giles meant.

"You want points for fucking a dude?" Miller asked incredulously as everyone regarded Giles with disgust and then exchanged nervous glances.

"I'm kidding!" Giles exclaimed. "I'm kidding, for Christ's sake."

"Well, just in case," Miller said, "banging a dude is an automatic forfeiture."

Everyone vigorously assented.

When Miller had jumped out to a comfortable ten point lead by mid-semester, Ezra angrily accused him of suckering them into a rigged contest, arguing that Miller, being the only contestant who pledged a fraternity, was hunting a baited field.

"Yeah," Todd Robert chimed in. "You're constantly going to parties with sorority girls."

"So?"

"So," Todd Robert said, "girls who feel the need to spend their parents' money to join a club to make friends obviously have very low self-esteem and girls with low self-esteem often use sex to get attention. Add alcohol and parties to the equation, and it's like shooting fish in a damn barrel."

"Well," Miller replied, smiling smugly. "If all that is true, it was also true when we made the bet. Y'all all knew I was pledging. So shame on y'all for not being smarter when it counted."

"I have a question," said Ezra. "How many of these girls that you had sex with were actually sober enough to consent?"

Miller scoffed and rolled his eyes. "Oh, so when y'all are getting hot and heavy with a girl, you're stopping to do a field sobriety test?"

"It's true," Giles argued. "You wouldn't hardly have any points if you only counted the sober ones."

Miller chortled. "Poret," he said, "you haven't put a single point on the board, and sober or drunk, fraternity or no fraternity, I could get more pussy than your fat ass even if I had *I've Got Genital Warts* tattooed across my forehead."

Giles weighed the idea in his head for a moment and then adjusted his glasses. "You know, it's incredibly depressing and demoralizing to have to admit it," he said, "but you're probably right."

They all laughed.

CHAPTER 39

On the last day of school before spring break, Giles was cramming for an exam when their dorm room telephone rang. "Hello?" he answered.

"Giles?" a vaguely familiar female voice asked.

"Yes. Who's this?"

"Ava."

Giles knitted his brow. "Ava *Mackey*?"

"Yes, how are you?"

"Oh hey, yeah, okay, hi," Giles stammered. "I'm good. Um, Ezra's in class. Do you want me to have him call you back?"

"Well, I'm in Iris, actually. I came home for spring break to visit my mom and sister. I was thinking about driving to Baton Rouge to surprise Ezra and see if maybe he wanted to hang out, I mean, unless you don't think that's a good idea. I mean, I don't even know if he has a girlfriend or whatever."

"Not unless you count Miranda," Giles answered.

Ava felt her stomach flip. "Oh," she said. "Who's Miranda?"

Giles chuckled. "Just a blow-up doll that our suitemate gave him as a gag gift for his birthday. But she's not the jealous type, so there shouldn't be any problems."

Ava let out a sighed relief and then forced a chuckle. "Okay."

"I'll tell you what," Giles said, "I get out of my last exam today at two o'clock, so if you want to meet me in the Kirby Smith lobby at about 2:15, I'll bring you up to the room to surprise him before I take off for Iris for the break."

"Oh, that would be perfect," Ava said with excitement.

Ava hurried into the lobby apologizing profusely for running late. "The traffic coming across the bridge was brutal!" she said as she gave Giles a big hug.

"No worries. Good to see you," Giles said. "Come on, it's this way."

"So, who was Edmund Kirby Smith?" Ava asked Giles as they rode the exceedingly slow dorm elevator up to the twelfth floor.

"It's funny that you should ask," Giles said, "because until my Louisiana History professor lectured about it last week, I had no clue. So, Kirby Smith was a West Point grad who fought for the Union in the Mexican-American War and then, when the Civil War broke out, being from Florida, he joined the confederacy and was made a general. Like a lot of Confederate officers did toward the end of the war, he fled the country so as not to be tried by the Union for treason. Then, when Lincoln started offering pardons for any Confederate officers and soldiers who took an oath of loyalty to the Union, he came back, and eventually became a college professor."

"So he taught here at LSU?"

"Nope, he taught at a couple of colleges in Tennessee."

"Oh. Did he attend LSU as a student or something?"

"Nope."

"Did he donate money to the school?

"Not that I know of."

Ava knitted her brow. "So why would LSU name a building after him?"

"That's a very good question," replied Giles. "The lecture didn't cover that part."

"You didn't think to ask?"

275

Giles grimaced. "You think I wanted three-hundred annoyed, hung-over freshman glaring at me when I raise my hand and ask a question to prolong a lecture?"

"Jesus, are the classes really that big?" Ava asked as they exited the elevator.

"Some are, yeah."

Ava chuckled. "So, these men were fighting a war to protect rich white men's right to own black people and a century and a-half later you're still honoring them with their names on your buildings as if they were heroes. I just find that so mindboggling."

Giles shrugged and grinned, nonplussed. "Yeah well, we southerners are a complex people, aren't we?"

Ava smirked. "A few of you seem okay to me," she said.

"Okay," Giles whispered as he stopped in front of Room 1213, "this is it." He unlocked the door and opened it slightly before whispering "good luck" and disappearing around the corner back toward the elevators.

Ava entered and found Ezra napping in a fetal position on top of an old comforter. She quietly approached, leaned over and kissed him on the cheek. When he did not wake, she tickled his nose with the fray of her ponytail. He startled and spun around in his bed, his eyes wide open, a stunned look on his puffy face. Ava was leaning over him, her hand resting on his chest.

"I'm sorry, I didn't mean to startle you," she said, smiling warmly.

Ezra stared at Ava in disbelief, his heart pounding against her palm. She grabbed his hand and put it on her chest so that he could feel the pounding in hers. They sat in silence, looking into each other's eyes for what seemed like a long time until Ava chuckled.

"What?" Ezra asked.

"You've got a pillow wrinkle line running all the way across your face."

Ezra blushed.

Ava leaned over and wiped a small amount of drool from the side of Ezra's mouth and then kissed the same spot. "I visited your mom before coming here," she said as she brushed Ezra's hair to the side with her fingers.

"Really?" Ezra replied, a little surprised given that Ava and his mother had never been particularly close.

"Yeah. We actually had a good talk."

"About?"

"About you mostly," Ava answered. "She encouraged me to come see you. To tell you how I feel."

"Really?" Ezra said, still trying to fully wake up. "How you feel about what?"

"About you silly," Ava replied.

"Hmm."

"Yeah," Ava replied, blushing.

"How did you get in?"

"Giles. He said he was heading back to Iris for the break."

Ezra nodded.

"It's quiet next door. Are your suitemates here?"

"Nope, one went home and the other is on his way to Fort Walton Beach with some fraternity brothers."

Ava smiled and assumed a seductive pose. Ezra returned the smile then turned to the shelf that ran alongside his bed and clumsily put on a Luther Vandross CD. They kissed and undressed each other slowly before she climbed on top of him and held herself above him with extended arms, looking down into his eyes as if peering into his soul. She gently licked the corner of his mouth and then looked into his eyes again to gauge his hunger. She licked the opposite corner of his mouth and was lifting her head again when she felt Ezra dexterously flip her onto her back and then kiss her hard, his hands finding hers and pinning them back over her head as she used the entirety of her body to match his intensity.

Ava was still sleeping soundly when Ezra woke. He slipped out of bed and returned a little while later with melting soft serve ice cream cones, waking Ava with a gentle kiss. They ate and chatted about nothing in particular until Ezra's curiosity and insecurities got the best of him. "So, what's dating been like in Rhode Island?" he asked.

Disappointed by the question, Ava regarded Ezra, carefully considering how to answer, trepidatious about where the conversation might lead. "No different from anywhere else, I'm sure," she said.

"Well, what are the guys like up there?" Ezra prodded.

Ava shrugged. She did not like the line of questioning, but she wanted to avoid coming across as defensive. "I don't know. The students come to Providence from all over the country so compared to here there's probably a lot more diversity."

Ezra nodded. "So do you have a boyfriend up there?"

Ava shook her head. "No. I mean, I did hang out with this one guy for a couple of months, but it wasn't super serious."

"It wasn't *super* serious?" Ezra echoed. "Well, if the stages of serious are *not* serious, *kind'a* serious, *very* serious and *super* serious, which level of serious were y'all, exactly?"

Ava shook her head. "God, you're still as hyper-analytical as ever, aren't you?"

Ezra made no response other than to stare at her with eyes that

278

made clear that he expected a direct answer.

"I don't know, Ezra," Ava said in an exasperated tone. "Why does it even matter? It's over."

"Because I want to know."

"*Kind'a* serious, I guess," Ava replied. "We really liked each other, but we didn't get to spend a whole lot of time together because of school and because he was on the basketball team."

"RISD has a basketball team?" Ezra asked, surprised.

"No, he goes to Brown, which is right down the road. RISD has some sort of partnership with Brown where RISD students can take classes at Brown and vice versa. That's how we met."

"So, he's black?" Ezra asked.

Ava scoffed. "You assume he's black because he's a basketball player?"

"Well, is he?"

"What difference does it make?"

"If it makes no difference then why are you evading the question?"

Ava huffed. "His father is of Nigerian descent and his mother is Portuguese. Are you happy?"

"Did you sleep with him?" Ezra asked, his jaw clenched.

Ava sat up in the bed and straightened her blouse. "How exactly is that your business?"

"Seriously?" Ezra asked, his tone cold.

Ava glared at him. She felt her face flush. "You wouldn't be asking me that if you knew he was white."

Ezra paused then opened his mouth with the intention of denying the accusation but realized that the moment had passed. "I'm not judging you," he said.

"Well that's not how it feels."

"Well I feel like you are judging me. I feel like you see me as this ignorant, cross-burning redneck."

"Well then don't act like one," Ava said sharply, returning Ezra's glare.

Ezra scoffed and shook his head. "Ava, black men target white women because it's a status thing for them," he said. "Like it or not, you're now forever a notch on Magic Johnson's belt."

Ava's face flushed and her nostrils flared in anger. "That's such a racist thing to say," she snarled, "and it's not true."

"Oh it is true. It's absolutely true," Ezra declared in a condescending tone.

"What about your black friends? What about Clayton? Is he like that?"

"Exception to the rule," Ezra said.

"But you automatically assume that the guy I was dating was a certain way? It's the bad actors who are the exceptions to the rule, Ezra. If you would get out of the south for a while, you would realize that. I know you were all fucked up from growing up down here and by that white girl getting raped by black men when you were young, but you don't think white men have raped black women? Jesus, how many black people in this country are descendants of black women who were raped by white men on plantations?"

Ezra rolled his eyes. He knew this was an argument that he could not win. They stared at each other in silence for a while. Ava finally took a deep breath and exhaled. "His name is Greer," she said. "His dad works in a lab at a chemical company. His mom is a high school English teacher. He made a perfect score on his SATs and got into Brown on an academic scholarship. He walked onto the basketball team. He's majoring in applied mathematics. He wants to work for NASA. He smells no different from

280

me or you, he doesn't like friend chicken or watermelon, and I'm pretty sure he's never stolen a bicycle."

Ezra snorted and chortled. He looked up at Ava and smiled ashamedly.

Ava smiled back. "And he's never been arrested, which is more than I can say for you."

Ezra regarded Ava curiously but did not reply.

"Yes, I know about your getting arrested for mooning the drive-through workers at McDonald's."

"I was fifteen years old," Ezra replied with an embarrassed grin. "People mature you know."

"Do they?" Ava replied with sarcastic dubiety. "Is this what maturity looks like on you?"

Ezra blushed with embarrassment. "I *have* changed," he said.

"Have you?" Ava challenged, her tone serious again.

Ezra stared at his feet for a few moments, thinking. Without looking up, he said, "I was nine years old when I got my first pellet gun," he said. "I would walk the rice field levees and the tree lines and shoot almost anything that moved. Frogs, snakes, birds, squirrels, rabbits, you name it. And when it came to birds, I killed any kind, no matter how small, no matter how pretty. Little wrens. Mockingbirds. Purple martins. Blue jays. Cardinals. Hell, I even shot an escaped parakeet one time."

Ava grimaced. "Why are you telling me this?"

"I know it was all despicable." Ezra said. "Especially the parakeet. I mean, that poor bird lived its whole miserable life in a cage until it finally got a taste of freedom—finally able to fly wherever he wanted. And he's singing his little heart out, so happy and free, and then, *bam!*—some stupid ignoramus with an air rifle puts a pellet through its breast just for kicks and it's lights out."

Ava frowned sadly but did not comment.

"Today, I would sooner jump off the Mississippi River Bridge than harm an animal. And you know that. I started out as a small town, small-minded ass, but I've evolved. I'm still evolving. And that includes breaking away from the racial indoctrination that I grew up with. I credit you, more than anything or anyone else, with helping me to do that. I mean it," Ezra said.

"I know," Ava said as she sat back down and gave Ezra a big hug. Then she pulled back and put her forehead against his and looked into his eyes. "But you've still got a ways to go. You know that, right?"

"Yes," Ezra replied. "I know that."

That afternoon, Ezra gave Ava a walking tour of the LSU campus. They ambled amongst huge, colorful crepe myrtles and beneath stately live oaks, many approaching two-hundred years in age. Ava stopped to touch the trunk of one and swore that she could feel its energy. They walked across the Parade Grounds where students were lying on blankets and reading or just relaxing in the sun while others threw Frisbees, kicked around Hacky Sacks or played fetch with their dogs.

They walked westward past the iconic one-hundred seventy-five-foot clock tower, through the quadrangle and toward Tiger Stadium, stopping to visit Mike the Tiger. Ava cried. She said she was so sad that such a majestic animal was having to live its entire life in captivity, never getting to run, hunt or mate as nature intended.

That evening they walked to the Varsity Theatre and bought tickets to see Dash Rip Rock, one of Ezra's favorite local bands. After the show, they stopped for a beer at The Chimes and then made their way to Louie's where Ezra introduced Ava to what he promised were "the best hash browns on the planet." She ultimately agreed.

On their way back to the dorm, they stopped at a convenience store and purchased a bottle of cheap wine. They walked through the Enchanted Forest and climbed the steps of the Greek Theater where they sat and drank from the bottle, watching the stars.

"Do you remember," Ezra said, "when you mistook a firefly for a zig-zagging meteorite when we were lying in the back of my El Camino back in Iris?" Ezra asked.

"Shut up," Ava said, giggling. "I'm pretty sure I was high."

"You were something," Ezra said, joining in the giggling.

"Do you remember us wondering how cavemen and cavewoman kept their toenails short?"

Ezra giggled. "I do. And you know what?" he asked, his eyes shining with happiness.

Ava smiled. "What?"

"If we got stranded on a deserted island with no toenail clippers, I'd chew your toenails for you so you wouldn't trip on them."

Ava looked at Ezra, grimacing and smiling at the same time. "I think that's the most romantic thing I've ever heard."

Ezra smiled. "I have my moments."

When Ezra woke the next morning, he found himself alone in his bed. He checked his radio alarm clock for the time then sat up, yawned and rubbed his eyes. Seeing no sign of Ava, he rose and went to the bathroom. Noticing that the bathroom door leading to Miller and Todd Robert's side of the dorm suite was ajar, he peeked inside to see if Ava had perhaps gone into their room to make a phone call or to read without waking him. He found it empty.

Assuming that Ava had stepped out to get coffee or to get them some breakfast, Ezra used the toilet and then stepped to the lavatory to wash his hands and his face. When he turned on the lavatory light, he noticed a folded note taped to the mirror with his name written on it. He opened it and read:

Ezra-

I have never been more disgusted by nor more disappointed in another human being in my entire life.

Do not try to contact me. Ever.

Ava

P.S.

Don't forget to update your score. I'm sorry I'm not worth more points.

Initially confused, Ezra read the note a second time at which point the meaning of her message hit him like a speeding train. He looked back at the open door leading to his suitemates' room, closed his eyes and threw his head back, covering his face with his hands in anguish. "Fuck!" he yelled. "Fuck! Fuck! Fuck!"

He swung the door open, crossed the room and tore the sexual conquest score chart off the wall, ripping it to pieces. He hustled back into his room and quickly threw on a shirt, some sweats and sneakers. He ran out the door and looked for Ava in the lobby and then ran outside. When he could not find her or her VW in the parking lot, he returned to his dorm.

He called at Ava's mother house and was told that she was not home. He waited an hour and called again. Her sister, who had always liked Ezra, confirmed that Ava had made it home safely but did not want to speak to him. He drove all the way to Iris and pleaded with her mother at the front door to let him see Ava, but Ava refused to come to the door and her mother refused to let him in.

Ezra was beyond contrite. For weeks, he telephoned Ava at least once a day. She refused every call. He wrote to her more times than he could count. He acknowledged the immaturity and vile nature of his behavior. He tried to explain without excusing his behavior. He apologized profusely. He pleaded with her to just talk to him and hear him out. After several months without a response he finally stopped.

CHAPTER 40

"Well?" Giles asked, trying to sound positive but doing a poor job of it.

Ezra let out a long, disappointed sigh. Then he took his time carefully folding the letter into a paper airplane before launching it and watching it fly across the apartment living room and into the kitchen where it crash-landed into the spiral electric heating element on the stovetop. He craned his neck backwards, laying his head on the back of the couch and stared up at the ceiling. "Missed it by two points," he said.

"Damn," Giles said with as much empathy as he could muster. "You'll just have to take it again."

Ezra shook his head dismissively. "There are no more LSAT exams before the fall semester starts. This was my last chance to qualify for this year's admission."

"Well," Giles said, trying to find a bright side, "look at it this way. At the end of this semester, you'll have been in school for seventeen years straight. And law school is going to be three of the most intense years of instruction that you will ever have. It would probably do you some good to take a year off, like a gap year, so you can recharge. Try to look at this as a blessing in disguise."

"It's just not fair," Ezra said.

"What's not fair?" Giles queried.

"Kenny Pearl—this black guy in my computer science lab—he got into LSU Law School with an LSAT score that is four points lower than mine. *Four* fucking points. And his undergraduate GPA is a whole half-point lower than mine."

"Affirmative action," Giles said with an expression that denoted a lack of surprise.

"But at my expense," Ezra said angrily.

"I know it's frustrating," Giles said.

"I know it's not the end of the world if you have an affirmative action personal injury lawyer and he screws up your auto accident claim. That's just money. But, what if you're wrongfully accused of first-degree murder and facing the death penalty and you have to rely on an affirmative action lawyer? Or what if you end up on the operating table with an affirmative action spine surgeon?"

Giles nodded.

Ezra continued. "And the sad part about it all is that it actually hurts them in the long run."

"Who?" Giles asked.

"Blacks," Ezra answered. "Think about it. When I told you that Liberty Burney got accepted to Columbia, what was your first thought? Honestly."

"Affirmative action," Giles admitted.

"Right. But what if she would have gotten in without affirmative action?"

"We would never know."

"Exactly," said Ezra. "It's gotten to the point that everyone just assumes."

Giles nodded. "What about Tulane or Loyola? Didn't you say their admissions standards are usually a little lower than LSU's, at least for law school?"

"They are and I could get in to either of those, but I can't afford their tuition. It's well over twenty grand a year for either one."

"Jesus," Giles said. "What about Southern?"

Ezra rolled his eyes and scoffed. "I'm not getting a law degree from a—"

Giles' eyebrows rose on his forehead with surprise and remonstrance. Ezra blushed with embarrassment over what he was thinking and almost said. Giles walked to the couch and sat next to him. "I get it. I'm pissed for you."

"I just want to fucking scream," Ezra said.

"Maybe give some more thought about applying to Southern," Giles suggested. "My lab partner's boyfriend graduated from Southern. She said the majority of the law students there are actually white."

Ezra shook his head resolutely. "I'm not going to Southern."

"Why not? Once you pass the bar, you get the same license no matter where you went to law school, right?"

Ezra shook his head. "Yeah, but when you hang a Southern law degree on your wall, you're essentially branded. It's like getting a medical degree from one of those medical schools in the Caribbean."

"So, what are you going to do then?" Giles asked.

Ezra sighed and stared up at the ceiling. "I'm think I'm going to do what you said—take a gap year. Recharge. I can move back home and get a full time job for a year and save up some money. I'll take the LSAT again and make sure I get a high enough score to get into LSU."

Giles nodded. "Well, if Southern is off the table, then that sounds like a good plan to me."

Ezra nodded.

"Now that that's settled, let's go get drunk."

"Dude, I'm already depressed enough," Ezra said. "The last thing I need is alcohol."

"I'm buying," Giles offered.

"Let me find my shoes."

As planned, Ezra moved home after graduation and found a full time job with a local landscaper. In the fall, he enrolled in an LSAT-prep course and drove to Baton Rouge three nights a week for six straight weeks to attend the classes. He re-took the LSAT and increased his score by four points, two points higher than he would have needed to gain admission to LSU the preceding fall. He reapplied. But because of the increase in the number of applications from higher performing applicants, the minimum threshold had increased by three points, leaving Ezra with a one point deficit and another rejection letter from the LSU admissions office. After wallowing in self-pity for a couple of days, he swallowed his pride and applied for admission to the Southern University Law Center. Based on his first year's performance, he was selected to be on the Southern Law Review and two years later graduated Order of the Coif.

After passing the Louisiana bar examination on his first attempt, he submitted his resume to more than forty law firms in Lafayette, Lake Charles, Baton Rouge, New Orleans, Alexandria and Shreveport. He was not invited to a single interview.

He then began sending his resume to every trial and appellate court judge in the Acadiana area, desperate for any type of work in the legal field, even if it was only as a temporary law clerk. A few days later, he received a call from the Honorable Felix Jordan, a young African American trial court judge in 15th Judicial Court in Lafayette Parish. The judge told Ezra that he was very impressed with his resume but that he had already hired a law clerk for the current year. He gave Ezra the name of a local attorney who was looking for a new associate and suggested that he contact him. Ezra thanked him profusely.

The local attorney was Rogers Musa, the only son of a working-class Nigerian immigrant father and a second generation Ethiopian-

American mother. Rogers was a tall, imposing figure with deep set eyes and very dark skin. His parents had worked in factories for years until they saved enough money to buy a small dry-cleaning shop in Bethesda, where Musa spent his formative years. He graduated at the top of his high school class and then, on full academic scholarships, earned a political science degree from Temple and then a two law degrees from Georgetown.

Musa moved to Lafayette in 1977 when his wife was offered a professorship in the biology department at the University of Southwestern Louisiana. After being passed over by all of the major firms in Lafayette, Musa rented some office space and hung his shingle. Though he initially accepted virtually any type of legal work that came through the door, he eventually focused exclusively on representing personal injury clients.

During the interview, Ezra quickly learned that directness and expediency were hallmark characteristics of his prospective employer. "If you're thinking," Musa said, before they had even sat down, "that I'm contemplating hiring you because you're white and that I intend to exploit your whiteness for monetary gain, you're correct," he said. "Once you have sufficient experience, you will handle virtually every case assigned to a white judge and every trial where we expect the juries to have a white majority."

Ezra made no reply.

"If you're thinking my intention is to treat you like a mule hitched to a wagon loaded so heavily that even with your most valiant effort you can barely make the wheels turn, you'd be right again. And I will expect you to turn those wheels, Mr. Brasseaux. I have over six hundred open files in this office. You would have your first bench trial within the first three weeks and your first solo jury trial within the first four months, all under my supervision and tutelage of course. You would be assigned over twenty files on your first day. Within six months, I will have you handling up to one hundred fifty files on your own. Within a year, you will be up to two hundred files. ”

Musa paused and regarded Ezra whose expression remained attentive, albeit stoic. “I've had associates come and go over the years usually because they were not cut of the cloth needed for this type of practice. I need a lawyer made of silk on the outside but with a burlap lining. Do you think you meet my criteria?”

“Yes sir, I do. I want to learn, and I'm not afraid to work hard,” Ezra said.

“You hunt or fish?” Musa asked.

“A little of both,” Ezra said.

“Don't bother renewing your hunting and fishing licenses.”

“Okay.”

“You play golf?”

Ezra shrugged. “Occasionally.”

“Put your clubs in the attic,” Musa said. “Won't be no time for none of that.”

Ezra nodded. “Consider it done.”

Musa noticed a fire in Ezra's eyes that lent credence to his words. “Of course,” Musa continued, “I am aware that this is a *quid pro quo* relationship. As a return on your investment of considerable time and energy, you'll gain invaluable experience. Law school teaches you what the law is. What it does not teach you is how to practice it. That's where I come in. I will teach you things that you would never learn and give you opportunities that you would never have had at one of those big firms that would use you like a high powered paralegal for ten years before letting you have your own cases and clients.”

Ezra smiled at the thought of trying cases while his contemporaries were still doing research projects and answering interrogatories. "That sounds good," he said in earnest.

"You want to know what the best part of this job is going to be?" Musa asked.

"Sure."

"It'll be when you go up against those uppity lawyers from big firms that overlooked you because of the name of the school on your degree, just like they overlooked me because of the color of my skin, and you'll have the advantage because they will underestimate you, just like they underestimated me."

Ezra's eyes narrowed as his nostrils flared and his pupils dilated. Musa had definitely struck a chord.

"The job starts with a three-thousand dollar a month salary for the first ninety days and then the compensation converts to a percentage yield, at which point you will receive thirty percent of the fees on every case I give you and sixty percent of the fees on every case that you bring in yourself. If you do what's expected of you, you'll easily make seventy-five thousand dollars in the first year and a hundred fifty the next year. Once you start bringing in your own cases, the sky is the limit."

Musa noticed a slight movement in Ezra's mouth and eyebrows and a sparkle in his eyes. "Now, don't start thinking about how you might spend all that money just yet because you're not going to have any time for that. We work very hard. Long hours. Early mornings. A lot of late nights and weekends. Holidays when necessary. If you're scared, now's the time to say you're scared."

Ezra smiled confidently. "I'm not scared, sir."

"Excellent," Musa said as he pressed a button on his desk and then released it.

292

Ezra could hear footsteps approaching.

"My office manager will show you to your office, get you started on the employment paperwork and give you a key. When you are finished with that, review the file that's on your desk. You will be second chair in that trial next Thursday. We'll meet in the war room at six o'clock tomorrow morning to discuss trial strategy and the division of labor. I expect you to have read the file from cover to cover."

"No problem."

Musa nodded and then grabbed a stack of documents from his desk and began to review them.

"Thank you, Mr. Musa," Ezra said. "I appreciate your giving me this opportunity."

Without looking up from his documents Musa said, "Here's lesson number one. Whether it's me or any other lawyer that you ever deal with, no matter their age, no matter how esteemed or intimidating they seem to be, you address them by their first name. You let them know that you are confident and that you sincerely believe that you are on an equal footing with them. Never give them any reason to believe that they are entitled to more respect than you or that you would show them any deference."

"Yes, sir. Got it."

CHAPTER 41

Almost immediately, Musa shattered every negative stereotype that Ezra had ever entertained about black men. He was a consummate family man. He did not do drugs or gamble and rarely drank, and then only in moderation. He did not have girlfriends on the side—in fact, he adored and made it a point of trying to spoil his un-spoilable wife. He rose every morning at five a.m. to cook breakfast for his family and still got to the office by six. He was very wealthy but maintained a frugal and unpretentious lifestyle. Though he could easily afford a full-time maid and to dole out generous allowances, he required his children to do daily chores and to get after-school and summer jobs. He ran his law office with military precision and was the hardest working individual that Ezra had ever met, bar none. His only vices, as far as Ezra could tell, were the butterscotch candies that he kept in ample supply on his credenza and Cuban cigars.

Musa had not exaggerated about the experience that Ezra would gain while in his employ. He learned quickly about the noble side of the practice—like helping families that were devastated by a wrongful death or catastrophic injury, and the ignoble side—like clients who faked and exaggerated injuries and chiropractors and orthopedic surgeons who diagnosed injuries that did not exist and ordered diagnostic testing and rendered treatment that was unnecessary. He soon learned which medical providers were willing to play the game and which were not.

Six months into his practice, Ezra was assigned a case in which he would be representing a woman who had accidently run over and killed another shopper's two-year old child in a local Wal-Mart parking lot. She wanted to sue Wal-Mart, claiming that she was suffering with PTSD as a result of the incident. She had medical records to support her diagnosis. Musa had explained to her that the claim against Wal-Mart was very questionable but that she did have a viable claim against the mother, i.e., for negligent supervision of the child. She agreed to proceed with filing suit.

After reviewing the file, Ezra went to Musa's office and informed him that he did not want to handle the case.

"Was the mother not negligent when she allowed her two-year-old to run loose in the parking lot?" Musa rejoined.

"Yes, but—"

"And do you believe that running over and killing a child did not cause our client severe emotional trauma?"

"That's not the point," Ezra explained.

"And what pray tell do you think the point is?" Musa demanded.

"That mother lost her child, Rogers," Ezra beseeched. "And she has to live with the guilt of knowing that she caused his death. Don't you think she is already suffering enough?"

"Of course she is," Musa said matter-of-factly. "But as soon as the suit gets filed, the mother's homeowner's insurance carrier will hire a defense attorney who will handle everything. They will settle quickly. They will not want to put the mother through a deposition and a trial. She will have minimal involvement. Besides, if we withdraw from the case, she will simply hire another lawyer."

"But what about the negative publicity that we'll get?" Ezra persisted. "The media will crucify us if they get hold of the lawsuit."

"When you're a personal injury law firm, there is no such thing as bad publicity," Musa replied. "Anything that gets our name out there is free advertising. And people aren't looking for lawyers that are empathetic to defendants. They're looking for hyenas who will lock on to the throat of their prey with vice-like jaws until they start bleeding money."

Ezra nodded in surrender, realizing that his objection to handling the case had no chance of being sustained.

"Did I in any way mislead you into believing that this job would be all peaches and cream?" Musa asked unapologetically.

Ezra sighed. "No, sir, you did not." He forced a half-smile and turned to exit Musa's office and then turned back. "Oh, by the way," he said, "Allstate's motion for summary judgment in the Knowles case was denied." When Musa displayed virtually no reaction to the news, Ezra said, "You don't seem surprised at all."

Musa almost grinned. "I was on the committee to elect Judge Precht for both his original bid and his re-election campaign."

"Why didn't you mention that to me?" Ezra said.

"Because if you knew that you were hunting a baited field, you might have not presented the case as fervently."

Ezra snorted. "So, the result had nothing to do with my preparedness or skills in the courtroom?" he said rhetorically.

"That's not necessarily true. Joel Precht is going to help us out when he can. However, we can't expect to walk into his courtroom and pour a bunch of rancid meat and moldy potatoes on the table and expect him to make a feast out of it for us. He's got to be able to maintain credibility and respectability."

Ezra nodded. "But we've only gotten past the motion to dismiss. I still have to convince the jury that L'Meeka didn't stage the slip and fall. I don't see how I'm going to be able to argue that to a jury with a straight face when this was her fourth slip and fall accident in a two-year period."

Musa nodded. "You will need to take the focus off of L'Meeka and turn it toward you. With your freckled baby face, the jury is likely to see you as innocent and honest—someone who wouldn't take a case unless it was legitimate."

"But that's just it. I don't believe in the case. And I'm afraid the jury will see that."

Musa allowed his head to tilt to the side and sighed before popping a butterscotch candy into his mouth. "Have you ever heard of a lawyer by the name of Juban Rothstein?"

"Sure. We studied several big decisions in law school in which he was one of the lead attorneys."

"Well by most accounts Mr. Rothstein was probably the most talented litigator ever to practice in Louisiana. He was that special breed of lawyer who would not only take cases that no one else would dare touch but would also find ways to win them, and he would always seem to win big."

Ezra nodded attentively.

"Anyway," Musa said after pausing to reposition the candy in his mouth, "very early in my career, I found myself alone on an elevator with him in the Orleans Parish courthouse and I was bold enough to ask him if he had any advice for a young lawyer. He looked me up and down as if to assess whether I was worthy of his advice and then asked me my name. I told him." Musa looked up at the ceiling and smiled nostalgically and then leaned back in his chair. "He looked me in the eye and with great conviction said, *Mr. Musa, listen very carefully, sir. The secret to success in the practice of law is sincerity . . . and once you can fake that, you've got it made.*"

Ezra began to chuckle and then stopped when he realized that neither Musa nor Juban were trying to be funny.

"Any lawyer can argue a case he believes in," Musa said. "Do you want to be just any lawyer?"

"No, sir."

CHAPTER 42

Ezra's third jury trial was in a Maritime personal injury case against Cradeur Drilling Company, a large gas and oil exploration company headquartered in Thibodaux, Louisiana. His client had lost an arm in an offshore drilling accident. CDC was represented by Jackson & Jumel, a preeminent defense firm in Lafayette. Leading their team of high-powered lawyers was Hank Jumel, one of the firm's founding partners and considered to be one of the most gifted civil litigators in Lafayette Parish if not all of Acadiana.

Though Jumel, as he so often did, won what seemed like an unwinnable case for the defense, he had been more than impressed with his young opponent's grit, preparedness and presence in the courtroom. Several weeks after the appeal was over and the case was closed, Jumel telephoned Ezra and invited him to lunch.

Jumel chose his "go to" lunch spot for their meeting, *Dwyer's Café* on Jefferson Street. They sat in a booth at the rear of the café and both ordered smothered pork chops over rice and sweet tea from a young waitress in a low-cut blouse who greeted them with a huge smile and knew "Mr. Jumel" by name.

The lunch meeting lasted nearly two hours. In contrast to the fierce and intimidating persona that he assumed throughout the litigation of their case, Jumel proved to be very warm, funny and self-deprecating. He shared with Ezra that his life had not always been a bowl of cherries, that he had been raised by a single mother after watching his father die a slow death from a rare form of throat cancer and that he and his wife had struggled with profound sadness and had their faith tested over never being able to have children of their own. He talked about his passion for literature and movies. He disclosed that maintained a comic book collection and attended what he called *Geek Fests* where he and several other collectors would gather once a year to show off their most recent acquisitions and *geek out* over recent developments in the comic book world.

"Do y'all dress up like they do at those ComiCon conventions?" Ezra asked, trying to mask his amusement while picturing Jumel in a superhero mask, cape and tights.

"It's called cosplay and no, we don't," Jumel said, smirking. "There are limits to our devotion."

Ezra chuckled. "I have to say, I would have never picked you out of a line-up for being a comic book collector."

Jumel nodded and smiled. "Well don't feel too sorry for me," he said, "the value of my collection is probably triple that of your home."

Ezra's eyebrows climbed as high on his forehead as they could reach, and he did a quick calculation in his head. "Holy investment portfolios, Batman!" he replied in an exclaimed whisper.

"Right?" Jumel replied, smiling.

When Ezra later mentioned that he was from Iris, an amused expression appeared on Jumel's face. He told Ezra that the first deposition he had ever taken as a young lawyer was in the context of a workers' compensation claim filed by a black man from Iris who was representing himself. "His name was Cedrick Watson," Jumel said.

"That name actually sounds familiar," Ezra said.

"Well, he was a cocky little banty rooster," Jumel said, chuckling. "Twelve kids with eight different women. Typical product of the projects."

Ezra nodded. "I know the type."

"Anyway, it was a case he could not win. We had a positive post-accident drug test which was an absolute defense to his claim. So I was just having fun with the deposition, knowing that my questions and his answers really didn't matter. Finally, he starts to get frustrated with me and pushes his chair back from the table. He leers at me and says, *'You know what, Mr. Jumel? I may not have a law degree, but I can do this shit just as good as you can. Because I'm intelligent. I'm very intelligent.* So, I decided to fuck with him a little bit, right? In a very serious tone I say, *Oh, I don't doubt that at all, Mr. Watson. By the way, do you happen to know what your I.Q. is, sir?* And I shit you not Ezra, he looks at me like he's a little confused for a second and then the lightbulb turns on and he says, *Shiiiiiiit, about 20/20."*

Ezra burst into laughter and began to shake his head. "That's not true," he said. "No way that's true."

"Verbatim," Jumel said.

'Wow," Ezra said, "that's hilarious."

Jumel smiled and glanced at his watch. "Wow, I didn't realize the time. I'm going to have to get going in a minute. But I wanted to talk to you about something before we leave."

"Sure."

Jumel's expression suddenly became more serious. "We all know the deal, Ezra. No offense, but practicing personal injury law doesn't require a whole lot of talent. It just doesn't. No one grows up wanting to be a personal injury lawyer. Shit, the overwhelming majority of them went into personal injury law in the first place because they didn't do well enough in law school or—and, again, no offense—they didn't go to a good enough law school to get hired by a defense firm or a corporation. They do it because they really don't have other options."

Though he did not entirely disagree with Jumel's premise, Ezra was not sure how he was not supposed to take offense to his comments. Notwithstanding, he maintained an expressionless countenance,

301

determined not to display his wounded feelings.

"And don't get me wrong. You don't have to have talent to make money. There are plenty of personal injury lawyers who make a lot of money despite their lack of talent, i.e., those that are lucky enough to get some big cases or because they work hard enough at developing a volume practice where they just sign up every client that walks through the door and then settle the cases for a discount to keep the fees rolling in."

"So," Jumel continued, "can you make a lot of money even with mediocre talent? Sure. Can you make a lot more money than a good defense lawyer? Absolutely. There's only so many hours a defense lawyer can bill in a day, right? But at the end of the day—and again, no offense, Ezra—but at the end of the day, even the ones who do really well have to live with the fact that they are carrion eaters and bottom-feeders, with the fact that no one in the legal world genuinely respects them."

Ezra had listened attentively, trying hard to resist the urge to defend himself and his mentor. He managed a smile. "Is this why you invited me to lunch? To insult me?"

"No," Jumel said, chuckling. "God, no. This is my fucked-up way of convincing you to stop what you are doing and come work for me. I'm offering you a job."

Ezra was caught off guard. As much as he respected and admired his employer, he knew that there was a lot of truth in what Jumel was saying. He had never gotten entirely comfortable with the personal injury practice. In fact, there were aspects of it that made him feel downright slithery, and the prospect of wearing the proverbial white hat more than titillated him.

When Ezra gave his notice, Musa was disappointed but did not seem surprised at all. When Ezra told him who had offered him the job, he was downright flattered. "Well," he reflected, "I'm more than sorry to see you go Ezra, but I guess when I've got the likes of Hank Jumel picking fruit from my tree, I must be doing something right. More importantly, you must be doing something right."

In that instant, Ezra felt their relationship change. Their superior-subordinate dynamic had come to an end. They were now colleagues who would become genuine friends.

Ezra made good on his promise to visit Musa from time to time. They could occasionally be seen smoking cigars and drinking Scotch on Musa's office balcony that overlooked Girard Park. They shared war stories and talked about current events.

When Musa learned that Ezra was writing a novel that largely centered on shining a spotlight on racial issues, he showed genuine interest and offered encouragement. "Want some advice from a well-seasoned Negro?"

Ezra regarded his former employer curiously for a moment, a little uncertain about how to respond. "Okay," he said.

"Don't let the white guilt propagandists influence you into writing a novel that perpetuates black victimization. There are already way too many people in this country doing that. The black leaders and liberal white politicians who push the victim agenda are doing nothing but feeding a cycle of poverty, welfare and underachievement, all clothed in fantasies of justice, reparations and equality."

"Black people need to finally assume responsibility for their own identity and stop trying to just rebrand it," Musa said. "First we were *Negroes*, then that word became offensive. Then we were *colored*, until that was no longer acceptable. Then, we were *black*. Now, you have to say *African American*. We're like a corporation with a sullied reputation that keeps changing its name without changing its product," Musa said, finally stopping to take a puff on his cigar. He exhaled and then chuckled.

"What?" Ezra asked.

Musa shook his head, laughing to himself. "My father," he said. "I remember toward the end of his life, him getting so outdone when he learned that American blacks were insisting on being called African Americans. *African Americans?* he would say in his thick Nigerian accent, *Less than one percent of the blacks here came from Africa and even a smaller percent have ever even been there. I am an African American. These people, they don't know what they are. They don't know who they are.*"

Ezra nodded.

"And he would go on about how *African American* is not a valid racial classification—how the term denotes geographical origin and current residence, not race. And of course, he was right. He would tell the same story over and over about his argument with his neighbor, Jackson Greene. He would tell Jackson that he was not an African American because he was not from Africa, but that the Van Ackers, Caucasians who owned the dry cleaning shop on the corner and who had migrated to the United States from Cape Town, *were* African Americans. Jackson would be outraged. They would argue for hours."

Ezra chuckled.

"You know," Musa said, "Caucasians believing Negroes to be inferior used to be the problem. Now, the problem is that most Negroes believe it. And every time a liberal politician, black or white, makes an excuse for black underachievement or gives a handout to the black community, it's just reinforcing the notion that blacks are not smart enough, determined enough, or hardworking enough to be successful on their own or to even take care of themselves."

Ezra nodded but did not reply, not wanting to interrupt.

"My family has perspective from both sides," Musa continued. "My father was an immigrant and my mother was born of immigrants who came to America post-slavery. In contrast, my wife's ancestors were American slaves. I know that there is still a lot of carryover from all of that. I get it. I know it's harder for Negroes in this country. In many ways, it's a lot harder. Hell, do you think I aspired to be a damn personal injury lawyer? In addition to my Juris Doctor, I have an L.L.M. in estate planning from Georgetown. But not a single white firm would give me an interview and there's just not enough affluent black folk in this area to support an estate planning practice."

"But regardless of what the Declaration of Independence and our Constitution say about equality, lighter skinned people tend to have it easier than darker skinned people. Men tend to have it easier than women. Prettier people have advantages over ugly people. Thin people have an edge on overweight people. This list goes on and on. Those are the realities. Is it fair? Perhaps not, but whoever said life is always fair? So, are we going to legislate anti-discrimination laws and affirmative action programs for ugly people and fat people?"

"As for racial prejudice, the answer is education, work ethic and perseverance. My wife and I are living proof of that. The answer is lifting ourselves up as individuals and as a community—just like other groups who have been discriminated against in this country, like the Jews and Asians. Playing the race card and assuming the role of victim to get what you want only perpetuates the cycle."

"I don't disagree."

"Let me ask you something, Ezra," Musa said.

"Sure."

"Do you think you are prejudiced?"

Ezra's face fell. He did not know how to respond. "I don't think that I am. I certainly try not to be."

Musa smiled. "Now if you weren't prejudiced, you would not have to try not to be, would you?" he said.

Ezra blushed.

"Of course you are prejudiced," Musa continued. "You're prejudiced. I'm prejudiced. So is every sentient human being with any kind of life experience. You prejudged me before you met me, and I prejudged you. We prejudge people every single day of our lives. *That man's harmless. That woman's promiscuous. Those boys are trouble. This is a bad neighborhood.* We're genetically programmed to assess situations and other people based on observation and past experiences," Musa continued. "The primitive man who never learned to prejudge did not survive and certainly did not thrive. It's just as true today. An affluent, well-dressed white man who fails to take another route when he sees a handful of black thugs admiring his gold watch is a fool. And the same is true for a young black man who, in the middle of the night, gets on a subway car occupied by a group of young blued-eyed, white men with shaved heads and neck tattoos."

Ezra nodded. "I see what you're saying."

"And when it comes to racial prejudices, they are held by everyone, in every group. No exceptions. White people have prejudices against blacks. Rich whites against poor whites. Blacks have prejudices against whites. Light skinned blacks against dark skinned blacks and vice versa. Hell," Musa said, remembering something that proved his point, "my little niece just started undergrad at Southern University in Baton Rouge. She wanted to rush AKA. She got blacklisted because she wouldn't pass the brown paper bag test. Do you know what that is?"

Ezra shook his head. "I don't think so."

"It's where your skin has to be no darker than the color of a

306

brown paper bag that you would get from a grocery store. Can you believe that? We're in the 21ˢᵗ century and the jealousies and divisions between the house niggas and the field niggas are literally still a thing. And the incredible irony is that most of the uppity light-skinned blacks who think they are superior to darker-skinned blacks get their lightness from their ancestral white slave-owners and overseers who raped their ancestral mothers on plantations. How do you like them apples?"

Ezra's eyebrows raised in befuddlement. "It sounds so crazy when you put it like that."

"And I'll tell you another dark secret—excuse the pun," Musa said before taking a puff from his cigar and then exhaling. "Blacks are every bit as racist against whites as whites are against blacks. The only difference is that, in this country, whites are in power. Go anywhere where blacks are in power and you will find evidence of the same types of discrimination, only against whites and other non-black races. The same is true for Asians, Hispanics, Native Americans, gorillas, baboons, dolphins, and trumpeter swans. Birds of a feather flock together. It's nature."

Ezra acknowledged Musa's diatribe with a nod but thought it best not to reply or comment.

"But you know what?" Musa said, leaning toward Ezra and lowering his voice, "you can't talk about any of this. At least not in public. A white man says what I'm saying and the ultra-left are going to brand him a racist and destroy his career. A black man brings this up and he gets ostracized as a sellout or an Uncle Tom."

Again, Ezra nodded tentatively.

"That's the problem in a nutshell," Musa said. "These people have succeeded in creating a culture in which true debate and meaningful discourse on the issue of race in this country has been completely snuffed out. And that's a damn shame."

"Agreed," Ezra said.

"So, that's my unsolicited advice," Musa said. "If you're going to take the time and effort to write about race, even in the context of fiction, don't be censored. Don't perpetuate an intellectually dishonest and self-defeating dialogue. That's my two cents."

Ezra took a deep breath and exhaled. "That's more like two-hundred cents," Ezra said.

"Probably so," Musa said, and they chuckled.

CHAPTER 43

Ezra adapted quickly to the defense practice. He progressed rapidly under Jumel's tutelage, making partner after just four years with the firm. He worked hard, developed his own book of business and after another ten years became one of the firm's top producers during which time he and Jumel, their age difference notwithstanding, became close friends.

"You know Hank, that stuff will kill you," Ezra said in the office kitchen as Hank was adding his usual extraordinary amount of powdered creamer to his coffee.

Hank shrugged. "Gotta die of something, right? How was your weekend?"

"I actually got invited to play a round of golf at English Turn. Nice track, but Jack Nicklaus did not design that course for recreational golfers, that's for damn sure."

Hank chuckled. "Yeah, I played that course about a month after it first opened, in '88 I think. The fifteenth hole sticks out in my mind—the par five with the island green."

"Yep, I put two balls in the water on that hole," Ezra said, as he poured himself a cup of coffee.

"Well I got one better," Hank said. "After a really nice tee shot, I had a two-hundred yard 4-iron to the pin. I hit the ball low on the club face but still very solid and it takes off like a bullet, never getting more than ten to fifteen feet off the ground, going straight at the left side of the green. The ball actually skids twice on the water and then hits this white bird that was wading on the edge of the bank."

"Oh no," Ezra said, grimacing.

"Yeah, the poor thing is squawking and flailing around like crazy. Golfers on the next tee box are running over to see what's going on."

"Jesus."

"So anyway, the poor thing is dead by the time we get to the green. So, I toss it in the cattails and start looking for my ball but can't find it. I presume that it must have ricocheted off the bird into the water, so I take a drop and I'm about to chip up onto the green when one of my buddies who putted out while I was getting situated started screaming. My ball is in the hole."

"Holy shit. Are you serious? So after all that, you end up with an eagle?"

"Yeah, though I kind'a *egretted* it."

Ezra's expression of amazement quickly turned into a frown and then a smirk.

"Gotcha," Hank said, grinning proudly.

Ezra shook his head, giggled and scoffed. "That was an awful lot of work for something that wasn't terribly funny."

Hank shrugged and smiled. "You'll be telling that one every time you play golf from now on."

"Doubtfully."

"You look like shit by the way," Hank said, gesturing toward the bags under Ezra's eyes.

"Thanks. Didn't get much sleep last night," Ezra said.

"Wait a minute, last night was your dinner date with that physical therapist, right? So, I presume it went well?" Hank asked.

"Hmm, not exactly."

"What happened?" Hank asked. "The way you described her, I had her pegged as a little hellcat in the sack."

Ezra sipped his coffee and sighed. "I'm not saying she wasn't."

310

"Well?" Hank asked, his prurient interests piqued, "what was the problem?"

Ezra shook his head and smiled, reluctant to share the details.

"Come on, man," Hank said. "I've been married for thirty years. My sexual gratification is mostly vicarious at this point. Don't leave me hanging."

Ezra scoffed and shook his head.

"Don't make me beg."

"It's in the vault?" Ezra asked.

"Of course."

Ezra paused, allowing the last layer of reticence to dissolve in his mind. "She's a crier."

"She cried afterwards?" Hank asked, curiously.

"During."

"*During*?!?" Hank's face twisted with confusion.

Ezra nodded.

"It couldn't be from pain, I mean, I've seen your—"

"Fuck you," Ezra said. "And no, it was not from pain. It was emotional crying."

"Damn," Hank said. "That's," he paused trying to think of the right word, "unconventional."

"Tell me about it."

What's her name again?"

Ezra glared at Hank as if to ask *what's the relevance?*

"Come on. We're in the vault," Hank promised.

"Whitney Thibaut," Ezra answered.

"Thibaut," Hank repeated, "you don't hear that name a lot. Is her father a football coach?"

"I think so," Ezra said. "I mean, I know she mentioned that he's a high school coach. I'm not sure if she mentioned which sport. Why?"

Hank chuckled. "My senior year, we made it to the quarterfinals in football and had to play St. Martinville High School. They had this 6' 4" two hundred sixty-pound beast who played both ways—running back and linebacker. I kid you not, we had five players leave the game with concussions, one on defense, four on offense, all caused by him. Guess what his name was."

"I have no idea."

"Martial Thibaut. I know he's coaching high school football in this area. I'll bet that's her dad."

"No. No way," Ezra said, shaking his head. "I remember Martial Thibaut. He ended up playing for LSU. He's black."

"Right."

"Whitney is white," Ezra said.

"Hold on," Hank said, gesturing for Ezra to follow him back to his office. He opened a filing cabinet where he kept all of his old LSU Alumni Magazines. He flipped through them for a few seconds and then pulled out the issue for March 2011. He held it up for Ezra to see. On the cover was a portrait of a large family posing in front of Mike the Tiger's cage on the LSU campus. "Is that her?"

Ezra looked at the photo and did a double take. "Let me see that," he said, snatching the magazine from Hank. He was flabbergasted. "Son of a bitch," he whispered. "I honestly had no idea. But when you look at her with the rest of her family, I guess you can kind'a see it."

Hank grinned.

"What? I swear I didn't know."

"What difference does it make?"

"None whatsoever."

"Are you sure?"

Ezra smirked.

Hank took the magazine back and gazed at the photo. "Damn. Her mother is a clock-stopper."

Ezra grinned.

Hank grimaced as though the woman's beauty was painful to behold. "Hmm, I do like cooking with some dark roux."

"Stop it."

Hank chuckled. "What?"

"Just stop," Ezra repeated.

"Hey, if it was good enough for Thomas Jefferson . . . ."

Ezra shook his head disapprovingly. "I'm going back to my office."

CHAPTER 44

Two months after the humorless Army administrator signed and presented him with his official discharge papers, Vance celebrated by evicting his on-again, off-again girlfriend of three years, closing on the sale of his house and purchasing a used Winnebago. Over the next sixteen months, he and Bruce, Jr., a/k/a B.J., whom he had rescued from the pound and who bore an uncanny resemblance to his namesake, embarked on a quest to visit every road-accessible national park on the North American continent.

After visiting over twenty sites in Canada and nearly fifty in the United States, their sojourn finally came to an end in 2008 when the motor home's engine threw a rod in the lower Florida Keys. Vance traded-in the RV "as is" for an old Toyota Land Cruiser, bought a used houseboat and took up residence at a marina at Big Pine Island. He taught himself to fly fish and, mostly to pass the time, worked part-time at a local tackle shop.

In the summer of 2010, Vance's younger half-brothers were killed in a boating accident. Their bodies were found floating near a railroad trestle on Two O'clock Bayou in St. Landry Parish between Krotz Springs and Port Barre. Their aluminum skiff had crashed into a concrete stanchion while they were night fishing and, judging from the damage, at a high rate of speed. Ezra reached out to Vance and offered him his extra bedroom if he was planning to come in for the funeral.

When Vance returned for the funeral, it was the first time he had set foot on Louisiana soil since leaving for Fort Benning over two decades prior. Before checking in with Ezra and Giles, he drove to the trailer park where he had grown up and found the old mobile home still anchored in the same back lot. Other than a treated pine wheelchair ramp and twenty-plus years of mildew and unrepaired wear and tear, nothing had changed, though everything looked much smaller through adult eyes.

Not sure if his father was still living in the trailer or not, Vance warily knocked on the door, first softly so as not to startle anyone inside, and then, when no one answered, more loudly. "Hello?" he called out.

"Who is it?" his father's surly voice called out from inside the trailer.

Vance opened the door and stuck his head inside. Through the smoky haze, he saw his leathery-faced father sitting half-dressed in an old, busted recliner, his hair uncombed, an unfiltered Camel in hand and several empty Schaefer beer cans laying on the floor behind a ratty wheelchair parked next to the recliner. He immediately noticed a scarred stump sticking out of his father's cotton briefs where a full leg had once been. He tried not to stare.

"It's Vance," he said.

His father squinted as he took a long drag from his short cigarette and then exhaled twin streams of smoke through his nostrils. "So it is," he said without so much as a hint of affection in his voice. He smashed what was left of the cigarette butt in an overfilled ceramic ashtray and lit another.

Vance stepped inside. "I'm in town for Bo and Luke's funeral." He had not spoken his half-brothers' names out loud in years and almost chuckled over the embarrassment of having siblings named after *Dukes of Hazzard* characters.

There was an awkward silence as he watched his father use his tongue to push a piece of tobacco to the edge of his lips and then spit it onto the dingy carpet where it landed amongst an assortment of lint, burnt popcorn kernels and nail clippings. Vance casually scanned the rest of the living area which fared no better.

"I got a bunch of shit piled up in the extra bedrooms," his father said, seemingly concerned that Vance was looking for a place to lay his head while in town.

"Not a problem," Vance said, "I wasn't planning on staying here."

His father looked relieved and leaned over the arm of the recliner to pull a can of beer out of a Styrofoam ice chest without offering one to Vance. "Where ya staying?" he asked.

"With Ezra Brasseaux."

"I remember him," his father replied. "I remember his daddy, too," he scoffed, "how he rode around town with his gun and his badge like he was big shit." He father took a drag of his cigarette, held it for several seconds and then exhaled the smoke. "Then he goes and leaves his family to run off with that younger woman. Real upstanding fella he turned out to be, huh?"

Vance shrugged. "Yeah well, we can't all hit the jackpot when it comes to paternity now can we?"

Vance's father did not react to the comment, though whether it was due to antipathy or not comprehending the slight was unclear.

"Where's Misty?" Vance asked.

His father belched and then coughed. "Shit. That whore left more than ten years ago. Cleared out with the boys less than a month after my work-comp got cut off. I hear she's done been married and divorced twice since we split and working on number four. Somebody else's problem now," he said matter-of-factly.

Vance thought of several things he could say in response but refrained.

316

"How 'bout you? You ever got married?" his father asked.

Vance shook his head. "Nope."

"Too bad," his father said. "Marriage is a fine institution, as far as institutions go." He chuckled at his own joke while scratching the skin between his thigh and scrotum and then drug his fingertips across his shirt to remove the yeasty moisture.

Vance did well to mask his disgust. He was also still trying in earnest not to stare at his father's stump. He recalled the many occasions on which his father had used that same leg to kick his sons in the rear when he was drunk, angry, or both—once so hard that Vance sustained a hairline fracture to his coccyx. Though he did not exactly subscribe in the Hindu or Buddhist versions of karma, Vance wanted to believe that there was a cosmic energy in the universe that tended to such things as balance and justice and that it perhaps played a role in his father's humbling dismemberment.

"Yeah," his father said before pausing to take another long drag from his cigarette, "I've learn't the hard way."

Vance regarded his father curiously. "Learned what?" he asked.

His father scoffed and spit out other another small piece of tobacco. "That when it comes to anything that flies, floats or fucks, you're better off renting."

Vance stifled a chuckle, not wanting to give his father the satisfaction.

"I heard you got wounded," his father said.

Vance smirked. "Just took a little shrapnel in my neck and under my chin," he said. "I've done worse shaving." He gestured toward his father's stump. "What happened to you?"

"Sugar diabetes," his father said. "Fucking doctors—they caught it too—" His response was suddenly interrupted with a coughing attack that

317

took nearly a minute to subside. "They caught it too late," he finally continued. "Found a tumor on my lung too," he said between lingering coughs.

"They stage it?" Vance asked, his tone and expression more curious than empathetic.

"It's a four," his father replied nonchalantly, almost proudly. "The cancer doctor wanted to give me chemo but I told 'em he could shove that poisonous drip up his ass. I'm thinking about calling one of those law firms on T.V. to see if I can get a settlement."

Vance mentally scoffed but did not change his expression. He wanted to change the subject. Then without much forethought he said, "Do you know what today is?"

"Thursday?" his father answered, though he was not sure.

Vance regarded him piteously. "It's August 3rd." When the date did not seem to register with his father, Vance said, "It's her birthday." His tone was more sentimental than he had intended.

"Who?" His father asked.

Vance sighed contemptuously under his breath. "Mom," he said.

"Oh," his father replied nonplussed.

Vance glared at his father. He felt a nearly irresistible urge to walk across the filthy living area and force a fist deep into his mouth while pinching his nostrils shut with the other, looking him in the eyes as he watched him struggle to breath and then expire.

He could not help comparing him to the other fathers that he knew growing up. How Ezra's dad always took time to joke with Ezra and his friends, how he coached Ezra's baseball teams, brought Ezra and his friends hunting and fishing and showed Ezra how to use tools and build things. How Giles' father brought his family on amazing vacations, how he never raised his hand or even his voice to his children and how he made

318

sure that Giles and his sister were never wanting.

But he also acknowledged to himself that, unlike Ezra's dad, at least his father had stayed. He was at least present, even if his presence was more often than not unpleasant, or worse. And unlike Giles, at least he had, whether by parental design or inadvertence, learned toughness and self-sufficiency from his father. To be sure, his father was right about one thing. He *didn't raise no pussies.* That was something, Vance thought. Likely he would never have become an Army Ranger otherwise.

But any redeeming qualities that his father may have had were far outweighed by his flaws. He had always struggled to keep a job and consequently was a mediocre provider at best. He smoked, drank to excess and was always rumored to have a woman on the side. And he was both verbally and physically abusive, both to his children and whichever woman happened to be sharing his name and his trailer at the time. In short, if ever asked, Vance would succinctly describe him as a piece of shit.

Thinking about his mother's last birthday led him to thinking of the last one she had while she was still alive. The treatment for her metastatic colon cancer had failed, and she was essentially sent home to die. Vance wanted to buy her a birthday gift but had no money of his own, so he rode his bike to the family's modest fishing camp just outside of town in search of his dad to ask him for some change. When he arrived, he found his father's old pickup parked out front and their old aluminum skiff gone. Figuring that his father was probably checking a trotline, Vance parked his bike, climbed high into the large mimosa tree on the bank of the bayou and waited. Within a few minutes, he heard the approaching putter of a boat motor. At the same time, he saw his uncle's truck turn off the highway into the camp's white shell driveway.

Vance decided to remain hidden in the tree until his uncle and father were beneath him and then jump down to scare them. As his uncle walked around to the back of the camp, Vance's father was pulling the skiff up to the dock. There was a woman sitting on the bow. He remembered so vividly the juxtaposition of her mussed bleached blonde hair and her dark roots. She held the tie-line in her hand and had a cigarette hanging out of her mouth. She was skinny and weathered looking.

As the bow nudged up against the tire-bumpers tethered to the dock, the woman leaned over and grabbed the dock cleat to steady the boat. Vance could see her cigarette flapping up and down in her mouth as she spoke, though her speech was muffled by the rumbling of the motor. After his father killed the engine, Vance could hear the woman cussing as she struggled to tie the line to the cleat as the two men laughed at her.

"She can't tie a boat off for shit," Vance's father said to his brother, then he grinned and winked, "but she can sure fuck though." The men erupted in laughter as the exasperated woman threw the rope down on the dock and climbed out of the boat, using expletives that would have made a sailor blush. When the adults were finally inside the camp, Vance quietly climbed down from the tree and rode his bike home where he made a card for his mother using scrap paper and colored markers.

Vance was jarred out of his trance when his dad snorted and scoffed loudly. "Look at this shit," his father said, gesturing bitterly with his chin toward the television and the media coverage of President Barack Hussein Obama II deplaning from Air Force One upon returning from a diplomatic trip to South Korea. "Whoever thought the people in this country would be stupid enough to elect a nigger president?" When Vance did not comment, his father continued his tirade. "What kind of name is that anyway? Sounds like a God damned terrorist."

Vance regarded his father and vacillated between amusement and disgust. Part of him wanted to laugh derisively in his face. Part of him was resisting the strong desire to castigate him for being a worthless excuse for a human being. But he ultimately decided that his father physically rotting away in a busted recliner in an old, moldy trailer, one limb and one lung at a time while festering in his own interminable ignorance was probably punishment enough.

"Are you going to the funeral?" Vance asked.

His father started to respond but was interrupted by a coughing fit. "Nah, I don't reckon. Ain't nobody gonna be there that I need to see."

"Well, I got my dog in the car, so I need to go see about 'em," Vance said. "I'll be heading out."

"If that dog shits in my yard, you be sure and pick it up," his father said.

"Roger that," Vance said and then paused and chuckled to himself, remembering one of the most humiliating moments in his life, courtesy of the man in the recliner.

He was ten years old and two girls in his class, Sidney McCarron and Taylor Leger, who were riding bikes in the neighborhood, had stopped to talk to him in front of his trailer. A couple of minutes later, his father drove up and noticed a large pile of canine excrement next to the sidewalk. In front of the girls, he ordered Vance to pick it up. Vance told the girls that he would be right back then turned and began to jog toward the shed.

"Where are you going?" his father inquired.

"To get the shovel," Vance answered.

"No, sir," his father said. "The time to use the shovel was when you first saw the dog shit in the yard. You've lost your shovel privileges."

Vance knew that if he disobeyed, his father would back-hand him right in front of the girls. Embarrassed beyond imagination, he walked back and picked up the soft feces with his bare hands as the girls watched in horror. Red faced, he walked to the rear of the lot and emptied his hand into the bushes and then hurried to the water spigot to wash up.

"You forget something?" his father said, bringing Vance back to the present.

Vance regarded his father for a moment. The corners of his mouth turned up, almost into a grin. "Not nearly enough," he said.

His father tilted his head slightly in reaction to Vance's comment but made no inquiry as to its meaning. They parted with neither saying good-bye.

Vance drove a few blocks to Jagneaux's Superette where he purchased a six-pack of beer and some ice. With B.J. at his side, he rode around town drinking and reminiscing, passing by the schools he had attended and the places where he had frequented or held part-time jobs. The video arcade was now a pay day loan business. The video rental store had been converted into a drive-through boiled crawfish vendor. But he was pleased to see that the skating rink, where he had his first kiss, and the movie theater, where he copped his first feel, were still in business, though both the worse for wear.

CHAPTER 45

Ezra parked on the side of the road in front of his mother's home where Giles, Vance and he would stay the night in anticipation of going to the funeral the next morning. Ezra and Giles were removing their bags from the trunk of Ezra's BMW when a speeding vehicle suddenly appeared from directly behind them, horning blaring and tires skidding on the asphalt pavement. Giles shrieked and in his panic fell backwards into the trunk of the car as Ezra instinctively jumped to the side, falling and rolling into the roadside ditch. The oversized tires on the old Land Cruiser screeched to a halt just a couple of feet shy of contact with the rear bumper of the BMW.

The driver rolled his window down and greeted Ezra and Giles with a huge shit-eating grin. "Hello, faggots."

"You bastard!" exclaimed Giles from the trunk of the car in a very rare exhibition of profanity, his heart pounding from what he was certain was going to be a fatal impact.

Vance chortled. "I think that's the first time I've ever heard you cuss, Poret."

"Fuck, dude!" Ezra angrily exclaimed as he attempted to extricate himself from the trough of the ditch. "You could have crushed us between those bumpers!"

Vance rolled his eyes. "With your cat-like reflexes? Not a chance," he said before climbing out of the Toyota and giving Giles his hand to pull him out of the trunk.

The three men stood on the side of the road, Giles and Ezra still waiting for their nerves to settle from their near-death experiences. "Give us a hug, asshole," Ezra finally said, before he and Giles took turns warmly embracing their old friend.

"Jesus, how long's it been?" Ezra said. "Since we had dinner in Enid when I was up there for depositions?"

"Yep," Vance said. "What was that, 1998?"

"1999 I think," Ezra said.

"Heck for me, it's been since you left for boot camp right after high school," Giles said. "Jesus, you haven't changed a lick."

"I wish I could say the same about you, buddy," Vance teased, gesturing towards Giles' balding head.

"Yeah," Giles replied, "the hair on my head is gradually relocating to my back and my buttocks."

Over the giggling they heard a bark from Vance's vehicle. "What do we have here?" Ezra asked.

"Come!" Vance called.

On command, a Malinois mix leapt through the open window of the Land Cruiser, hurried to Vance and sat obediently at his feet. "Gentlemen," Vance said, "meet B.J."

"Wait, you named your dog *Blow Job*?" Giles asked.

Vance smirked. "No dickhead. B.J. is for *Bruce, Jr.*"

"Holy shit," Ezra said, bending down to affectionately scratch the beautiful dog behind his ears, "he's the spitting image of old *Bruces from Opelousas*. He's gorgeous."

Vance smiled and instructed B.J. to shake hands with Ezra and Giles. B.J. promptly complied and then turned his attention back to Vance to eagerly await his next command. Vance pointed to the lawn of Mrs. Brasseaux's next door neighbor and said, "Go do your business," at which point B.J. made a beeline for the neighbor's flowerbed and squatted.

"Whoa Dude," Ezra said in a low voice, "that's Mr. Baumfelder's house and he's a fucking Nazi about his lawn."

"Relax," Vance said.

On cue, the front door of the house opened and an old man stepped onto the portico. The screeching tires had grabbed his attention and he had been watching the canine trespass unfold from his window.

"You got a bag to pick up after your dog?" the man called out to Vance. His tone and expression bore an unmistakable condescension, the same tone and expression that he used with Iris High students for more than thirty years.

Vance waved at his old principal and smiled. "Oh, hey there Mr. Baumfelder," he said, it taking the full capacity of his self-restraint not to call him *Mr. Bum-fucker,* the not-so-secret nickname given to him soon after he joined the Iris High administration in the early seventies. "I'm not sure how much urine we'd be able to scoop into a bag, but if you want to grab one, we can give it a go."

Ezra turned his back to Mr. Baumfelder so as not to be seen laughing at his expense.

The retired principal's face turned red with embarrassment and anger. "Well, the ammonia from the urine kills the grass," he snapped.

"That's why I train him to go in the mulch," Vance retorted with a huge grin, basking in the glory of one-upping his old persnickety principal.

Mr. Baumfelder's face grew two shades redder before he stepped back inside the house and slammed the door without another word.

"Dude," Ezra said. "That was epic."

Vance grinned and shrugged. "I always hated that motherfucker."

"And what's all this?" Ezra said, gesturing toward the menagerie of abstract animal images on Vance's arms. "You look like the side of a box car after spending the night in a Detroit train station."

Vance smiled. "These are my totem spirits," he said. "They've

325

been with me through a lot of shit."

"And what about that?" Giles asked, gesturing toward the band on Vance's right ring finger. "You got married in some sort of counterculture ceremony that requires you wearing the wedding band on the opposite hand?"

Vance scoffed. "You know better than that. I had this made years ago out of the leash ring on Bruce's old collar."

"Awww, that's so cool," Ezra said.

"Yeah man, I love that you did that," Giles added.

"You sure your mom doesn't mind hosting all three of us?" Vance asked, gesturing at the house.

"Yeah, I mean no, she's actually excited about it," Ezra replied. "She made a sweet dough pie and she's cooking a seafood gumbo because she figures you haven't had any good Cajun food in forever."

"Your mom bakes and cooks now?" Vance asked, surprised.

Ezra shrugged and smiled. "Go figure."

After having dinner with Ezra's mother and then helping to clean up, the trio made a campfire in the backyard in the same spot where they used to camp out as kids. They sat around the fire in old aluminum-framed lawn chairs, drinking, talking and teasing each other late into the night, their old dynamics virtually unchanged notwithstanding that more than twenty years separated their reunion from the last time they were all together.

When Vance expressed an interest in hanging around for a week or so after the funeral before returning to Florida, Ezra said he was more than welcome to stay with him as long as he wanted. A week turned to two and two weeks to three. Then one morning Ezra found a note from Vance on the kitchen table. He had left in the middle of the night to race back to the Keys to make storm preparations at his houseboat in anticipation of Tropical Storm Bonnie.

Over the weeks and months that followed their joyous albeit short-lived reunion, Vance seemed to disappear into the ether once again, not answering his telephone or returning calls or texts. When Ezra proposed to Giles that they take a trip to the Keys to surprise Vance with a visit, they realized that he had never shared his address, and they were unable to confirm one online.

"Well," Giles said, "I'm sure we'll see him again when his dad kicks the bucket. You know he won't pass up the opportunity to piss on his grave."

"Or dance on it," Ezra proffered.

"Or both," Giles said, chuckling.

"Well, if he does both, let's hope he dances first."

"Definitely."

Ezra's phone began to vibrate. "Well, speak of the devil," he said when he answered the phone. After a brief conversation, for most of which Ezra did the listening, he hung up and smiled. "Let's go," he said.

"Was that Vance?"

"Yup."

"Really? What's up?"

"He sold his houseboat in Florida and bought another one at Butte LaRose. He wants us to come see it."

"Are you serious?"

Ezra shrugged. "That's what the man said."

"Well, I'll be a monkey's uncle," Giles said as he followed Ezra to his car. "By the way, do you know the origin of that phrase?"

"No, and I'm really not interested," Ezra replied.

"It was first used as a sarcastic—"

"*Not interested!*" Ezra sang out in a long, poorly vocalized operatic response, which he often did when discouraging Giles from offering word or phrase origin trivia.

"—by creationists when they—"

"NOT IN . . . TER . . . ES . . . TEEEEEEEEED," Ezra sung out at the top of his lungs when Giles persisted, holding the *-ed* note as long as his lungs would allow.

"—when they wanted to—"

Ezra quickly inhaled and sang ". . . IN THE SLIGH . . .TEEEEEEEEST!"

"—make fun of evolutionists," Giles blurted out, giggling triumphantly.

When they turned into the driveway leading to the pier where Vance's new—or at least new to him— houseboat was moored, a small, dusty Datsun passed them coming from the opposition direction. A young female was behind the wheel donning large frame sunglasses and mussed hair. She gave them a cursory wave as she went by.

"Who was the chick in the old rice-burner?" Ezra asked when Vance stepped out onto the pier to greet them.

Vance answered with a coy smile.

"Jesus man," Giles said, appalled. "She barely looked sixteen,"

"Old enough to bleed, old enough to breed," Vance replied.

"Please tell me you're not fucking a minor," Ezra said, glaring at Vance disapprovingly.

Vance scoffed. "Don't be stupid."

"Because you know I don't handle criminal cases," Ezra added.

"Whatever," Vance said, grinning and shaking his head. "Just take your shoes off before you come in."

"Take our shoes off? What is this, a floating dojo?" Ezra asked.

CHAPTER 46

When the elevator doors opened, Ezra was using his smart phone to reply to a work email and made no attempt to enter. A small, elderly man with smiling eyes and wearing an Iberiabank maintenance uniform stood inside waiting patiently. "You coming up, neg?" he said in a thick, Cajun French accent.

"Oh sorry, yes, thank you," Ezra said apologetically.

"Where to?" the old man asked.

"I'm dropping something off for someone in the Knowles Financial Group. I think it's on the fifth floor?"

"The fi't floor it is, then," the little man said before pressing the corresponding button.

The man's inability to pronounce the "th" consonant blend reminded him of his paternal grandparents whose first language was Cajun French. When they spoke English, the "th" sound was sometimes replaced with a "t" sound and in other words with a "d" sound, there being no rhyme or reason as to which. For example, when the weather was getting bad, a *t'under* storm was coming. Articles and pronouns such as *the, this and them* were *da, dis* and *dat*. His cousin *Elizabeth* was *Elizabet'* or *Bet'*.

"*Merci*," Ezra said with a warm smile.

Hearing Ezra respond in French caused the old man's expression to brighten. "*Ah, tu parler Cadjins Francais?*"[4]

Ezra shook his head, blushing. "*A petite, a très peu.*[5] I know some phrases and quite a few words, but I'm nowhere close to being fluent,

---

[4] Ah, you speak Cajun French?
[5] A little. Not very much.

unfortunately."

The old man smiled and then turned to watch the elevator doors close. The car jerked upward, stopped briefly and then jerked again before easing into a smooth, upward motion. "I work in dis building," he said. "It does dis all da time, all da time, all da time. I tell my boss to call the technician to fix it, but dey tight, tight wit' da money. Dey don't do nothing to fix nothin' 'til it breaks all da way."

Ezra smiled, regarding the old Cajun with mild amusement. Judging from the deep wrinkles and assortment of liver spots on his face, Ezra surmised that he well past traditional retirement age. "How long have you worked in this building?" he asked.

"*Mais*," the old Cajun said, "I got here wit' da bricks."

Ezra considered the age of the structure and chuckled. "That's a long time."

"*Oui.*"

"Your accent sounds familiar. I'm guessing you're from either Evangeline Parish or St. Martin Parish. Maybe Mamou or Cecilia?"

The old man smiled. "Close. I'm from Chataignier," he said. "Lived dere my whole life."

"Chataignier?" Ezra replied with a mild expression of surprise as the elevator began to slow down in anticipation of reaching the fifth floor. "So, you commute an hour each way for work in Lafayette?"

The old man scoffed. "Commute shit," he said as the elevator door opened, "I drive back and fort', me."

Ezra resisted the urge to laugh as he was unsure of whether the old Cajun intended his response to be humorous. "Well, this is me. *Bonne soirée, mon ami,*"[6] he said to the old man as he stepped out into the hallway.

---

[6] Good evening, my friend.

"*Bonne soirée, mon frère,*"[7] replied, the man with a warm smile, it being obvious that being able to converse with someone in Cajun French, even if it was just at a very basic level, had made his day.

Ezra found the office he was looking for, but it was half past five and the receptionist was already gone for the day. He wrote a note on the package, left it on the counter and then found his way back to the elevator where an attractive, light-skinned African American woman was waiting.

"Man, come five o'clock it's a ghost town in this old building," he said, trying to be friendly.

The woman managed a faint smile but did not otherwise reply. When the elevator car returned and the doors opened, Ezra followed her in. "Going to the first floor, I presume?" she asked.

"Yes, thank you," Ezra answered.

The woman hit the button and they watched the doors close. The car bucked—more roughly than it had on the way up—before continuing its descent. Ezra glanced at the woman out of the corner of his eye and then turned to face her. "I'm sorry," he said. "But I think I might know you from somewhere."

The woman turned toward Ezra and regarded him for a moment. "Yeah, you look vaguely familiar, too. Are you from Iris, by chance?"

Ezra's face lit up slightly and then he knitted his brow, trying to place the woman. "I am."

"I lived there until the third grade, before we moved to California. I actually just moved back to Louisiana a couple of months ago, so I figured that might be the connection."

Ezra was still unable to place the woman. "What year did you graduate from high school?" he asked, not wanting to be rude by asking a

---

[7] Good evening, my brother.

woman her age directly.

"Class of '89."

"Okay, I was class of '87. My name's Ezra Brasseaux," he said extending his hand.

The woman smiled and gently took Ezra's hand. "Yeah, you probably knew my sister, Deidra. She was in your—"

Suddenly, the elevator car jerked and started again before halting abruptly. Ezra instinctively grabbed the handrail as the woman grabbed his other arm to prevent herself from falling to the floor.

"Are you alright?" asked Ezra.

"Yeah, I'm fine," the woman said. Realizing that she was still holding Ezra's arm, she blushed and released it.

When the car did not move and the doors did not open, Ezra hit the button for the first floor again, but there was no response. He tried all the other buttons to no avail. "Nothing's working," he said, stating the obvious. "Sounds like the emergency brake kicked in for some reason."

"Great," the woman muttered with annoyance.

Ezra picked up the emergency phone and hit the button several times. "It's dead," he said. He patted his pants to feel for his cell phone. "Dammit," he said. "I left my phone in the car. Do you have yours?"

The woman rifled through her purse and pulled out her phone. "No bars," she said. She lifted it higher and moved about the car to find a signal. "Nothing," she said.

They exchanged nervous smiles and then, in a half-panic, the woman began punching the elevator buttons again, one at a time, harder and harder. When there was no response, she began screaming for help and pounding on the doors of the elevator with the heels of her hands until the pain caused her to stop. "Shit!" she yelled.

"Let me try this," Ezra said as he wedged his fingers between the doors and strained to separate them. The doors moved slightly, just enough to see the inside of the elevator shaft. He released the doors and stepped back. "We didn't reach the bottom," he said. "I'm guessing we're somewhere between the second and third floors."

"Lovely," the woman replied sarcastically.

Ezra took out his keys and used the blade to tap loudly on the steel doors. He suggested that the woman take one of her shoes off and do the same with the heel. They tapped five times and then yelled "help" in unison, waited several seconds for a response and when there was none repeated the process. After a few minutes, they took a short break and then tried again, though they received no return signals.

"Somebody surely heard us, right?" the woman asked, desperately.

"I would hope so," Ezra said, trying to offer some assurance as he looked at his watch. "It's well after five, but hopefully that old maintenance man is still around."

They waited a few minutes and then repeated the distress signals. There was still no response.

"Might as well get comfortable," Ezra suggested as he lowered himself down to sit on the floor of the elevator car.

The expression on the woman's face revealed that she was not ready to give up just yet. "What about going through the top?" she suggested as they examined the ceiling tiles.

Ezra chuckled, "You watch too many movies," he said.

"Well, then, what are we going to do?"

"We just have to wait until they come for us I guess," Ezra said in a defeated tone. "There's nothing else we can do."

The woman was still not mentally prepared to surrender to the situation. For a moment, she considered allowing Ezra to lift her up so that she could go through the elevator car ceiling, but she immediately dismissed the idea, remembering that Ezra had hit all of the buttons and afraid that even if she succeeded in getting outside onto the roof of the car, the elevator might start again, but with her on the outside, maybe crushing her against the top of the elevator shaft.

"What happens when we need to pee?" the woman inquired.

Ezra chuckled and gestured to the Prada handbag at the woman's side. "I guess we can use that."

The woman scoffed with indignation. "Boy, please! I paid over two thousand dollars for this bag, and it's only a couple of months old."

"What's our alternative? If we pee on the floor, it will spread all over. At least if we do it in your purse, it's contained."

"Nope. If it comes to that, we can use your shoes," she said, pointing with her chin to Ezra's black leather wingtips. "We each get a shoe."

Ezra laughed. "Well, let's hope someone lets us out before we get to that point."

"Yes, please, Jesus."

"By the way, if I'm going to agree to let someone urinate in my shoe, I should probably know her name."

The woman chuckled. "Celee. Celee Auzenne."

"Okay," Ezra said, "yeah, Deidra Auzenne, your sister, I remember her, actually."

Celee nodded and smiled.

"In fact, it's funny, you know what I remember most about Deidra?"

"What?"

"She ate bananas using a fork. The only other person I've ever seen do that is my best friend, Giles."

Celee let out an ambiguous chuckle as if there was a story behind why her sister ate bananas that way, though she did not share it. "Do you work here?" she asked.

"No, I was actually just dropping off a copy of the manuscript of my novel to a friend who offered to read it and give me some feedback."

"You're a writer?"

"Well, I'm actually an attorney. Writing is just a hobby."

"Really? You trying to be the next John Grisham?"

Ezra shook his head. "Nah, I'll be very, very lucky to get it published at all. I'll probably self-publish."

Celee regarded Ezra, trying to size him up. "Was your daddy a lawyer?"

"Nope," Ezra said.

Celee sensed a subtle change in Ezra's expression when she mentioned his father. "What does your daddy do?" she asked.

Ezra sighed as if he was not particularly keen on discussing his father. "Well, when I was young, he was in law enforcement, but frankly I don't know what he's doing now. He left when I was in middle school."

"Oh," Celee said, "I didn't mean to—"

"—nah, it's fine," Ezra replied, trying to downplay the awkwardness. "But, what about you?" he asked, obviously eager to change the subject. "What do you do?"

Celee smiled. "A good lawyer ought to be able to read people," she said. "Guess."

"Well, I'm a very mediocre lawyer and an even worse guesser," Ezra said.

"I doubt that." Celee replied. "I'll give you three chances."

Ezra smiled. "I really, really suck at this."

"Give it a shot."

336

"Nurse?"

"No."

"CPA?"

"Hell no."

"Yoga instructor?"

Celee burst into laughter. "You really do suck at this," she said.

"I told you," Ezra said with a grin. "So, what do you do?"

"College professor. I just accepted a position at UL, teaching psychology."

"Very impressive. So, is it *Dr.* Auzenne?"

Celee smiled. "Not yet, but soon. I'll be finished with my doctoral work in a few months."

"Nice," Ezra said.

"A lot of people think that psychology is a bunch of quackery," Celee said, as if fishing for Ezra's thoughts on the subject.

"Yeah, well, a lot of people think all lawyers are shysters."

Celee grinned. "Have you ever tried therapy?" Celee inquired.

Ezra nodded. "My mom made me go see a counselor when I was in high school when she thought I was spiraling downward, you know, because of my dad leaving us."

"Did it help?"

Ezra chuckled. "It helped me to feel better about myself for a little while by teaching me to place blame on others for my own shitty behavior," Ezra said. "No offense to your industry."

Celee smiled. "None taken."

"So, let's see how good *you* are. I've got a couple of recurring dreams you can interpret."

"Oh, I'm not a clinical psychotherapist."

"Well, give it your best shot anyway."

337

Celee smiled. "Okay."

"The first one is that I'm young—like three or four years old, and this little boy—his name is David—and it's one of those weird dream things where, you know, I know him but I don't know how I know him, and he keeps calling for me to come with him, that he wants to show me something, and we're running through these fields and along these levees with water for as far as you can see on both sides. I get close to him but I never catch up to him. I never get to see what he's trying to show me."

"Hmmm," Celee said. "That's an interesting one. There could be several things going on with that one. The little boy, David, is not someone in your life?"

"Negative."

"That's is a curious manifestation. Did you lose a sibling or a close companion early in your childhood?"

"No. I'm an only child and I haven't lost any friends, childhood or otherwise."

"Okay. Well, do you know if maybe you were a twin and that the other twin didn't make it all the way through the pregnancy?"

"Nope. I would have been told if I was a twin. My mom is not the type to hold back on stuff like that."

Celee paused to think for a moment, then said, "This is going to sound a bit out there, but we're just brainstorming, right?"

"Sure."

"So, I don't know if you've ever studied Jung or believe in the collective consciousness, but it could be coming from that, like maybe you had a half-brother on your father's side, you know, after he left, or maybe a sibling that was miscarried or—you know, something like that, and they're trying to connect with you."

Ezra nodded reflectively. He had always assumed that his father had probably started another family in Texas but never gave much thought to whether he might have half-siblings and certainly had no desire to connect with them if he did. "Do you believe in the collective consciousness?"

Celee shrugged. "I'm not sure. When it comes to the psychological world, I think I know just enough to doubt nothing."

Ezra smiled. "I like that. I might use it."

"What's the other dream?" Celee asked.

"So, this one is really weird. I'm like some kind of fish-person thing—not a merman exactly—I'm more fish than man, and I'm swimming in a really huge school with millions of other fish-people just like me, and we are moving in a huge circle and every fish-person, including me, is biting and eating the tail of the fish-person in front of him until the school gets smaller and smaller until I realize I'm the only fish left, biting my own tail, and I've got it halfway eaten off when I realize it's me, and I wake up."

Celee's face twisted in curious amusement.

"That's it. What do you think it means?"

"What do you think it means?" Celee asked.

Ezra shrugged. "That I'm chasing my own tail?"

"Well, but you're doing more than that, right? You're consuming others and in the process consuming yourself. It sounds like a manifestation of your awareness of some kind of self-destructive behavior," Celee said.

"Hmm," Ezra said, contemplatively.

"So, what type of law do you practice?" Celee asked.

"Mainly maritime defense for big oil and gas companies, some big chemical companies, too. I also do some coverage and defense work for insurance companies."

"Ah," Celee said. "So maybe your dream is a subconscious metaphor for doing legal work to protect and fortify big business whose primary means of making huge profits is the perpetuation of monetary exploitation of the masses, of which, ultimately, you are a part."

Ezra's face fell. He felt simultaneously impressed and depressed. He regarded Celee in silence for a moment. "Damn," he said. "You're good."

Celee smiled bashfully.

Desirous of lightening the conversation, Ezra said, "Anybody ever told you that you have a *doppelganger*?"

"No."

"That's kind'a my gift—identifying people's *doppelgangers*."

"So, who's mine?"

"Zoe Saldana."

Celee snorted and shook her head. "The actress from *Avatar*? I wish! I thought you were supposed to be good at this?"

"I am."

"Okay, whatever," Celee said, blushing. "Who's yours?"

"You're not allowed to name your own *doppelganger*. That's the rule," Ezra said. "Who do you think it is?"

"Hmm," Celee said, as she scrutinized Ezra's facial features. "I don't know. Maybe—I don't know his real name—the guy who played Potsie on *Happy Days*, but with freckles."

Ezra grimaced and chuckled. "You suck."

Celee giggled. "Well, it's true."

"I know," Ezra admitted. "I've actually gotten that before."

"Or maybe Paul Rudd, but with freckles. You have that same goofy handsomeness about you."

It was Ezra's turn to blush. "Well," he said, "thank you, I guess. I hadn't heard that one before."

Celee shrugged as if to indicate that she had given it her best shot.

"So have you kept up with anyone from Iris?"

"Not really," Celee said. "I mean, I never had many friends *in* Iris proper. We were one of the few Creole families that lived in town. I didn't really fit in well with the black kids because I was so light skinned, and I didn't really fit in with the whites because I was black. Most of my people lived in Swords and Frilot Cove and around those areas, and most of them went to school in Plaisance or Lawtell."

Ezra nodded. "Yeah, I knew a few people from those communities. Some Papillions, some Coutees, some Delahoussayes."

Celee nodded. "Yeah, those of some of my cousins."

"Yeah?"

"Yep." Celee gestured toward Ezra's left hand. "I don't see a ring," she said. "You divorced? Or you never got married?"

"Never married," Ezra answered as he regarded his naked ring finger, trying to mask his regret.

"A charming, nice-looking guy like you, how come?"

Ezra blushed again. "I don't know. I was really head over heels for my high school sweetheart and ultimately screwed that up, and I've just never felt like that about anyone else. What about you—ever been married?"

"Not yet," Celee said. "I've been asked five times but I'm still waiting on my prince charming."

"Five proposals?" Ezra echoed, impressed.

Celee laughed. "Yep, though in full disclosure, three of them were made by the same fool."

CHAPTER 47

When Celee heard her stomach growl, she began digging through her purse and found a chocolate flavored protein bar. She held it up for Ezra to see. "This is all I've got. You want half?"

"Can't, but thanks," Ezra said. "I'm allergic to chocolate."

"Allergic to chocolate? I've never heard of such a thing," Celee said as she unwrapped the bar and bit off a piece.

"It's technically an allergy to the proteins in the cocoa beans," Ezra said. "And it's very rare. Lucky me."

"What about chocolate women," Celee asked while still chewing, covering her mouth with her free hand, "are you allergic to them, too?"

Ezra chuckled. "I don't think so."

"So, you've never gone out with a black girl?"

Ezra considered the question for a moment and then replied, "Actually, I have."

A skeptical expression appeared on Celee's face. "You had to think about it?"

"Well, I went out with this light-skinned black gal a while back, but I didn't find out that she was black until after the fact. So, I'm not sure I get credit for that one."

"So, did you see her again after you found out?"

"No."

Celee glowered at Ezra disapprovingly.

"But it had absolutely nothing to do with her being black, I swear," he said defensively.

Celee smirked skeptically.

"What about you? Have you ever dated a white guy?"

"Once," answered Celee. "Travis Ambrose was his name." When she said the boy's name, she noticed a subtle reaction in Ezra's expression. "What?" she asked. "You don't know him. That was in California."

Ezra shook his head. "No, I didn't think I knew him. My middle school principal's name was Mr. Ambrose. I hadn't thought about him in a long time."

Something about Ezra's body language told Celee that there was more to the story. "What about 'em, this Mr. Ambrose?"

"Nothing," Ezra said, unconvincingly.

"Nuh-uh," Celee replied. "I can tell you're lying. Tell me," she insisted.

"It's nothing, really."

Celee glared at Ezra, making it clear that she was not going to relent. When their eyes met, he blushed. "I'm waiting," she said.

Ezra sighed and regarded Celee for a moment. "You would think really low of me," he said.

Celee shrugged. "I might. I might not. If I do, you'll just deal with it. So, tell me."

"I really don't want to," Ezra said sincerely.

"Tell me," Celee insisted.

"Okay," he said fretfully before letting out a deep sigh.

Celee smiled triumphantly.

Ezra sighed and crossed his legs to get more comfortable. "So when I was in the seventh grade, I was going out with this girl named Monique Landry. After a couple of months, she dumps me to go out with an eighth grader, and I'm pissed about it. Then one of the girls in my class tells me that us breaking up was really a blessing in disguise because she heard that Monique's family is part black. Of course, this is the mid-1970s, and a white person being outed for being part black was scandalous. So, I

343

end up telling a few of my friends about Monique being part black, and we thought it would be funny to draw pictures of Monique as a girl that had white features on one half of her face and exaggerated black features and dark skin on the other side."

Ezra paused to judge Celee's reaction.

"Go on," Celee said with a stoic countenance.

"Of course, no one had any intention of showing her the pictures."

"That was very thoughtful of you," Celee replied with thinly veiled sarcasm.

"Well after class, a couple of my classmates dug my drawing and my friend Vance's drawing out of the trash and without us knowing, gave the drawings to Monique."

"Oh, snap!"

"Yeah. And of course she was very upset. She ends up showing the pictures to her mother who was furious. Her mom not only calls our parents to tell them what we did, but she also takes the pictures to school and complains to the principal."

"Mr. Ambrose," Celee said.

"Yes. So, Vance and I got called out of class to go to Mr. Ambrose's office. In front of Monique and her irate mother, Mr. Ambrose shows us the pictures that were pulled from the trash and asks us if we had drawn them. When we admitted that we did, he proceeded to berate us and makes us apologize to Monique and her mother. And we had to pick up trash after school every day for a week."

Celee turns her head slightly and regards Ezra with a perplexed look. "I'm not getting it. It's like this story is missing a punch line," she said.

"Well, I wasn't finished. The punch line," Ezra said then paused and sighed, "the punch line is that Mr. Ambrose was black."

Celee's eyes widened and she covered her mouth. "Are you serious?"

Ezra nodded.

"So, this white woman is expressing her outrage and indignation about rumors of her family having black ancestry . . . to a black man?"

"Yes," Ezra said.

"Wow."

"I know. I felt so bad for Mr. Ambrose. He was really a nice man."

"Jesus. I mean yeah, you were definitely some little shitheads, but you were kids. It's just really hard to imagine how a full-grown woman could be so ignorant and insensitive," Celee said, shaking her head.

Ezra nodded in agreement.

They sat for a while before anyone spoke again. It was Celee who finally broke the silence. "So," she said, trying to mask her grin, "did you eventually outgrow your racist ways?"

Ezra blushed with embarrassment. He knew that Celee was asking in jest—at least partially—but did not know how to respond. "I sure hope so," he finally said.

"I'm just giving you a hard time," Celee said. "I'm not judging you. If there's anything that I've learned from living in the South and in California is that southern blacks sow a lot of what they reap when it comes to prejudice. While I hate to admit it and I'm not saying that true racism is at all justified—because it's not—I know that black culture is just different down here in a lot of ways."

Ezra did not know how to respond and so didn't.

Celee's face softened as a melancholy smile formed on her face. "You wanna know why you saw my sister ate bananas with a fork?"

Ezra regarded Celee curiously but did not reply.

345

"It was because our mother made us. You know why?"

Ezra shook his head.

"So as not to give white folks cause to see us as monkeys."

Ezra felt all of the color drain from his face. He was dumbstruck. "That's really awful," he finally said, "I mean, not that she made y'all do that, but because she felt she had to in order to protect you."

Celee nodded. "Yeah, it's pretty fucked up."

Ezra nodded in agreement.

"Why do you think your friend—the one that ate bananas with a fork—why do you think he ate them that way?"

Ezra paused to ponder the question. "I've never really thought about it much. I guess I just assumed that's the way he was taught, or maybe it's something he just started for no particular reason on his own. He's a little quirky."

Celee furrowed her eyebrows and turned up the corner of her mouth. "Was he effeminate?" she asked.

Again Ezra did not answer right away, taking time to consider the question. "Not blatantly, but I guess you could make that argument. Why?"

"So maybe he was afraid his peers would tease him about the banana being phallic and that he was fantasizing about giving someone a blowjob if he ate one the conventional way?"

"Hmm," Ezra said. "That's an interesting theory. Maybe."

"Is he gay?"

Ezra shook his head and shrugged his shoulders. "I don't think so, but I'm not entirely sure. I've always kind'a wondered in the back of my head, but if he is, he's never come out."

"Would it matter to you?"

"Not in the slightest. Maybe when I was twelve, you know, but

346

no, not even a little bit."

CHAPTER 48

After closing her eyes for several minutes without being able to fall asleep, Celee sighed. "I'm getting hot. You?"

"I'm okay," Ezra replied.

"So, give me the Cliff's Notes on your novel," Celee said. "What's it about?"

Ezra chuckled. "You don't want to know."

"What you talkin' 'bout, Willis!?" Celee replied, stealing a line from Arnold Jackson's character, Arnold Drummond, on *Different Strokes.*

"Trust me."

"Well," Celee said, straightening her posture and shifting her legs to get more comfortable, "now you have to tell me."

"Well," Ezra said, "if you must know, at its core, my novel is about racism."

Celee scoffed and laughed. "Are you serious?" she said.

"I know, right?"

"So what's the plot? I mean, don't spoil it. Maybe I'll want to read it someday, so just give me the dust jacket summary."

"A pretty white teenage girl is raped by two black men in a small Louisiana town. It's told from the perspective of a white boy who, in middle school when the rape occurred, finds himself inextricably connected to the post-rape narrative."

Celee knitted her brow. "It's about the rape rumor in Iris?" she asked.

"Rumor?" Ezra asked, furrowing his brow. "It wasn't just a rumor."

"Well, I mean, was it ever proven that she was raped? Or that she was raped by black men?"

Ezra scoffed. "Maybe not in a court of law, but that's not uncommon, especially in rape cases when the victim doesn't want everything outed in a courtroom."

"Well, we had already moved when that happened, but we heard about it from relatives. I can tell you that the people in Iris' black community were very skeptical."

Ezra smiled, almost condescendingly. "Why do you think a pretty, popular white girl with everything going for her would lie about getting gang-raped by black men? It just wouldn't make any sense."

Celee smirked. "I don't know. Still, no matter how perfect their lives appear on the outside, everybody's got issues, and people lie about all kinds of things for all kinds of reasons."

Ezra nodded. "I guess, but it's just really difficult to imagine in this context."

"Okay, well anyway, I've decided that I definitely want to read your book. If it's about race and racism, I might have to write my own book just to correct all the stupid shit in yours."

Ezra laughed. "Okay."

Celee nodded. "How long have you been writing, you know, in general?"

"Since middle school, I guess. I won a short story contest when I was in the seventh grade and I've been writing ever since."

Celee nodded. "What was your award-winning short story about?"

Ezra laughed nostalgically and looked up toward the ceiling as if he were reviewing a mental image of the cover page. "It was about this little boy who discovered time travel after his socks kept disappearing in the washing machine. He developed a theory that when the wet clothes inside the machine caused the machine to become unbalanced, it led to the wash tube spinning and wobbling in a certain way that caused a fissure in time, and that's where the missing socks were going. So, he used some of his dad's tools to turn the washing machine into a time machine and traveled back in time to 65,000,000 B.C., shortly before dinosaurs were made extinct. He finds an unguarded nest and takes a couple of eggs back with him to present time."

"That's pretty creative. I like it," Celee said. "Did he incubate the eggs? Did they hatch?"

Ezra chuckled. "The short story ended when he returned with the eggs, leaving it to the reader's imagination as to what was to come. But it's funny that you ask that because when I first got the urge to write a novel and was contemplating what I would write about, I actually gave some thought to turning my old short story into a novel and expanding on it to detail what happened when he got back, you know, the havoc the hatched dinosaurs created on modern earth, but—"

"But Michael Crichton stole your thunder with *Jurassic Park*."

"Yes he did," Ezra said, chuckling.

"That bastard," Celee teased.

Ezra nodded.

"What's the most recent thing you've finished, I mean, other than the rape-race novel?"

"Another short story," Ezra answered.

"About?"

Ezra chuckled. "It's a little cheesy."

"I think I can decide if it's cheesy or not."

Ezra sighed.

"What?" Celee scolded. "You've got something else to do?"

"Well, it's called *The Tragic X*. It's kind of a modern *Romeo & Juliet* with a twist and sans the fatalities. It's about this young boy who lives in a small house with his mother on a small Greek island. He's befriended by a retired journalist who lives next door and likes to sit on the sidewalk every morning, drinking coffee and having great conversations about life and love and philosophy. When the old man dies, he leaves the boy his old vintage typewriter. It becomes his most prized possession and inspires him to start writing, only the "x" key on the typewriter doesn't work, and the boy's mother can't afford to get it fixed.

"Meanwhile, another family with a beautiful young girl moves in next door. Her name is Xandra—which is a very common name for girls in Greece. They become close friends, and of course, he falls madly in love with her, though he doesn't have the courage to tell her how he feels. Instead, he bangs on the typewriter all night writing love poems that trumpet his love for her, but of course he never gives any of them to her because he is too bashful.

"Unbeknownst to him, she has fallen madly in love with him too, but she also, is too timid to say anything. One day while the boy is out working with his father, the girl, curious about all the tap-tap-tapping coming from the boy's window at all hours of the night, sneaks into his room to see what he is writing about and finds the loves poems. Only, because the "x" key on the typewriter is broken, she assumes them to be about another girl named Andra, which unfortunately for our characters, also happens to be a common Greek name for a girl."

"Oh, no!" Celee exclaimed.

"Anyway, in her despair, she decides to take her own life. She starts to type a suicide note using his old typewriter. But when she tries to type out her name, she notices that the "X" key does not work and realizes that all of the poems were in fact written about her."

Celee smirked.

"What? I told you it was cheesy."

"No, it's very clever," Celee said.

"But?"

"But it's all about perspective. A white girl hears that story and is all *awwww, that's so sweet!* A black girl hears that story and is like *suicide over some teenage crush? Boy, please!*"

Ezra chuckled and shrugged. "If you say so."

When Celee raised her arms in the air to stretch, Ezra noticed a tattoo on the inside of her bicep. "Tell me about your body art," he said, gesturing toward her left arm.

Celee turned her arm so that she could see the tattoo better. "It's the tree of life. It symbolizes our connectedness to everything around us, to the earth, to the universe, to each other."

"I like it," Ezra replied. "Do you have any others?"

Celee was about to respond when the elevator jerked and they felt it moving downward. They both exclaimed excitedly and braced against the walls, praying for the elevator car to reach the bottom without stopping again. As soon as the doors opened, they both rushed out past the uniformed elevator technician and the old maintenance man in search of the nearest restrooms.

"I'm suing!" Celee yelled over her shoulder at the technician as she followed Ezra around the corner in a full sprint. When Ezra did not reply, she said huffing, "I know how white people think black people are all sue-happy. That was a joke."

"Yeah, it was a funny one," Ezra said sarcastically as he hurriedly pushed open the door to the men's restroom and raced inside.

CHAPTER 49

Upon arriving at his office early the next morning, Ezra threw his keys into the small ceramic bowl on his desk and proceeded to the kitchen to get a cup of coffee. After filling his mug, he retraced his steps back to his office and was just getting settled when he heard a light knock at the door.

"Come in."

His secretary, a mousy brunette with narrow-set eyes, poked her head into his office. "Good morning," she said.

"Good morning Vo," Ezra replied. "What are you doing here on Saturday?"

"I'm going to miss most of Monday to bring Natalee and Cristina to the doctor in New Orleans. I'm making up that time."

"Everything okay?"

"Yeah, routine stuff for their Crohn's."

"Okay."

"Oh," she said, pointing at a short stack of records sitting in the middle of his desk, "those are the records we received from Savoy Memorial in Mamou in response to our subpoena in the Kelli Miller auto accident case. They came in yesterday afternoon after you left. I figured you would want to take a look at them before the depositions next week."

"*Merci.*"

"Oh, and Mr. Jumel was looking for you. He said you weren't answering your cell yesterday evening."

"Yeah, I was stuck in an elevator downtown for a couple of hours."

353

"Oh my God, really?"

"Yeah."

"Oh God, I would have totally freaked out. I get so claustrophobic."

Ezra smiled and then turned to his computer screen to start working.

"Oh, and by the way," Vo added, "I'm not sure those are the right medical records for *our* Kelli Miller. The date of birth is correct, but spelling of the names doesn't match exactly. It could be a typo, I guess."

"Okay, I'll take a look," Ezra replied. "Thanks."

After his secretary closed the door, Ezra began working on an appellate brief that was due the following week. By noon, he had a rough draft hammered out and decided to call it a day.

When he woke early on Sunday and could not fall back to sleep, he got dressed, made some coffee and drove back to his office to prepare for the depositions in the Kelli Miller case. After settling into his leather chair, he regarded the medical records on his desk, estimated the time it would take him to thoroughly review them and quickly typed a billing entry into the computer.

After sliding on his reading glasses, he read the certification page: *The attached are a photocopy of the records of Kelly Mueller, DOB 11/14/60, in custody of Savoy Memorial Hospital, maintained in the ordinary course of business.* Ezra removed his glasses, rubbed his eyes, put his glasses back on and read the name again. Still not trusting his eyes, he took a sip of coffee and read the name a third time. *Kelly Mueller.* "What the hell?" he asked the portrait of Cicero hanging on his wall.

He turned to the first page of the records but then paused for a moment. He knew that he had an ethical duty to *not* read confidential medical records sent to him in error—that to do so would constitute a serious breach of the patient's privacy rights. But this was too big of a coincidence, he told himself. For years he had been working on a novel inspired by the rape of a Kelly Mueller, and now the medical records of a Kelly Mueller, by pure happenstance, had made their way to his desk? This was providence, he rationalized, and providence would certainly supersedes any privacy rights or rules of professional responsibility created by man. And regardless, unless he read further he would not be able to rule out the possibility that maybe it was a typo on the certification page. Maybe these were actually the records of his plaintiff, *Kelli Miller*. And the only way to be absolutely sure of that was to read on.

Ezra set the certification aside and perused the admissions page from top to bottom. *Kelly Mueller,* spelled the same way each time, appeared on the document in three different places. He began thumbing through the rest of the records. Every reference to the patient's name was *Kelly Mueller.* There was no reference to a *Kelli Miller.*

He knew he should stop reading but could not resist. He scanned the billing information, searching for the patient's billing address. He found an Iris, Louisiana post office box. "Holy shit," he muttered to himself. He was certain that there were no other Kelly Muellers from Iris. The chances of this being a different Kelly Mueller were virtually nil. *Why was she at a hospital in Mamou, twenty miles away, when there's a hospital in Iris?* he thought.

He next checked the date of admission: September 3, 1976. Using the patient's date of birth, he did a quick calculation in his head. She would have been nearly 16 years old at the time of the visit. "Son of a bitch," he said to himself. It was *the* Kelly Mueller. It had to be.

Ezra leaned forward in his chair, took another sip of his coffee and began to peruse the records in greater detail. He found the nursing triage entry. The patient had arrived at the emergency room accompanied by her mother at 10:55 p.m. The Chief Complaint was noted as *Sexual Assault/request for D&C*. Ezra instinctively covered his mouth with his hand as if to stop himself from exclaiming uncontrollably.

Adrenaline pumping through his veins, Ezra looked around the room at nothing and took a deep breath. "Holy shit," he muttered in an exclamatory whisper. "Holy fucking shit!" he repeated, as he stood up and paced around the room. These were not just medical records for Kelly Mueller. These were the medical records from when she was raped. "Oh my God!" Ezra whispered to himself as he plopped back down into his leather chair and excitedly spun himself around like a sugar-charged kid spinning on a swiveling bar stool.

He stopped, took a deep breath and began to read again. The next several pages consisted of what appeared to be standard medical literature detailing the procedure and risks associated with both general anesthesia and a D&C procedure. *Dilation and curettage entails the insertion of progressively larger metal rods in the cervix until the desired dilation is reached followed by the insertion of a metal loop used to scrape the pregnancy from the uterine wall,* he read, wincing at the images in his head. He continued flipping through the records until he found a report detailing Kelly Mueller's physical examination by the attending ER physician.

The doctor noted *no visible signs of trauma* but that the examination was *thwarted by the patient's refusal to disrobe and/or submit to a vaginal inspection.* There was an entry indicating that a social worker consult was ordered. Ezra thumbed through the rest of the pages and could find no record of a D&C having been performed.

Toward the bottom of the stack of medical records, he found a

356

handwritten narrative on a Social Work Consultation Form. He read the short consultation note to himself out loud:

> *Pt admitted to ER for D&C secondary to reported sexual assault. SW consult ordered when Pt. refused vaginal exam. In private consultation (mother not present), Pt admitted that there was no sexual assault and affirmed pregnancy for boyfriend. Pt stated she does not want parents to know she was sexually active and therefore told parents she was raped because she believed that was the only way they would allow her to terminate pregnancy. Pt states that upon arriving at ER, she had a change of heart and no longer wishes to proceed with D&C. After encouragement was offered, Pt requested the undersigned's assistance in relating this information to her mother. Mother was supportive and escorted Pt from ER.*
>
> *-Maria Soileau, L.C.S.W. (11:48 p.m.)*

Ezra removed his reading glasses and laid them on the stack of documents. He swiveled around in his chair and stared out of his window at the adjacent wetlands park, focusing on nothing in particular, his brain trying to process this new information about Kelly Mueller against the information that had been stored in his head for over thirty years. He glared at the medical records and shook his head. "She lied about the whole God damned thing," he said aloud, angrily.

He stood up and once again looked out of his office window, staring aimlessly into space. The streets were still damp from an overnight shower. He covered his hands with his face and sighed as he massaged his eyebrows, a nervous habit triggered by stress. He picked up his iPhone, scrolled through his favorites and made a call which was picked up after the third ring.

"Dude," a raspy voice answered. "What the heck? What time is it?"

"Man, I'm sorry," Ezra said with genuine compunction, "but I couldn't sit on this any longer. This is huge. Like wooly mammoth huge."

"What's going on?" Giles said groggily.

"The Kelly Mueller rape," Ezra said.

"The what?" Giles asked, still trying to wake up.

"You know, when we were in middle school, Kelly Mueller getting raped," Ezra said, "the fucking premise of my novel."

"What about it?" Giles groaned.

"Well, the whole story. It's all bullshit. She made it up," Ezra exclaimed in a hushed whisper.

"What are you talking about?"

"Kelly Mueller was not raped. She made it up."

"Wait, how do you know this?" Giles asked.

"It's a long story. Just trust me, I know. She was pregnant for her boyfriend, and she told her parents she was raped so that they would let her get an abortion."

There was a moment of silence on the phone as Giles absorbed the information. "Well," he finally said, "I guess I get it. What sixteen-year-old girl wants to go through the shame of being pregnant in high school?"

"But the whole town thought she was raped by black men."

"You sound angry," Giles said.

"You think?" Ezra said with bitter sarcasm, missing the irony in Giles' tone completely.

"You're angry that a young white girl did *not* get raped by black men?" Giles asked with a hint of condescension in his tone.

Ezra paused, temporarily stymied by the query. "Don't be a smartass. I'm angry that she lied about it. I'm angry that she made me angry at black men who did nothing to her. I'm angry about how this fed unjustified prejudices. I mean, that rape played a huge role in how I viewed black men for most of my life. And not just me."

"Okay."

"Okay? The rape was the literary predicate—the nucleus—of my novel, which by the way, I've been working on for over eight years. The truth guts the whole thing."

There was more silence before Giles spoke again. "I have to admit that I'm a little confused."

"About what?"

"Your indignation. You know, as it relates to your book."

"I don't get it," Ezra said.

"Isn't it supposed to be fiction?"

"Well yes, of course. It's a novel."

"Then what difference does it make if the original inspiration for it was true or not? If you want to write it as a rape story, you can still do that, right?"

"No. Even though it's fiction, I want it to be honest."

"Honest fiction?" Giles said in a tone that stopped just short of being patronizing.

"You know what I mean," Ezra replied, frustrated that Giles did not seem to share his umbrage.

"I don't see how it matters. It only needs to be plausible. And surely there's nothing implausible about black men raping a white girl, right? I mean, surely it's happened before."

Ezra sighed in exasperation. "You don't get it. It's like if Mona Lisa had passionate sex with Leonardo de Vinci and told him that she loved him right before he began painting her, and then after he was finished, she confessed that she really had no feelings for him at all. No artist wants to create fraudulently inspired art."

"Are you—"

Ezra cut Giles off. "No, I'm not comparing my talents to that of de Vinci—God, you are so fucking predictable."

"Well," Giles replied, chuckling. "But seriously, do you think maybe your indignation might be a little misplaced?"

"What the hell are you talking about?"

"I think the rape was an allegory for black behavior that you were using to illustrate and justify white prejudice. And maybe now, you are beginning to realize the illegitimacy of your thesis."

"What are you trying to say? You just admitted that black men raping a white girl is a very plausible storyline."

Giles sighed. "Now you're the one who's missing the point. I think you need to ask yourself a tough question. Were you writing the novel to explain racial prejudice, or to justify it?"

"I'm not racist," Ezra said defensively, "if that's what you're insinuating."

"Hmm," Giles replied. "Doth the lady protest too much?"

"I don't know, do you?"

Giles giggled. "I think you are confusing who the lady is in this metaphor."

"Well, I think you don't know what a racist is if you think I am one," Ezra said.

"It's too early for this," Giles said through a yawn.

"Well, you started it," Ezra said.

"Maybe so, but," Giles said, wanting to redirect the conversation to the reason Ezra had called so that he could bring it to an end and go back to sleep, "isn't this what you really wanted to accomplish with your novel? To get people throughout the color spectrum to engage in introspection and healthy dialogues about race? To re-examine their racial attitudes and predispositions?"

"Yes, of course."

"And why should you be the only one exempted from that?"

"Exempted from what?"

"Self-reflection. Self-examination," Giles answered. "Asking yourself why you are so upset about learning that the object of your childhood adoration was *not* in fact gang raped by black men."

Ezra reflected in silence for several seconds and then scoffed, as if to realize that he had been caught in his own net and was now being filleted by his own knife. "Well," he finally said, "If I'm a racist, then so are you."

Giles expelled the subtle hint of a chuckle. "I can't say that I'm not unequivocally disinclined to disagree with you on that."

"What?"

Giles scoffed and smiled. "I'm going back to sleep. I'll talk to you later."

CHAPTER 50

Ezra spent the next four days in Biloxi conducting depositions in a wrongful death case in which a thirty-two-year-old roustabout was crushed to death when a piece of defective drilling equipment malfunctioned on a jack-up platform in the Gulf of Mexico. Being deposed were seven eye-witnesses to the incident and his young widow. Ezra had the unenviable task of defending the drilling company.

On his long drive home, he called Giles just to check in. He was about to end the call after the fourth ring when Giles answered. "Hello?" He sounded like he was trying to control his breathing.

"What took you so long to answer?" Ezra asked.

"I was just walking in—I had my hands full with groceries," Giles said.

"Groceries, huh?" Ezra replied in an incredulous tone, suspecting that it was more likely that Giles' breathlessness was due to sexual activity instead of a short walk from the car with a bag of groceries.

"Where are you?" Giles asked, obviously wanting to change the subject. Ezra could hear him holding his hand over the mic on his phone when he was not speaking.

I'm on my way back from Mississippi," Ezra said. He thought he heard a man's voice in the background. "Is there someone else there?"

"No, why?"

"I thought I heard someone else talking."

"Must have been the TV," Giles said.

"I thought you just walked in?"

"I did, but I had left the TV on. What is this, an interrogation? Where are you, anyway?"

"I just told you; I'm on my way back from Mississippi."

"What?"

"Nothing," Ezra said. "Hey, you sound preoccupied. I guess I'll let you get back to your *groceries*."

Giles started to protest Ezra's suspiciousness, but then decided to let it go. "Okay. Be safe."

"Bye."

When he returned to his office later that evening, Ezra grimaced at the sight of an incredibly large pile of mail on his desk. Sitting beneath the pile was a cardboard box sealed in packaging tape with only his name and the words, "PERSONAL & CONFIDENTIAL" written across the front with a felt tip marker.

He pulled a pocketknife out of his desk drawer and cut open the seams on the top of the box, wincing at the thick, moldy smell coming from within. Inside were three very weathered hardbound books. The exterior of each book was stained and mildewed in varying degrees, particularly around the edges. Ezra surmised that they had probably been in storage for many years where they were subject to humidity. He flipped open one of the books. It appeared to be a handwritten journal.

A clean white envelope lay at the bottom of the box. He pulled it out and opened it. Inside was a one-page, unsigned, handwritten letter addressed to him.

Dear Attorney Brasseaux,

These are the journals of the late Hedi Patterson Pugh. She was married to Ferrell Pugh. Her older sister was the late Sue Patterson Mueller who was married to

Abel Mueller. The journals speak for themselves.
Other than our turning these over to you, we are
regretfully powerless in this matter but we are hopeful
that you are not.

"The sins of the father are visited on his children."
Exodus 34:7

God bless.

Ezra scratched his head and then read the letter again. Then he quickly turned around and pulled out the Kelly Mueller hospital records from inside his credenza. He flipped through the records to find the billing information and then scrolled down to the bottom of the page. *Susan Mueller* was identified as the "responsible party." Her relationship to the patient was indicated as "mother."

"What the fuck is going on here?" Ezra said out loud to himself in disbelief. He looked at the journals and then the Kelly Mueller medical records and then the journals again, hovering somewhere between denial and dumbfoundedness. He opened and scanned each of the journals in order to find the entry with the earliest date, which was September 1, 1976. He began to read.

The September 1 entry detailed an old fashioned *boucherie*—a picnic style gathering of several families for the butchering of a hog—held under a canopy of live oaks at Hedi's older brother's farmhouse. Ezra skimmed ahead to the next entry dated September 3, 1976. Some of the words had been smeared by water or perhaps tears.

I woke at 3:15 a.m. to the sound of someone frantically
pounding on the carport door. I turned to wake Ferrell but

364

found nothing but his pillow on his side of the bed. I put on my housecoat and hurried toward the front of the house. Before going to the door, I peeped through the window and saw that it was Sue. When I opened the door to let her in, she was crying inconsolably and begging for me to help her. I brought her to the sofa and did my best to calm her down.

Sue took several deep breaths, trying to settle her nerves. She started by telling me that she and Abel had been watching television in the living room the evening prior when Kelly came home distraught and sobbing. Kelly said she had stopped at the drugstore next to the nursing home on her way back from studying at a friend's house. She said that when she got back to her car and was getting ready to leave, a colored man stepped out in front of her car and asked her for a ride. When she shook her head no, she said a second colored man opened the front passenger-side door and jumped into her car and then the first man climbed into the back seat. She said they made her drive to the baseball park where they showed her a large knife and threatened to cut her throat if she screamed. The first man held her arms while the second made pulled off her pants and panties and raped her while the other one watched. Then the other man took a turn. She was not able to offer detailed descriptions of either man except to say that they were both tall, large-framed and very dark-colored and possibly in their thirties. She said they smelled of alcohol and sour sweat.

Abel told Kelly to get in the truck and instructed Sue to stay home. He did not say where they were going but Sue assumed that he was taking Kelly to the police station or to the hospital, but when they returned about forty minutes later, Kelly told Sue that they rode by the drug store and then through the colored section of town to see if she could identify her attackers. When she could not, they drove back home.

About an hour after Abel and Kelly returned, Sue heard voices outside her home. She peered out of the window and saw Abel talking to a couple of Sheriff's deputies. She could see one of the deputies shining a flashlight into the faces of two colored boys who were sitting in the back of the car. After checking on Kelly, Sue returned to the kitchen and upon looking through the window again discovered that the sheriff department cruiser and Abel's pickup were gone. She brought Kelly some hot tea and coaxed her out of bed and into the car. Fearing the gossip and rumors that would surely surface if she brought Kelly to the hospital in Iris, she drove thirty miles to Savoy Memorial Hospital in Mamou.

The journal entry concluded with details of the hospital visit that were very consistent with the medical records that Ezra had recently read. He stopped and took a deep breath. His head was whirling. He felt nauseous, excited and incredulous all at once. It was all so surreal. He physically pinched himself hard to make sure this was not some sort of fantastic dream or fatigue-induced hallucination, unable to get over the extraordinary coincidences at play. It all seemed too contrived, he thought, like a trite made-for-television movie. Feeling like the butt of some cosmic prank, he stood and looked out of his window to see if he could see faces forming in the clouds snickering and laughing at him and then thought himself crazy for doing so.

CHAPTER 51

Ezra went to the office kitchen to get a fresh cup of coffee and then returned to his office. His head still whirling, he sat down and took a deep breath in an effort to prepare himself for more reading.

Sue said that when she and Kelly returned from the hospital, Abel was not home. Sue called me to see if Ferrell might know Abel's whereabouts, and I told her that Abel and Errol Frey had picked up Ferrell but that they did not say where they were going, though I noticed them turn right out of the driveway toward Abel's crawfish ponds. She remembered the sheriff's unit and it immediately occurred to her that the deputies had likely picked up one or more colored boys that they suspected of the rape. She told me that she had to go and hung up. She rushed to her car and sped out to the farm property. As she neared the back of the property, she saw the silhouette of a vehicle parked near the main pump shed and parked as near as she could without risking getting stuck in the large, muddy tractor ruts. She walked by moonlight in mud-caked shoes, taking care not to slip into the flooded rice field. She stopped when she heard moaning and then high-pitched screaming from inside the shed.

She saw Errol and Ferrell were sitting on the tailgate of Abel's pickup smoking cigarettes, their backs to her. A young colored man wearing medical scrubs and a burlap sack over his head was sitting in the bed of the pickup with his back against the cab, his wrists bound to the truck's roll bar. When he jerked at the rope in an effort to free himself, Sue saw Errol reach over and strike him on the hand with a tire iron to get him to quit.

Sue heard Abel's voice coming from inside the shed, chastising someone about putting his "nigger lips" on his daughter, and then there was a loud, blood-curdling squeal. As she rushed past the pickup, Errol saw her and grabbed her around the waist, stopping her progress, telling her she did not want to go inside.

Sue fought for Errol to let her go, clawing her fingernails into his flesh until he finally released his hold on her. She ran to the shed and swung open the door, freezing where she stood, transfixed. Her husband, unaware of her presence due to the wailing and shrieking, was hunched over a colored boy wearing the same color medical scrubs as the other boy. The boys bottom lip was missing and Abel was pulling the boy's top lip taut with pliers as he cut the lip from the boys' mouth with a box cutter. Sue felt paralyzed. She looked on helplessly as Abel picked up a cutting torch and used it to cauterize the wounds around the boys mouth as he continued to writhe in pain and scream at decibels she did not think possible from human vocal chords. She tried to yell at Abel to make him stop but her voice would not come.

Ezra felt his stomach turn. He stood up and paced around his office, not wanting to read any more but unable to stop. Finally, he sat back down and continued.

The smell of the burning flesh caused Sue to grow even more nauseous. She felt her stomach lurch and then watched its contents empty onto the ground. She looked up again at the boy. He could not have been older than seventeen or eighteen, she thought. Beyond exhausted, the boy allowed his head to fall until his chin rested on his chest. She could see a large patch of hair and scalp missing from his head, his legs splayed out before him, one badly broken and twisted unnaturally to the side.

When Abel shifted his stance, he caught sight of Sue in his peripheral vision. He turned around to find her looking at him in horror, unable to speak. He angrily chastised her for not staying home and then viciously scolded Ferrell and Errol, who were both standing in the door, for allowing her to enter. When Ferrell put his arm around her shoulders and attempted to guide her out of the shed, Sue finally found her words. She wiped vomit from her mouth and pleaded with Abel to stop. When he growled at her to go home and turned his back to her, she screamed that Kelly had lied about the rape, that she was not raped, that the colored boys were innocent.

Abel scoffed, muttering that the boy had already confessed. She saw Errol and Ferrell exchange horrified glances, both obviously thinking the same thing—that the boy would have admitted anything to stop the torture.

She told Abel that she brought Kelly to the hospital, that Kelly told the social worker that she made the rape up because she's pregnant. Sue explained that Kelly only said she was raped so that they would allow her to get an abortion.

Abel told Sue to shut up and go home. Sue knew that to say anything more or to disobey her heavy-handed husband would have injurious consequences. She glanced at the young man whose one opened eye was now desperately fixed on hers, realizing that she was his only hope. Again, she pleaded with Abel.

Abel went into a rage, raising his arm to backhand Sue before Ferrell pulled her out of the way and out of the pump shed. Tears streamed down her face as she put her hand over her mouth, turned and ran down the dark, muddy road. She drove home; reciting Hail Mary's the whole way.

That night, I didn't sleep, waiting for Ferrell to come home. Just after four o'clock in the morning, the phone rang. It was the Evangeline Parish Sheriff's Department. Ferrell had been in a serious motor vehicle accident but was in stable condition. I rushed to the hospital and found Ferrell in a fog. He was concussed and heavily medicated.

371

As soon as we had privacy from the nursing staff, he began telling me everything, how they were just supposed to rough the boys up a bit, how Abel took things way too far, how he continued to torture the colored boy even after learning the truth from Sue, how things spiraled out of control when the other boy escaped, how they chased him for a quarter of a mile in the moonlit darkness through mud, across levees and through crawfish ponds, how he was running for his life with his hands tied behind his back, crying out for his mother, how, after he was caught, he promised not to tell anyone if we just let him go, how Abel knocked the boy down face-first in to the crawfish pond and stepped on the back of his neck with a heavy boot, burying the boy's face in the soft mud, how he continued to apply pressure as the boy squirmed and writhed and then stopped moving altogether.

There was a huge argument between the three men, Ferrell said. Ferrell and Errol were telling Abel that he had gone way too far and that they had not signed up for this. Abel became irate and threatened them. He told them to take his farm truck and go dump the bodies deep in the Atchafalaya Basin while he cleaned up the mess at the pump shed. They didn't know what to do. Eventually, they reluctantly obeyed. While on their way, they had a head-on collision with an eighteen-wheeler that killed Errol.

The next journal entry was dated September 29. By then, Hedi had pieced everything together as best she could. The journal detailed how the collision had occurred in Evangeline Parish, near its border with St. Landry Parish. The colored boys had been found just inside the St. Landry Parish line a day and a half later. The collision was investigated by the Evangeline Parish Sheriff's department. The investigation of what happened to the colored boys was handled by the St. Landry Parish Sheriff's Department. The respective law enforcement agencies had not made the connection between the vehicular crash and the colored boys being found in the woods and therefore did not share any information. Or if they had, it was being swept under the rug. As such, neither Ferrell nor Abel were questioned or suspected of having been involved in what happened to the colored boys. She went on to state that the colored boy who had been tortured and mutilated in the shed had somehow survived but that brain damage had apparently left him a near-vegetative state, unable to communicate or care for himself.

For weeks, Ferrell barely slept, worrying that, notwithstanding Abel's powerful connections, law enforcement would somehow connect them to the heinous crimes. And even after a couple of months, when no detectives had come calling, he never stopped worrying that the boy who survived would regain the ability to speak or communicate in some way, and that he would somehow be able to identify them.

Though I tried to talk her out of it in order to protect Ferrell, Sue, at one point, had come within an inch of reporting what happened to the police. After a series of sleepless nights, she could take the worry and guilt no more. She waited until Abel left for work and then drove

373

to the police station in Iris and asked to see Chief
Brasseaux who she knew from high school. But when the
chief's administrative assistant told her that the chief was
in a meeting with Horace and Bernice Chaisson, the
parents of the colored boy who Abel had drowned, she
panicked and left, never finding the courage to return.

There were no subsequent journal entries until Friday, December 11, 1976. A few months after the dust had seemed to settle, Hedi wrote that she and Sue were having coffee in Sue's kitchen when Chief Bernard Brasseaux pulled into the driveway in his old Bronco. He was looking for Abel. She commented that Abel had a lot of connections with law enforcement and that it was not uncommon for them to visit him at home, but in light of all that had transpired, the women were justifiably anxious about his visit. They had heard that Chief Brasseux had a colored officer asking questions around town, trying to see if anyone saw or heard anything that might give them a lead on what happened to the two colored boys.

Chief Brasseaux was very friendly and did not seem
especially concerned about anything in particular,
although he did not mention what it was that he needed
with Abel, which we thought was a little suspicious. Sue
asked if everything was okay and he went out of his way to
assure her that everything was just fine. Sue gave him
directions to where Abel was using an excavator to
reinforce the levees of a crawfish pond at the back of the
farm. After he left, I called Ferrell at home and told him
about Chief Brasseaux's visit. Ferrell told Hedi not to

374

worry, but he seemed anxious.

The next journal entry was on December 20, 1976. It read:

> *Sue and I ran into Melody Poret at Jagneaux's. She said*
> *that Chief Brasseaux was discovered to be having an*
> *affair with a young lawyer at the D.A.'s office and that he*
> *and Eve were getting a divorce. She said that he had*
> *resigned and had already moved to Texas with the other*
> *woman. She said poor Eve was devastated—that she*
> *thought Bernard was happy and never saw the affair*
> *coming.*

Three days later, on December 23, 1976, the entry read:

> *Ferrell came home this afternoon in good spirits. It's the*
> *first time I've seen him smile since everything happened.*
> *He said Abel spoke to the interim police chief who*
> *confirmed that the investigation involving the colored*
> *boys had been closed. Thank you, sweet Jesus!*

The blank pages that followed suggested that it was the last entry
Hedi had made, at least in the journals that had been delivered to Ezra.

Ezra set the journal down and sat back in his chair. Though the
journals did not expressly confirm that his father was in the know relating
to what happened to Cedric Chaisson and D'Arius Cole, the implication
seemed clear. The only plausible conclusion that Ezra could draw was that
prior to leaving office to start his new life, his father had given Abel and

Ferrell assurances that they would not have to worry about being investigated or prosecuted—that any suspicions about their involvement had been swept under the rug and that the investigation into the crimes had been closed. He shook his head in disgust. "Priceless," he heard himself say out loud, not having believed prior to reading the journals that he could have thought any less of his father.

After closing his office door behind him, Ezra went to the restroom and splashed cold water on his face. He was at a loss in terms of what to do. He felt a strong urge to knock on Hank's door. Hank had always had an uncanny ability to make sense of the nonsensical, to find order in chaos, and to untangle the tightest knots. But fearing that Hank might think him distracted from his law practice, he abstained.

CHAPTER 52

The next day Ezra placed a call to J.B. Thibodeaux, a trusted private investigator from St. Landry Parish. He stressed that what he was calling about was highly confidential.

"Always," Thibodeaux replied.

Ezra explained that he had a few questions about Abel Mueller, Ferrell Pugh and Errol Frey. Thibodeaux said that he was very familiar with Mueller and Pugh but only knew Frey by reputation. "Abel, Ferrell, your dad and me, we all were in the military at the same time, me and Ferrell in the Navy and your dad and Abel to the Army. They went to boot camp together."

"I didn't know that," Ezra said.

Thibodeaux told Ezra that Frey and Pugh were nothing special but that Mueller was really bad news. "His family came down here from Concordia Parish when Abel was just knee high," Thibodeaux said. "So said, his father was connected to the Silver Dollar Group."

"Who's that?" Ezra asked.

"It was a small offshoot of the Klan—a handful of bad apples who thought the Klan was too soft," Thibodeaux said. "These boys were just as nasty as they were ignorant, and they were as ignorant as they come. God only knows all that they were doing. I do know that they were implicated in the murder of a shoe repairman up in Ferriday in the early 1960s— burned that poor man alive in his shoe shop just because they didn't like that he accepted business from white women."

"Jesus."

"Yeah. Now that was his father. As for Abel," Thibodeaux continued, "I've heard that he's been involved in some bad shit. I don't know what he saw or did over there, but he came back from the Korean War a much-hardened man, and he wasn't exactly a box of jelly rolls when he left."

"Okay."

"What you asking about this man for anyway?" Thibodeaux asked, more out of concern than curiosity. "You got yourself crossways with him?"

"No, no, nothing like that," Ezra assured.

"Well, make sure you don't. Abel Mueller is dangerous, Ezra. And what makes him even more dangerous is that he's got a lot of connections, especially in law enforcement."

"I kind'a already suspected that," Ezra said, "but I'm hearing you loud and clear. I'll keep my distance."

After the call with Thibodeaux, Ezra texted Giles and Vance and asked them to meet him at Eula's. He waited for them in a booth toward the back of the bar. After swearing them to secrecy, he told them every detail of what he had learned about the crimes committed against the Chaisson boy and the Cole boy. Giles was horrified. Vance just listened without much reaction.

"Man," Giles said, "I'm really surprised Ferrell Pugh was involved in all that. You remember when we went to his house for your term paper interview? He seemed so nice."

Ezra nodded. "Well, maybe he was. Maybe he just got sucked into the whole thing by Mueller."

"But still," Giles said.

Ezra noticed that Vance was being unusually quiet and seemed distant. "What's wrong with you?" Ezra asked.

"Abel Mueller," Vance said.

378

"What about him?"

"You don't remember?"

"Remember what?" Ezra asked.

"He's the mother fucker who cracked Bruce's skull with a pipe and left him to die."

Giles and Ezra exchanged a quick mutual glance. "Holy shit, that's right," Ezra said. "I had completely forgotten about that."

"Me too," Giles said. "Damn." "And I'll tell you who else he is. Y'all remember when my Uncle Gary and his friend Gene got beat up real badly at the Swine Festival in Basile? This was when we were in elementary school at the time. They were in college."

"Not really," Vance said.

"Vaguely," Ezra replied.

"Well, they got jumped in the parking lot by a couple of men. My uncle Gary was in the hospital for a few days with his jaw wired shut. His friend Gene had a broken nose and some broken ribs. It was all sort of kept hush-hush at the time, but I found out much later that it was Abel Mueller and a couple of his buddies who did it."

"Why?" Ezra asked.

"Because that believed my uncle and his friend Gene were queer."

"Jesus," Ezra said, shaking his head in disgust.

"Were they?" Vance asked.

"Were they what?" Giles said.

"Queer."

"What difference does it make?" Giles replied somewhat angrily.

"Relax dude," Vance said, "I was just curious." He glanced at Ezra who was already looking at him and apparently thinking the same thing.

379

Giles took a sip from his drink, as if pouring fresh coolant into an overheated radiator. Vance and Ezra followed suit. They sat in silence for a few moments, contemplatively avoiding eye contact with each other.

"Well?" Ezra finally said, desirous of reclaiming the direction of the discussion.

"Well what?" Vance queried before taking another swig from his beer.

"What are we going to do about Mueller and Pugh?" Ezra asked.

"What do you mean?" Giles asked.

Ezra sighed. "We've talked about how we live unremarkable lives, how there was no wild west for us to tame, no epic world war for us to fight in, how we were too young for the civil rights movement, how we missed the opportunity to be a part of something special—to really make a difference."

Vance looked at Giles and Giles at Vance, both curiously.

"We have literally never spoken about any of those things," Giles said.

"Yeah never," Vance affirmed. "Not even once."

"Well," Ezra replied, "if we didn't, we should have. I mean Vance, I know you fought in a war, but it wasn't exactly defending the world against the Axis Powers. And it wasn't much of a fight at that."

Vance shrugged as if to say that he felt no disrespect or even disagreement.

"And even if the conversation was only in my head, isn't it true that we've all lived exceedingly ordinary lives? Isn't this our opportunity to do something that really matters? And maybe make up at least a little for being a part of the racism that has existed for all of those years?"

"What in the name of Little Big Horn are you talking about, Crazy Horse?" Vance said.

Ezra smiled and then took a deep breath. "I know this is going to sound hokey, but I really think this is—" he paused, "I really think this is our calling," Ezra said.

"Our calling?" Giles replied, not masking his incredulity. "Like a calling from God?"

Ezra nodded. "I know how it sounds. I do. But I believe it is. The coincidences are just too much for it to be anything else."

"But you don't even believe in God."

"I never said that," Ezra retorted defensively.

"Dude, are you serious?" Giles said, daring Ezra not to retract his statement.

Ezra blushed. "I may have said that I questioned the existence of God, that's different. That's normal. And that was a long time ago, when I was trying to impress Ava Mackey."

"Whatever," Giles said.

"I absolutely believe in God," Ezra insisted. "I go to mass almost every Sunday. And whether it's God or the universe or whatever, some higher power brought us to this point. I really think we're being used as instruments for justice. I really do."

Giles snickered. "Higher power? What is this, an AA meeting?"

"Suck me, Giles," Ezra said.

"Don't tempt him," Vance quipped.

"Fuck you, Vance," Giles snapped.

"Guys, guys, guys!" Ezra interjected, his tone filled with exasperation. "Come on, please. I'm being serious."

Vance snorted. "You want us to be instruments for justice, huh?"

"Yes, I do," Ezra said earnestly. He looked back and forth at Giles and Vance, begging for someone to acknowledge that they agreed, or were at least open to the idea.

"But what if I don't believe in God or in any higher power?" Giles said. "Where does that leave me?"

Ezra furrowed his brow. "What do you mean? You went to Catholic school for Christ's sake. You thought about being a priest at one point."

Giles smirked. "That was a long time ago. I have awakened."

"Well, I don't care what you call it," Ezra said. "God, karma, cosmic justice, whatever. I know you have to see it. Even if you put it in different terms or attribute it to something different, I know you have to feel what I'm feeling, at least a little bit."

"I wouldn't be so sure about that," Giles said.

Ezra sighed. "Come on, man. Don't you see that you're tied to this because you're the one who found D'Arius Cole? And also because of what Mueller did to your Uncle Gary, and God knows how many other gay people."

"Wait, are you trying to make me the patron avenger of all gays?" Giles asked, defensively.

"I'm not. You are just closer to that issue because of your Uncle Gary, that's all." Ezra shot a quick glance at Vance as if to get some indication that his reply did not sound as disingenuous as it felt.

Vance smirked.

"Anyway," Ezra continued, "whether you see it as a calling or not, all I'm trying to say is we all have cause to want to be a part of bringing some justice to the situation. I'm tied to it because it's my father who swept the investigation under the rug and because Kelly Mueller's medical records and her aunt's journals, coincidentally, were dumped in my lap. Vance, you're tied to this because Mueller is the son of a bitch who did what he did to Bruce."

Giles and Vance made no reply.

"I know in my heart that we're supposed to do something about this. I mean, I'm not advocating that we become vigilantes, but we need to do *something*."

Giles noticed that Vance had a thoughtful expression, which was out of the ordinary for him. "What?" he asked, tapping Vance's arm.

Vance looked up as if he had been startled out of a trance and then glanced at Giles and then Ezra. "I'm not saying I believe in this *calling* bullshit, but I've actually got another connection to this whole thing, you know, besides Bruce."

"What?" Ezra asked.

"The mother of D'Arius Cole's kids, Jayla, she's my housekeeper," Vance answered. "And we've become friends."

"Really? There you go!" Ezra said. "A double connection."

"Your cheap ass has a housekeeper?" Giles asked incredulously.

"I cleaned enough latrines when I was in the service, bitch. That's one of the few things I don't mind spending my retirement money on."

"Have you ever talked to her about, you know, what happened and everything?"

Vance shook his head. "Sort of but not in great detail. We mostly talked about how fucked up D'Arius is. I know she does a lot to help take care of him because his mother is a strung-out crackhead."

Ezra nodded and then looked at Giles and Vance for some sign of affirmation. "So, are we together in this or what?" he asked.

"Do you think Mueller and your dad were buddies? Is that why your dad swept everything under the rug?" Giles asked.

"Probably. I know that served together in Korea. So it was either that or my father was a racist who didn't think crimes against blacks were worth prosecuting," Ezra answered.

"Or both," Giles said.

"Or both," Ezra agreed.

"Why don't we just send the journals to the police?" Giles said. "You know, anonymously."

"No," Ezra replied. "Mueller's too well-connected. Chances are that whoever gets put in charge of the investigation will bury the evidence, or worse might even show him the journals so he can figure out who sent them to me." Ezra took a big swig of beer and then belched into his hand. "Excuse me," he said. "Besides, the journals could not be used to convict him. It's all hearsay."

"Well, do we want him to get caught or do we want him to suffer?" Vance said.

"Both," Ezra said.

Vance grinned. "Okay, have you heard of the rat bucket torture?"

Giles and Ezra both shook their heads.

"Well, you tie the person down, put a large rat on his belly and then cover the rat with a small metal bucket. Then you use a torch to heat the bucket up, and the only way for the rat to get away from the heat is to scratch and bite his way through the person's belly."

"Isn't that from a scene in one of those *Fast and Furious* movies?" Ezra asked.

"Yeah, but in the movie, they were just trying to get the guy to talk. With Mueller, we could let the rat finish the job."

Ezra grinned and nodded. "As appropriate as that sounds, we are not putting ourselves in a position to physically overtake Abel Mueller and then kill him slowly with a rodent. I would prefer to lead him to his retribution without risking a capital murder conviction and lethal injection."

"I thought Louisiana had the electric chair?" Vance said.

"It did until 1999," Ezra replied.

"Then what's your idea?" Giles asked Ezra.

"I don't know yet," Ezra answered. "I just think we have to do something. We just have to be smart about it. Give me a little time. I'll think of something."

"Oh brother," Vance said with a foreboding tone.

"I'll second that emotion," Giles said.

"How about you let me propose a plan before you shit all over it, okay?" Ezra retorted.

"How about you not get so defensive about a plan that you have not even come up with yet?" Vance shot back.

"Yeah," Giles said, finding it odd to be on the same side of an argument as Vance. "If it's a good plan, we can always wash the shit off."

Ezra shook his head and smiled. "Fair enough."

Giles looked at his watch and then immediately started scooting out of the booth. "Gotta run. See y'all later."

"You sure?" Ezra said, "I'm buying another round."

"I've had too much already," Giles said. "And I'm late."

"You gotta date?" Ezra called out as Giles was nearing the door.

"Maybe," Giles called back over his shoulder.

"What's his name?" Vance yelled as the door was closing behind Giles.

Ezra punched Vance in the arm. "Don't be a dick."

After they had a few more rounds, Ezra set his empty beer bottle down on the table with a loud *thunk*. "Let's take a drive," he slurred.

"Where to?" asked Vance.

"Iris. My mom's house."

"Why?"

"I'm going to initiate you into a little ritual that I started after you left for the military."

"Give me your keys." Vance said.

"Why? I'm fine."

"I just want to see if that Bavarian beast of yours is really *the ultimate driving machine.*"

"Fine," Ezra said, handing Vance the keys to the BMW.

After stopping to buy a six pack of beer from Circle K, they began driving toward Iris, both worn out by the heavy conversation and desirous of lightening things up.

"So whatever happened with Ava Mackey?" Vance asked, his curiosity piqued by Ezra's reference to her earlier in their discussion. "Do you keep up with her at all?"

Ezra shook his head. "We never talked about that?"

"Nope."

Ezra sighed. "It's a fucked up story," he said.

"Give me the *Reader's Digest* version," Vance said.

"So after we broke up, me, Giles and our suite-mates came up with this sexual conquest contest where we each put up ten dollars and you get a certain amount of points for each girl you sleep with, winner take all at the end of the semester. Well, Ava surprises me with a visit over spring break, and everything is going amazingly well until she discovers the poster board with everybody's points on my suite-mate's wall. She hall's ass and refuses to talk to see me, refuses to talk my calls, doesn't respond to my letters. I don't hear from her for well over a decade. Then out of the blue she friends me on Facebook and then sends me this really long private message wanting to make amends, apologizing for judging me and for shunning me, telling me that she found Jesus after going through some really fucked up shit."

"Ava Mackey, the queen of atheism, found Jesus?" Vance asked incredulously.

Ezra nodded. "That's what she said."

"What kind of fucked up shit?" Vance asked as he jerked the steering wheel to the left to miss a pile of opossum roadkill in the middle of his lane.

Ezra grimaced as if it was going to be painful to recount Ava's story. "Turns out that a couple of years after finishing college she got pregnant and had a kid. Then one night when the kid was like eighteen months old, she and the kids' father got totally baked in the backyard while the kid is sleeping in the house. It was never definitively determined, but they think their cat must have knocked over a lit candle and caught the house on fire. And they were too out of it to even notice until it was way too late."

"Mother fucker," Vance said. "That's hard to come back from."

Ezra nodded. "Yeah. But it gets worse. She was so irretrievably mind-fucked by what happened that she tried to commit suicide by chugging a bottle of Drano."

"Aw, hell," Vance said, grimacing.

"Yeah. It basically burned and destroyed virtually everything in her mouth, esophagus and stomach. She had like seven surgeries and spent over sixty days in the hospital and now lives on a feeding tube."

"Damn."

"The only good thing about the whole situation is that during all of this, she met a social worker who was a born again Christian, and long story short, she found Christ. She actually said that she'd rather be in the physical condition she is now having a relationship with Jesus than being physically healthy and damned."

"Damn."

"Yeah."

"Did you ever consider going to visit her?"

Ezra shook his head. "I don't think I could bear seeing her that way. I really don't. I know that's cowardly, but I just don't have it in me."

Vance nodded. "I get it. I've seen some guys get really fucked up in combat. It's hard for everybody." Vance paused contemplatively. "So you would think that after learning about what happened to Ava would allow you to finally move on."

"What are you talking about?"

Vance shrugged. "I don't know. Giles had mentioned a while back that the reason you never got married or even got serious with anyone was because you never really got all the way over Ava."

Ezra's opened his mouth to categorically reject the premise but then stopped short. "I don't know if that's true. Maybe. Or maybe I'm just not relationship material. I don't know."

Vance smiled but did not otherwise respond.

Ezra nodded. "Let's change the subject. You dating anybody?" Ezra asked.

"I don't really date," Vance said. "I'm like Muhammad Ali. I stick and move."

Ezra snorted and this time, did choke on his beer. "I'm almost afraid to ask," Ezra said, coughing through the question.

"Ask what?"

"How many—how many women have you been with?"

Vance cogitated on the question for a few moments, doing calculations in his head. "How many would you guess?"

"I don't know. Thirty-five? Forty maybe."

Vance laughed. "Seriously?"

"What? Is it more or less?"

Vance grinned. "It would be over a hundred and twenty."

Ezra's eyebrows rose nearly to his hairline. "Are you serious?"

Vance nodded. "You learn very quickly to lower your standards when you're in the military. And if you lower them enough, the sky is the limit. There's always a chick out there looking to hook up with a soldier. You can have a different woman every night if you want."

Ezra chuckled. "So, what's your type?" he asked.

"I'm not too particular," Vance said. "All I really need is a pussy and a pulse."

Ezra laughed and shook his head in amused disgust.

"And frankly if I've had enough to drink, a pulse becomes optional."

Ezra grimaced. "It's times like this that I regret knowing you well enough to know that you're not joking."

Vance smiled and took a swig of his beer as he turned into Ezra's old subdivision. "Almost there," he said.

Vance parked the BMW on the side of the road in front of Ezra's mother's house. Instructing Vance to be quiet, Ezra led him through the side gate and down the fence line to the rear corner of the property where a lone Chinese Tallow stood tall. He put his hand on the old tree and looked at Vance with glassy eyes. "You know why they call these chicken trees?" he asked.

"I don't know. Because chickens like to roost in them?" Vance guessed.

"No, because Chinese Tallow seedlings are the only kind of plant matter around here that a chicken won't eat. So, when birds drop the seeds in chicken yards, it's the only thing that has a chance to grow."

"Truly fascinating," Vance replied with thinly veiled sarcasm.

"Fuck you," Ezra said, chuckling almost inaudibly as he fumbled to get his phone out of his pocket. He turned the flashlight on and began kicking at leaves, twigs and dirt until he found what he was looking for.

"What is that?" Vance asked.

Ezra sighed. "That, sir, is my piece-of-shit father's Bronze Star."

Vance looked at the medal and then back at Ezra, curiously. "That's a real Bronze Star?"

"Yep. From when he served in Korea."

Ezra took a short step backwards, unzipped his pants and, struggling to keep his balance, began urinating, moving his penis in figure eights to create a zigzagging stream on and around the medal until it was completely submerged in his frothy piss. He sighed, shook his penis clumsily and then zipped his pants and stepped backwards. "Your turn," he said.

Vance regarded Ezra for a moment and then looked down at the urine-saturated medal which was becoming visible again as the bubbles in Ezra's urine were quickly disappearing. He shook his head. "I'm good," he said.

"Come on, go ahead man," Ezra said, struggling to get his jeans buttoned.

"No, I'm good," Vance said.

"Dude," Ezra argued, "I brought you all the way out here for this. I mean, I know yours wasn't a great father, but at least he stuck around."

Vance looked at Ezra and then back down at the ground at the medal. "Yeah, well, I'm not going to debate you on who had the shittier dad, Ezra. And I'm not pissing on your father's Bronze Star."

"Fine," Ezra said, before turning and stumbling back toward the side gate.

Though Vance empathized with Ezra and understood his bitterness toward his father, he did not share it. His perspective was just different. Ezra's father had always been kind to him and made him feel welcome when most other parents discouraged their children from associating with him, it being the popular sentiment around town that the Duhons were *white trash*. But what stood out most in his mind about Ezra's father was the day he showed up at their mobile home when Vance and Ezra were around eleven years old.

Vance was crawling underneath the trailer to retrieve his football when he saw Chief Brasseaux's Bronco pull into their drive. He heard his father step out onto the front porch and tell Chief Brasseaux that Ezra wasn't there. Chief Brasseaux told his father that he wasn't there for Ezra—that he was there to talk to him.

"What about?" Vance's father wanted to know.

Chief Brasseaux told Vance's father that he happened to be passing by Ezra's bedroom when Vance was sleeping over at their house the night before last and saw bruises on his buttocks and lower back when he was getting changed.

Vance's father offered no reply or explanation.

Chief Brasseaux went on to say that if he ever saw something like that again that they were going to have a serious problem.

Vance's father mouthed off to Chief Brasseaux about it not being a crime to discipline your own kid. Chief Brasseaux said he wasn't there as the Chief of Police.

If that was the case, Vance's father said, he might just have to come down off the porch and give Ezra's father a good ass kickin' for being a pervert that watches naked boys and for sticking his nose in other people's business.

Chief Brasseaux was not exactly a big man. He was at least a couple of inches shorter and about twenty pounds lighter than Vance's father. Vance was therefore not surprised when Chief Brasseaux turned back to his Bronco and opened the door, apparently not interested in a physical altercation.

But instead of getting into the Bronco, Chief Brasseaux removed his sunglasses and set them on the dash. Then he shut the door, took a couple of steps into the yard and proceeded to roll up his sleeves. There was a look in his eyes that Vance had never seen before.

Vance knew he could not let Chief Brasseaux get pummeled by his father over something to do with him. He began crawling out from under the trailer as fast as he could when he heard his father mutter something. He stopped and listened. He heard his father say to Chief Brasseaux, "you're lucky I'm too drunk to scrap" and for him to "get the fuck off my property" before retreating into the trailer, slamming the door behind him. And he remembered that his father had never laid a hand on him again.

Vance had never told Ezra about the encounter. He was too ashamed when they were younger. And when he thought about telling him later in life, he knew that Ezra was so entrenched in his bitterness and resentment that it would not make a difference, so he abstained as he would again this night.

"You know what," Ezra said, regarding Vance with disappointment, "I get it. You not wanting to piss on the medal. Military loyalty and all that shit. Whatever."

Vance shrugged. "Come on. Let's go home you drunk fucker."

CHAPTER 53

Over the ensuing weeks, Ezra, Giles and Vance gathered on several occasions to talk about a plan. Collectively, they proposed and rejected a number of ideas as to how they could deliver justice to the Chaisson and Cole families. And to Uncle Gary and his friend, Gene. And of course to Bruce.

Giles wanted to anonymously turn the information over to the state police or the FBI and allow them to handle everything, but Ezra rejected this idea out of concern that someone would eventually leak the information to Mueller and that Mueller would trace the journals back to whomever his unnamed source was.

Vance's ideas were much more direct and violent, usually involving some form of torture, mutilation or both, and were immediately rejected by Ezra and Giles.

After several weeks with no fresh ideas, when it seemed that efforts to formulate and execute a plan might be dying on the vine, Giles and Vance received a text message from Ezra asking them to meet him at Eula's for a drink. He said it was important.

Upon squeezing into the booth next to Giles and across from Vance, Ezra placed a folder on the table. "Take a look," he said.

Giles opened the folder and found what appeared to be a photocopy of a newspaper article.

"Read it," Ezra instructed.

Giles held the paper to the side so that he and Vance could read it at the same time.

Feds Investigate Old St. Landry Parish Hate Crimes

Baton Rouge, Nov. 18 (AP) — Using shared technology developed by a consortium of scientists from the United States, France and Sweden, the U.S. Department of Justice has opened a federal investigation into an alleged murder and aggravated battery of two African American men that occurred in 1976 in St. Landry Parish, Louisiana. Sources with the DOJ confirm that the men are believed to have been the victims of racially motivated hate crimes, and the newly developed technology is being used to analyze recently harvested brain cells from the surviving victim's memory bank for visual images that could be helpful in identifying the assailants. The investigation will be one of three test cases in the United States.

"What the hell?" Giles said. "You called the FBI?" His volume was louder than he realized.

"Shhhhh," Ezra said, shaking his head. "No, I did not call the FBI, knucklehead," he whispered. "It's a ruse."

"I don't get it," Giles said.

"Me either," Vance said.

"So, I've stayed in touch with Dew over the years. He's a computer genius, it turns out. He has his own IT company."

"Dew? As in Dewey Bordelon?" Vance asked.

"Yes," Ezra replied. "And at some point, when he was telling me about all the things computer hacks were doing with identity theft and whatnot, I came up with this idea that he could create for us a digital profile and email address for a fictitious AP reporter."

"For what?" Giles asked, impatiently.

"We could use them to deliver this article to local newspapers for publication."

Giles and Vance both still looked confused.

Ezra sighed impatiently. "Dew can send this article to the editors of the *Iris News* and the *Daily World*, making it look like it's coming from a bona fide AP source. With a little luck, one or both of the papers will run the article. Since these local papers are always desperate for something other than obituaries, school lunches and the most recent Garden of the Week to print, I think the chances are pretty good. Might even make the front page."

"Okay, let's say they publish it. What's the end game?" Vance asked.

"There're all sorts of possibilities," Ezra said. "For starters, it could put so much pressure on Mueller and Pugh that they turn themselves in."

"Or turn on each other," Giles said.

"Yes. And it could get people talking about the crimes again, and hopefully, someone who knows something might decide to finally come forward, and maybe some new detective with no ties to Mueller who wants to make a name for himself decides to dig deeper."

"So how much does Dew know?" Giles queried.

"I had to tell him most of the story to get him to play ball. He was begging me to let him do it after I told him what it was all about. I knew he would."

"Why?"

"Have you kept up with him at all? Have you seen his profile picture on Facebook?"

"No," Giles said.

"I don't do social media," Vance said.

"Well, his wife is as black as the ace of spades," Ezra said in a hushed tone.

"Holy shit," Giles whispered.

"Yes sir," Ezra said.

"So old Dew, the biggest racist of us all back in the day, turns out to be a nigger lover?" Vance posited.

"Take easy, George Wallace," Ezra said reproachfully.

"Yea, I'm pretty sure you have always held the title of biggest racist," Giles said.

"Agreed," Ezra said.

"Bullshit. What makes you say that?" Vance asked with surprising sincerity.

"Oh, I don't know," Ezra said with sarcastic bemusement, "maybe it's because you're the only one who created a so-called *nigger trap*, or maybe it's because when you found out that they might be creating a holiday to honor Martin Luther King, Jr., you said you hoped that they would kill four more coloreds so that we could have the whole week off."

Giles chuckled. "That's right, you did say that."

"I was obviously joking," Vance insisted.

"Well, what was the so-called N-word trap?" Giles said.

"I don't recall anything about a nigger trap," Vance said, feigning ignorance.

"Yes," Ezra said, "you wired a boat battery to your bike, covered the battery with leaves and leaned the bike against a tree near the road in front of your trailer, the idea being that when a black person tried to steal it, it would electrocute them. You said, and I'm quoting, *I'll probably have a pile of niggers stacked up six feet high in front of my bike by the end of the day.*"

"But a boat battery wouldn't electrocute anybody. Not enough voltage," Giles said.

"Yeah, but he didn't know that," Ezra explained.

Giles chuckled. "Did you catch any?"

Vance smiled mischievously. "No. My little idiot half-brother tried to get on the bike and it shocked him so bad that he shit his pants. When my dad got home my cunt of a stepmother told him what I did, and he tore the hide off my ass with an extension cord."

They all laughed.

"In fact, that was the last time I took a beating," Vance said. He almost brought up the story about Ezra's father confronting his but decided not to.

"Well, I think it's genius," Giles said, tapping the fake newspaper article with his finger. "And it's safe. I love it."

"I know, right?" Ezra said, obviously very pleased with himself.

"How soon can Dew send it to the papers?" Giles asked.

"Well, he's already started sending legit AP articles from this fake source just to get the local papers used to seeing the name and email address. If I give him the green light, he can do it next Friday, in time for them to run it in next Sunday's edition."

CHAPTER 54

Abel was washing a coffee mug in the kitchen sink when he heard brakes squealing and then the sound of an automobile engine in his driveway. He pushed the curtain aside and saw Ferrell getting out of his pickup truck with a rolled-up newspaper in his hand. He was moving quickly or at least quickly for a man with a bad hip, and he looked anxious. Before Abel would reach the door, Ferrell was at the top of the steps rapping loudly on the windowpane.

"Did you read the paper?" Ferrell asked when Abel opened the door.

"Not yet."

"Well, you'll want to," Ferrell declared, his Adam's apple bobbing in his neck as he swallowed nervously. "Right there on the front page, bottom left." Abel took the paper from Ferrell and walked to his kitchen table where he grabbed a pair of cheaters and began to scan the front page with a deliberate air. "Right there, bottom left," Ferrell repeated.

"Yes, yes," Abel said, calmly. "Let me read." After perusing the article once and then a second time, Abel set the paper down, took his glasses off and set them down on the table next to the paper.

"They're gonna be coming for us Abel," Ferrell said, his tone filled with trepidation. "They're going to pull pictures out of that nigger boy's head and figure out who did that to him."

"Now don't going get yourself all into a lather, Ferrell," Abel said.

"Don't you think we need to get ahead of this thing?" Ferrell asked excitedly.

"How do you figure?"

"We could go to the authorities. We could say we just tried to talk to 'em and they attacked us or something like that."

Abel scoffed and glared at Ferrell condescendingly. "You want to go to the police and tell them that back in the 70s a little hundred thirty-pound jig came at us and that we fractured his skull, cut off his lips and jammed a mop handle up his ass in self-defense? And that we went ahead and drowned his buddy because we were scared of him, too?"

"Shit, I don't know," Ferrell wailed. "All I know is that I'm plenty scared, Abel. I really think we should consider turning ourselves in. I always heard that they are more lenient on you if you turn yourself in. I can't go to prison. I just can't."

Abel's face reddened with anger. "And what would you tell 'em, Ferrell? That you was just waiting outside and doing what you was told, and it was me that did everything so I could go to death row and you get a slap on the wrist?"

"No, no, I would never do that, Mule. But we could blame most of it on Errol. We could say we found out what Errol was up to and was trying to stop him."

Abel's countenance hardened. "If it ever comes to that, that's what we'll need to do. But we ain't turning ourselves in. And you're not going to tell nobody nothing about nothing. Do you understand me?" When Ferrell did not respond immediately, Abel repeated, "Do you fucking hear me, Ferrell?"

Ferrell shuddered. "Yes," he muttered.

Abel stepped toward Ferrell until their noses were almost touching. He poked Ferrell hard in the chest with his finger as he spoke. "I swear to God, Ferrell Wayne Pugh, if you even think about turning yourself in or saying anything to anybody, I will get to you, and I will snap your neck like a God-damned twig, do you hear me?"

"I won't say nothing if you don't want me to," Ferrell said

nervously. "I promise. You don't have to threaten me. I ain't said nothing to nobody all these years."

"I mean it, Ferrell," Mueller said, poking Ferrell in the chest again.

"I know you do, Mule," Ferrell said.

Abel lowered his hand, turned and walked back to the table. He sat down haggardly and leaned back in the chair. Ferrell thought that he looked ten years older than when he had arrived a few minutes earlier.

"You okay, Mule?" Ferrell asked.

Abel stared at the wall and said nothing.

"Mule?" Abel turned and looked at Ferrell as if he had forgotten that Ferrell was in the room. "Are you okay?" Ferrell repeated.

"Yeah," Abel replied. His face had lost most of its color.

"You don't look so good."

Abel gave no indication of having heard Ferrell's comment.

"Abel?"

"What?"

"I said you don't look so good. Are you alright?"

"I'm fine."

"So, what are we going to do?"

"Nothing for now," Abel said. "I need to think on it for a little while. You go on home."

After Ferrell was gone, Abel poured himself a double shot of bourbon and sat in his recliner in the dark, drinking and thinking. After a few minutes, he began to feel flush and lightheaded. When he tried to lift himself out of his recliner, he became weak and disoriented. He eventually pulled himself out of the chair and made his way to the bathroom where he leaned against the lavatory counter to catch his breath. He poured himself a glass of water from the faucet, drinking thirstily before setting

400

the glass down in the sink. He looked at himself in the mirror and thought he noticed the left side of his face drooping. He tried to turn the light off with his left hand, but his arm felt too weak to lift. He shuffled to his bedroom. He lay down on top of his bedding staring at the ceiling, exhausted, his legs hanging over the side, his mind whirling, his vision beginning to blur . . . .

As he slowly regained consciousness, Abel realized that he was in the hospital. The nurse asked him questions to determine if he was oriented to person, place and time. He was only able to grunt and to some extent shake and nod his head. She explained that he was in the hospital's ICU ward after having a series of strokes. He was found by a neighbor. He was lucky to be alive.

CHAPTER 55

"Yes, ma'am?" Ezra answered.

"Mr. Brasseaux, I have a call for you from the Evangeline Parish Sheriff's Office."

"Put it through."

"Yes, sir."

"Ezra Brasseaux," Ezra answered.

"Mr. Brasseaux, this is Deputy Terrell Truitt. I'm a detective with the Evangeline Parish Sheriff's Office."

"Okay. Wait, Terrell Truitt," Ezra said slowly as if trying to awake a reposed memory. "You know, your name sounds familiar, Deputy Truitt. Do I maybe know you from somewhere?"

"Kind'a, sort'a. I grew up in Iris, too. I was a couple of grades behind you in school. I believe you were in the same class as my first cousin, Clayton Chaisson."

"Yes, yes, yes," Ezra said, happy to make the connection. "I think I remember you now. You had a twin brother, right?"

"Yes, sir."

"Yeah, I remember Clayton telling me about what happened with your brother and your father. I know it's been a while, but all the same I'm very sorry for your loss in that regard."

"Thank you, sir."

"So, now that we got that figured out, what can I do for you, Deputy Truitt?"

"Well," the deputy said, "the sheriff has us lookin' into somethin', you know, runnin' down some loose ends in an investigation. One of the D.A.'s distant relatives was found dead in a crawfish pond yesterday afternoon. It looks like a suicide, but the family thinks there may be, you know, foul play or something like that, so the sheriff needs to make a good showing that he's givin' it a thorough look-see. So, that's what I'm doin'."

"Gotcha," Ezra said. "So how can I help?"

"Well, this old boy was found drownded with his hands bound behind his back with his jacket cuffs buttoned together and his shoes tied together with his own shoestrings. Could'a done it himself, you know, to make sure he couldn't change his mind or something. But somebody else could have done it, too, you know?"

"Damn," replied Ezra. "Is this individual someone that I'm supposed to know?"

"That's what I need to find out. The old man they found in the crawfish pond—his name was Ferrell Pugh."

Ezra felt his stomach flip when he heard Ferrell Pugh's name. He immediately wondered if Pugh's death was really a suicide or if Abel was involved. He then began to wonder whether any of it had anything to do with the fake AP article.

"Hello?"

"Yeah, I'm here. I'm sorry, my secretary walked into my office while you were talking and I got distracted. What was the guy's name again?"

"Ferrell Pugh," Terrell said.

"Okay yeah, from Iris, right? I actually met Mr. Pugh when I was in college. I interviewed him about the Iris Mardi Gras for a term paper. But I don't think I've seen him or talked to him since."

"Well actually, your name was scribbled on a piece of paper that they found in Mr. Pugh's desk."

Ezra instantly felt nauseous. "Hmm," he said, trying to sound somewhat surprised but not anxious. "That's odd. Unless it was something he had written all those years ago and just never threw it away."

"Yeah," Deputy Truitt said, "my boss wants to know if maybe you have represented him with regard to anything that might serve as a lead, you know, some nasty litigation or a business relationship gone south, or anything really."

Ezra felt a sense of relief. If the deputy suspected Ezra of being involved in any way, directly or indirectly, he was doing a masterful job of hiding it.

"I know I didn't do any legal work for him, Terrell," Ezra said, switching to a first name basis without thinking about it. "I would definitely remember that." He was trying very hard to sound confident but casual. "It's possible that he called for some type of legal service that I don't handle, you know, like for a will or a property transaction or something like that. He could have spoken to my staff. We always refer that kind of work out. But if he did, it wasn't communicated to me. Does the note have a date on it or anything like that?"

"No, it sure don't. It's just your name with some illegible scribblin'."

"Or maybe someone referred him to me for some type of legal services and he wrote down the name in case he wanted to call me," Ezra said.

"Would you mind checking with your staff to see if they have any records or memory of talking to him?"

"Not at all."

"I appreciate it."

"Of course," Ezra said. "Anything to help."

"Well, listen man, I know you're busy and I've got a few more calls to make myself so I'll let you get back to it. Just needed to check the box on this one if you know what I mean. Thanks for your time."

"No problem," Ezra said, "I'll get with my staff and let you know if there's anything involving Mr. Pugh."

Ezra picked up his office phone and dialed the number to Giles' company landline. When the receptionist answered, he identified himself as Ricky Stelly and asked for Giles.

"Giles Poret," Giles said. "How can I help you?"

"It's Ezra."

Giles scoffed. "Why did you give another name?"

"I didn't know if your receptionist logs the calls that she transfers."

"Why didn't you just call my cell?" Giles asked with curiosity.

"I didn't want there to be a cell phone record of me calling you at this very moment," Ezra said. "That's why I'm calling from a landline."

Giles was silent for a moment. "Okay, you're freaking me out," he said anxiously. "What's going on?"

"I just got a call from a detective from the Evangeline Parish Sheriff's Office. Turns out that Ferrell Pugh was found dead—drowned in a crawfish pond."

"Seriously?"

"Yeah, something about his hands being bound with this jacket sleeve buttons and his shoes tied together. They think it was probably suicide, but the D.A. is distantly related and he's apparently pressing the sheriff to investigate it in order to rule out foul play."

"Jesus," Giles replied, his voice filled with anxiety. "So why in the hell did they call you?"

Ezra sighed nervously. "He said they found my name scribbled on a fucking piece of paper in Pugh's house."

"What?!" Giles exclaimed. "Are you serious?"

"As a heart attack," Ezra answered.

"Christ," Giles said in an exclaimed whisper. "What did you say?"

"I told him that Vance Duhon, Giles Poret and I were involved in a scheme to trick the local newspapers to print a fraudulent article in the hopes that Mueller and Pugh would turn on each other or turn themselves in for hate crimes committed against two black boys in 1976. *What the fuck do you think I told him, Giles?*"

"I don't know, that's why I asked," Giles answered. "You don't have to be a jerk."

Ezra sighed. "You're right. I apologize."

"So?"

I played it off like he might have called me for legal services and my staff might have referred him to another lawyer."

Giles was silent. He was not understanding why Ezra was not more freaked out by the situation at hand.

"What are you thinking?" Ezra asked.

"What am I thinking?" Giles echoed. "What am I thinking?" he repeated. "I'll tell you what I'm thinking. I'm thinking about the Chuck Will Widow."

"The what?" Ezra asked.

"The Chuck Will Widow," Giles explained, "is a very small bird that has a very wide mouth that it uses to feed on very large moths. A few years back, I read an article about a birder in Florida finding one dead. When he examined it, it had a tiny bird lodged in its throat, which it apparently had choked on. It had literally bitten off more than it could chew—although birds don't bite or chew, but you get my drift."

"That's not helpful," Ezra said.

"I didn't say it was. You asked me what I was thinking."

"Okay. Meet me at Eula's at 5:30. I'll call Vance and tell him to meet us there."

"Okay."

After ending the call with Giles, Ezra checked with his staff about any calls coming in from a Ferrell Pugh. There were none. He then called Terrell Truitt back to give him that information. Truitt thanked him for getting back to him so quickly and did not have any other questions or requests. Ezra told him not to hesitate to call if there was anything else he could do. Truitt thanked him.

"Where's Vance?" Giles asked as he slid into the booth where Ezra was sitting in front of two beers, one already half gone. He looked even more panicked than he sounded over the phone.

"Never responded," Ezra said, pushing the untouched beer toward Giles. "Here, this one's for you. You look like you need one."

"Thanks. I may need more than one," Giles said before taking a huge gulp and then another. "I wonder where he is."

"No telling. Probably rocking the houseboat again with that sixteen-year-old."

Giles shook his head and grimaced. "You don't really think she's underage, do you?"

Ezra smirked. "No, but she ain't far from it." He peeked over his shoulder and then turned back toward Giles. "Speaking of, you see that gal at the bar in the white blouse?"

"Yes."

"She walked past me in those yoga pants to go to the restroom before you got here," Ezra explained. "I swear to God that she's got the most amazing ass I've ever seen. I'm glad I hadn't had more to drink

407

because I had this irresistible urge to literally reach out and grab it as she walked by me."

"So, you grabbed her ass?" Giles asked.

Ezra looked at Giles as if wondering if his brain was hemorrhaging. "No Giles, I didn't grab her ass."

"So, it was a *resistible* urge," Giles replied, trying to maintain a serious expression.

Ezra regarded Giles for a moment and then rolled his eyes. "I now feel an irresistible urge to punch you in the throat."

Giles giggled victoriously. Ezra in turn, smiled contentedly, his efforts to distract Giles from his panic having proved successful, at least temporarily.

Their conversation of course turned back fairly quickly to the sheriff department's investigation of Ferrell Pugh's death. They speculated about whether it was suicide or whether Abel Mueller had turned on him. They even pondered, though mostly in jest, whether Vance had gone rogue and had something to do with it. Mostly they brainstormed about why Pugh might have had Ezra's name written on a piece of paper. They left more paranoid than when they arrived.

CHAPTER 56

The next afternoon, Ezra's office phone rang while he was editing a pleading. It was his secretary. The Evangeline Parish Sheriff's Office was calling again.

Ezra's vision flashed white, and he instantly broke into a sweat. His mind began racing, clouded with paranoid theories, both plausible and absurd, as to why the sheriff's department was calling him back so soon or at all, though the fact that they were calling and not showing up at his office with handcuffs was probably a good sign. He considered letting the call go to voicemail before finally grabbing the receiver after the third ring. "Ezra Brasseaux," he said in the calmest tone he could muster.

"Ezra," the voice on the other end of the line said, "It's Terrell again. I'm sorry to bother, man." Terrell's tone was very somber, not at all friendly like the day before

"No, it's no bother at all Terrell," Ezra said, trying not to let his voice crack. "What's up?" he said.

"Listen," Terrell said, "We're going to need you to come to the station. You will probably want to clear your calendar for the rest of the day."

Ezra felt his stomach flip and a huge lump form in his throat. He felt nauseous and paralyzed. He forced himself to take a breath. "Uh, I'm supposed to be leaving in a few minutes for meeting with a client in Baton Rouge," he lied. "Can you give me some idea what this is about?"

"This is not something to do over the phone, man. You're going to want to reschedule that meeting. This really can't wait," Terrell said solemnly.

"Okay, yeah, I'll reschedule. I'll be there in about an hour, depending on traffic."

"Ask for me when you arrive."

"10-4," Ezra replied, trying to sound nonchalant.

On the drive to Ville Platte, Ezra contemplated every conceivable scenario as to how the meeting might go, whether they just planned to arrest him upon arrival and read him his Miranda rights right there in the lobby or whether they planned to soft pedal it and treat him as a witness, trying to get him to implicate himself before making the arrest.

He considered that what he had done with the fraudulent newspaper article might be a violation of some federal law and that the sheriff would have no jurisdiction to prosecute a federal crime. He then began to wonder whether the FBI or some other federal agency was involved and whether they would have agents, all dressed in dark suits and dark ties, just like in the movies, present for the meeting and prepared to make an arrest.

He began to think how all of this would impact his career. He and his law school friends were always quick to call each other when one of their classmates had been the subject of a state bar disciplinary action. Melanie Johnson had been put on probation for comingling her client's funds with her business funds. Jay Lewis was suspended for sleeping with a client. Lester Pedigo got disbarred after being convicted for possession of child pornography. Now, his classmates might be making the call about him. He would almost certainly lose his license.

The bar association had probably never had the occasion to discipline a lawyer for something like this, he thought, but surely it would take the matter very seriously and hand down a harsh punishment. He imagined receiving a ruling from the Louisiana Office of Disciplinary

Counsel. He would open the envelope and pull out a document bearing its official seal. It would be short and to the point.

> *In the matter of In re Ezra Paul Brasseaux, Esq., it is the finding of the Office of Disciplinary Counsel for the Louisiana State Bar Association that Respondent engaged in fraudulent manipulation of the press which constitutes a breach of the public trust and conduct unbecoming an officer of the court. Effective immediately, the status of Respondent's license to practice law in the State of Louisiana is as follows:*

PERMANENT DISBARMENT.

He thought about calling Giles and Vance but rejected the idea because the authorities would surely be gathering his phone records and might even have tapped his cell phone for all he knew. Upon arriving at the sheriff's office, he drove around the parking area, scanning the lot for any sign of a vehicle with federal government plates but saw none. He parked his car in the lot reserved for judges, court personnel and attorneys. He chuckled to himself at the thought of his parking a car being the last act he engaged in as a licensed attorney before being arrested and disbarred.

Upon entering the police station, he was somewhat relieved to be greeted with a handshake instead of handcuffs, though Deputy Truitt's countenance was noticeably grave. As he was escorted to a conference room in the rear of the building, he scanned the station for any sign of federal agents but saw none. He was shown into a room with a large table and several chairs on either side, and he was asked to have a seat while they waited for the sheriff to join them. Deputy Truitt excused himself, promising that the sheriff would not be long. Ezra thanked him and stared at the pitcher of water on the table in front of him. With trembling hands, he filled a plastic cup with water, downed it and then filled it again. He waited only a few minutes though it felt like hours.

Sheriff Rives "Joey" Deshotels, a portly, pie-faced man with a thick, handlebar mustache arrived and shook hands with Ezra in a cheerless, almost apologetic manner. Terrell and the sheriff sat down, taking their time to get comfortable in the padded folding chairs positioned on the other side of the table.

Ezra waited anxiously for one of them to begin, though neither seemed very eager to take the lead. His impatience bordered on anger. He tried hard to mask his emotions but was not sure of how good a job he was doing. He wanted to take a sip of water but was afraid that Terrell and the Sheriff would see his hands shaking.

"Ezra," the sheriff finally began, "I know that Terrell informed you about our investigation of Ferrell Pugh's death."

"Yes, sir."

"Well, his body was found in a crawfish pond toward the back of a tract of farmland owned by a man named Abel Mueller. The property extends into Evangeline Parish, and the body was found on this side of the parish line. That's how we're involved."

"Okay," Ezra said.

"Do you know Abel Mueller?" the sheriff asked.

Ezra shrugged. "Not personally. Growing up in Iris, I knew of him. I knew of his twin daughters, but they were several years older than me."

"Well anyway," the sheriff continued, "when our guys were pulling Pugh's body out of the crawfish pond, the laces of his boot were snagged on something in the mud. One of our men reached down to free it, thinking it was probably a piece of a crawfish trap. He found that the lace was actually tangled up on or maybe even deliberately tied to an antenna."

"An antenna?" Ezra asked, his curiosity overcoming his determination to remain quiet. "Like a T.V. antenna?" he asked.

"No, a car radio antenna," Terrell interjected.

Terrell and the sheriff both sat in silence regarding Ezra, each waiting for the other to deliver the punch line. Though it was just a few seconds, the silence was too much for Ezra to bear. He felt the wild impulse to punch them both in the face for creating so much suspense at his expense.

"After we realized the antenna was attached to a vehicle," the sheriff continued, "we got an excavator back there and dug it up. It was buried directly under the spot where Pugh's body was found."

"Like maybe it was a suicide, and he wanted us to find it," Terrell said.

Ezra stared at Terrell then glanced at the sheriff, still waiting for the other shoe to drop.

"Anyway," the sheriff said, "We pulled the vehicle out and pressure washed it. It was on older model Ford Bronco."

"With the remains of a body inside," Terrell added.

"We ran the VIN and plates on it," the sheriff said. "The vehicle was registered and titled in your father's name."

413

Ezra's face went blank. His brain went through a series of mental triangulations, few of which were completely rational. He was confused, skeptical and wary. He looked at Terrell and then at the sheriff and then at nothing, trying with his fatigued brain to absorb and process the information.

Terrell looked at Deshotels and he reciprocated, as if each was deferring to the other. Finally, Terrell spoke. "We confirmed that the remains are your father's, Ezra."

Ezra stared at Terrell in silence for a moment. "My father?" he finally said, uncertain of the implications.

Terrell nodded. "I'm sorry I couldn't say anything about it before, but we were waiting on the results from forensics."

Ezra scoffed in disbelief. "I don't understand. My father left Louisiana over thirty years ago and never returned. I don't see how it could be him."

"The pathologist used old x-rays from his medical and dental records to verify his identity," Deshotels said. "It's a one-hundred percent match. I'm really sorry to be the bearer of this news."

Ezra resisted the urge to laugh. *This has to be a bad joke*, he thought. "I really don't understand," he said.

"A full autopsy is being conducted but the coroner's preliminary impression from the post-mortem changes is that death occurred at least twenty years ago, maybe thirty," the sheriff explained. "There was also oil change records in the glove compartment of the Bronco that didn't get wet and were still legible. And the latest one was dated June 23, 1976."

Terrell gave Ezra a moment to absorb the information and then cleared his throat. "So, our working theory is that your dad was killed and buried very close in time to when he was believed to have left Iris in 1976. Nothing else seems to make sense."

Ezra's face contorted into an anguished smile and then transitioned into a grimace. He nodded and then shook his head. His mind was racing, his heart fluttering. Finally, he took a deep breath and exhaled. He chuckled nervously. "This is not at all how I was expecting this meeting to go."

Terrell nodded. "I'm sorry that I couldn't give you a heads up on the phone. Hopefully, you understand why."

"All this time," Ezra said, shaking his head, still struggling to absorb the altered reality, "we thought he had left and was living in Texas."

Terrell nodded. "We spoke to the people he worked with at the Iris P.D. That was their belief as well. Apparently, he had made plans to move there with an Isabella Vadas, a former A.D.A., right?"

Ezra nodded. "That was my understanding."

"Well, just to cover all our bases, we reached out to her. She was not easy to track down. Anyway, we learned from her that the day before your father was supposed to leave for Texas to join her, he telephoned and told her that he had changed his mind. He had decided to stay."

"So he never went to Texas?"

"Apparently not. She said that she did not take the news very well and that they had a very ugly fight over the phone. She said she tried calling him a few times several days later after she had cooled off but that he never answered or returned her calls, so she eventually got the message and stopped trying. Now we know why she never heard back from him."

Ezra took another deep breath. "Has the cause of death been determined?"

The sheriff sighed. "The roof of your dad's Bronco was totally smashed-in like maybe an excavator bucket came down on it," he said. "We don't have the coroner's final report yet, but it looks like he was crushed inside the cab and then the vehicle was pushed into a hole and buried."

Ezra mashed his eyes shut and bowed his head. Competing emotions were wrestling within him, each struggling to take center stage—anger towards Mueller and Pugh, guilt over harboring so much resentment and animosity toward his father all these years, trepidation about how he was going to break the news to his mother, relief over the fact that he had not actually been abandoned by his father and finally, jubilation that he was not going to lose his law license. He was overwhelmed.

"We still have a ways to go before we've completed our investigation," Deshotels added, "but our working hypothesis is that your father was investigating Abel Mueller, probably for some really bad shit, and that somehow Mueller found out that your dad was on his trail—maybe someone leaked it to him—maybe one of his own people—and unfortunately Mueller got the drop on 'em."

Ezra closed his eyes. "I think I know."

Terrell and Deshotels exchanged a quick glance and then both regarded Ezra curiously.

Ezra paused to gather his thoughts for a moment. "In 1976," he began, "Cedric Chaisson was killed and his cousin, D'Arius Cole, was mutilated and beaten nearly to death. It was mostly Mueller, but Pugh and a guy named Errol Frey were also involved. I'm guessing my Dad was getting close to figuring it out and maybe went out there to question Mueller or look around his property for evidence."

"How do you know this?" she sheriff asked.

"It's a bit of a crazy story, but I've got Pugh's wife's journals. I know it's all hearsay, but they have a lot of the details that will help put all the pieces together."

"You're shitting me," Deshotels said in disbelief.

Ezra shook his head. "No. I don't even know who sent them to me. They just showed up at my office a few months back with an unsigned letter. I guessed it was someone in Pugh's family. You can send someone to pick them up at my office, or I can bring them to you, whatever you want."

Terrell and Deshotels looked at each other with surprised expressions and then turned back to Ezra.

"Why didn't you take the journals to law enforcement?" Terrell asked.

Ezra shook his head. "I don't know," he said. "It was all so overwhelming for me. I mean—and I know this is going to sound crazy but—before I received those journals, I was actually writing a novel that was inspired by the rape of Abel Mueller's daughter, Kelly. I had been working on it for years. When I got the journals, I don't know, I freaked out. I did a little digging and learned that Mueller was really dangerous and that he had some close connections to local and state law enforcement. But I didn't know who, so I didn't feel safe going to anyone."

Ezra considered telling Deshotels and Terrell about Kelly Mueller's medical records and the AP article but rejected the idea. He needed to think everything through first.

"Do you know why this unknown person sent the journals to you specifically?"

Ezra shrugged. "There was an unsigned letter that came with the journals. It was very cryptic. It said that they hoped I could do something about what happened. I'm presuming they chose me because they believed that my dad helped to sweep everything under the rug, and that maybe I would want to make up for all that. They quoted something from the Bible

417

which I interpreted to mean that sons are responsible for the sins of their fathers."

"Jesus," Terrell replied.

"Have y'all made any arrests?" Ezra asked.

Terrell looked at Deshotels who sighed. "No," he said. "Abel Mueller had a series of strokes recently. Can't walk. Can't talk. Can't do anything really. He's on round the clock care with home health. He's not supposed to get any better."

"And of course Frey and Pugh are dead," Terrell added.

"What I want to know," said Ezra, "is if my dad was after something that big, how could no one else at the police department or the D.A.'s office have known about it?"

The sheriff nodded. "We have the same questions, and we are going to look into it, Ezra. We're getting the state police involved. But half of the people that we could have talked to are dead by now. And if someone who's still alive does know something, how likely are they to be willing to cooperate? So, it's going to be tough. But I promise you we are going to do our best to get answers to those questions. Especially if it means having to go after dirty cops."

Ezra nodded. "I appreciate that."

"And Mueller's medical condition is not going to lessen our resolve to get this crime solved. There could be others involved," Deshotels added.

They paused to give Ezra a moment. "I know this is a lot to take in," Terrell said.

Ezra stared down at the table, his thoughts and emotions still competing with each other for dominance. "My mom," he finally said. "I've got to go talk to my mom."

"Of course," Terrell said. "Would you like me to go with you?"

"I don't think so," Ezra said. "I think it would be better if it's just me for now. Thank you, though."

"We understand," Deshotels replied. "I'm sure you will have more questions once all of this sinks in. Call us any time. And we'll call you if there are any significant developments."

Terrell walked Ezra to his car, neither of them speaking along the way. When they arrived at the car, Ezra stopped and looked up at the sky and sighed.

"I wanted to tell you something about your father that you probably never knew," Terrell said. Ezra turned and leaned against his car to hear what Terrell had to say. "You probably remember that I was a real punk growing up. Always in trouble. Always hangin' with the wrong crowd."

Ezra had a vague memory of what Terrell was referring to but did not acknowledge as much, waiting for Terrell to continue.

"Well, in late 1975, which would have been just a year or so before your dad went missing—" Terrell paused, "—me and some podnas got busted breaking into a Radio Shack and I got put in jail. The other two dudes got bailed out by their moms. When nobody came for me, your father came and got me out of the holding area and brought me to his office. He was the first person that ever asked me what I wanted to do with my life. I had never even thought about it before. Unless they get an athletic scholarship or they real smart, niggas in the hood just be, you know, they just go with the flow. Well, we talked and he got me thinking. He's the one that encouraged me to start doing better in school and that if I stayed out of trouble, he would help me get into the police academy, if I had any interest in pursuing that. He even bailed me out of jail with his

419

own money. Made me promise not to tell nobody. Well, he wasn't there to help me get into the academy when the time came, but it was him who inspired me. And if it wasn't for him taking the time with me, I'd probably be in prison or maybe even dead by now."

Ezra smiled warmly and nodded. "I appreciate you sharing that with me, Terrell."

"I just thought you should know," Terrell said.

CHAPTER 57

After Terrell and Ezra shook hands and said good-bye, Ezra got into his car and sat behind the wheel for a few minutes trying to gather his thoughts and get a handle on his emotions. He took a few deep breaths and then called his office to tell his secretary to clear his calendar for the rest of the week. He would explain later.

As he drove slowly in the direction of Iris, it occurred to him that his memory of what his father looked like was very vague. On the one-year anniversary of the date that it was presumed that his father had left for Texas, he and his mother had built a fire in the backyard and burned every photograph of him that they could find.

He recalled him having a nice smile and that he was tall with an athletic build. He remembered the smell of his Old Spice aftershave. But he was not sure about the exact color of his hair or eyes or any distinguishing facial features. Then, it occurred to him that he was approximately the same age now as his father was when he last saw him and that everyone had always said how much they resembled each other. He tilted his rearview mirror to look at himself, hoping to trigger a more vivid memory of his father. It did not.

He suddenly felt the weight of everything crashing down on him like a huge wave. He pulled over onto the shoulder of the highway and put the car in park. He rested his head on the steering wheel between his hands and began to sob. Tears flowed down his cheeks. His nose began to run. He could hear vehicles passing and imagined their occupants staring at him as they passed. He did not care. He cried until he could cry no more. He rifled through his console and found a stack of fast-food napkins that he kept in reserve. He blew into one, and then another, and then one more until his nose was as free of mucous as he could get it. He put the car in drive and drove on.

After a few miles, he called Terrell.

"Hey man, everything okay?" Terrell said when he answered, not expecting to hear back from Ezra so soon.

"Yeah. Yeah, I'm fine," Ezra said with surprising composure. "Hey, I've got a favor to ask. I was wondering if you could give me Isabella Vadas' telephone number. I promise I'm not going to harass her. I just want to know if she can tell me anything else about my dad during those last few months, you know, just so I have something."

There was a pause before Terrell spoke. "I'm really not supposed to give out that kind of information, Ezra."

"I know," Ezra said. "But these circumstances are a bit unusual. And I'd really appreciated it."

Terrell sighed. "Okay. But please do not tell anyone where you got it."

"Of course."

Ezra knew that it would be best to wait a few days or weeks before calling Isabella, but patience had never been his strong suit. To his surprise, she answered. When he identified himself, she did not seem surprised to hear from him. He explained why he was calling. It was apparent that the sheriff's office had not given her much information. He gave her a quick summary of all that had transpired. He could hear sniffles over the line. In a quivering voice, she expressed her sincere condolences.

She stated that she would really want to attend his services, if they were planning any, but realized that it would be best for Ezra's mother if she abstained. She would find her own way to pay her respects, she said.

She told Ezra that she genuinely loved his father and that even when he changed his mind about moving, they were still committed to working things out. She said that she was so heart-broken and devastated when she thought he had cut her out of his life. "I guess, in a way, we had that situation in common," she said.

"Yeah, I suppose we did," Ezra said. "It's hard, isn't? I mean, believing a certain truth about someone for so long and then learning that it was in reality exactly the opposite."

"Yes," Isa said, her voice full of emotion and empathy.

"I mean, I'm not trying to put angel's wings on him or anything. He still left my mom. That caused her a lot of pain. And I guess I still have some resentment about that. But—" Ezra stopped.

There was an uncomfortable pause. Finally, Isa spoke. "It may not be my place," she said, "but I'm going to tell you anyway because if I were in your shoes, I would want to know. And because of that resentment you just referred to, I think it's only fair that you know the truth, the truth about your parents and what happened to their marriage."

"Okay," Ezra replied warily.

Isa paused, struggling to find the right words. "I want you to understand that I'm not trying to canonize him either. But I can only imagine what people said and what unfair assumptions were made—by people in the community, by you, about your father leaving the marriage. And of course I'm biased and feel responsible to some extent because of my role in that. But I want you to know that it was a very, very difficult decision for him and that although we were very much in love and wanted more than anything to be together, his first priority was always you. I also think you should know that when I came along, their marriage was already dead. And it had been dead for a very long time, Ezra."

Ezra was silent, trying to reconcile this characterization of his parents' marriage against his own conflicting memories and impressions. "I don't think that's true," he said. "They never fought. They seemed pretty normal to me."

"I know. They did their best to create that perception for you. And I'm sure they got good at it."

"What does that mean exactly?"

Isa paused and swallowed, beginning to second guess whether she should share such sensitive information with Ezra.

"Please, just tell me," Ezra pleaded.

"Your father shared with me that when you were around four years old, your mother became pregnant with their second child. When she learned that there were genetic abnormalities, she elected to have an abortion. Because your father was so staunchly Roman Catholic and *pro-life*, she kept it from him. She told him that she had a miscarriage.

"Later, when she could not get pregnant again, they consulted a fertility specialist and it came out that the reason she could not get pregnant was because of scar tissue from the abortion. That's how he found out. Your father was devastated and felt very betrayed. Your mother was unrepentant, believing that she had done nothing wrong. And they were unable to reconcile their differences. They resolved to stay in the marriage as long as they could for your sake. Your father and I of course met many years later.

Ezra remained silent for a while. Finally, he spoke. "On some level I knew," he said.

"Oh?"

"His name is David," Ezra said, referring to the little boy in his recurring dream.

"Whose name is David?" Isa asked, confused.

"My brother," Ezra said. "I've dreamed about him all of my life—well, beginning when I was about four and a-half, apparently not long after the—" he hesitated, finding it difficult to say the word, "—after the abortion. He looks just like me but without freckles and with darker hair and lighter eyes. He told me that an angel gave him his name. After my dad disappeared, the dreams took on a new theme. It's like David was always trying to lead me back to my dad, though I would always wake up just before we found him."

Emotion was thick in Isa's voice. "That's beautiful," she said. She could hear Ezra taking a deep breath through the phone. "You know," she said, "until just now, I didn't really know if I believed in angels."

"Me either," Ezra said as tears ran down his face. "This is so overwhelming."

"I can only imagine, Ezra."

Ezra thanked Isa for everything, and she thanked him for reaching out. She told him to feel free to stay in touch if he had any desire to do so. He thanked her, although he thought that it was unlikely that he would.

He telephoned his mother to let her know that he was stopping by for a short visit. He sat her down at the kitchen table and did his best to tell her everything that he had learned from the journals and from the sheriff's department. Her reaction was much more placid than he expected it would be. She did not get very emotional or ask many questions. It was clear that the new information did not change things for her nearly as much as they had for Ezra, which was to be expected. She said that they would have to arrange a funeral service. Ezra agreed.

"Is there anything else?" she asked, sensing that Ezra was holding back something.

"No," Ezra lied. "That's pretty much everything." He decided to spare her the embarrassment and pain that might come from him mentioning anything about talking to Isa Vadas. About the abortion. About David.

When they were done talking, Ezra stepped out of the backdoor and walked to the giant Chinese Tallow at the rear of the property. He kicked the leaves and dirt around with his shoe for a while and when he did not find what he was looking for, he went into the shed and found a garden rake. He walked back to the dirt patch and gently scraped the ground with the tines of the rake. After a few strokes, he felt metal striking metal. He used his fingers to separate the dirt from his father's medal. The bronze had corroded to varying hues of green. The tattered nylon ribbon was stained from years of exposure to water, mold and decomposed leaves but was otherwise intact. He held the medal in the palm of his hand and wept.

After leaving his mother's house, Ezra called Clayton Chaisson and asked if they could meet at Eula's. They found a table near the rear of the bar where they could have some privacy. Despite his emotional exhaustion, Ezra told him everything. He began with the lie about the rape and the resulting price that Cedric and D'Arius had paid. He disclosed his grand plan to bring Mueller and Pugh their comeuppance. He ended with explaining the theory about his father's efforts to investigate the crimes and how that had gotten him killed while everyone believed he had swept the crimes under the rug and then abandoned his wife and son.

Clayton expressed his sincerest condolences. He promised to share the information with his parents. Ezra thanked him.

"*The Lord is good to those who hope in him,*" Clayton said, "*to the person who seeks him. It's good to wait in silence for the Lord's deliverance.*"

Ezra nodded with agreement. "Is that from *Proverbs*?"

"*Lamentations* 3:25," Clayton replied.

Ezra smiled. They stood and embraced.

CHAPTER 58

Abel lay restlessly in his homecare bed, staring blankly at his living room ceiling. Each miserable day felt like a lifetime and the brief respites that came from sleep seemed to come and go in an instant. Every moment of his waking existence was a hellish struggle with feeling claustrophobic in his own body and one in which death felt imminent but was never quite delivered.

The forlorn silence was suddenly interrupted by the sound of metal tapping on glass. With considerable effort, Abel turned his head toward the noise. It was dark outside, but he was able to make out the silhouette of a tall man standing on his front porch just outside his living room window. The tapping stopped and Abel watched the man use his finger to write something in the pollen that had built-up on the windowpane. The letters were inverted so that Abel could read the message from the inside. *Bruce – 1976.*

As Abel was trying to make sense of the message, he heard voices in the kitchen, then the sound of a door close followed by footsteps into the living room. He turned his head just as the overhead light was turned on to see a dark-skinned, heavyset black woman wearing mauve medical scrubs. As his eyes adjusted, he could see that she was carrying a medical chart. She glanced in the direction of the window and Abel expected her to react to the man, or to the message in the pollen, or both, but she did not. Instead, she walked to the whiteboard that had been hung on the wall across from Abel's bed. She erased the name that was written next to "CNA" and wrote her own.

"Good evening, Mr. Mueller." the woman said in a very pleasant voice. "My name is Jayla. I'm your new night shift caregiver. I heard all about you, so I got myself reassigned here just to be able to take extra good care of you myself."

Abel regarded the large woman as she sat in the chair next to his bed and flipped through the pages of his chart. "Pervasive muscle weakness," she read out loud. "Aphasia. Neurologically intact," she continued. "Comprehends but unable to make needs known other than to respond with head movements and blinking."

She turned to Abel and smiled. She set the chart down and stood up, facing Abel. "So, if I pinch your toes Mr. Mueller, you should be able to feel it real good and let me know you feel it, okay?" As she said this, she reached under the linens and pinched Mueller's little toe on his right foot. Mueller grunted affirmatively and blinked once. "Very good," Jayla said before pinching his big toe on the opposite foot. Again, Mueller grunted and blinked. "Excellent," she said. "And how about this?" she asked as she moved her hand under the linens without making contact with Mueller's feet. Mueller did not grunt this time, but blinked twice for *no*.

"Outstanding," Jayla said, chuckling. "That's because I didn't pinch you. That means you not going crazy."

Abel regarded the CNA curiously, his gaze softening. She pulled Abel's sheets up closer to his neck and lifted his head with one hand as she fluffed his pillow with the other. When he was settled, she used her fingers to comb his hair to the side. "I think I smell a wet diaper, Mr. Mueller," she said in a kind voice. "I'm going to roll you over to get that changed. I need to do a skin audit on your backside anyway."

With powerful arms, the big-boned CNA rolled Abel over and held him steady on his side with one hand while dexterously removing his diaper with the other. She examined the red skin around his rectum and patted it softly with a moist, medicated towelette and then very gently applied ointment to the affected area. He grunted loudly and his body tightened when he felt her touch the sore area around the edges of his anus.

"Is it sensitive down there?" Jayla queried in a compassionate tone. "You're starting to get a little rash. I'll bet them nurses at the hospital was letting you stay with a dirty diaper too long," she said, as she made a note in the chart. "We see that a lot. Then, when the patient gets to home health and the family sees it, they want to blame that on us. No, ma'am. Not on my watch," she said with a prideful chuckle.

When she came around to the other side of the bed, Abel noticed a faded tattoo on the left side of her neck, the details of which were obscured by the darkness of her skin. She noticed Abel looking and smiled. She stood up straight and said, "Are you trying to read my neck, Mr. Mueller?"

Abel did not respond but his eyes moved from hers to the side of her neck and then back.

"D'Arius is my baby daddy name," she said. "I got two babies with him: D'Arial, he a truck driver, and D'Arienne, she work at the post office. We had talked about getting married and having some more kids, you know, but he ended up getting hurt real bad when my babies was little. In fact," the large woman continued as Abel followed her with his eyes, "my man, he been pretty much like you for nearly thirty years. Probably shouldn't still be alive."

Jayla pulled on Abel's covers to straighten them out as she talked. "The Lord Jesus only knows how, but my man, he got mixed up in a real bad situation, Mr. Mueller. Yes he did. Somebody did a real number on him. Big chunks of hair and scalp were ripped right out of his head. Broke most of the front teeth out of his mouth. Broke his leg real bad to where it turned to the side. Spinal cord damage. Brain damage."

Jayla continued as she straightened an assortment of medication bottles on the bedside table. "And whoever got a hold of him, they had to be full of hate. They rammed a mop handle up his backside and cut off his *hmm-hmm*. The whole thing. Left him with what looks like a deformed vajayjay. And they cut his lips off and torched the skin around his mouth, I guess so he wouldn't bleed to death 'cause maybe they wanted to torture him some more. Can you believe somebody could be so cruel?" she said, shaking her head piteously.

She sucked her teeth as if she were still in disbelief of all the injuries her boyfriend had survived. She glanced at Abel and saw him glaring at her, his mouth beginning to twitch. "And now," Jayla continued, "with his brain injury, he just stare at you with those dumb, anxious eyes, eating through a tube and urinating and defecating into a bag. And that's all day, every day."

Jayla stopped what she was doing and put her hands on her hips and met Abel's stare. "You know what's freaky? Because he ain't got no lips to cover his teeth, it always looks like he's got this crazy smile on his face, you know? Like one of them evil clowns you see in the movies. And he just stares at you with that crazy clown smile. But it ain't no smile. He ain't got nothin' to be smiling about and couldn't if he did. His own kids been scared of him their whole lives."

Jayla adjusted the incline of Abel's bed using a remote control as she continued to go on about her boyfriend. "He stay at his momma's house, but she a drug addict and can barely take care of herself much less take care of him, so I do what I can, Mr. Mueller. But I can't always be there, you know?"

"I don't mean to bad-mouth his momma though. She was a good momma for a long time. She raise five kids all by herself. D'Arius was the youngest. She was working three jobs for a good while. Life finally wore her to the nub, you know, to where there was just nothin' left of what made her good. Starting using meth to try to lift herself up and be able to keep going, keep working, and then the meth got the upper hand, just like it always do."

Jayla paused and smiled at Abel. "But listen at me. Going on and on about me and my man like you care to be burdened with all that. I can be silly like that sometimes Mr. Mueller, so you'll have to excuse me." She laughed at herself and looked around the room to see if anything else needed to be straightened.

"When all that happened to him, he was with his cousin, Cedric. Cedric Chaisson. They worked at the nursing home together. Cedric and D'Arius was first cousins on their mommas' side. Cedric was my second cousin on his daddy side. Seem like everybody related somehow in the hood," Jayla said chuckling to herself. "He was with D'Arius when they went missing. Poor Cedric, he come back dead—drownded and dumpted in the woods with D'Arius. They said they was found by two little white boys hunting blackbirds. That was something, huh? White boys hunting black birds but finding black boys," she said, chuckling.

CHAPTER 59

Abel continued to glare at the large CNA anxiously, the corner of his mouth now twitching more violently. His body jerked as if he were trying in vain to get out of bed. Suddenly, he remembered the man in the window and laboriously turned his head to shift his gaze in that direction. But due to the glare of the overhead light, he was no longer able to see him.

As Jayla folded a hand towel and placed in on the bedside table, she gestured with her chin toward the window. "Quiet out here in the country, huh?" She looked around the living room, admiring the grandfather clock and antique furniture. "You got a real nice house, Mr. Mueller," she said as she held a cup and straw in front of in his mouth, "here, you need to keep hydrated."

While continuing to glare at Jayla, Abel wrapped his lips around the straw and sucked cold water into his mouth, his eyes fixed on her as he did. When he began to cough, Jayla quickly pulled the straw out of his mouth. "Hey now, don't you go choking to death on me. No, sir," she said, chuckling.

Abel watched Jayla walk to the front door, open it and look outside. He thought he heard her say something but was not sure whether she was mumbling to herself or talking to someone else. She closed the door and then turned the overhead light off. Abel turned and was again able to make out the outline of the man who was still standing outside the living room window. The man had cleared a circle of pollen from the glass so that Abel could see his grinning face more clearly. Abel did not recognize him.

As he nervously glared at the strange man in the window, Abel heard Jayla's cell phone vibrating in her pocket. She pulled out her phone and spoke softly enough to where Abel could not hear what she was saying. He saw her put the phone back into her pocket and walk back toward him. He thought he heard a vehicle pull into the driveway and then the sounds of car doors being shut.

Jayla leaned over his bed and, again, combed Abel's hair to the side with her fingers. He could see more tattoos on her breasts but could not make out what they were. "I've got a surprise for you, Mr. Mueller," she said in soft voice. "You gonna have some visitors tonight."

Abel regarded Jayla suspiciously. He heard a light tap on the front door. Jayla opened the door. "Y'all come in," she said. Abel watched a badly disfigured man sitting in a wheelchair being rolled into the room under the direction of a very large black man dressed in a dark suit. The large man entered slowly and closed the door behind him. He nodded at Jayla and parked the wheelchair in the corner of the room where the disfigured man and Abel had an unobstructed view of one another. Their eyes met. The disfigured man was staring at Abel with a lipless faux smile. Abel's pupils dilated and he began to murmur and twitch in his bed.

"Dis my D'Arius, Mr. Mueller," Jayla said as she patted D'Arius gently on the arm. "I thought it would be good for him to come visit for a little while. He don't get out enough. And this," she said, gesturing toward the large black man, "well, he gonna introduce hisself." She turned to the large man and said, "He can't speak, but he understands."

The huge man nodded to Jayla and pulled a wooden chair to Abel's bedside and sat in it, the legs creaking under his weight. He closed his eyes, took a deep breath and drew his hands together in front of his face, the tips of his fingers nearly reaching the end of his wide nose. His lips moved in silent prayer for several minutes as Abel watched anxiously. When he was finished praying, the large man opened his eyes and looked at Abel. He saw the anger and confusion on Abel's face and studied him for a moment without expression. Finally, he said, "Mr. Mueller, my name is Clayton Chaisson. My older brother was Cedric Chaisson, the young black boy that you murdered back in September of 1976."

Abel leered at Clayton bitterly, unrepentantly, his nostrils flaring and eyes narrowing. He tried to speak but produced only incomprehensible sounds as foamy saliva gathered at the corners of his mouth.

"Mr. Mueller," Clayton continued, "I want you to know something about the young man that you drowned. I want you to know that my brother was walking kindness, sir. He had a contagious laugh and did nothing but bring joy to people with his gentle disposition and his God-given musical talent." Clayton paused to wipe tears from his face, then began to speak again. "I want you to know that when you killed my brother, you also broke my mother. You robbed my whole family of the peaceful life my parents had made for us."

Clayton closed his eyes again, took a deep breath and leaned toward Abel's bed. "I am not here to harm you, Mr. Mueller," Clayton said reassuringly. "Actually, I came here to pray for you. And to forgive you."

Abel glared at Clayton, his body squirming and jerking as if he were trying to get up.

"My family and I forgive you not because you deserve forgiveness Mr. Mueller, but because the Lord Jesus Christ commands that we give it." Clayton placed his large hand on Abel's forearm. "And forgive you, my family and I do. May God have mercy on your soul, sir."

Abel's eyes looked upon Clayton unashamedly as his lips began to move. He tried to spit but the saliva intended for Clayton's face only oozed from his lips and ran down his chin and neck. Clayton reached for a tissue and wiped Abel's chin and neck clean as Abel's eyes burned with ire.

Clayton smiled piteously. "The good Lord knows that people who are the hardest to forgive are those that need it the most. God bless you, Mr. Mueller," he said.

Clayton turned and stepped back toward the door, facing Jayla. "Thank you," he said.

"No problem," Jayla said.

"You sure you don't want me to take D'Arius back home? I don't mind."

Jayla shook her head. "No, he needs a break from his momma house. He'll be fine here, and I'll bring him home when my shift be over."

Clayton nodded and quietly left the house, shutting the door behind him.

After the door closed, Jayla pulled the chair closer to Abel's bed and sighed. She gently put her hand on Abel's arm and smiled. "The Chaissons, they good people Mr. Mueller. *Good, good* people. Every last one of them. And Cedric, he might have been the best of them all, that sweet, sweet boy."

Jayla pulled her phone out of her pocket, quickly typed a text message and then returned it to the pocket. She turned back to Abel and smiled. She sat without talking for several minutes until the silence was interrupted by metal tapping on the glass again. Abel turned in that direction and saw the tall man still there, staring at him. The man was grinning with the tip of his nose pressed against the glass.

Jayla watched the interaction between Abel and the man at the window and smiled. "You know who that is, Mr. Mueller?" she asked. When Mueller did not make an attempt to respond, she continued. "You used a pipe to crush the skull of that man's dog when he was a young boy. Do you remember doing that? I know he sure does," Jayla paused. She glanced at the man standing at the window and then back at Abel. "You sure have a knack for crossing the wrong kind'a people, Mr. Mueller. Yes sir, you sure do," she said, chuckling.

There was another knock on the door. Jayla went to the door and opened it. A tall, thin elderly black woman with pink-dyed hair and gold-capped teeth stuck her head in the door and smiled mischievously. "You ready for 'em?" she asked in a loud whisper.

Jayla smiled. "Yeah. He good?"

The tall woman chuckled. "Aww, yeah. I kept him off his meds since yesterday, and I ain't let him relieve hisself since. He been trying to grind up against everything in sight all day long," she said.

"Good," Jayla said as she opened the door wider.

Abel and D'Arius watched as a short, dark-skinned, developmentally disabled man waddled in. His undersized Aquaman t-shirt did not quite cover his naval, and his oversized corduroy cut-offs hung loosely on his hips, exposing the elastic band of his dingy cotton briefs. He had scraggily patches of black and gray beard stubble about his face and chin, a wide-set nose and large, bulging, jaundiced eyes. His mouth and extraordinarily thick lips were contorted, exposing bluish gums and large, misaligned teeth, one of which remained outside of his mouth even when it was closed. His eyes shifted back and forth excitedly between Jayla, the gold-toothed woman, D'Arius and Abel, grunting as drool began to form at the corner of his mouth.

"You stayin'?" Jayla asked the gold-toothed woman.

"No, girl. It smell like piss up in here. About to make my ass gag."

Jayla chuckled. "Yeah, you get used to it."

"Not me, no," the gold-toothed woman insisted.

Jayla shrugged. "Go smoke you a few cigs and then come back to get 'em."

437

The gold-toothed woman smiled and nodded as she pulled a cigarette out of her vinyl cigarette case and slid it between thick, painted lips.

"Don't worry, Queep," Jayla said to the developmentally disabled man, gently leading him into the room and closing the door behind them, "Auntee Vee gonna be back for you soon."

As his musky, rancid odor began to fill the room like a malodorous fog, Queep began to breathe more rapidly, snorting and grunting incoherently, his drooling increasing as he pulled at his massive phallus through the thick denim of his cut-offs. Abel stared apprehensively.

Jayla removed Abel's covers and pulled his gown up to his neck and then strained to roll him over onto his belly. She turned his head back toward D'Arius and Queep. Laying naked, prostrate and helpless and with an angry albeit forsaken look in his eyes, Abel watched as Queep slobbered and waddled back and forth, lifting one periwinkle-socked foot into the air and then the other, over and over again like a blue-footed booby engaged in a mating ritual.

Abel's eyes widened with disgust and then horror as he noticed Queep's swollen, uncircumcised glans extend past the waistband of his underwear, his deformed naval hidden in its shadow.

"Mr. Mueller, this is my cousin, Queep," Jayla finally said. "He's gonna be visiting you on a regular basis. Twice on your birthday if we can manage it," she chuckled.

When Queep heard his name, he was unable to contain his excitement. He squealed, clapped his hands and began running in place, his eyes sparkling with jubilation as copious amounts of drool hung from his mouth.

Jayla shushed Queep and instructed him to settle down and to remove his pants, which he did with surprising alacrity, still grunting and squealing in anticipation, pulling at his engorged penis, his bulging eyes fixated on Abel's exposed orifice with a salivating eagerness. He tried to move toward Abel, but Jayla held him at bay with a powerful hand on his chest.

Jayla turned back to Abel, her countenance still soft and pleasant. Their eyes locked. She savored his terrified expression for what seemed like an eternity to Abel. She glanced at Vance and the corners of her mouth rose slightly. She turned back to Abel. "Like I told you," she said to Abel, "the Chaissons—they good people. But as for me—well, let's just say . . . I ain't no Chaisson."

Holding Abel's gaze, Jayla's soft smile transformed into a cold grin as she removed her hand from Queep's chest and stepped aside.

Following a soft knock, the front door opened and the gold-toothed woman poked her head inside. Jayla had Queep standing naked from the waist down in the center of the room while she used towelettes to wipe his abdomen and genitalia clean while he bashfully covered his eyes with his hands.

The gold-toothed woman peered at the old white man lying naked and prone in his bed and let out a peculiar sound that was part laughter and part gasp as she covered her mouth. "Good Lord!" she whispered. There was a mixture of loose excrement, semen and blood smeared about Abel's anus. "Good Lord!" she repeated, grimacing.

Abel glared at the woman then shifted his eyes to D'Arius, who was still in the corner of the room. D'Arius stared back at Abel with a blank expression. Whether he comprehended what was happening or even recognized the man responsible for his condition was unclear.

When she finished with Queep, Jayla looked at Mueller and snickered. "I don't know if he shit himself because he was scared or if he thought maybe it would make Queep stop, but I think it just made Queep more excited."

The gold-toothed woman nearly retched and then stuck her tongue out for emphasis. "Lord," she said, with disgust.

Jayla giggled at the woman's reaction as she turned and looked at Abel again. "You know, I almost feel sorry for 'em."

"Do what?" the gold-toothed woman growled with an indignant scowl on her face.

"I said *almost*, bitch."

The two women belly-laughed.

"What you gonna do with that?" the gold-toothed woman asked, gesturing toward Abel.

"Wheel him to the back porch and hose him off," Jayla answered.

"If I was you, I'd make him sleep in his shit. Wait 'til early morning to clean 'em."

Jayla shook her head. "Uh uh. I don't want his rectum gettin' infected. They might send him to the hospital for that."

"True that," the gold-toothed woman said. "Okay. Same time next week?"

Jayla turned to look at Abel and smiled when she caught his eyes. "Yes, ma'am," she said. "Same time next week."

CHAPTER 60

It was rainy and colder than usual for March in Acadiana as the sun began to rise unseen behind the thick fog and overcast skies. Ezra was sitting with his back to the wall, sipping coffee and scanning articles on his internet feed when he came across a post about how leg-crossing is one of the best ways for women to identify a "non-toxic male." He looked down at his uncrossed legs and tittered. He was typing a quick search for ways to spot a non-toxic female when he heard the splattering sounds of rain come from the direction of the café entrance. He watched as Celee held the door open with her foot as she shook water from her umbrella. He waited until her eyes found his and then made a show of looking down at his watch and then back up at her with a reproving scowl. She smirked and began making her way to his table.

"If you give me any shit about being on CPT, I will pour that very black coffee on top of your very white head," Celee threatened.

Ezra feigned confusion. "I'm not sure I understand the reference," he said.

Celee rolled her eyes and smiled as she slid into her chair. As she was getting settled, a young waitress with puffy eyes and a forced smile appeared.

"I ordered you an AML," Ezra said as the waitress set the mug of coffee on the table in front of Celee.

"Thank you," Celee said to the waitress and then turned back to Ezra. "A what?"

"Oh, when you led with CPT, I thought we were going with acronyms this morning," Ezra said with a sly grin. "Almond milk latte."

Celee smiled and shook her head. "Can you do me the favor of allowing me to have my first dose of caffeine before you start with the foolishness?"

"Of course," Ezra said. "But before we get off topic, I do want to footnote that I regard it as a major affront to female mammals everywhere, humans included, to refer to that stuff as almond *milk*," Ezra said. "I mean, think about it, milk by definition is produced by mammary glands. I'm pretty sure almonds don't have mammary glands. That nasty liquid they add to your coffee is just hydrated nut paste posing as milk."

Celee smiled. "Well on behalf of dams and does of every mammalian genus and species, I appreciate you looking out for us, Mr. Brasseaux," she said just before taking a sip of her coffee. "Mmmm, that is one good, hydrated nut paste latte. Thank you."

Ezra smiled and nodded.

"So how was your Mardi Gras?" Celee asked.

"Good. I met Vance and one of his Army buddies at Fred's in Mamou. But we didn't stay long. Everybody was packed in there like sardines. The cigarette smoke was so thick that you could almost sit on it."

"Gross. I thought they outlawed smoking in bars?"

"That's a municipal thing," Ezra said. "Each municipality decides for itself. And Mamou of course is the town that time forgot. Hell, some of the older doctors still smoke while seeing patients."

"That is not true," Celee said with extreme dubiety.

"Swear to God," Ezra declared. "My cousin is a medical assistant over there. Old Dr. Marcantel and Dr. Soileau still do. They have ashtrays in the examination rooms."

"That is so crazy."

Ezra chuckled and nodded. "So, how was your Mardi Gras? Did you go to any parades?"

"Christ no," Celee said. "It was nice and quiet. I snuggled up in front of the fire with a book and read all day."

Ezra nodded. "Nice."

"Aren't you going to ask me what I was reading?" Celee asked with a sly expression.

Ezra's face lit up. "Really?" he asked.

Celee nodded.

"How far did you get?"

"Finished it."

"Wow." Ezra said.

"Yeah."

"Well?"

"It's good," she said. "Hard to read at times you know, because of the content, not the writing, but it's good. Really good, Ezra."

Ezra smiled and blushed. "Thank you."

Celee took a sip of coffee and then set her mug back down gently on the table. She looked like she was about to say something but could not find the words.

"What?" Ezra asked, sensing that she had some constructive criticism about the novel but was reticent to offer it. "Just say it. I can take it."

Celee smiled uncomfortably. "It's not criticism," she said. "I was just wondering . . . did white people really think and talk like that back then?"

Ezra nodded with embarrassment. "A lot of them, yeah. A lot still do, unfortunately."

Celee nodded contemplatively.

Ezra sighed. "Yeah. Ugly."

"So," Celee said, deciding to change the subject, at least for the moment. "Are you doing okay?"

Ezra shrugged. "Doing fine."

Celee tilted her head and squinted her eyes as if she were peering into Ezra's soul. "Are you really?"

Ezra felt his face flush. "Yeah," he replied. "I mean, truthfully it's a little harder than I thought it would be."

"What is, exactly?"

Ezra shrugged. "I don't know. It's hard to explain. It's like the part of my brain that controls my feelings can't entirely let go of the abandonment history, even though I know now that it's not true."

Celee nodded. "That's because it *was* your truth for so long, and that truth caused some deep wounds, and those deep wounds left scars."

Ezra nodded but did not reply. Celee sensed that he was not interested in being psycho-analyzed over coffee. "It'll come," she said before changing the subject. "So, what else is going on?" she asked in an uplifting tone. "Any interesting cases? Any new love interests?"

"Nothing worth mentioning," Ezra replied.

Celee peered at Ezra above the rim of her mug as she sipped her latte.

"What?" Ezra asked.

Celee smiled. "I was just wondering. The protagonist's high school sweetheart in your book—did you have someone in your life like that? I mean, someone who introduced you to a new way of looking at race?"

Ezra considered the question for a moment. "Yeah, I did. She introduced me to a new way of looking at a lot of things, actually. Not all necessarily good though. She was very anti-religion, for example. At least back then she was."

Celee nodded. She could see that Ezra was deep in thought and holding back. "It comes across as somewhat confessional. It's powerful," she said. "Compelling."

Ezra snorted and smiled. "Powerful. Compelling. Despicable. Shameful. Probably a lot of words to describe it, huh?"

Celee frowned disapprovingly. "That's not how I see it."

"Well, I suspect you'll be in the minority."

"Would you hold it against a butterfly for having been a caterpillar?"

Ezra smirked.

"It's called growth, Ezra. And none of us get to choose our early influences."

"I guess not."

"There's another way to look at it," Celee said. "Have you ever heard of *kintsugi*?" she asked.

"I don't think so."

"Well, it's the Japanese art of repairing fractured pottery using gold or silver. Most collectors view the repaired pottery as being more valuable than a piece that's perfectly intact. Psychologists use *kintsugi* as a metaphor for boldly embracing our imperfections and turning ourselves into something even more beautiful and meaningful than what would have existed had the imperfections never existed."

Ezra allowed himself to absorb the concept. He nodded and smiled. "Not bad."

They sat in silence for a moment sipping their coffee before Celee set her mug down and straightened her posture. "Hey, I almost forgot. I have something to show you," she said.

"What?" Ezra asked warily.

Celee rolled back her sleeve so that Ezra could see the Tree of Life tattoo on the inside of her bicep, which he recalled from their first meeting in the elevator. "Notice anything different?" she asked.

Ezra studied the tattoo for a moment. "You had one of the leaves shaded white?" he said.

Celee nodded.

"Cool."

"Yep. And you inspired that," she said.

"Me? How?" Ezra asked, genuinely puzzled.

"Our intimate and sometimes painful conversations that started in the elevator," Celee said, "and the friendship we have developed since then. It's honestly the first time that I ever felt like I really and truly connected with a white person. And it gave me hope and optimism that I never had before."

Ezra blushed. "I'm truly flattered."

"You should be. And I also want you to know that I release you."

Ezra's face contorted into a confused expression. "From what, exactly?" he asked.

Celee's countenance assumed a very serious expression. "From your past ignorance. From your past prejudices." And then the corners of her mouth turned upward subtly despite her efforts maintain a serious expression. "And—when we were stuck in the elevator—from the guilt you should bear from wanting to piss in my Prada."

Ezra snorted and burst into laughter as Celee's phone began to ring.

After ending the call, Celee frowned. "I'm sorry. I have to go," she said as she quickly stood and looped the strap of her handbag over her shoulder.

"I thought we were going to have breakfast," Ezra said.

"That was one of my colleagues. She is sick and I have to cover her 8 A.M. class." She leaned over and kissed Ezra on the cheek. "Talk to you soon."

"Yep."

CHAPTER 61

After Celee left, Ezra began composing an email to his secretary, instructing her to schedule a meeting with the client in a new barge collision case that had been assigned by the insurance carrier. As he was typing out the message, he heard the sharp clip-clopping of a woman's heels crossing the wood floors of the café's seating area. He thought nothing of it until the clip-clopping drew nearer his table and his acute olfactory senses picked up a very subtle but familiar scent.

Like some people were good with faces, Ezra was good with smells. The jasmine and saffron undertones of this particular aromatic signature were unmistakably from a very expensive Parisian perfume, the same expensive perfume worn by woman that Ezra had come to refer to in his own mind as *The Cryer,* i.e., Whitney Thibaut, the beautiful, very light-skinned African American physical therapist with whom he had a date six months prior and then never called again after she had repeatedly cried during sex.

Cringing with embarrassment, Ezra kept his head down, pretending to be focused on his phone, hoping that the Chanel pumps would continue clip-clopping past his table. They did not.

Ezra braced for public humiliation, his mind already working on an exit strategy. Then it suddenly occurred to him that Whitney had not called him back either. *This wasn't the 1950s,* he argued in his head. *Women were just as free to call men as vice versa. That would be his defense,* he thought. Then his mind began to question why she had not called him. *Was his sexual performance lacking? Probably it was. After all, who can concentrate on pleasing a woman sexually when she's sobbing the entire time? Or wait, was it his missing testicle?* He had not anticipated that their first date would lead to sex and things developed really quickly after drinks at her condo—too quickly to give his standard warning and disclaimer. *Did she notice? Was she grossed out by it? Was she maybe stopping to apologize to him?*

Mentally preparing himself for anything, Ezra slowly lifted his head and looked up to discover that the strikingly beautiful woman standing before him was in fact not Whitney Thibaut. He let out a deep breath and smiled with embarrassed relief. The woman watched his reaction but did not smile back.

"I'm sorry," Ezra said, nervously bungling his words, "I didn't—I was—I actually thought you were someone else for a moment."

The woman's face wore a complex expression, neither friendly nor hostile. She allowed Ezra to stew in his awkwardness for a moment before speaking. "You're Ezra Brasseaux, right?"

Ezra's eyebrows rose on his forehead as he regarded the woman with more scrutiny. He thought that she looked vaguely familiar but he could not place her. "I am," he said. "I'm sorry, do we know each other?"

"Well, we've never actually met, if that's what you're asking," the woman replied.

When she did not elaborate, Ezra became anxious and racked his brain trying to figure out who the woman was. They had never had a romantic encounter—he was certain of that. He had not had very many and he would definitely have remembered being with someone so beautiful. But she did look familiar. More familiar by the second.

"I read your novel," the woman finally said.

"Oh okay," Ezra said, feeling more relieved but still unable to get a good read on the woman. "Well, my very small, hanging-on-by-the-skin-of-his-teeth publisher and I thank you for that." He hoped to evoke a chuckle if not a smile but got neither. When the woman did not comment further, Ezra's discomfort returned. "Well, what did you think?" he asked.

The woman stared at Ezra contemplatively for a moment before she spoke. "That would be a complicated answer," she finally said.

Ezra regarded her curiously and smiled. "Well, I appreciate your politeness. Some of the reviews have been pretty brutal. The fact that I was trying to attack racially indoctrinated prejudices by shining a light on it seems to have been lost on a lot of readers. One lady emailed my publisher pointing out that I had used the N-word thirty-eight times."

"I actually thought it was very well-written," the woman said without any warmth in her tone.

Still a bit bemused and wary by the direction of the conversation and the woman's demeanor, Ezra nodded and said, "Thank you."

"Do you mind if I sit for a minute?" the woman asked.

"Actually," Ezra said as leaned over, pulled out his wallet and placed money on the table, "I was just getting up to head back to the office, but you're welcome to the table."

As Ezra began to stand, the woman pulled out a chair across from him and sat, placing her purse in her lap and both hands on top of her purse. She leaned toward Ezra and in a low voice smiled and said, "I'm Holly Francois."

Ezra froze halfway between a seated position and standing erectly, his eyebrows climbing on his forehead with surprise. His mind began to race. He regarded the woman curiously. Holly Francois was the name of a character in his novel, the name he had chosen for Kelly Mueller in fact. He began to study the woman's face. The single dimple, the tiny, slightly upturned button nose, the mesmerizing gray-blue eyes that turned to half-moons when she smiled, the perfect teeth. It was all familiar. Her hair color and hair style were a little different and her breasts hung a little lower, but it was her. It was Kelly Mueller in the flesh, sitting right across the table from him.

An almost imperceptible smile seemed to appear on the woman's face as if she sensed his recognition, but she did not speak.

"I don't understand," Ezra replied, futilely trying to feign ignorance. Feeling tension in his back from still being hunched over, he sat back down.

"I'm also the one who sent you the journals," the woman said.

"Journals?" was all Ezra could think to say in his state of profound discombobulation.

A disappointed grin appeared on Kelly's face. She knew that Ezra knew exactly what she was talking about and she had no interest in playing cat and mouse. "Yes," she said in a slightly irritated tone, "the journals that contained a lot of the background information that you used in your novel." She paused to gauge Ezra's reaction. "Though you didn't find them hidden amongst a box of old books at an estate sale like the lawyer character did in the book."

Ezra held Kelly's stare but did not reply.

"You know, if I had known you were going to write a book about it, I would never have sent them to you—my aunt's journals, I mean."

"Well," Ezra said, finally willing to admit, at least implicitly that the cat was out of the bag, "in my defense, I had started writing my novel years before I ever saw those journals."

"Really?"

"Yes."

"But why—if you don't mind me asking?" Kelly asked with a pained look on her face. "What made you want to write about that in the first place?"

"That's a good question," Ezra said.

He had contemplated how Kelly Mueller might react to the book a thousand times over the years, both while he was writing it and after it was published—whether she would be flattered on some level—whether she would feel insulted—whether she would view it as an invasion of her privacy. But ultimately, he would reason and correctly so, that the book was not about her *per se*. The rumors of her rape had merely inspired the storyline. The book was about something much bigger.

"It's a fair question," Kelly replied.

Ezra held Kelly's stare for a moment and then broke eye contact, trying to think about how he had rehearsed the response to this question at least a hundred times. "I guess," he finally said, deciding to speak from the heart instead, "because the rape—or the rape *rumor* I should say—was such an impactful event in my life."

Kelly furrowed her brow. "How so? I mean, we didn't even know each other."

"No, I know," Ezra said, "but you were—" he felt himself begin to blush and stopped—"well," he continued, looking down at his coffee to avoid direct eye contact, "when my friends and I were in middle school, you and your twin sister, you, you were—" he stammered nervously, "—you were basically goddesses in our eyes. You really were. We all thought you were the prettiest girls we had ever seen in person, and frankly, we were all madly in love with y'all—or at least one of you. I don't know why," Ezra said, trying not to blush any more than he already was, "but we each picked a favorite twin." He stopped short of confessing that she had been his pick.

Ezra glanced up at Kelly to get a glimpse of her reaction, but there was none that he could detect. It was as if she had been told how beautiful and loved she was so many times throughout her life that it no longer affected her.

"And when we were told that you had been raped," Ezra continued, "that in itself was horrific enough. But when we heard it was by black men, it was just—I don't know—with the ignorant racist attitudes that we all had back then, there was this truly overwhelming outrage—the prejudice that we held toward blacks was amplified exponentially. More than that, it turned to hatred, to true animus. I mean, I remember so clearly how we all wanted to hang every black man in town—hell, the black boys too, because we knew they would eventually grow up to be potential rapists."

Ezra paused to consider his own words and the depths of ignorance in which he had wallowed for most of his childhood. "And I realized later in life how, at least for me in particular, how big of a role the whole rape thing played in my attitude towards black people." He stopped and regarded Kelly for a moment, this time it being his turn to gauge her reaction, though she still showed none. Nor did she reply, as if she were not yet satisfied with his response and wanted to hear more.

Ezra felt his mouth getting dry. He nervously picked up his mug to take a sip of coffee only to find it empty. "To be honest with you," he continued, putting the mug down, "when I first started writing my novel, my intent was to make the rape story part of the explanation or justification for prejudice against blacks—you know, to show that prejudices and stereotypes don't just get invented out of nothing—that there is a cause and effect—that yeah, sure, there's discrimination and there's certainly been oppression, but that they still need to be accountable for their behavior. I was of the mindset that they earned the prejudices or at least a lot of them. The bad hygiene. The crime. Black mothers spitting out babies in the projects just to get a bigger welfare check. Gang activity in urban areas. Black boys and black men walking around in public with their pants hanging below their asses. I remember thinking, is there anything that better captures a snapshot of what is wrong with their culture? I wanted the black community to own that and everything else that had spawned these prejudices and to send a message that if you don't like the prejudices that you've created, then do something about it as a community instead of making excuses and getting a pass for it by playing the race card over and over again in perpetuity."

Kelly nodded subtly but said nothing, allowing Ezra to continue.

"Then when I learned that—" Ezra paused, trying to choose his words carefully so as not to insult Kelly, "—when I learned the truth, well it hit me really hard and I slowly started to rethink some things. Like, you know, that every black individual is just that—an individual—who should be judged on his or her own merit, not what some other black person or persons did. Just like it wouldn't be fair to judge me or you for despicable behavior of other white people. White people who historically have systematically enslaved, raped and oppressed blacks. White people who treat blacks like animals and then feel justified in doing so when they succeed in getting some of them to act like animals."

"The more I thought about it, the more shame I felt," Ezra continued. "True shame. And the plot flipped. The book just assumed a life of its own. And though I'm not super religious or anything, I felt like the book and its new storyline became my calling."

"And your confession, apparently," Kelly interjected.

"And my confession, yes."

The corners of Kelly's mouth turned up slightly, but it was not a real smile.

"I have a question," Ezra said.

"You want to know why I sent the journals to you?"

Ezra nodded.

"Would you laugh if I told you that I thought it was some form of divine intervention?" Kelly asked.

Ezra scoffed inaudibly. "I don't imagine that I would think anything about any of this is funny."

"Well, my aunt Hedi had the journals hidden. The only person who knew about them or where they were was her sister, my mom. After Aunt Hedi died, my mom collected the journals and hid them again. She never shared them with us. When she died, she left a safe deposit box for just me and my sister. The journals were in there. When we read them, we were of course mortified. All along, we had no idea about what happened to those black boys. Our mothers kept all that from us. And well, we were scared to death of *him*."

"Your father?"

"My adoptive father," Kelly said. "Abel married our mom when we were almost two and he adopted us. My mom changed our last names to Mueller. Our real dad was killed in a gas explosion on an offshore rig not long after we were born."

"I had no idea," Ezra said. "And I'm sorry about your dad."

Kelly smiled politely and nodded a thank you. "But anyway, we were afraid to go to the police because well, we knew Abel was well-connected with law enforcement and the district attorney's office. Then one day, my sister—she lives in Covington now—she was in Lafayette for a soccer tournament and she brought her son to get some lunch at this little hamburger joint—the Judice something—"

"Judice Inn," Ezra said.

"Yes, so anyway, they were in line to pay and heard one of the workers call out the name Ezra Brasseaux."

Ezra's eyebrows rose slightly on his forehead but he did not comment.

"So, she called me from the soccer game and tells me about it. We both are thinking the same thing—that Brasseaux is not a common name and that you're probably related to the Brasseaux who was the Chief of Police in Iris at the time all that stuff went down."

"Ah," Ezra muttered mostly to himself, starting to get a feel for where the story was heading.

"So, we got online and did a search for obituaries with your last name, and we found one that listed you and your father amongst the survivors. I think it was the obituary for your paternal grandfather. Anyway, we looked you up online and found out that you're an attorney. Ultimately, it was my sister, Kim's, idea to send you the journals."

"But why?" Ezra asked. He suspected that he knew but wanted confirmation. "Why me?"

"Well, after reading the journals, we both thought that your dad knew who was responsible for what happened to those black boys and that he decided to sweep it under the rug, probably because of his relationship with Abel. And we thought maybe if you knew that, maybe out of some sense of family accountability, you would want to clean up your dad's mess. And of course being a lawyer, we thought you would know better than us what to do."

"But what if I had done nothing?"

Kelly shrugged. "I don't know. We didn't think it through that far."

Unconsciously, Ezra let out a little huff. She was right. He had felt a sense of vicarious responsibility. He also wondered to what extent Kelly felt responsible for what happened to those "black boys." He felt irritation over the fact that she did not seem to know their names. "Cedric Chaisson and D'Arius Cole," he said, enunciating their names slowly.

Kelly looked at him blankly.

"The two African American boys."

She nodded, blushing slightly with embarrassment. "Did you know them?" she asked.

"I was friends with Cedric's younger brother, but I didn't really know Cedric. I didn't know D'Arius at all."

Kelly nodded. "I know we were grasping at straws, but we were desperate and scared. And we were too afraid to do anything ourselves, so I guess sending the journals to you made us feel like we were doing something. Does that make sense?"

Ezra shrugged. "I guess. I mean, it worked. And it led to me learning the truth about my father. And I'm certainly grateful for that." He wondered if Kelly knew that Abel was also responsible for his father's death, but before he could ask, she cut him off.

"I'm really sorry about your dad by the way," Kelly said. "I don't know if you knew this, but even though they couldn't bring him to trial because of lack of sufficient evidence and because of his medical condition, they went ahead and charged Abel with your father's murder, in addition to the crimes he committed against those black—against—"

"Cedric and D'Arius."

"Cedric and D'Arius," Kelly said, feeling compelled to say their names out loud.

Ezra nodded. "Yes, I'm aware."

Kelly nodded. "I'm just sorry that my Uncle Ferrell got drug into all that. I know this might be hard to believe, but he really was a sweet man. He was just weak-minded, and he didn't know how to say 'no' to Abel. It's really a shame."

They sat in silence for several moments allowing Ezra to take in everything. Finally, a faint smile appeared on his face.

"What?" Kelly inquired.

"The truth," Ezra said. "It's been quite the roller coaster ride getting to it. I mean, there's just been so many things that I thought were the truth for so long that ended up being just the opposite."

Kelly nodded.

"It makes me think of one of my favorite quotes that I sometimes use in jury trials when my opponent is trying to confuse or mislead the jury," Ezra added, "but I guess it applies to life in general, too."

"What's that?"

"*Three things cannot long be hidden: the sun, the moon and the truth,*" Ezra recited.

"I like it. Is that Shakespeare?" Kelly asked.

"Buddha," Ezra answered.

Kelly smiled and then the smile suddenly faded.

"What?" Ezra asked.

She took a deep breath and exhaled. She looked out of the window and then back at Ezra and smiled sadly. "Well, the funny thing is—" she stopped as if she was not sure she should finish her thought. "The thing is that you still don't know the truth. Not all of it."

Ezra's eyes narrowed slightly, though his expression remained stoic. "How do you mean?" he asked.

Kelly looked Ezra in the eyes. "If I tell you, will you agree to keep it strictly confidential?" she asked.

Ezra paused to consider the request. "Of course," he said.

"Like you could lose your law license if you divulge my confidence, right?"

"That's true."

"And, I mean, I don't want you writing another novel inspired about what I'm about to tell you," she said.

458

An embarrassed grin appeared on Ezra's face. "No more novels."

"I really don't even know why it's so important to me for you to know the truth," Kelly said. "I guess I just feel like, through all of this, that maybe we have some kind of cosmic connection, you know? Like God was working through both of us. Does that sound crazy?"

"No," Ezra said. "Not at all."

Kelly bowed her head, then opened her mouth to speak but nothing came out. A tear rolled down her cheek and she wiped it with the palm of her hand and took a deep breath and exhaled.

"You really don't have to—"

Kelly cut Ezra off. "The truth is—" she said, finding her voice, speaking slowly, "—the truth is, I *was* raped."

Ezra was beyond befuddled. The journals had made clear that Kelly had made up the rape story. The social worker's report from the hospital had confirmed it, too—though he had no intention of letting Kelly know that he had seen her medical records.

With a confused expression and choosing his words carefully, Ezra said, "But the journals—"

"I know what the journals said," Kelly replied.

Ezra leaned back in his chair with a wary countenance, waiting for the other shoe to drop.

Kelly closed her eyes, took another deep breath, held it, and then exhaled. She finally lifted her head and looked at Ezra for a moment before she spoke. "I did lie about being raped by black men. Then I lied about not being raped. I was raped over and over again, starting when I was thirteen. It had been going on for a few years. The only thing that was different this time was that I got pregnant."

Ezra did not know what to think or how to respond. "That's horrible. I'm sorry," was all that he could think to say, though Kelly sensed his skepticism.

She cleared her throat and straightened her posture. "I lied about being raped by black men because I knew that's the only way my mother would allow me to get an abortion." She paused. "Then I couldn't go through with it. I couldn't do that to my own child. So, then I lied about not being raped."

She pulled a tissue from her purse and blotted her eyes. After a few very uncomfortable moments, she lifted her head and looked at Ezra again. Only this time there was genuine bitterness and anger in her voice. "It was *him*," she said.

Ezra's brow furrowed deeply as he attempted to solve the pronoun-antecedent riddle. Then, like a light switch, his brows shot upward on his forehead when he remembered who Kelly Mueller's long term boyfriend was. "Your old boyfriend? Perry Fuselier?" he asked.

Kelly grimaced and shook her head sorrowfully. "No," she said, "no, not Perry. Perry was nothing but good to me."

Then who? Ezra thought to himself, racking his brain. Then gradually, like a fluorescent lamp that requires warm-up time for the electrical current to fully heat the cathodes and reach their full lumen output, the epiphany came. His thoughts went back to the discussion he had with Celee when they were stuck in the elevator—when Celee had expressed skepticism about Kelly Mueller being raped by black men. He had argued that to doubt Kelly's story was nonsensical. And his argument had been sound. A smart, beautiful, popular girl would have absolutely no reason to falsely claim that she was raped by black men . . . unless of course the truth that she was trying to hide was even worse than the lie. *Son of a bitch.* It all made sense to him now. Of course it was *him*.

"Abel?" he whispered, though he knew the answer.

Kelly closed her eyes and nodded subtly. Another tear rolled down her cheek.

"Oh my God Kelly," Ezra said. "I'm so sorry. I really am so sorry."

"I never told anyone. I was so ashamed. And the fact that it was just me and not my sister, too made me think I was somehow to blame—that I had done something to encourage it."

Ezra shook his head empathetically but abstained from speaking. There were simply no words.

"And when my mom told Abel that I was pregnant and that I had made up the story about the rape so that I could get an abortion and then changed my mind, do you know what he did?"

Ezra shook his head subtly, not certain that he wanted to know.

"He waited until we were alone in the house to confront me. He came into my room. I just wanted to get away from him. When I stood to walk out, he punched me with all of his might in the belly."

"Oh my God," Ezra said, grimacing in horror.

"I started spotting within the hour and by the next day had miscarried. That's why you never saw me big and pregnant or with a baby if you were wondering what happened to the pregnancy," Kelly said.

"Jesus."

Kelly wiped tears from both sides of her face. "And the injury to my uterus, I found out later was permanent. I was never able to get pregnant again."

Ezra was speechless, his own eyes moist. "I—I don't—I don't know what to say. I'm so sorry."

Kelly sniffled and dabbled her nose with her tissue. "Well, at least I can take comfort in the fact that he's presently rotting in hell, right?" she said, the nares on her tiny, perfect nose still flaring subtly with anger.

"Well," Ezra said, "I heard about his last few months. It might comfort you a little to know that regardless of what happens in the afterlife, he suffered greatly before he died."

Kelly scoffed. "Maybe so, but not nearly enough, I promise you."

Ezra smiled wryly. *Probably not. But pretty close,* he thought to himself.

ABOUT THE AUTHOR

Troy Allen Broussard was born, raised and still makes his home in the heart of southwest Louisiana's Acadiana region where the rich Cajun-Creole culture and the rice fields, bayous and swamps shaped his identity and inspired his creative endeavors. He balances his love for family and the outdoors with a busy civil law practice spanning more than three decades. His debut novel, a fifteen year project, is a work born of deep introspection, cultural pride, a daring sense of humor and a passion for story-telling.